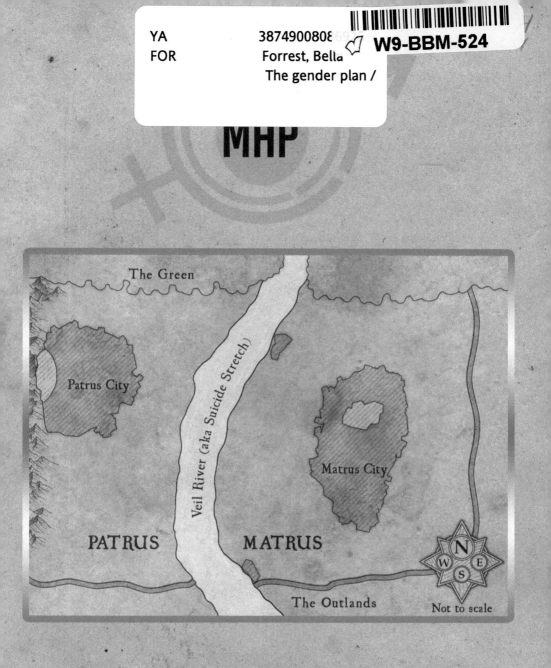

The Green

Patrus City

Veil River (aka Suicide Stretch)

Matrus City

PATRUS

MATRUS

N
W · E
S

The Outlands

Not to scale

NIGHTLIGHT PRESS

First Edition

THE GENDER PLAN

BELLA FORREST

CHAPTER 1

Viggo

The road was dark, barely illuminated by the headlights of the emergency vehicle we barreled along in. Clouds blocked the light of the moon—the darkness was almost oppressive. Thomas swerved, the tires squealing slightly under the strain of moving too fast at a strange angle, and I grabbed the dashboard, steadying myself. I gave him a quizzical look, but he simply shrugged, his dark eyes unwavering from the road ahead.

The rattle of gunfire behind us broke the silence of the night, cutting through it instantly. I gritted my teeth together and turned to peer into the back of the ambulance, looking at where Amber stood, her face peeking out the small window.

"They're still behind us, Thomas!" she shouted, turning slightly and ducking farther down. I checked the mirror on the passenger side door—the larger military vehicle was so close that if Thomas tapped the brakes even slightly, their front end would be forever entangled with our rear.

"I don't exactly have the proper skillset for this, Amberlynn!" Thomas grated, swerving again to miss yet another pothole on the ridiculously rutted and bumpy backroad he had retreated down.

"DON'T USE THAT NAME!" Amber shouted back, her violet eyes seething and her face turning a dark red that rivaled the curls on her head.

"No fighting," Ms. Dale ordered sternly. Amber scowled, then returned her attention to the back window, muttering under her breath. Ms. Dale shook her head, her braid bouncing against her neck, and reached up to steady herself with a hand against the ceiling as the back of the bay rattled and weaved wildly under Thomas' erratic driving.

Once again, we were going to be lucky if we made it out of this alive.

"We have to lose them soon," Ms. Dale said. "Or else we're going to have to miss the rendezvous back at the farmhouse we burned. We can't bring these people down on the rest of our base."

I knew no other way to respond except for leaning out of the passenger-side window, using my knee as a brace against the door. The sharp night wind whipped at my face as I looked back at our pursuers in their grimy Matrian combat vehicle. They would be unable to see any faces through the ambulance's rear windshield due to the glare of their lights—which was probably for the better, all things considered. I sighted down the barrel of the gun in my hand and exhaled, squeezing the trigger three times.

It didn't help much. The bullets ricocheted off the heavily armored vehicle, the noise of their impact swallowed by the rattle of the wheels on the dirt road and the coughing roar of engines. The driver of the other vehicle swerved away, though not before one of their headlights shattered.

It was barely a victory, considering the bullets I'd lost, but it was the most damage we had done to their vehicle thus far.

Pulling back in, I fell back down onto the seat and ejected the magazine of my gun. "I'm out," I shouted, irritation churning my stomach. "Anyone got anything?"

"I've got three left, one in the chamber," Amber announced.

"I'm so sorry, I've got nothing," added Jeff, his thick mustache twitching in displeasure.

"I'm out too." Cad made an effort to eject his magazine, as if he could manifest more bullets in doing so, and I couldn't blame him. Even I wanted to double check the clip, just in case I had gone completely blind in the last thirty seconds.

"Sorry, my friend," Cruz said cheerfully. "But I used all the bullets in that rifle on the last vehicle."

That had been the first of our pursuers, evidence of our messy exit from the city. We'd made it to the checkpoint at one of the larger arteries to and from the city, pulling slowly through the barrier just as the order had come down to stop any vehicles attempting to leave the city. In fact, as luck would have it, we had been right next to the warden in charge as she'd received the order. All it had taken was a look from me to Thomas, and he had gunned the ambulance's engine, getting us out of there before they could stop us.

The vehicle Cruz was referring to, the first of three to come after us, had caught up with us almost immediately and opened fire. We had returned the gesture, and ultimately, it was Ms. Dale who had saved us by managing to take out the tires. Then all it had taken was for Thomas to swerve around a sharp dip in the road—we'd gone left, and they'd gone up and over the side, into the steep irrigation ditch that ran alongside the road.

"I've got two left in this clip," Ms. Dale said, shaking her head. She looked at me, her eyes flat and hard. "We have five bullets between us. Any thoughts?"

The roar of the engine in the truck behind us grew louder, and I strained over to see the thing hurtling up on Thomas' side. I recognized the maneuver. Whoever their driver was, it was clear she was both skilled and confident. She was attempting to hook the rear corner of our vehicle with her own, probably just trying to nudge it slightly. But a nudge at this speed…

I shuddered, suddenly longing for my motorcycle—in this case, it would be far safer and way more nimble than the hulking box of a vehicle we had 'borrowed' from the emergency response team earlier that day.

"Thomas," I said, tension making my voice tight. "They're—"

"I know," he snapped, twisting the wheel to the left and cutting them off. The back of the vehicle swayed under the sudden shift in the truck's gravity, and I heard somebody in the back, probably Jeff, give a grunt as they were thrown into something. Equipment in the back rattled and clanked angrily. I looked at the small man driving, noting the pallid color of his skin and the sweat trickling down his forehead to stain the collar of his shirt. "At this rate, it won't even matter!" he sputtered. "No doubt a heloship is incoming."

"I don't think that's likely!" Ms. Dale said, her voice carrying over the whipping wind flowing through my open window and the two bullet holes in the center of the window between Thomas and myself. "Elena's going to need every soldier she can get her hands on in order to try and find anyone who saw that video!"

She had a point: the video we had uploaded and played in

all the stadiums throughout Patrus was the counterpropaganda tool we had needed to expose the lies and deceptions Elena had used to gain control over the city. Obviously she had recognized its dangers—within minutes of its showing, she had ordered her soldiers to fire into crowds of helpless civilians, trying to keep the message from getting out. We'd done what we could to help on our way out of Starkrum Stadium, but the message had been broadcast all over the city. Who knew how many of the viewers in the other stadiums had made it out alive?

There was a pause, punctuated by more gunshots being fired at us as we sped ahead. "You're absolutely right, of course," Thomas announced in answer to Ms. Dale's question, seemingly oblivious to the gunshots filling the air. "I forgot to factor in that part of the equation. Actually, it shifts the equation enormously, to a whopping—"

"Another time, Thomas!" I yelled.

I nearly bounced out of my seat as Thomas hit a pothole hard, the entire vehicle going airborne for a moment afterward. As I landed hard enough to make me run a tongue across my teeth, making sure they were still in place, the equipment clattered around in the cabinets and drawers installed in panels along the back sides of the vehicle. There was a heavy metallic clink, just behind me, and I focused on it, my mind working furiously.

It took the span of four heartbeats to remember what was positioned right behind my seat. When I did, I snapped into motion, climbing over the hump into the narrow passage that led into the already overcrowded bay. I motioned Jeff out of my way, and the older man squinted at me in confusion before standing aside, moving into the short, narrow passage I had just vacated.

I unhooked the red top strap that secured a large

silver canister of oxygen to the wall. "Cad! Get ready to open the doors," I shouted, grabbing the canister by the nozzle and lifting it out. It was surprisingly heavy for a tank that basically contained air. Anello Cruz was there within moments, helping take some of the strain off of me as we lifted it straight out. I had to bite my tongue to keep from insisting he let me handle it. After all, not long ago, he had been our kidnapping victim. But he seemed to have had a change of heart after witnessing the video... We hadn't had trouble from him yet. Maybe he'd changed his mind about what we were doing for Patrus—he certainly seemed eager to join in on the action against the Matrians. Right now, I wasn't going to question having another pair of hands. Later, though, I would definitely be doing a more thorough background check.

"I'm ready for you," said Ms. Dale from her position behind Thomas. She had dropped to one knee, her gun out, her eyes trained on the doors, and I could see from the sharp light in her eyes that she understood my plan. Cad had his hand on the door handle on my side, Amber on the other. Cruz helped me adjust the canister in my arms and then stepped away.

"Ready! Count me down!"

More gunfire sounded behind us, and I heard the metallic thunks as the bullets impacted on the doors. Amber closed her eyes, and as soon as the fire paused, hopefully due to the owner needing to change out the magazines, her eyes snapped open and she began to count.

"Three! Two! ONE!"

Amber and Cad twisted their handles and pushed, dropping low to avoid catching a bullet. I staggered forward and heaved, tossing the oxygen into the air toward the vehicle maybe five feet behind our bumper. The silver canister twisted oddly in the air.

Ms. Dale squeezed the trigger twice, the sounds of her shots nearly deafening in the confines of the bay. The first bullet hit the side and ricocheted—but it opened up a small hole in the process. When the second bullet hit the container, it created a spark too small to notice as the canister exploded against the hood of the enemy truck, lighting up the night with orange for just a moment. Tires squealed and glass shattered. The truck swerved violently to the left, one wheel slipping off the side of the road onto the slope of the irrigation ditch on the shoulder. And then the whole thing flipped off the road, rolling out of my eyesight. It all happened so fast that I could still feel the jolting force of the explosion, and I was almost thrown off my feet as the rear end of the ambulance shook erratically around us, the back doors clanking in their frames.

Amber gave a small cry, thrown off balance, and I saw her pitching forward, toward the open doors—but Cad reached out and hooked her around the arm, pulling her back and over to his side. I pushed to the edge, using the metal frame as a handgrip as I leaned out and began pulling the left door closed. Ms. Dale was on the right side already, doing the same thing. Between the two of us, we slammed the doors closed, cutting off the sight of the dark road behind us.

I sat down almost immediately in the relative silence of the fully enclosed ambulance bay as the adrenaline seemed to completely desert my body. Wiping my hand across my brow to clear off the dots of perspiration that had formed there, I looked around the bay. Everyone was sitting or leaning heavily on something, their breathing ragged, cheeks stained red from exertion.

I couldn't help but smile as I took them all in. "Good job, everyone," I said.

Five pairs of eyes stared back blankly, and a chuckle escaped me—they might not want to enjoy the awesomeness of still being alive right at that moment, but damn it, *I* was going to.

CHAPTER 2

Violet

"Are you insane?" I whispered harshly, still finding it difficult to speak through the lump in my throat.

Owen didn't answer my question. Instead, as I struggled to my feet, he pounded loudly back up the small set of stairs toward Ashabee's hidden basement entrance door—which, I noticed, he'd slid closed behind him—and shouted in the voice of a man whose triumph was turning to terror, "I've got her! I've got—oh God! She's got a—"

The moment he'd said 'I've got her,' a chill had gone down my spine, and I had almost swung my backpack around to grab for my gun—the gun Owen himself had given me. But before I could even figure out the implications of what that might mean, Owen had spun his own weapon up and shot at the ceiling, two loud blasts. At the same time, I saw his other hand pressing the button that locked the door from the inside, a glitter of lights next to the handle turning on as Ashabee's technology secured the lock.

Silence reigned for a moment. Owen stared at the door. Then I heard the sounds of pounding feet from outside, more shouting, voices I didn't recognize: "Hey, what happened in there? Where are they?"

"Help me get this damn thing open!"

In almost complete darkness, Owen came back down the stairs toward me, a wild kind of excitement in his voice. "I bought us some time. Violet, we can do this!"

I gaped at him.

Owen's face was partially hidden in shadows cast by the dim ensconced lights on the wall of Ashabee's secret armory. This basement had stronger lighting, but neither of us had stopped to flip the switch. Then again, considering that Owen had just sold me out to Desmond, nationalist psychopath and Queen Elena's right-hand woman, neither of us had spared much thought for the lighting. Even if he had just *pretended* to sell me out, if I were to believe what he was saying.

I *wanted* to believe him. He was my best friend, and some unshakable part of me refused to believe he would truly throw me to the wolves like that. We'd been through so much together. And the hatred in his voice when he spoke of Desmond had been so clear.

My heart's desperate urge to believe Owen would never really betray me wasn't making things easier or less confusing. If anything, it was making this whole thing worse—and I didn't have time to be confused. I shook my head, at a loss for words, raging that, despite everything, I couldn't bring myself to just shoot him in the leg and leave him there to rot while trying to make my own escape.

Nothing could make up for the fact that I'd been hoping to

find my brother and instead I'd found *her* waiting for me. Or for him dragging me out here on false pretenses and lying to my face about it. Since I couldn't figure out how to feel about anything, my brain settled on anger. I was *furious*.

As I continued to not speak, Owen's eyes bored into mine. In the soft light, I could see he was trying to look reassuring, but his desperation made the idea nonsensical. "Violet, please, we can stop her," he whispered. "It's going to be all right. We've got her now. She believes me. We can put an end to all this."

From up the stairs came the sound of banging. Like it or not, I was stuck with Owen right now. I needed him to help me escape, and moreover, if he was trying to double-cross—*double double-cross?*—me once more, I needed to at least play along until I could escape *him*, too.

"What's your plan?" I bit out.

Owen looked feverishly into my eyes. "Desmond is up there right now. We have a bit of a scuffle, shout at each other, and then I bring you upstairs—I'll go for Desmond, you go for the guards… No, you can shoot her, if you—"

"Do you even *hear* yourself?" I recoiled, trying to keep my voice low while taking a horrified step away from him. The fear lurking in my stomach raised its ugly head again, but I pushed it down into the river of anger roaring up my insides. I felt like the whole room was spinning around me. "Killing Desmond isn't some kind of prize that's going to make everything better!"

Owen's blue eyes burned even in the dim light as he held my gaze; then he looked away, pain clenching his face. He opened his mouth as if to reply.

The pounding at the door above us stopped momentarily, just long enough for me to wonder if they'd pulled back—and then a honey-sweet voice called out through the door, clearly audible, making my stomach crawl. "Do hurry up, Owen dear," it said. "Every second you spend down there makes me doubt your intentions."

Desmond was there at the top of the stairs right now. And she suspected. Oh, of course she suspected.

Owen shot me a glance and then turned in her direction.

"Say something!" I hissed at him. "Fix this!"

"No! I was pretending you shot me, remember?" he whispered back. My eyes narrowed at the back of his head, suddenly wishing I had free use of both hands so I could slap this stupid idea out of his head. I had use of my left, but the slap that this level of delirious stupidity deserved was one I wasn't currently capable of delivering. "Then how are you supposed to open the door without blowing your cover? Do you want me to *really* shoot you as a cover?"

"No, I don't know! I—I—" Finally, he was flustered. "I imagined it going differently than this, okay?"

"You—"

This time, Owen didn't let me finish the angry remark on my tongue. "I needed this all to be over!" he said. "I'm tired of everybody around me getting hurt! I'm tired of this war, I'm tired of everything falling apart and going wrong, and without Ian, I have nothing to look forward to anymore. It's all so out of control and wrong, and it's all Desmond's fault. We can stop it. We can stop it right now. All we need to do is kill her."

"Do you really think that is going to solve everything?" I snapped, my voice getting louder. A moment later, I caught myself, my hand fluttering to my mouth, but there was still a loud banging coming from the door.

Owen sighed. "No," he said in the smallest breath imaginable. "But it felt so right."

I sucked in a deep breath, trying not to let my imagination drift into dark places... scenarios where Desmond kidnapped me... and... I shut my eyes and tried to filter all the thoughts out. Those thoughts would get me nowhere, and neither would this argument. I tried to clear my head.

The banging stopped for a moment as Desmond's voice spoke to us again.

"Owen, I very much hope you are truly injured, because that will make the rest of this much easier for you. Cease this charade. My guards and I are growing impatient—bring her up here, or neither of you will like the result."

Owen turned to me, his blue eyes imploring, and whispered desperately, "Okay, new idea. We pretend to surrender, then..."

My fingers on my right hand twitched in response, trying to form a fist in spite of the cast preventing it. "She shoots us both. First me, then you."

Owen glared at me, but he didn't answer. I pushed on. "I'm not going up those stairs, Owen. It's too dangerous. I'm going out of Ashabee's tunnel while they're distracted. If you try to stop me, I'll... I'll... Please don't try to stop me."

I didn't want to say what I would do, but I didn't have to. From the barren look on Owen's face, I knew he understood. His stupid plan was going to fail. He would have to drag me back to Desmond kicking and screaming. My teeth were clenched and my right hand's fingers dug into the cast. If he tried to persist—if he really *did* want to sell me out to Desmond—this would be the hardest moment of my life.

Up above us, the pounding on the door had resumed, and it

sounded less like random pounding now and more like deliberate use of force. I winced at the sound of splintering and scraping. The more time we spent here, the less time I had to escape.

"Come with me," I pleaded, begging him not to fight me over this. "We'll find some other way to kill Desmond. We'll fix things."

Instead of trying to fight me, Owen did the only thing that might have been worse: he turned back toward the basement door and pulled out his gun.

"You were right," he said. "I'm sorry. I shouldn't have dragged you into this. Get out of here while you still can, Violet."

I had already taken a few steps back before the gravity of that statement fully registered. "You don't really think you can take them all down by yourself—"

"I have to try! You said yourself that I've got to fix things!" Owen wasn't even trying to whisper anymore. A moment ago, I had been furious enough to leave him behind and escape, but now, my heart rushed into my throat and the dizzy feeling flooded back in. A thousand emotions surged through my brain at once, paralyzing me for a split second.

It was a split second too long. There was a final crash, accompanied by excited shouts from the guards, and a big slice of pale light flooded down the stairs above us as Desmond's voice drifted down the stairwell in the flood of debris and settling dust.

"Time's up, Owen," she said, her voice arctic cold.

Owen whipped his gun up to face the stairs, and I had time to swing my backpack around, fumbling for the gun as I took frantic steps backward, when, instead of the rush of footsteps I was expecting, I heard something clink. A small object made an arc in the air as it sailed down the stairs, hitting the landing with a metallic noise.

My brain recognized the object but refused to believe what it was. I was frozen, trapped in a nightmare all over again—bombs going off around me while I was dying. Owen shouted something, but it was impossible to hear over the panic causing my heart to skip beats and my ears to ring.

Owen turned to face me, his eyes wide, and my shock barely registered as he grabbed me, like he once had in The Green, throwing my stomach over his shoulder and running toward the back of the garage.

I barely noticed the throb of pain that pulsed through my ribs, focused on the grenade as it bounced, up off the landing, down toward us. We weren't far enough. We weren't going to make it through this.

And then, a shadow detached itself from the dark edges of the room, moving quickly in the dim light. I had time to register a tall, lanky frame and mop of tangled dark curls, all too familiar, racing the opposite direction that we were, toward the stairwell.

Time seemed to slow. In a motion almost too fast to understand, the figure stooped down and grabbed the grenade, making my heart leap up my throat. Then, almost before I could think, his arm drew back and he threw the object back up the stairs. Whirling, he ran toward me and Owen. I reached out for him over Owen's shoulder, my arm straining to touch him.

Tim's name was on the tip of my tongue as Owen knelt and slung me to the ground, hunching his body over mine to shield me just as the blast went off. The sound of the explosion was loud but oddly faraway, and I had time to wonder exactly how far Tim had managed to throw the grenade. I clasped my hands over my head as I felt the force rumble through the house, the lights in the basement flickering.

A wash of heat, dust, and small debris washed over us, and for a moment I hoped that was all. Then, with a huge creaking and a groaning, the room around us went dark, and I heard the sounds of timbers splitting and cement cracking. I felt Owen jerk above me as rubble rained down around us, and then he was falling down on me, pushing us both the short rest of the way to the floor.

CHAPTER 3

Violet

For a while, it seemed like everything around us was rumbling. I couldn't see anything, and I was pinned to the ground by Owen. There was no way to tell whether moving or staying here would be safer. All I could do was pray, Tim's name still on my lips.

Slowly, silence fell. I started counting after the noise of debris falling stopped, wondering whether there was still more of the house above us slowly falling apart. When I got to thirty, I began to hope it was finally over.

I realized I'd closed my eyes during the cave-in. I opened them again. Blackness greeted me, and I blinked once, then twice. Now that I'd realized I was alive, I also began to notice the new set of aches running through my body. I struggled with the warm weight holding me down: Owen was lying on top of me, his chest pressed to mine, his hair tickling my chin. And he wasn't moving.

A throb of fear pulsed through me as the blackness did not

lessen, the feeling unfurling slowly in the pit of my stomach as awful possibilities raced through my head. What if we were trapped underneath this building? What if Desmond was digging us out as we lay here? What if she left us for dead? What if I had gone blind? What if Owen was… I cut that one off. Had I really seen Tim? And if so, where was he now?

A fear unlike anything I had ever known gripped me. I had survived a lot of things, but I wasn't sure I could handle any of those possibilities, let alone all of them at once. It was too… too terrifying a thought. My vocal cords clenched, and my body started to shake. When I caught myself whimpering, I stopped and took a deep breath.

I worked through the questions, starting with the silliest. I wasn't blind. My eyes would have been in pain if they'd been injured. More likely, the lights in this part of the basement had broken. If there was no light, at least they hadn't started a fire. If we were buried under here—another wave of panic flushed my chest, and I struggled with the question. I couldn't know for sure that we were trapped unless I checked. That went for most of the other questions too. Except—

Tim. He was the one who had saved us from the grenade. It had definitely been him. The memory was crystal clear. He must have been in the basement the entire time, hidden in the shadows at the edges of the huge room. Why hadn't he come to us when we'd raced down there? Why hadn't he said anything? Why wasn't he saying anything now?

I focused on Tim, pushing the rest of the questions back into the farthest recesses of my brain. If I tried to find him, the rest of the things would fall into place. They had to. I hoped.

First things first. "Owen?" I whispered.

There was no response. But the steady feel of the man's heart beating from inside his ribcage, and the sound of his breathing, softer than my own, reassured me he was still alive.

I shoved awkwardly at Owen, trying to push him off me. My left arm wasn't as strong as my right, but I continued straining with my whole body, first wriggling my hips out from under him, and then my shoulders, making for freedom, ignoring the pain. Nothing seemed that dire, though I was sure, as my chest heaved, that my bruised ribs were going to be set back in their healing process. Dirt and rubble on the floor gritted under me as I shifted, scraping loudly across the floor.

Shoving a final time with my hips, I pulled free of Owen. He slumped, his breath coming out in a grunt, but he showed no signs of waking—well, from my limited perspective. My guess was that some of the rubble that had missed me had hit him on the head during the cave-in. Maybe his attempt to protect me had helped after all.

My anger at Owen was still there, but it was pressed deep down beneath a layer of fear. I couldn't process all these feelings right now. I just needed to make sure he wasn't injured too badly. *And find Tim,* I thought, but one thing at a time. I needed to find a light first.

Sitting up, I began running my hand over the floor, trying to feel for my backpack. My fingers sifted through fine dust and chunks of wood and concrete, but found nothing. Irritated, I turned and reached for Owen's still form, running my hands over him. His backpack was still on his back, though it was covered in dust and debris.

I fumbled with it, the darkness suffocating, until I managed to work the clasp open. Getting on my knees, trying to ignore my growing anxiety, I began pulling things out hastily, letting them shift down and clatter to the floor before feeling them one at a time. There were several items I couldn't identify in the dark, then a long plastic tube that felt promising. I found the button on the side and clicked it back.

Nothing. I clicked the button three or four times, harder each time, without success. I shook the stupid contraption and heard a clinking sound. Whatever had happened to it, it wasn't working.

Breathing out in sour disappointment, I checked the bag again, and then began searching his pockets. Each second felt like an eternity, like this nothingness would forever be my reality.

I gasped when I felt something rectangular and metal brush against my fingertips as I dug my hand into one of Owen's pockets. Grasping it between clumsy fingers, I was pleased to find that it had a familiar weight. I pulled it out and held it to my nose. The smell of the flammable liquid teased my nostrils, and the smile that broke on my face must have looked kind of manic. It had to be a lighter.

Flipping open the lid, I struck the spark awkwardly, and was rewarded when the device ignited, its bright orange-and-blue flame erupting bright enough to make my vision gray for a second.

"Tim," I whispered, turning to the stairwell. The flame bounced and flickered, the darkness rushing in and out as I spun it around, but it remained lit, casting a circle of hazy orange light around me. The light cut over Owen's face, and I paused as I saw the trickle of blood coming from his forehead. I spared a moment to check his eyes, peeling back the lids. His pupils responded to the light, even if he didn't wake up. The rest of his body seemed thankfully intact.

"Tim?" I repeated as I began to move slowly toward the stairwell. Stepping around a twisted, broken metal shelf, I picked my way around overturned boxes, screws and bolts that had spilled out onto the floor, and large bits of rocks. It looked as though some of the sides of the secret room's walls leaned in, and most of the area around the door to the stairwell had collapsed. Something overhead creaked, and I stopped, raising the lighter up and looking at jagged, deep cracks in the ceiling where the broken concrete, brick, and mortar bits seemed to barely cling to each other, radiating outward from the area of the door like fingers.

I lowered the lighter and moved forward a few steps before stopping again, realizing that the pile of debris blocking my way toward what had once been a stairwell was bigger than I'd thought. A long counter was lying on its side, partially obstructing my path. Draped across it at an angle were several thick wooden boards, topped by broken bits of mortar and brick that looked precarious in their positioning. The boards were holding for now, creating a small gap in the rubble underneath them, and that was my only way through toward where I remembered the door was. A massive shelf had fallen on it at an angle, the objects and boxes under it propping it up slightly. It was a maze of chaos. Nothing looked sturdy at all.

I knelt down to try to peer down the accidental tunnel, and then gave a small, involuntary cry as I saw Tim lying there. His eyes were closed, his cheek resting on the floor. Blood was running from his nose in slow drips. I scooted forward into the hole, sticking my fingers over his mouth and nose before I had time to think. My heart beat twice before I could feel his slow and steady exhale. I held my fingers there for several more seconds, reassuring myself that he was breathing. Then I sat down, close to the boards. Eyeing the distance between myself and Tim's hand, I braced my foot against the cabinet. I pushed on it a few times to ensure that it wasn't going to shift as I began to pull. Taking a deep breath in, I closed the lighter. I carefully placed it in my pocket, and then leaned slowly forward, stretching out my hand for where I remembered Tim's was. I had to adjust my hand a few times, but eventually I grabbed his arm, just above the wrist, and pulled.

Tim shifted forward easily, and I gasped as my ribs pinched together painfully with the effort I was exerting. I didn't let go of Tim, but relaxed my effort before taking another deep breath and pulling again. Once Tim's shoulders were clear of the boards, I slid both arms under his armpits, and then squat-walked back with him a few feet. I stumbled on pieces of brick and banged the backs of my calves on a fallen table, but I made it clear of the worst of the debris.

My baby brother definitely wasn't a baby anymore, I thought as I sat down for a moment and let the warm, dusty, stifling air of the basement do its best to dry the perspiration that had formed on my skin. My breathing was ragged from exertion and fighting through the pain, and my head had begun to ache. After a few moments, I reached into my pocket and pulled out the lighter, flicking it on again.

Tim's pants were torn in a few places, and there were cuts on his legs and thighs. He wasn't bleeding profusely, but he *was* bruising horribly, the skin around the wounds already almost black. This was another side effect of Queen Rina's experimentation—not only was Tim hypersensitive to touch, so much so that it bordered on pain, but the capillaries just under his skin would rupture more easily and in greater amounts than an ordinary person's. He was going to hurt for the next few days.

I stroked my fingers through my brother's hair and then stood up. Ashabee's secret armory had another exit on the opposite side of the room, a secret driveway for the cars. When Viggo and Owen had explored it—I found myself thinking bitterly of the days when Viggo and Owen worked together, and had to refocus—they had found that there were tunnels that branched off out of this room, one to the fields, another to a location inside the house's walls. They were both well-disguised on the outside, so there was a good chance Desmond didn't know about either of the hidden exits. However, opening it now would reveal that advantage to her and her guards, and if she was alive and looking for me, there was no way I would be able to get Owen and Tim out as well. At that moment, I wished desperately for Jay's strength, knowing that with only my own two arms, it would never work.

Which meant I needed, somehow, to fight them. And not only to fight them, but to beat them. My mind whirled, leaping to and discarding a dozen ways to avoid a fight, and then a dozen more ways of bringing the fight to my opponents. There wasn't enough data, I realized. I had no idea what I was working with.

So, I scavenged. I started with Owen's bag, then dug up my own from a pile of rubble that had barely missed me, scraping my hands and feeling the dust build up beneath my fingernails. I found a counter against the wall much farther back that was untouched by the cave-in, and placed the bags atop it. I pulled out every item we'd packed one by one, giving myself a quick inventory, and then began searching the room. When I found my flashlight, I almost grinned again, immediately shutting the lighter off to conserve its fuel.

My search wasn't nearly as detailed as I would have liked, but it would have to do. From what I remembered, it had been almost six when Desmond had shown up. I was surprised to find, based on the watch on my wrist that was miraculously still working, that it had been under an hour since then—it already felt like I'd been here in this basement for hours.

It took the better part of twenty minutes to search the room and give first aid to Tim and Owen with the half-used, mouse-gnawed first-aid kit that I'd uncovered in a drawer underneath the counters. It was nearly seven thirty by the time I finished my hurried exploration. My search had yielded more than I'd thought it would, but then again, my group had left Ashabee's in a hurry, and they'd all said multiple times that there hadn't been enough room in all the vehicles for everything.

Which was very lucky for me. My eyes took in my overall haul in the glow of the flashlight. I had found a small bottle of kerosene, six grenades, some string, and, best of all, a rifle that had slipped behind one of the shelves and was lying on its side on the floor, as well as a bulletproof vest that I'd dragged out of an unmarked box on one of the back shelves. I also had a roll of duct tape from Owen's bag, his pistol, mine, and four clips of ammunition. I only had one magazine for the rifle, but reloading would have been too awkward for me to handle anyway. Still, I did have an idea for its application.

I just had to get up to the next floor somehow. Now that I had the beginnings of a plan gestating in my mind, the darkness around me didn't bother me as much—it was just another obstacle to be tackled like all the rest. I turned to the next problem. I couldn't use the once hidden door—it was buried now, behind the rubble Tim had been stuck under, but maybe I could find a ventilation duct. I wasn't keen on the idea, not after having been stuck navigating one in the facility in The Green, but it was the only idea I had.

It took me another fifteen minutes to realize that none of the vents I could find in the room were big enough to fit me, let alone me and all my gear. Clenching my teeth in annoyance, I swung back around, trying to see if I had missed any. I paused in the wide-open area where the cars had been kept, my light cutting over something on the wall almost quickly enough for my brain to dismiss it. Almost.

I swung the flashlight back around and frowned when I noticed that one small sliver of paint seemed brighter than the rest. I studied it closely. There was a nearly imperceptible difference between the paint here and the rest of the wall. It sat a millimeter or two back, just a small gap, barely noticeable.

Tucking the flashlight under my arm, I touched the area, and felt it give slightly under my left hand. Biting my lip, I placed my hand flat and dragged it to the left. The flat panel slid open, revealing a hollow, square chute just behind it, carved out of the bedrock. Hanging inside was a metal cage, just big enough to sit in, with a series of pulleys and ropes that seemed to attach to the top. These went up into the darkness beyond the roof of the cage.

It was an elevator. A ridiculously small one, but I didn't care what size it was if it led to one of the other levels of the house. This was my ticket up. I moved back to the counter and threw all my gear into my backpack—everything I could reliably carry, keeping the rifle in my hands. I was just going to have to set it down to fit into this strangely tiny box.

I moved back to the miniature elevator, opening the cage door and thrusting the rifle into the back, pressed against the mesh. Then I turned around and sat backward into the metal cage, ducking my head under the bit of wall overhanging the entry. I scooted back until I felt my shoulders touch the mesh, and then pulled my legs in, adjusting myself to the small space. It wasn't completely uncomfortable, but I wouldn't want to be stuck in it for any length of time.

Swinging my flashlight around the chamber, I looked for a switch that would make the thing go. I hoped it was simple and easy to figure out... and that the electricity here was still working, for that matter. For a moment, I was afraid that after all this I'd be stymied by complicated machinery, and then I saw a little panel awkwardly wired into the heavy mesh next to the cage door. There were only two buttons. I pushed the top one.

The small elevator made no noise, not a chime of the kind I'd expected based on the few elevators I'd seen in my life. But a little light above the button pulsed a soft green, and then, more silently than I could have hoped, it began to ascend. The cage shifted and swayed gently, and I swallowed, trying to still my nerves, hoping this plan would not get me killed. My brother—and Owen, too, though he might not deserve my help—were counting on me. I had too much at stake here to die.

CHAPTER 4

Viggo

A bright red hue lit up the horizon, glowing like a beacon, inviting anyone nearby to come check it out. But in the deserted countryside, we seemed to be the only ones around. It was just as well. As we turned down the narrow dirt road that led us toward it, I could see hazy wisps of smoke in the air, whirling around us as we drove past. The corn in Mr. Kaplan's field was turning brown in death, the strong stalks sagging, almost weeping, for the loss of their caretaker.

The vehicle bounced over the bumps in the road, the shocks squeaking under the weight. The glow grew brighter as we approached the trees on each side of the road, their branches obscuring the view of the house, creating a little archway. Thomas sped through it, and I blinked as the smoldering remains of the farmhouse came into view.

Part of the second floor had collapsed, and everything was a charred black. The flames were mostly gone, but embers still burned brightly on the ground. I could see Lynne near the house, grabbing a bucket and splashing liquid on the ground just outside the perimeter. I had instructed her and Morgan to make sure the fire we'd started in order to call in the ambulance we'd hijacked didn't rage out of control, and thanks to their efforts, it seemed that it hadn't.

Thomas pulled the car up to where the other vehicles were parked and shut off the engine. Within moments, we were all stepping out, each of us with a clear destination in mind. Except for Cruz, of course—he stood near the back of the ambulance, his eyes studying the fire. I moved closer to it, keeping an eye on him as I headed toward Lynne.

"How'd it go?" she asked as she splashed more water on the dirt. She wiped the sweat off her brow with her forearm, exchanging her bucket for a full one from the supply they'd brought from the well and taking a big step over, splashing the next patch of earth.

"We got the broadcast out," I replied grimly, and she turned toward me fully, giving me a meaningful look.

"Their response?"

I met her gaze flatly, shaking my head at the brunette before me. "Kill the messengers. And anybody... anybody who heard it, too."

She frowned. "It's going to get bad."

"It always does."

"Pardon me?"

The voice behind me was startling, but I tried not to spin around quickly—I didn't particularly want to show my surprise to this person. I turned and regarded Cruz. Lynne put a hand on her hip and blew a lock of hair away from her eyes. "Who's this?"

Cruz's eyes lit on Lynne, his gaze sliding up and down her curves. He smiled, his white teeth flashing red in the light of the embers, and he managed a small bow. "Please, allow me to introduce myself. I am Anello Cruz."

Lynne's face stayed carefully blank, and I bit back a smile as Cruz blinked, waiting for a reaction. His dark brown eyes flicked to me, and then back to Lynne. He straightened, shrugging. "Surely it sounds just a small bit familiar?" he repeated, and Lynne shook her head—but this time, a little smile turned the corners of her mouth up.

I wasn't sure where that was coming from. I shook my head at him, deriving a small amount of pleasure from disillusioning the man. "She's from Matrus," I informed him, and Cruz's eyebrows leaped into his hairline.

"Ahhhh, a Matrian! Are they all as beautiful as you over there, or are you just extraordinarily blessed?"

I blinked, feeling like I had just been sucker punched. Had Cruz—a man who had not so long ago been accusing me of treason while we'd had him tied up with zip ties—actually interrupted our conversation so he could flirt? My mind sputtered and stalled in the face of that frankly illogical action.

Lynne's reaction, however, baffled me further. Her hand was still on her hip, but she was eyeing Cruz up and down with wary interest. "Are you serious right now?"

Cruz raised his hands, an eager smile on his lips. "As the night is long in winter."

At that, she chuckled, her smile broadening. "What a gentleman," she said finally, though she seemed more amused than seduced. "Are you a refugee as well? Will you be joining us?"

"Your cause is my cause now, madam," Cruz replied, not

missing a beat.

Lynne gave another chuckle at his use of the word 'madam,' and I had just about had enough. "Lynne, would you excuse us for a minute?" I said, managing not to drawl, and took Cruz by the shoulder, guiding him far enough away that our conversation wouldn't be clearly overheard.

"What is it, Croft? Do you have a problem?" he asked, his dark eyes serious. I peered into them, trying to figure out the motivations hiding there, then looked for a way to phrase my question.

I settled on, "Are you just putting on a show for her? Or are you serious?"

"About the beauty of the lady over there?"

"About joining our cause," I said, the words coming out perhaps more dry than I'd been trying for. I didn't have a problem with new recruits, but this one seemed a little suspicious to me. His help had been useful in our escape, but how could I know that he wasn't, once again, siding with whoever wouldn't get him killed? Frankly, the man's manner grated on me, but I wasn't going to deny another fighter we desperately needed just because of that. Cruz was a former Power Fight League fighter, and in many ways, he seemed a typical Patrian male—so I felt my concern was justified. If he couldn't get behind the females who were also leading our little cadre, then things were not going to go well.

Cruz stared back at me. From what I remembered of the ring, he'd never backed down from a challenge. "I am very serious," he said. "I want to be a part of it. I mean, that's why you kidnapped me, hijacked the feed, and broadcasted your little message, eh? To get people to help you fight the Matrian invaders? Well, I listened. I want them all to go back to where they came from and stop destroying my country. I'm already here, and I want to help."

"And me zip tying your hands to a pipe didn't leave you with any hard feelings at all?" I said, letting my skepticism leak into my voice.

Cruz raised his eyebrows. "My personal feelings about that incident put aside, I can forgive a few mistakes here and there, Croft."

I stiffened automatically. Even though the message was conciliatory, the remark grated on my pride, and Cruz knew it. But I was controlling my alpha male urges right now.

"If you were to join us," I tested, "what help could you offer us?"

Cruz smiled. "Well, for one thing," he said with complete confidence, "I can tell you that the way you are going about controlling this fire is completely mad."

Now that was interesting. "How do you know that?"

"I see you were not paying attention to my tour earlier today."

"I had bigger things on my mind."

That shut him up for a moment, but his mouth did not remain closed for long. "I helped put out the fires in Patrus when they started. When everything started. I learned much from it."

I would listen to his idea, even if I found the man himself irritating. "Do you have a suggestion?"

"First, we need to dig a trench around the house. About… as wide as my arm, and as deep as from my finger tips to my elbow."

"That's a lot of work," I said dubiously. "We might have some time, but not that much."

"If you want to keep this under control until it goes out, it's the only way. But hey, have no fear, my friend! I saw a big digger over there by the farm. I'll just start it up—shouldn't take long at all."

"You know how to drive a digger?" I asked. The question went straight to his back, as he was already jogging toward the barn. He raised his hand, flashing me a thumbs-up sign, and I rolled my eyes. I wanted to see this idea at work—I wouldn't deny that it could be useful—but if Cruz stayed, this discipline thing was going to have to be addressed. I wandered back over to Lynne, deep in thought.

"I'm sorry about that one," I said to her.

She turned to me, empty bucket in hand, and smiled. "It's okay. I thought he was kind of sweet. It's hard to explain why... Maybe because he's just confident or something, but he's got a certain... charm."

"I thought he was kind of a jerk, myself."

Lynne laughed, unaffected by my grumpiness. "A lot of people are jerks when they're threatened. And I'm sure you have no idea why any guy would be threatened by *you*, Viggo."

I shrugged and crossed my arms, choosing not to rise to that bait. "He's going to have to work with me a lot if he joins up. So he'll have to get over it."

"Well, he seemed sincere in wanting to help," Lynne said thoughtfully. "Maybe we just need to give him a chance."

I thought about this. "You're probably right," I said. "But that doesn't mean we shouldn't be cautious. He was working with the Matrians not too long ago. He gained their trust enough that they let him walk around the station unattended. And that worked out very poorly for them. I can't just trust him blindly. Too much riding on it."

The woman nodded. "That's true."

For now, if he got the digger working and helped control the fire, I would keep the guy around. But he was going to have to prove himself. Not just to me, but to all of us.

"Thanks for your input, Lynne," I said. "I can't spend too much time on this—gotta catch up with Ms. Dale. Can you just watch him for me for now?"

"I got you, Viggo," she replied, giving me a warm smile. "I'll keep an eye on him."

"Thanks," I said sincerely.

She gave me a mock salute and then turned to the rest of the men, who had been keeping the wet line going behind her, already telling them to take a break—they had another plan to implement. I turned and headed back to where Ms. Dale was standing in front of the bound emergency crew, the light of the video causing their faces to glow. It was nearing the end of the message, from what I could tell. Sure enough, she reached down and clicked it off.

"I'm sure this is a shock to you, and I understand that. Give it a minute to percolate. And while you do, I want you to consider this: in a few minutes, I'm going to let you go. You're free to take your vehicle and go wherever you want. You can also feel free to alert whoever you want. We won't be here when you get back. However, if you believe in what you just saw in that video, then you'll know we're not your enemies. We're here to help. You have the choice to stay with us, if you want, but we won't force you."

I stopped, content to let Ms. Dale continue with this crucial job; she had this under control. I moved away as she continued to speak, heading for where Amber, Thomas, and Jeff were standing near the front of the ambulance. "Any word from Tiffany?" I asked, referring to our spy still in the city.

Jeff shook his head, his mustache drooping sadly. "No. We keep trying to reach her, but she isn't picking up. Do you think…?"

I met his eyes, noting the shimmering fear lurking in the shadowed recesses of his gaze. "We don't know anything yet, and before we left, the place was turning into a madhouse. She might be on the run, or trying to hide—we just don't know. Make sure whoever's on guard duty knows to keep the handheld on them at all times, and get one of us if she calls."

Amber nodded. "I'll handle that."

"Excellent. Now, do you mind if I use that thing to call Violet? I want to let her know we're all right."

Thomas extended the handheld he had been holding. "I didn't do it yet. It occurred to me that if I did I would be denying you an emotional outlet."

I smiled, resisting the urge to pat him on the shoulder. I wasn't entirely sure how he'd react to that. "Thanks."

Tapping the screen, I selected the handheld designation that connected to the one they kept at our base and waited for the call to connect. Amber shifted, catching my attention. She had a bemused expression on her face, her finger tapping the corner of her eye. I gave her a confused look, and her smile grew, her finger still tapping… I reached up and touched my eye, thinking something was stuck there, and my fingers were brought to a halt by the spectacles I was still wearing. I snatched them off just as the handheld connected. I shoved the glasses into a pocket and looked down, surprised to see Dr. Tierney's heart-shaped face filling the screen.

"Dr. Tierney? Where's Violet?"

Dr. Tierney frowned, a crease forming in the middle of her forehead. "She left. I thought you knew."

I froze, trying to process what she was saying. "What do you mean, she *left*?"

"Owen came for her. Said Thomas sent him information on where Tim could be. That he was going to go looking and Violet could join. I think they went out around five, five thirty. Was that not… Viggo?"

I wasn't looking at the screen anymore, which was probably why Dr. Tierney was calling my name. I didn't care. Thomas shifted under my gaze, his posture screaming his discomfort to me. "You sent it to Owen?"

"I thought it would be best," he replied defensively. "That he was the best choice, all things considered."

"Owen's brother just died, Thomas. He isn't exactly thinking straight."

"But he wouldn't do anything crazy. He probably just took her to look."

"Yes—in the countryside, where sightings of other people become slimmer every day, and… more importantly, we have soldiers who are going to be hunting for us very, very soon, if they haven't started already."

"I see." Thomas frowned pensively, his eyes shifting back and forth as if deep in thought. After a moment, he squared his shoulders. "I may have miscalculated, although to be fair, I asked Owen to check it out and hold off on telling Violet, as you asked me to."

I blinked, absorbing this information. "Then why would he take her?"

Thomas shrugged, looking completely baffled. "I have no idea."

The wrongness of everything about this was causing my gut to churn. "I've got to find them," I said.

Looking down at Dr. Tierney, who was still trying to get my attention on the handheld, I bade her a quick goodbye and shut the device down. "Send me the coordinates to those sightings and keep things going here," I said to the assembled group, then turned toward the cars. "Try to get out in an hour or less—any longer and we're pushing it. I've got a radio in my bag. I'll be on channel three."

I shouted the last part behind me, breaking into a jog, and then a run, across the dew-soaked grass toward the group of cars we'd brought here from our home base. I checked my watch. It was seven thirty. She'd been gone for hours, and it was dark. Something was terribly wrong—I wasn't even sure how I knew it, I just did.

Throwing my bag into the backseat, I leapt into the driver's seat and started the engine with the keys that still dangled from the ignition. It turned over with a dull roar, and I threw it in reverse. Turning so I could see behind me, I started to accelerate, when the sound of the passenger-side door opened and Ms. Dale hopped in.

"Ms. Dale, I—"

"Oh, for heaven's sake, Viggo," she chided as she buckled her seatbelt with a click. She met my gaze, her eyes unmoving. "I'm responsible for her too."

It took me a moment to absorb what she was saying, but once it hit me, I closed my mouth and nodded. "Right."

The engine roared as I hit the gas, propelling us backward until we could turn around. I quickly turned the car, threw it into drive, and then headed out, trying to let the motion of the vehicle and the fact I was out here, trying to find Violet as soon as possible, soothe the worried knot in my stomach.

It didn't help.

CHAPTER 5

Viggo

I gazed out the window, the road flying under us as I held down the accelerator. It took everything I had not to just speed up, but I didn't want to miss a single thing in the dark. Ms. Dale sat behind me, her eyes on our map of the country roads, surveying it and comparing it to the information Thomas had recovered about Tim's possible location.

"These files are eyewitness statements," she murmured in the silence of the cab.

I glanced over at her, the blue light of the handheld illuminating the sharp lines of her face. "By whom?"

"People who live out here," she replied, shifting slightly in her seat. "Taken from their debriefing reports when they went into the city to register. One man saw him lurking around his farm—that's the one we just left—and another two spotted him on the road… heading south, but he cut into the tree line before they could stop to ask him for help, so no help there."

"And this last one?"

"As odd as it seems, on top of a hill. It's apparently very popular with lovers, and the two in question decided to take a small break from their drive. It's only a few kilometers from this road."

"It makes sense," I said. "He'd be staying in a small area, trying to find us."

She sighed and shook her head. "We were idiots to focus so much on the idea he'd been captured. We could've been scouring the area for him. None of this would need to be happening."

Her statement caught me by surprise. I shot her a glance and then shook my head. "That's not necessarily true. You know that."

She pressed her lips together in a tight frown and then looked away, leaning heavily in the seat and lapsing into silence.

The road continued to slip by, jouncing us as we rode in silence. It was gut-churningly painful, all that silence. It gave my mind the freedom to focus on the worry that had settled into every muscle of my body, making me feel like gelatin. All I could think about was Violet and Owen, hours earlier, searching on the very road we were driving on now… Them being taken… or… or worse.

"Talk to me," I barked at Ms. Dale when it became too much.

I could feel the surprise radiating from her, even before she uttered, "What?"

"This quiet. It's not doing me any favors."

There was a pause. "Oh." The silence rushed back in for a second as the old spy fidgeted slightly in her seat, readjusting herself. "What do you want me to talk about?"

"Anything. Nothing. I don't know… How's Henrik?"

I turned and saw her eyebrows rise in surprise. "Henrik?"

"Yeah. He's awake now, right? Growing stronger every day?"

"He is." Her tone was cautious, waiting. "So?" I gave a little chuckle and shook my head at her, meeting her gaze briefly before focusing again on the road. "What?" she asked insistently.

"Nothing—you're just really bad at this."

"What? Talking about another member of our team?"

"No, talking about your relationship, Melissa."

I heard her tsk and smiled in the darkness. It always struck a nerve when I called her that. I still wasn't entirely sure why. We all called each other by our first names—except her. Somehow calling her 'Melissa' over 'Ms. Dale' had never sat right. I couldn't even think of her that way.

"Mr. Croft, my personal life is not for public dissemination," Ms. Dale said archly. "Whom I spend my time with is really none of your concern."

"Oh, come on. We all know that something's going on with you two. How is hiding it—"

"Look, just because some of us choose to be more discreet in our relationships—"

"At least you admit that you're in one."

Another quick glance at Ms. Dale made me grin. Her mouth was a circle of surprise, her eyes wide. As soon as I looked, she closed her mouth with a cluck of her tongue and then looked out the window.

The quiet returned, and I sighed. Maybe I had pushed her a little too far. Maybe I should—

"Did you have problems with Violet? With how hard she's been pushing herself, in spite of barely being out of her sickbed?"

I blinked. She was actually asking for my advice? That was new. And... nice. "Yeah, actually. It wasn't easy to come to terms with."

"How did you manage?"

"Well, first I had to resist the urge to tie her to the bed," I said, and she chuckled.

"Yes, well, I can understand that."

"Henrik's pushing himself too hard?"

She looked at me, a sardonic expression on her face. "Of course he is. He keeps getting out of bed and trying to move around, despite Dr. Tierney's advice. Oh, that's the turn."

I slowed, turning the wheel, and stopped when the headlights cut over the grass of the hill. Ms. Dale sat forward, and I knew her eyes were glued to the same thing mine were. We got out of the vehicle, squatting down in front to peer at the dust on the side of the road. Fresh tire prints marred the surface, the tread identical to that of the vehicle we drove in now—like all of Ashabee's cars, designed by him, Amber had said, to be bulletproof.

"They were here," I said.

Ms. Dale stood up, her eyes following the lines. "But they're not anymore. I think they went that way," she said, pointing down the road in the direction we had been traveling.

"Is there a back way to the camp I don't know about?"

She shook her head and went to the car to retrieve the handheld. I climbed in too, not wanting to waste a moment. Ms. Dale began moving the map around on the screen, scanning. Then she made an irritated noise.

"Ashabee's," she said in disgust. "Of course—what an idiot I've been."

"What? Why?"

She looked at me, her eyes holding my gaze. "Viggo, we're within a mile of Ashabee's property. It's the last place Tim saw us, so..."

"So he went back and has been hiding out there? No, then they would've found him. They'd be watching the place."

"Yes, they'd be watching for anyone coming or going, sure, but they might not be watching the entire property. Look, the dates on these sightings were right after the palace fell. He walked back—probably slept in the barn for warmth, walked down this road to travel more easily, and then climbed the hill to try and find it. He's very likely to be there."

"Do you think Owen and Violet went there?" Ms. Dale nodded, her face solemn. "Of course they did," I muttered.

I threw the car into gear, and Ms. Dale frowned. "We should call for backup," she said.

"There's no time for them to get here. Besides, a two-man team draws a lot less attention."

She exhaled sharply. "That's the stupidest thing you've ever said. I would've accepted something like 'our enemy is distracted and probably not paying attention' or 'we know the property better than they do,' but that one was pretty lame."

I gritted my teeth together. "Yes, for those reasons too, but mostly because we can't just leave them there."

Ms. Dale rolled her eyes and patted my forearm. "Relax, Viggo, I didn't say we weren't going. So stop growling at me and start driving."

I readjusted myself in the seat, tamping down the sudden rage that had formed in my stomach, and then pressed the gas, throwing us forward. It took a few heartbeats for me to completely calm down. When I did, a question instantly popped into my mind.

"You said earlier that I wasn't the only one responsible for her."

"I did." Her tone was guarded, but I forged on.

"Was that because of what you did?"

She shot me a glance and then looked away, clasping her hands together in her lap.

In a moment of duress, back when we were more enemies than friends, Ms. Dale had confessed to me that *she* had been the one to select Tim as a test subject during the Matrian screening process for boys. At the time, she had been following orders from her higher-ups, testing young Violet's loyalty to Matrus, but I knew it had eaten her up inside ever since she had seen the true horror of how the boys were "trained" in the Facility. I was picking at a sore spot, I knew that. But I wanted to understand. Needed to, really.

I turned right down the road that would lead us to the mansion, and Ms. Dale sighed. "Of course it is," she confirmed. "I… set Violet down this path. Regardless of my intentions, I did. And in doing so, I hurt her, and more specifically, her brother, more than I thought was possible. The suffering she's endured all stems from me, from a decision *I* made."

"Not all of it is your—"

"Spare me, Mr. Croft. I am looking for neither forgiveness nor platitudes. Yes, I was ignorant of the use of the boys, and yes, I didn't have a choice about whether or not to send Violet to Patrus. I just put her in a position to choose, when she shouldn't have had to. And from that moment, her fate was sealed. Every step on this path exists because I forced her to choose."

I fell silent, uncertain how to respond. After a moment, Ms. Dale added, "I owe Violet a debt I can never repay. And given that disaster seems to follow her around, I realize that maybe I have spent too much time trying to fix the problem, and not enough time trying to take care of her. Just like I spent too much time fixated on what she could do for Matrus, and not enough time trying to learn who she really was. Maybe if I had, I would've realized—"

She drew silent as we both noticed it at the same time—a bright red glow on the horizon that I recognized. Something was on fire, something bigger and more out of control than the little blaze we'd set at Mr. Kaplan's. And I knew, within my core, that it was Ashabee's mansion.

I pressed down on the accelerator, watching the speedometer needle drag upward, climbing to its zenith, the engine roaring noisily, and we raced down the road next to the wood.

Slowing enough to make the turn, I pressed down on the brakes hard, stopping short with a jerk that caused the seatbelts to lock up. I unhooked mine as I rolled down the window, leaning over and clumsily keying in Amber's code. The unbroken side of the huge gate rattled as the machine whirred, pulling back before us and revealing the mansion—half of it ablaze, thick black plumes of smoke reaching out into the sky.

Even from the distance, I could see a lone, dark figure standing on the driveway, watching it burn.

CHAPTER 6

Violet

The tiny elevator creaked under my weight, and I looked up, through the mesh, as the darkness around me continued to press in. I didn't know where the ceiling was, couldn't see it in the gloom. Whatever Ashabee had designed this tiny elevator for, he hadn't done a good job. Why wouldn't he have included proper lighting? I fidgeted and checked my watch, my nerves making it hard to sit cramped up in this tiny space, my feelings swinging from impatience to nausea.

It had been another twenty minutes of gear gathering, planning, and searching since I'd last checked. Not good—who knew what Desmond was up to? Maybe she'd already found another way into the basement. I'd have no way of knowing in this black hole. My heart beat faster, and I felt the sickness rising in my stomach again, but pushed it down. I tried to calm myself, if only a little. Maybe she'd decided we were dead and left.

I shook my head at myself. As appealing as it sounded, that

idea was the dream of the hopelessly naïve.

Just then, the green light, which had been blinking slowly as the cage rose, became steady again. Then it went out, and the cage shuddered to a halt. This was it, then. A new type of fear gripped my shoulders as I realized it was time to see if I would even be able to implement my plan.

Licking my dry lips, I turned my focus onto the gate in front of me, sliding it open. A panel sat in front of me, cool to the touch. I felt my way around the edges, and detected a small bump under my fingers. It was about the size of the tip of my pinky, and spherical. Even in the shadowed light cast by my flashlight, which I'd lain on the floor of the elevator cage, it was hard to see.

I grasped it between my fingers and then twisted, freezing when I heard a small click. The panel gave a little, and slowly, very slowly, I opened it a crack, peering through it for any sign of life. Heartbeats passed as I strained for any indication that I wasn't alone. Silence greeted my caution with open arms, beckoning me forth. So far, so good.

I gently pushed the panel with my fingertip, watching the gap grow wider as it swung out into a dim room. When I heard it bounce off the wall with a little thunk, I froze, my heart skipping a beat, my eyes searching the darkness for signs of Desmond or her entourage. Nothing stirred.

I grabbed the flashlight and swung it around, illuminating the room. The beam of light cut across a door on my right, a shelf with several books and picture frames, a wardrobe, a nightstand, a bed… Gauging from the narrow stature of that particular piece of furniture, I was in the servants' quarters on the second floor. Carefully, I unfolded my legs and slid out from the elevator, letting my feet land softly on the hard wooden floor. I crouched, and immediately let out a gasp as my legs almost gave out on me. My muscles were deadened from the position I'd been sitting in, pins and needles already jabbing around my feet and shins.

I held on to the frame of the elevator, using my left hand and my right shoulder as a brace to keep from falling, and waited for the numbness to recede. As soon as my legs felt relatively normal again, I straightened my knees and grabbed my bag and the rifle from inside the elevator.

Leaving the grate open, I closed the panel, and then studied it. On one side it was stone, but the side facing the room was covered with wood, with nobs fastened to it—a garment or tie rack, clearly, judging by the row of long strips of fabric in simple navy blues, browns, and blacks that hung from the knobs. Actually, though… The tie on this particular knob had a flashy design with bold geometric patterns and colors shooting through it. Clever.

Secure in the knowledge that I could find my way back to the elevator, I turned and tossed my bag onto the bed, glad to be rid of its heaviness for a moment. I moved toward the door, getting ready to turn my flashlight off, when a picture caught my eye. It was a picture of Jeff—Ashabee's former manservant. He had his arm thrown around an elderly woman with thick round glasses. They were pressed cheek to cheek, her hand on his other cheek, his arm draped lovingly around her.

The scene was nice. It seemed strange that Jeff had left it in the move. Maybe he'd forgotten it?

Something made me shove the picture into my pocket, and then I put the thread of curiosity aside. I needed to know what was going on. I stuffed the smallest handgun into my waistband, leaving the rest of the backpack on the bed. Then I clicked off the flashlight and moved toward the dim light shining under the door. I opened it gently, trying to mute the click as much as possible. I pulled it open a fraction of an inch, then a bit wider, until I could stick my head out into the corridor beyond. I was alone.

I pressed my head against the door and exhaled in relief. Then I moved, creeping as silently as I could back toward the servants' stairs at the rear of the house—the ones Ashabee's secret doorway sat above.

Jeff's room was very close to the stairs—probably since he was the most called-upon member of Ashabee's staff—so it took me only a few moments to reach them. I circled the still intact landing carefully, pausing when I heard the distinct sound of Desmond's voice wafting up from below.

"—again, requesting update on a heloship evacuation route at my position."

There was a burst of static, and then a nasally voice piped through. "With regrets, ma'am, the queen has ordered all heloships on standby. There is a crisis in the city, and we're still assessing the risk."

Desmond spat out a curse. I crept closer to the stairs, testing my weight on each floorboard before I moved onto it. With all the rubble below, I had expected this thing to be a mess. But somehow, it continued to be structurally sound. Ashabee must have brought in a brilliant architect when he had the mansion built. At this point, it wouldn't have surprised me.

"Thanks for the update, Control," said another female voice. I bit back a smile—clearly Desmond was tired of talking. I was glad that she was frustrated. It wasn't much to make up for the horrors she had put us through, but it was a start. I slid farther behind the landing, trying to find the place where I could peer down and see how many guards there were. So far, I'd heard one.

"Keep sifting that rubble out of the way. We need to get down there. Find out if she's dead or if she's managed to escape us. Again."

Desmond's voice held an angry bark to it, reminding me of a savage dog. *I'm not dead,* I thought to her, as though she could hear me. *And I'm going to make your life a lot harder.*

"With respect, ma'am, there are pieces of stone here too big for us to move on our own. We need a full team here to—"

"Haven't you heard, Warden? There is rioting in the streets, people looting and gone wild over one little propaganda video made by a team of rebels. And not just any rebels, no, but the same one *that* girl in the basement happens to lead. She's a criminal, ladies, and dangerous to boot. Not to mention, she is the only suspect in the assassination of Queen Rina. I don't care how hard it is; we have a duty to Queen Elena to get her and drag her back to Matrus for questioning. So stop arguing with me and dig!"

I finally got an angle by going to my belly, peering around the wraparound stairs. It was hard to see all the guards, but from the little flashes and the softer exchange of voices, I counted three. I waited for a while. Desmond paced the area around the stairs like a wild beast as I watched, and I fantasized about going to get my rifle and just unloading a clip into her. But I knew it would be a rash move. Killing Desmond would only get me killed by the guards. While I'd held stairs like this before, I'd been in better shape then, in a pitched battle with backup if I failed. If they all charged up the stairs at me, I was likely to be able to take most of them out—but what if one came around behind me or ran away? Or what if one hit me, and Tim and Owen were left to fend for themselves in the basement with unknown injuries?

Or I could take them all out at once… I thought about just

tossing a grenade down the staircase at them, a brutal parody of what Desmond had done to me and Owen—and, inadvertently, Tim. But down there, the walls were already compromised. Who knew what another concussive blast would do to the structures down in the basement? It could do nothing. Or it could cut off more than the lights in the front part of the basement. I knew the hidden doors needed electricity to run—what if the wires were already damaged? I still had the tiny elevator, but it needed electricity, too. If I had to risk more structural damage to the house, I wanted it to be farther away from the part where my brother was still effectively prisoner.

I breathed out silently. I was wasting time here imagining fanciful revenge stories and big triumphs. Really, I just needed the guards out of the picture, and that meant using something other than a straight-out fight, which I would never win in my condition.

I crept back to Jeff's room, feeling secure about my safety for the next few minutes, grabbed my backpack, and dumped its contents onto the bed. I stared at the things I'd collected, my heart already racing at the thought of what I needed to do, focusing on the items, trying to piece them together… Almost before I had my plan fully mapped, I slipped what I needed back into the bag and stared at the bulletproof vest, wondering if it would slow me down too much to put it on now. I went out into the halls again without its unnatural weight on my ribs and prayed I had not made a grave mistake…

Then, once I felt I'd gotten sufficiently far enough away from the back wing of the house to avoid damaging more of the basement, I began setting up traps using the grenades.

It was tricky business, creating a tripwire with a live explosive.

I knew a lot about it in theory, based on conversations I'd had with Viggo and Ms. Dale. I was always interested in listening to them talk about this kind of stuff, which wasn't surprising, considering the course my life had taken.

I knew two good ways to rig a tripwire using the supplies I had, but given that I only had one good hand, my choice was whittled down to one option. I used duct tape to secure my precious supply of grenades to things in the house, swearing under my breath as I fought each time to rip off the long strands with my single useful hand and my teeth. The grenades looked more like silver cocoons than weapons by the time I was done, nesting on a wall under a chair here, a table leg there—I wanted to make sure the tape held them harder than the jerk it would take to pull the pin loose. With this method, I attached the trip wire directly to the pin, running it at an angle to something across a doorway or a hall and tying it off. Hopefully, the guard who passed through it would walk fast enough so the pin was ripped out. I tried my best to make that the only option while not thinking too hard about what would happen if one of traps didn't go off. My backup plan was desperate but simple: shoot them before they shot me.

As I crept around upstairs, stepping lightly, barely daring to breathe, I felt as though every closed door held a guard behind it, and around every corner I expected to see a search party coming to find me. I kept reminding myself they had no reason to believe I could escape the basement—but this was Desmond I was dealing with. Wouldn't Desmond think to search the house? My breath hitched at creaking floorboards, and I fought to keep my hand steady on the grenades even as I cursed my ever-present cast. My fingers slipped as I set up the traps, and I checked my watch constantly. Every minute passing told me I had been up here too long. Every time I looked down at my watch and saw that even more time had slipped away, I was painfully reminded that Tim and Owen were depending on me.

Once I had everything in place, or as best as I could get it at the moment, I wavered on running through the trap locations one more time. I had to remember exactly where the wires to the grenades were, or else my whole plan would backfire on me—but it had already been twenty minutes, and I didn't think I could afford the time. Any moment, they might choose to stop digging and go search the rest of the house. I would just have to trust my memory and risk it.

I crept back to Jeff's room and put the bulletproof vest on, then shrugged my shirt back on over it, its clumsy weight settling over my ribs as if to say that we were really getting serious now. I took the gun Owen had given me out of my waistband and wrapped it up in a shirt I'd pilfered from Jeff's wardrobe.

Moving confidently down the hall, I slowed as I approached the landing to the servants' stairs, creeping silently past it. I paused, listening to the sounds of grunting and straining that came from below. The guards were working on moving a big chunk of debris now, and from the sound of it, they weren't making much progress. A part of me still wanted to try my luck with shooting them... but I'd already gone through that logic. I couldn't risk taking them all at once.

At least they were distracted. I approached a window that looked out on the grounds behind the manor. It was a smaller window than the others found around the house—I guessed Ashabee had figured his servants didn't need a view. Sucking in a deep breath, I drew back my gun, wrapped in Jeff's shirt, and slammed it hard on the corner of the window.

It shattered noisily, and I froze, my ears and eyes focused on the landing. Seconds went by without a sound, so I began to knock at the glass still standing in the frame, sweeping it away.

"Someone's up there," a voice said loudly.

"Of course someone's up there," Desmond's voice came snidely. "Get up there and find out who!"

I'd known they were going to hear me—that was the point of the maneuver—but even so, my heart jumped into my mouth at the sound of the order to come find me. I heard footsteps clattering up the hall and jumped into action as quickly as I could. Which wasn't very fast.

I awkwardly shoved the muffled gun—safety on—into my waistband and moved down the hallway at a fast walk, heading deeper into the servants' quarters, hearing cautious footsteps on the floor behind me. Despite all my preparations, I spotted my first trap only in the nick of time, managing to step over it and ignore thoughts of what would have happened if I hadn't seen it there. When I moved around the corner, I paused, my heart beating fast, to peek out into the hallway I'd just left… just in time to meet the brown eyes of a Matrian warden stepping out of a door.

Her eyes widened, and then the shout went up: "Over there! She went down that hall!" I darted back, stumbling on my feet with a little jolt of panic at the footsteps behind me accelerating into a run. I didn't have to get away, I reminded myself. I just had to avoid…

Three steps down the hall. Four. The footsteps grew louder and louder, and I held my breath, wondering whether to start running.

Then the explosion went off, debris flying down the hall and impacting against the wall behind me.

I let out the breath I'd been holding, risking a moment to hope. Peeking around the corner once more, I winced when I saw the still form of one guard, blood soaking into her uniform, making the heavy olive-green fabric appear almost black. The other two guards were also sprawled on the floor, but they were stirring, slowly sitting up.

I turned back and began to move, heading toward the next trap. I didn't want to draw too far ahead of them—which was good, because my ribs made it hard for me to run much faster than this. I couldn't have beat them, even if I wanted to. Even at a pace that seemed agonizingly slow, I made it to the next corner and was just moving into the adjacent hall when gunfire exploded behind me.

Hunching my shoulders and gritting my teeth against the impending pain in my ribs, I threw myself into the bedroom on the left side of the hall, the door already standing open for me. From what I'd gathered during our time here, these were some of Ashabee's more 'practical' guest rooms, which meant not grand enough for a politician or someone of great wealth, but rather a merchant or some kind of representative.

It was still such a luxurious chamber that it made this whole maneuver seem more surreal than ever. I slammed the door shut behind me, wincing at the loud noise it made; as soon as it was shut, I slid down onto my stomach, wriggling myself under the bed, trying not to think of hands grabbing my feet and dragging me out while I was exposed like this...

I made it under, feet first, and waited, my breaths whooshing loudly in my ears, my handgun pressing uncomfortably into my hip. I grabbed the string running down the bedpost to my left and anxiously rubbed it between my fingers, hoping for luck.

It felt like ages before footsteps approached the door, and I felt my heart skip a beat as I heard the knob begin to turn. *This is part of the plan*, I reminded myself, trying for a deep, calming breath while making as little noise as possible. The door swung slowly open.

As soon as I saw the warden's boots stepping forward clear of the door, I yanked on the string, tightening the simple noose knot I had been able to make using my fingers and my teeth.

Immediately the sound of gunfire filled the room as the automatic rifle I'd tied the string to erupted. The string continued to compress the trigger, round after round of ammunition tearing out toward the door, and the bedframe rattled as the gun's recoil strained it against the huge knot of tape and string I'd used to secure it to a bedpost.

I didn't wait to see if it had been successful—I knew it had been even before her body toppled to the floor. I slid out from under the bed on the side, away from the gunfire, my chest aching as I squirmed up, scrambling for the bathroom in that direction as the gun finished expending its clip and slamming the door behind me.

Not a moment too soon, either. Wood went flying as bullets tore through the door, and I ducked down low, crashing into the neighboring bedroom through the shared bathroom. I moved to the door, yanking the handgun from my pants and fumbling at the shirt I'd wrapped it in. I would come back around behind her and—

The plan died instantly as the door swung open and I saw the barrel of a gun pointed right at my chest.

CHAPTER 7

Violet

The gun shook slightly in the warden's hand. I swallowed hard and slowly raised my arms, letting the shirt fall to the floor. Her pale brown eyes flicked to the gun in my hand, pointed at the ceiling. I could tell she was nervous.

"Put it down, and step into the hallway," she said, her obvious fear giving the order a desperation that I understood.

"Okay," I said softly, slowly leaning over. My ribs pinched as I reached too far, but I powered through it, not wanting to risk any sudden gestures or deviate from the expectations of the woman in front of me. The gun slid to the floor with a clunk, and I straightened up, very slowly, raising my hands to shoulder height. I moved into the hallway with her. "See? Harmless."

The warden took a small step back, her eyes darting all over me. "Don't talk unless I ask you to. The bag. Hand it over."

Taking deliberate care once again, I shrugged off my backpack, hooking it on my wrist and swinging it around. I held it out to her, and she took another step back.

"You open it. Slowly."

I gave her a hard look, and then looked down at the cast on my arm. Another look up told me she didn't care. As I glanced past her right shoulder, I could see the cause of her fear and rage. Lying a few feet away was a warden, her torso draped out into the hallway, blood seeping into the carpet. I swallowed my own nerves and carefully shifted the bag onto the cast, using the straps to hang it, my arm protesting against weight it was no longer used to. My fingers trembled as I fumbled with the clasp for a second.

Then it was open. I began to awkwardly tilt the bag forward, about to tip the items in it out. "Stop." I glanced up at the woman, and was surprised to see she had fought back some of her nervousness. A thin thread of steel had wormed its way into her voice, hardening.

"One at a time—I remember now. You like bombs."

The way she said it, with such bitterness and rage, it was like I was a dirty taste in her mouth. I gulped, and began pulling out items as I touched them, one by one. Her eyes narrowed as she took in my one remaining grenade, but I sat it on the floor and kicked it away. She tracked its movement for a few seconds, and then, like a hawk's, her eyes were back on me.

Each moment dragged on like an eternity, and I could feel a mounting pressure as each second ticked by, weighing heavily on me, urging me to do something, to get away. Yet I couldn't—I was locked in the hallway with her. She had me at her mercy. My mind was punishing me already for the blunder, reminding me of all the other times I'd been trapped with no way to escape. Tabitha's torture room, the palace when the blast went off, The Green's facility, the Porteque gang's den…

Each time had gotten harder and harder to endure. Another fight to try to overcome with no way out. I couldn't endure it again. I wouldn't. Viggo had come to rescue me from most of those moments, and I trusted him with my life, but he wouldn't always be able to reach me even if he would always, always try. I had come this far, too far, to ever let something as precious as my freedom be taken from me again.

I reached into the bag again, pausing when my fingers touched the squeeze bottle full of kerosene. I pushed down farther, tilting the bag more and giving it a little shake, and was rewarded with the heavy weight of Owen's lighter. I palmed it awkwardly and then grabbed the kerosene, pulling it out.

At that moment, I had no idea what my plan was. I wasn't even sure I had one. Just the knowledge that these two items could mean the difference between my freedom and a high probability of death. Even then, I still leaned over to set the kerosene bottle on the ground.

"Stop. What is that?"

I looked up at her, hesitating a moment. Maybe if I lied, she'd let me keep it? "It's water," I said a heartbeat later. She met my gaze, and I pressed on, emboldened. "It was dusty. In the basement. I got some water to take with me."

"Hand it over," she said. I straightened slowly, suddenly confused. Why did she want it?

After a moment's deliberation, I held the squeeze bottle out in front of me, taking a careful step forward. The warden reached out and snatched it quickly from my fingers, and I almost fainted as the lighter clenched between my bottom two fingers slipped. I jerked my hand back to my stomach, pressing the lighter against it. Looking away for a moment, certain she had seen and all too cognizant of the gun pointed at me, I started to take a slow step back. The warden's voice stopped me.

"Open it."

In her hand, the bottle remained outstretched toward me, the white plastic container held out like an offering, or a gift that nobody wanted. Licking my dry lips, I stepped forward again, clutching the lighter more tightly to my palm. My hands felt sweaty and clumsy, my heart beating staccato against my ribcage. I pinched the lid of the bottle between my thumb and forefinger and twisted, relieved that the seal gave easily. I twisted twice more, my movements hurried and jerking to disguise the lighter in my hand.

The lid lifted up easily after the third twist, and I pulled it, and the lighter, back slightly. The warden pulled the bottle toward herself—to her nose or her mouth, I had no idea. In that moment, I seized the opportunity.

My left hand flashed out, quicker than I could ever imagine, pressing forward on her hand and upturning the bottle, while my casted hand lashed out at the pistol in hers, connecting awkwardly, the gun pointed at me flying out of her hand as the woman gave an 'oof.' The liquid sloshed out of the bottle in an arcing spray, splashing down on her mouth, chin, and chest.

The warden had a moment to shout. Then I was pressing forward with my left hand, using my thumb to slide the lighter up into my fingers and flipping open the lid. It was already coming down on the spark wheel, my hand pressing in close to her chest, when I fully registered what I was about to do.

And then it was too late. My thumb hit the spark wheel, viciously spinning it around. There was a whoosh of noise as the kerosene ignited, and then the woman before me was burning, fire licking up her torso and head in blue and orange flames. I saw her eyes widen above the flames around her mouth, which was opening to scream, but nothing came out save a harsh, brittle whoosh of air.

I took a step back, the lighter slipping from my fingers and onto the floor as the flames began to spread, the heat from it causing my eyes to sting. The woman tried to bat at the flames on her chest, but her shoulders were already beginning to burn. And the smell… The smell of burnt hair began to flood the hall.

I covered my mouth with my hand, recoiling at what I had just done as I watched her race away. I noticed the gun still lying where I'd thrown it on the floor. I bent down to grab it, a roar of panic sounding in my head. Levelling it at her, I squeezed the trigger until she dropped.

I moved over her and put one more in her head, just to be sure.

Then I tossed the gun to the side, stumbled away a few steps, and very noisily emptied the scant contents of my stomach onto the floor, next to a small table, while the woman's body still burned next to me.

I took several calming breaths and sat there, shaking, waiting for the relief that it was over to come. But it just… wouldn't. That was probably the most gruesome, most hideous death I had ever been a part of. I hadn't known myself capable of that level of… If I could kill someone with that much unnecessary pain and suffering, what was I fighting for? What had happened to the days when Viggo and I had tried to take everyone down nonlethally, promising the guards that we didn't kill? And over those thoughts, the sight of the woman's face, the noise of the oxygen getting sucked out of her lungs by the fire, played through my head, over and over—

I shook my head and stopped myself. This train of thought would get me killed. Just sitting here trying to process it all would get me killed. It was survival. I'd acted on instinct, like I had always done in my life when I was in danger, but this time… I had stopped it. I had ended her life before she could suffer any more. I had done what I could. I had…

Desmond. I couldn't keep wasting time. I had to deal with what I had just done later. I looked up and down the hall, half expecting my enemy to be standing there, watching me. She wasn't, but she could be anywhere. Wiping the back of my hand over my mouth, I stumbled over to the gun I had tossed aside and picked it back up. Resting against the wall another moment, I looked at the body still burning on the floor, forcing myself to witness the horror of it.

"I'm sorry," I whispered to her. Not that it would help now. The flames on her body were consuming her quickly, but they didn't seem to be dying down. Grimacing, I ripped off some curtains from the nearest window and threw them over her body, then went back and tore down another set, waiting until I was sure I'd smothered the fire before I could go on my way. As much as my skin crawled standing here, vulnerable in the open, with the horrible sight of the woman I'd killed obscured by ruined curtains, I needed to make sure the fire didn't spread.

Then I staggered back down the hall, heading deeper into the house. I carefully picked my way through the traps that hadn't yet been sprung, looking to see whether any had been tampered with. They hadn't, but the emptiness in the house was eerie. I had no idea where Desmond was. Every corner I turned, I half expected to see her looming in front of me. I checked behind me at every tiny noise.

As I crept into the foyer over the main stairwell, I hesitated, my mind noticing the discrepancy before I could even register it. A foggy haze seemed to be filling up the room, permeating it with the scent of something burning. I turned back toward where I had come from, almost expecting the still burning woman to be crawling her way toward me, but the hallway was deserted. Had I missed something about the fire? Had it caught anyway?

Coming around the banister, I saw that the room beneath me was lit up with a red glow in the area just under the place I'd emerged from, casting long, dark shadows that seemed to twist and writhe in the presence of a moving light source. I took a few steps down the staircase, my heart in my mouth. Then my blood ran cold when I saw the bright orange flames spreading through the left side of the house. Through *Tim's* side of the house.

This wasn't the fire I had put out. This had Desmond written all over it—she had to have set the fire. Probably as soon as everyone had raced upstairs. She hadn't waited to see if her people had been successful; she clearly wanted me too badly for that.

The fire in front of me roared and crackled, the flames seeming to grow with every second that passed. I thought fast, but each thought felt as though it was coming too slowly. How I could get to my brother and Owen? Desmond knew I wouldn't leave them if they were still alive. Which meant she had set the place on fire to get me to show my hand—show where I'd been hiding.

I didn't have a choice. I raced up the stairs, back the way I had come, barely avoiding triggering any of my traps. The haze of smoke behind me seemed to become thicker, darker, even as I ran, drowning out any lingering light. As much as I hated it, it looked like I was heading into the blaze. I switched on my flashlight, my breathing sharpening the ache in my ribs, but even its light seemed weak compared to the diaphanous cloud forming in the halls.

When I reached the servants' stairs above Ashabee's secret entrance, I had to throw an arm over my face. The flames were more intense here, starting to crawl up the staircase from the first floor. I leaped past their reaching arms, using the sleeve of my shirt as a makeshift mask.

Adrenaline lending speed to my muscles, I rushed to Jeff's former chambers, yanking open the secret panel and throwing myself into the elevator leading to the basement. Closing the door behind me, I furiously punched the button, trying to still my nerves as the green light waited a moment before turning on. Good—the fire hadn't shorted out the wiring that ran this thing yet.

The green light started flashing. Though it seemed to go impossibly slowly, the cage began to descend. As it rattled and whirred, I exhaled sharply, trying to will some calm into my already jumbled emotions. Even after a few deep, clearing breaths, I still couldn't get my mind in order. Fire was suddenly a huge presence in my life. The woman's face, the smell of her burning underneath the curtains… Everything seemed to cycle around and around. If the fire in the house got to the electrical system before I was all the way down, I would be stuck here, swinging in a metal cage in an elevator shaft until the house burned down around me. If the controls to the doors that opened up the basement driveway burnt out before I could reach them, Tim, Owen, and I wouldn't be in a much better situation.

It seemed like forever due to the pain in my squashed limbs, but the elevator ride was less than a minute. I checked my watch enough to know.

When the light finally turned off, I fumbled desperately at the latch and burst out of the stupidly tiny elevator. The depth of the darkness in the basement blanketed my eyes, confusing me, but I managed to reorient myself after a few stumbled steps. The solidity of the basement, even partially collapsed, comforted me a tiny bit. This part of the house was made of concrete and surrounded by earth; the fire would have to burn through a wall of rubble to reach us. It would take a long time—I hoped. No, the more immediate danger, after the worry that the doors would stop working, was that the house would collapse on top of us and trap us in here.

I stumbled over to where Owen and Tim still lay, their condition unchanged. I studied them closely, and then turned toward the back of the room, my eyes seeking out in the darkness the entrances to the tunnels that led up from the secret room. I could just make out the two Viggo and Owen had explored: the longer one that led out to the fields beyond Ashabee's house, and the gently sloping ramp that led up and onto the drive. That one was closer to me, the bottom of it barely visible at the edge of the pool of light from my flashlight. Unfortunately, I hadn't found any vehicles left in the armory during my search for weaponry. That meant I needed to get out under my own power as quickly as possible before the electrical circuits were damaged—and I had to find the car that Owen and I had come here in. Which was out on the driveway, presumably where Desmond was parked, and where she could still be lurking, too. As much as I wanted to take my brother and Owen all the way out into the fields and be away from this awful place, I didn't have the time, the energy, or a way to get us home from there.

Going out onto the driveway was a horrible plan, but I didn't have any other options left. I leaned over and wrapped my arms under Tim's armpits, dragging him a few feet toward the other side of the room and the ramp. Then I headed back, and did the same with Owen, dragging his heavier body toward the ramp and then setting him down a bit harder, my breath coming in sharp gasps.

I hobbled over to my brother, took a deep breath, and then repeated the process, dragging both of them, one at a time. I knew it was probably the least efficient way to handle it, but I couldn't bear the thought of leaving one behind, and then coming back to find his body engulfed in flames. I'd had more than enough fire today—I was done.

The process was agonizingly slow. I had just gotten both of them up the final parts of the ramp, my head spinning, when I caught the first haze of smoke hanging in the air, somehow drifting in from above. At this point, I didn't know if the dizziness was from the smoke, lack of oxygen, or just sheer exhaustion. I sank onto my backside. My thighs, butt, and back were aching from the exertion, and I was parched, but there was no water. I hadn't had any since Owen and I had gotten out of the car on the hill. When had I last eaten? Sometime this afternoon. At the moment, I was finding it hard to remember.

All I wanted to do was flop to the cold concrete ground and lie there mindlessly, but I needed to get Tim and Owen out and safe first. I rotated my shoulders and then stretched out my stiffening legs, laying them flat on the ground for a few moments. It helped alleviate some of the aches and pains in my battered body, but not by much.

Then I was up. I found the controls for the hidden exit point and hit the button, my heart in my mouth. I swung around, pulling out my gun, flicking off the safety, and holding it ready with my left hand.

For a moment, nothing happened. I considered the darkness all around me, and a swell of horror rushed through my stomach—what if all the electricity to the basement really was already gone? The little elevator had worked, but it had been a while since I'd gotten out of it. What if I'd gotten this far, only to be separated from freedom by an immovable steel barrier?

The thoughts all shot through my head in the space of a minute. And then the door hummed, revealing a little gap in the ceiling that grew as the door shuddered back farther. I glimpsed the night above the dying lawn along a looping part of the drive away from the house. Relief rolled over me, but my eyes probed the shadows as the door opened, looking for any sign of Desmond. Then I risked climbing partway out to see if I could spot her lying in wait—there was almost no way she could know this was where I would be coming from. As my eyes came up level with the lawn, I became aware of the red glow from behind me, contrasting the deep, dark shadows.

There was no sign of Desmond in my immediate range of vision, no glitter of eyes, dark shadows, or glints off weaponry in my line of sight. But a vehicle parked some ways away from Owen's car must have been hers… and it was still here. I scanned the area again, paying close attention to any overlooked detail. Maybe she thought I was still inside? At the very least, she was probably camping by one of the doors, looking toward the mansion… I had an advantage in that she was unlikely to be looking out into the grounds for me.

I'd been resisting the idea, but now I had to turn to the house, and I paused at the sight. Half of it was on fire—the half we were just coming out from under. The rest of it was still intact, seeming strangely whole, as though nothing had gone wrong there at all. The heat from the blaze touched my cheeks, and little wisps of ash floated through the air.

I continued to search for Desmond among the various lawn ornaments, looking withered and unkempt by now, but I couldn't see any sign of her. Satisfied, at least for the moment, I headed back down to retrieve my first charge. I started with Tim, and moved him out among some ornamental bushes a few feet farther away, back from the house and the fire, completely clearing him from the hidden driveway. Then I went back to grab Owen.

It took considerably longer to get the man's unconscious body the rest of the way up the slope, especially as I was constantly checking over my shoulder, paying attention to every time my neck prickled and every sound around me. When I finally had him hidden, I fell back on the grass, my chest heaving and sweat making my clothes stick to me. I let my breath catch, coughing periodically when I got a small bit of smoke. After a couple of minutes, I picked myself up off the ground. I had to find a way—one of the cars—to get them out of there.

I moved toward the two vehicles sitting on the drive, slowing to a stop when I took in the full extent of the flames devouring Ashabee's house. They were magnificent and terrifying, spilling from the double doors at the front, the giant, opulent manor taking on the form of an angry monster erupting from the ground. I shivered, thinking again of the guard's burning face, then forcing myself to think of the house instead: all the time we'd spent here, disgusted by the unnecessary grandeur, continually nagged by the figure who headed the house, a brilliant Patrian weapons designer who also happened to be bigoted and abusive... Even with all the pain that had gone on here, the disgust I felt for Ashabee, I had never pictured it ending like this.

I felt the weariness building up in my body again and promised myself I would move in just a moment. For now, I stood and watched the manor as it burned.

CHAPTER 8

Viggo

I pushed up the drive, noting the two cars in the driveway, drawing nearer to the lone figure who stood back a ways on the looping driveway, watching the house burn. Red reflected off the patches of Violet's scalp, shining brightly under her crop of ever-growing hair. I had already exhaled in relief, preparing to stop, when I saw someone step out from the bushes just to Violet's right.

It took a moment for me to register the gun the person carried in her hands.

Slapping my foot on the gas, I angled the car toward the figure. Even through the windows, I heard the crack of gunfire—Violet turned, her head flicking toward the figure, and then she was falling, toppling to the ground.

"NO!" I roared, my fists clenching the wheel, my foot trying to stomp even harder, even though the gas pedal was down as far as it could go. The headlights cut over the figure, and I caught a glimpse of Desmond's eyes going wide as we barreled down on her. She flung herself right, away from the car, but by then we were almost upon her, my rage overshadowing all sense of reason.

It grabbed control of my body, working with the muscle memory and my reflexes. My hand shot down, grabbing the emergency brake. I swirled the wheel one way and then ground the emergency brake up, locking up the wheels. The right rear end slid around, straight into Desmond's path of escape.

I heard the thunk as the side of the car impacted her body, a dark part of me feeling a savage rush of satisfaction to know I had hit her. Then it was gone, and my foot was on the brake, bringing us to a shuddering halt. I frantically threw open the door, practically slipping on the dew-slick grass as I rushed over to where Violet lay.

My mind was going wild, unable to cope with the thought of seeing her lifeless, broken form lying on the ground. *Not again, not again, not again*, it screamed, the thought trying to force its way out of my vocal cords and into the night in a primal howl.

I clamped it back, dropping to my knees next to Violet's still form. Her eyes were closed, her face and body lax. I stared at the bullet holes, unable to comprehend their perfection and the lack of blood. All I could see was death clinging to her, while Ms. Dale's words rattled in my ears.

Then Violet coughed, her eyes snapping open wide as she tugged at something bulky under her shirt. Frowning, I lifted up the edges, and saw the bulletproof vest resting on her skin—and the two bullets lodged in it. I carefully eased my hands up under her shirt to her shoulders, releasing the nylon tabs that held the top of the vest in place, and then the ones at her sides. Violet gasped again, giving me an appreciative nod as I carefully pulled the vest off.

I knew exactly how she felt: getting hit with a gun from such a close range was the equivalent of getting kicked in the chest by a horse. But she was alive. God, she was alive.

"Desmond?" she asked, her breathing ragged. She held out a hand to me, and I gently hoisted her up into a sitting position.

"Ms. Dale?" I called over my shoulder. "How's Desmond?"

Ms. Dale's voice carried over the sound of the crackling fire. "Still alive, but unconscious—I think. Should I get back in the car and hit her again?"

Violet gave me a concerned look and then carefully pulled herself to her feet. Her knees and legs were shaky, so I climbed to my feet with her and wrapped my arm around her shoulder. She held me around my waist, and together, we picked our way across the yard toward our car. Ms. Dale was standing on the other side, a healthy distance from Desmond, her gun still trained on the other woman.

Desmond lay curled sideways in the grass, her body looking like it was trying to go two ways at once—her front curled up, her legs splayed out. Her left leg was bloodied and lay at a not-quite-natural angle. Her eyes were definitely closed, but whether she was faking unconsciousness or not, I wasn't sure.

"I found her gun and patted her down," said Ms. Dale from where she was standing. "But honestly, it would just be safer for all of us if we put a bullet in her."

I looked down at the scene before me, feeling my blood curdling. This woman had just shot Violet without a second thought, and even looking at her was making the anger pump through my veins. But I hadn't been trained to give in to the rage that boiled in my blood. I had learned as a warden to evaluate the situation fully.

"We… shouldn't," I said.

"Viggo." Ms. Dale's voice was sharp, and she didn't lower her gun from where it pointed at Desmond. "Don't do this mercy thing. Now's the best chance we're ever going to get to take her out once and for all. She's dangerous. Too dangerous."

"It's not that. She has *information*," I insisted. "We can get her in a position where we'll make her talk. Take her in now, while she's unarmed and unconscious."

"Can we not have this argument? If we let her wake up, then she'll be back to being armed again," retorted Ms. Dale. I opened my mouth to interject, and Ms. Dale shook her head, her entire stance adamant. "I don't care what you say, Viggo, there's no reason strong enough to convince me to let this snake of a woman live. She's toxic, and she has a way of worming her way in. Even her mouth is a weapon. You both know it."

I looked down at Violet, who was wearing a faraway look, her silver eyes staring at Desmond. "Violet?"

The haunted shadows fled across her face as she jerked back and looked at me. "Tim's here," she said blankly. "Over by the driveway from the basement. Owen, too."

I'd thought she was paying attention to the discussion, but now I realized her voice was hollow and flat, and I cupped her cheeks between my hands, peering into her eyes, my excitement at the thought of seeing her brother alive—and my current rage at Desmond—eclipsed by worry.

"Violet?" I asked, concern softening my voice.

Eyelids fluttering, she gazed back up at me, and then seemed to do a double take. "Viggo?"

"Are you all right?"

"Of course," she murmured after a moment. "I'm just… I'm really tired. Desmond is too dangerous."

"She's the key to everything," I said. "We can use her."

A hard edge appeared in Violet's eyes then, even in her distracted state, and she shook her head. "We don't need her," she said fiercely. "Let's just… get it over with. She's too dangerous."

"Good," said Ms. Dale. "My pleasure." Her face held no sign of guilt or humor, devoid of anything that could allow me to question her sincerity.

I sucked in a slow breath, then nodded stiffly. She cocked her gun, the cold click of the metal seeming loud in the night.

But before Ms. Dale fired, another voice spoke up.

"I wouldn't do that… if I were you."

Her voice was weary and tight with pain, but it still managed to convey that sense of silky, easy superiority that instantly put my nerves on edge. I cursed under my breath. Desmond was conscious again. How long had she been listening? We would never know the answer to that one.

Ms. Dale hesitated, keeping her gun pointed, and she gritted her teeth as though controlling her trigger finger. "You have ten seconds to convince me not to blow your brains out."

"So angry, Melissa," Desmond murmured. I saw now that her eyes were open and glittering in the light from the mansion fire. "I always knew that would bring you down in the end."

"Nine," Ms. Dale said without missing a beat.

"The boys," Desmond said quickly. "You wouldn't want anything to happen to the boys."

"Killing you is the best thing I could do for the boys," Ms. Dale replied, but now there was the barest bit of hesitance in her voice, and Desmond, lying helpless and weaponless on the grass, knew it.

"Seven days," Desmond said dreamily, ignoring the jab.

I sensed what she was doing—lying to save her skin—but now I had to know what she was talking about, too.

"Seven days 'til what?" I growled.

"Viggo, dear, don't try to play the bad cop. Even Melissa here can do it better than you, and she's a sorry excuse for a—"

Desmond's laconic drawl cut off sharply as Ms. Dale fired her gun, the explosion deafening. I was shocked for a moment—until I saw there was no blood or bullet hole. Desmond had simply flinched, jerking her head to the side as though she'd been stung. The shot had hit the ground close to her face. Expert control on Ms. Dale's part.

"I am this close to killing you," Ms. Dale spat. "Answer the question."

Desmond's voice was just a little higher when she replied, "If I'm gone longer than seven days, my people will order all of the boys under ten into the river and let them drown. The boys younger than fourteen on the next day, and so on and so forth. Elena and I discussed it, in the eventuality that you people got a hold of me like you did King Maxen. The older boys are much easier to work with, so she may keep *them* alive, at least for a while longer…"

"You're lying," Ms. Dale snarled, not losing her focus on Desmond as Violet and I stared. My stomach twisted into knots. She'd sprung her trap, and now we were flailing in it.

Desmond's lips twitched up. "Shoot me and find out," she crooned.

"Fine," Ms. Dale said, and before I could voice the shock of alarm that coursed through me, she'd spun her gun around in her hand, stepped forward, and knocked Desmond on the head with the butt of it. The older woman's neck snapped backward, and she slumped.

"We've heard enough out of you," Ms. Dale snapped, then pulled back, huffing, and looked at me and Violet.

"I know what you're going to say," she said, bitterness oozing from her words.

"We can't take the risk?"

"Yes. And, as much as I hate to say this, I agree. Until we can find some way to verify that all the boys are safe from the Matrians... even the possibility of this being true..." Ms. Dale's voice became sharper. "She's got our hands tied. Viggo, you get your wish. We have to take her with us."

"I'm starting to reconsider that wish," I growled.

Ms. Dale shrugged. I'd rarely seen her this visibly angry, her posture rigid and her teeth clenched. "Too bad."

Violet shifted in my arms and put her face against my chest. "Viggo?"

"Yes?"

"Let's get out of here, please. Desmond was on the handheld earlier—calling reinforcements. We need to go."

"Of course, baby," I said, everything falling away except my need to get her back to safety as quickly as possible.

That seemed to be all Violet needed to hear in order to let go completely. She sagged in my arms then, and I gently took hold of her knees and pulled her up to my chest, supporting her weight with both my arms. Ms. Dale studied us for a moment, her eyes reflecting her concern. "Is she all right?" she asked, taking a step closer without letting her weapon lose its bead on Desmond.

Violet's eyes were closed now, her breathing deep and even. I looked up at Ms. Dale and shook my head, baffled. "She just… fell asleep."

Ms. Dale frowned and took a step closer, using one hand to peel back Violet's eyes. Violet murmured something, her left hand coming up to bat Ms. Dale's hand away before nestling in closer to me. "She's exhausted. Whatever happened in there must've been a very draining experience for her physically."

I clutched her tighter. "It was definitely mental as well. Her eyes were all right, though?" I murmured, remembering how Violet had seemed… well, sort of all right after the palace, but had slowly started to slip away as we watched, her mind becoming more and more fractured as blood had pressed into her brain.

Ms. Dale responded with her eyes back on Desmond. "Her pupils were responsive, and she woke up when I began to probe her. It's physical, for sure. Probably overexerted herself. We'll have Dr. Tierney take a look when we get back, but I think she's fine."

The breath I had been holding came out in a slow huff, and I nodded. "Great. Let's get out of here—one of us will have to take Owen's vehicle, and we'll have to load up the guys."

Tsking under her breath, Ms. Dale whirled and stalked away, back toward the car. She came to a halt right in front of the driver-side door, seemingly torn. After a moment, she whirled back and moved up to me. "Desmond better go in your car," she warned. "Because if I take her in Owen's, she won't get back to base alive."

Turning, I took a look at the other two cars in the drive. One I recognized as Ashabee's, but the other clearly belonged to Desmond. "How long do you think we have?"

Ms. Dale checked her watch, frowning. "Before this place is

crawling? Hard to say. Why?"

"I'm just wondering if you think Desmond put a bug in Owen's car, just in case. Or if…" I paused. "If she's had a tracker installed in her body."

"She *would*. Ugh, all these complications." Ms. Dale curled her lips in distaste as she considered the thought. "Best not to risk it, of course… We'll have Thomas meet us somewhere and let him do a sweep. We can use both his device and the one that Dr. Arlan uses."

"All right. Can you make sure Tim and Owen are okay? I gotta get Violet loaded, and make sure our newest prisoner is tied up."

Ms. Dale's mouth flattened into a line of disapproval, but she nodded. "I might need your help with Owen. And Tim, actually. They're a bit too big for me to handle."

I opened my mouth to say that Violet had done it while injured, but I didn't really want to argue with Ms. Dale in her current state of mind. Besides, it would be easy for me to move them—no need to make the older woman force herself into un-comfortable physical labor. "I gotcha. Just drive the car over there and watch them, and I'll be with you in a minute." Ms. Dale nod-ded and jogged off. Owen would've left the keys in the car—he usually insisted upon it as a security measure, in case one person on a mission died and the other needed to get away.

My gut churned when I thought of Owen. I wasn't even sure what to say to him at this point. Half of me wanted to hit him hard enough to knock some sense into him. Another part of me softly but painfully reminded me that he had just lost his broth-er… and it was still my fault. At least partly.

I sat Violet gently in the passenger seat of our car, then came back and got to work on Desmond, using some leftover zip ties I kept in my bag on her wrists, binding them in front of her so I could keep an eye on them. Then I went to work on her feet. As far as I could improvise, I used all the tricks I'd learned as a warden backward, making sure that Desmond wouldn't be able to escape from her bonds the way I would usually try to escape them. It didn't make this feel any safer, any less like we were making a horrible mistake, but at this point, we had little choice.

Finally, when she was as secure as I could make her, I picked her up, a part of me surprised at how light she felt for a creature filled with so much evil. As I worked, I heard Ms. Dale start up Owen's car and drive carefully around toward the secret entrance.

I thought about putting Desmond in the trunk—I didn't want her waking up on the drive and causing havoc—but resigned myself to keeping her in the backseat so I could keep an eye on her. Once I had her loaded up, I drove the car around, parking it next to where Ms. Dale had parked hers, so I could see inside.

Ms. Dale was on the handheld, the blue light cutting a bright contrast against the flickering red flames. "We need a location and a timeframe, plus any suggested driving routes, Thomas. We're worried their vehicle may have a trace on it."

"Affirmative—we're just wrapping things up here. The emergency staff decided to go back to the city, by the way. Something about the people needing them after what we did."

"It was their choice," she said. "Just send us a message. Being this close to yet another fire tonight is creeping me out."

"Understood. Expect something in under a minute."

Ms. Dale clicked off the handheld and placed it on the hood, running a hand through her hair. Her ever-present braid had slipped out, and I could see the strands of silver in her hair shining a bright iridescent red as they reflected the fire. "Owen's got a head injury, but it might be superficial. Tim… Tim's not so good. I don't see a sign of a head injury, but his pupils are sluggish. I'm not sure why."

I stared at where Tim rested on the ground, noting the dark bruising all over his body, disappearing under his clothes. "Me neither. I'll grab him and then help you with Owen."

"Owen first. I want to jostle Tim as little as possible." The handheld chirped, and Ms. Dale turned and tapped a few buttons on it. "Thomas came through—we'll meet him forty-five minutes from here. I have a route. Let's move."

There was no arguing with that tone, even if I wanted to. And I didn't.

CHAPTER 9

Violet

I jerked awake, the acrid smell of smoke thick in my nostrils, expecting to see the warden's shocked face bathed in a halo of flames. The sudden movement caused a wave of pain to ripple through my muscles, stretched taut and stiff against my bones. I gasped and flopped back against the pillows, staring up at the canvas tent overhead.

It took me a minute to remember that we had moved out of the farmhouse—the small room Viggo and I had been staying in was now reserved for the sick or wounded, and now, since I was able to stand up and get around freely, and my arm, ribs, and skull were healing with no complications, I would just have to visit every so often. Besides, it was kind of hard to lead an army of refugees camping in tents when they saw us come out of our comfortable bedroom every morning. Viggo had insisted we move to be on the same level of comfort that they were, and I had gladly agreed.

It wasn't even uncomfortable. Thanks to Viggo's knowledge, our little nest on the ground was cushioned enough to support all my stiff limbs, and warm and cozy in spite of the mucky conditions outside. We were right next to Cad, Margot, and their two children, too. It was nice, all things considered.

I breathed through the stiffness and bruises, shaking off the lingering tremors of the nightmare. Instead, I turned my mind toward the familiar sounds of the camp, the birds singing in spite of the lateness of the season, and the feel of the sun overhead, trying desperately to warm up the cold earth below. It helped chase away the anxiety that had haunted my dream, and gave me a little time to stretch out my legs and arms.

Lifting up my shirt, I groaned when I saw, even from the weird angle of looking down at my own body, the two purple splotches that marred my chest and collarbone. I was more grateful than ever that I had found that vest—Desmond would have ended my life.

It was a sobering thought, and one I didn't intend to dwell on. I was alive, safe with the people I loved—and we'd found Tim. I should be cheerful and relieved. But we'd been forced to take Desmond back to our base on the off chance that she had really arranged for the boys to be killed if she went missing. And we now had less than seven days to figure out what to do with her… The notion poisoned my joy and sent anxiety churning through me.

I'd hated the idea of shooting my enemy while she was down, unarmed. But in this case, it would have been the safest thing we could do. I didn't want to live in this constant fear of Desmond anymore.

Too late for that now. Desmond was dangerous—I was

keenly, intimately aware of that—but we had to make the best of it. I knew we would have to go to great lengths to keep our camp safe from her, including keeping her from seeing any of the Liberators who were now working with us—that was a secret we needed to keep badly.

I tried to be optimistic. Maybe, just maybe, we could get something out of her. Anything, even something small, would be helpful. When that didn't really work, I simply pushed the nerves aside, knowing I couldn't really change them until the situation was better.

Besides, I had more important things to do. Like see my brother.

Oh, and deal with Owen.

I sank farther into my pillows, and considered the real possibility of staying in bed. With everything that had happened last night, the emotional high of discovering my brother, right in the middle of the emotional blow of Owen selling me out to Desmond, was a strange mixture of relief and a gut check to the stomach. Both left me breathless, nervous, and uncertain.

It took me a moment to realize that I *was* nervous to see Tim. Was he mad at me for not finding him sooner? Did he blame me for not trying harder to find him? I prayed he didn't view this as I did: another failure to protect him.

And with Owen, I wasn't even sure what to expect. I knew Viggo and the others would want to know what happened with everything. Knowing the rest of our crew, they probably suspected this situation was an accident, or bad timing. But Owen and I both knew the truth. I hoped he didn't expect me to lie for him—I didn't think our relationship could take another hit on that level.

I shook my head and threw back my covers, the cool air

making my skin prickle. Last night had been one of the most difficult nights I had ever faced—worse, in some ways, than when I'd squared off with Tabitha at the palace—and I had survived. I was not going to sit back on my laurels, today of all days, when so much was happening. Tim wasn't going to blame me, and so help me, I was going to find a way of handling Owen.

I got dressed slowly, taking my time so as to not aggravate my injuries. A quick check of my watch marked the time as a few minutes before ten. Viggo had probably opted to let me sleep, something for which, today, I was extremely grateful.

Slipping on my socks, I padded slowly toward the flap over the entrance, pulling it back some and sitting down right at the edge. My boots were right outside on the ground, under the edge of the rain fly—another of Viggo's tricks for keeping the tent as clean as possible. I quickly slipped them on and began to tug awkwardly on the laces, hating that I still only had full use of one hand.

I looked up as Margot stepped around the tent, a basket of clothes on her hip. She raised her eyebrows in surprise, and then a smile broke out on her face, her white teeth practically glistening under the winter sun.

"Violet!" she exclaimed brightly. "Viggo told me to keep an eye out for you. He made you a plate of food, but didn't want to wake you up this morning. I'll go get it."

I smirked as she set down the basket and disappeared into her tent, reappearing after a moment with a battered tin plate covered with a clean cloth. "Here you go, dear," she said affectionately, pushing the plate into my hand. "You eat this, and I'll help you with your boots."

"Margot, you really don't have to—"

Her brown eyes twinkled as she knelt down at my feet, her fingers already attacking my laces. "Of course I do," she chided. "You're family, and you're injured. There's no shame in needing a little bit of help, y'know."

I gave her a crooked smile and pushed my foot out more, relinquishing the argument. I pulled off the cloth and began eating, using my lap as a table while Margot tugged on the laces. The fare was simple, but good. The best part was the little portion of canned peaches; while they would never compare to the real thing, they were a sweet treat, all things considered.

Once I was finished, I handed the plate over to Margot and stood up, brushing my hand over my lap and chest to clear away the crumbs. "Thanks, Margot. Do you know where everyone is?"

"Oh! Well, Viggo is in the house. Ms. Dale, Cad, and a team left this morning to go raid some of the weapons depots. We're apparently running desperately low on fuel. Thomas is fiddling around with the silver egg thing that you had with you in the palace, and Amber is currently teaching some of the cadets how to fly the heloship."

I blinked. "Wow. You are really well informed."

Margot laughed and shook her head. "Nah. Your fiancé thought you would want to know when you got up."

I chuckled and nodded. "That sounds like Viggo. Well, if you'll excuse me, I want to go check in with him, and then go check on my brother."

Margot nodded, pressing her hand against my cheek, her smile deepening. "Of course, dear. Cad and I looked in on him this morning. Dr. Tierney assured us both that he's going to be fine, but I'm guessing you'll want to hear it from her."

"Yes. And also, I'm just worried."

"Well, stop talking to me about it and go see for yourself. Unless you want some help getting there? You are looking a bit… stiff."

I drew in a deep breath and nodded. "That's a word for it. Another word would be bruised and battered." She frowned, and I reached out and took her hand, inexplicably happy that I could do that, because she was family. "I'm okay," I reassured her. "And I'll take it easy. I promise."

She gave me a long, considering look, and then nodded. "All right. But you hear me now, Ms. Violet Bates: if you *do* push yourself too hard, then I'll make you go to bed myself, even if I have to carry you there. Don't mess with me, either—I've already seen my children through toddlerhood."

I laughed, remembering Tim when he was a toddler. "Message received, Commander," I said with a salute.

I was bolstered by the sound of her laughter as I turned and walked down the lane between the rows of tents running along the tree line. The grass was worn down and muddy from all the foot traffic the last few weeks, so I picked my steps carefully, heading to the familiar brown, dilapidated farmhouse that had become our new home.

I was just leaving the row and crossing the yard when Morgan jogged up to me.

"Violet!" she said, coming to a stop just in front of me.

I frowned. Morgan and I didn't talk much. In fact, she seemed to let Lynne handle most of the meetings between us and the Liberators. "Hey, Morgan. What's up?"

"Have you seen Owen? I mean, is he okay?"

My frown deepened, and I shook my head. "No, I'm sorry, but I was just on my way to check on him. Do you want to—"

"No!" she said, practically shouting. She took a step back, and then looked around, fidgeting slightly. "Sorry," she said after a second, looking chagrined. "I just… I know Quinn's in there, and I heard… I heard about what happened to him." She frowned, and met my gaze, her turquoise eyes haunted with shadows. "I don't do well with stuff like that."

I completely understood. It was hard seeing what had happened to Quinn. The wounds Tabitha had inflicted on him, in order to make Amber talk… they were difficult even for me to stomach. But still, that didn't make Quinn any less of a person, and I was certain he would love a visit from Morgan.

"You should come with me," I said softly. "Quinn's injuries, they're hard, but I'm sure he'd love to see you too."

Morgan frowned and shook her head, her short black hair fluffing wildly around her face. "Lynne's said the same thing to me, but you both don't get it. It's fine. Just… if you hear anything about Owen, let me know, okay? I gotta go."

I opened my mouth to argue, but she was gone, running back over to the firing range. I felt jealousy pulse through me for a moment, envying the way she could just break out into a run like that, effortlessly. I shook the feeling off. I was on the road to recovery, bumps and all, and I would get back to fighting form. It would just take patience—something not entirely within my skillset, but I could learn.

Viggo was sitting at the dining room table, examining some papers, a radio sitting in front of him. He looked up as I entered, his green eyes meeting mine and a smile growing on his lips.

"Hey, you," he said, making as if to stand up. I waved for him to stay in place and then moved over to him, risking the pain to bend over for a chaste kiss.

"Hey yourself," I said. "Have you checked on Tim? Is he—"

"Before you go off with your million questions, Dr. Tierney says he's going to be fine. He is in shock, however, so it might be a little bit before he wakes up. By the way, *you* were in shock too."

"I was?" Surprise radiated throughout me for just a moment at his revelation, and then the obvious signs started to fall into place. It made sense, when I thought about it. Still, I felt fine now, in spite of the nightmare from this morning. Then again, it seemed like nightmares were a constant phenomenon in my life at this point.

He nodded, his smile faltering a second. "Intense emotional and/or physical trauma," he said, sounding like he was quoting somebody. "Want to talk about it?"

I frowned, suddenly wary. I had dreaded this confrontation, dreaded telling him about Owen, but knew I had to. I just didn't want to do it now.

"I do," I hedged. "But I need to talk to Owen first."

Viggo frowned, confusion making the green in his eyes darken. "Why would you need to—"

"As soon as I tell you, you'll understand. I just need you to trust me on this."

Viggo's frown continued, the lines on his face deepening. He studied me closely, and then gave me a bewildered nod. "I always trust you, Violet. Owen's in the back with Dr. Tierney."

"He's all right?"

"His head wound was mostly superficial. He's got a mild concussion but nothing else, so he should be fine to get to work. Do me a favor and ask him if he intends to stick around, and if so, let him know about our meeting? It's at noon."

I smirked at him, crossing my arms. "And when was I going

to hear about this meeting?"

"Just now," he replied tartly, a smile on his lips. "Now go—I know you're dying to see your brother."

"Hey, I'm also dying to see you." I paused, considering my phrasing. "And you know, no more using the word 'dying.' It's beginning to sound too close to my daily life."

Viggo sighed and then reached out and tugged me close, gently maneuvering me until I was sitting on his knee. He rested his forehead against mine, lacing our fingers together. "How bad?" he asked, his breath caressing my face.

I exhaled and closed my eyes, resisting the urge to just curl up against him and fall asleep. "Bad," I replied honestly, and his response was to wrap his arms around me, holding me close. "I'm so glad you came for me. Did I thank you for that?"

"No, and I never get tired of hearing it. By the way, am I winning yet?"

I rolled my eyes, but a smile tugged at my lips. "I thought we weren't playing that game anymore."

"We're not, but let's just call it an oldie but a goody."

"Oh, just like you," I teased, and a deep rumbling laugh burst from his chest as he cradled me closer, resting his chin on my head.

"Just like me," he agreed. He held me like that for a few seconds longer, and then pulled back. "Did that help?"

"A little," I admitted, taking just a moment longer to soak up his love and support. Then I stood. "I'll be back in a little bit," I said.

He nodded, and I felt his eyes watching me as I turned and walked down the hallway, moving toward the first bedroom. It was partially open, and I pushed through, letting my eyes adjust to the dimmer light. The curtains were drawn, perhaps to keep the patients from having to stare into the sun, and I blinked at the change.

Dr. Tierney was hunched over by one of the walls, and when she turned, I realized she was examining Owen, who sat in a chair with his back to the wall. His eyes widened when he saw me, and then he looked away.

"Hey, Violet," Dr. Tierney said. "Your brother's still not awake yet, but—"

"That's okay, Doc," I said, leaning against the doorframe. "Viggo filled me in. But why did he go into shock?" I moved over to the bed where Tim was lying, noting the dark bruises mottling his face and arms. "Also, is that much bruising okay?"

Dr. Tierney sighed and moved up next to me, resting a hand on my shoulder. "In terms of blood loss, it's negligible, but I did give him a blood patch, just in case. And as for going into shock… Well, to be honest, I don't know. Best guess, it's probably a reaction to the extreme pain he must have experienced due to the side effects of Dr. Jenks' experimentation. Owen mentioned he was close to a hand grenade going off—much closer than you two. The kinetic energy alone, even with a wall in between, must have been agony for him. I'm sure he'll wake up soon, though. I've got him on some mild painkillers."

I nodded, the worry I had been keeping at bay slipping past my defenses. I hated seeing Tim like that, lying still, in a bed. A small part of me was grateful he hadn't been able to see me that way—I could only imagine the toll it would've taken on him.

Turning, I looked at where Owen still sat in the chair, looking very guilty. His eyes met mine in a flick and then shot away, toward the ground. "Dr. Tierney, is Owen okay to leave?"

I turned my head back to her, and she blinked, her brows drawing together in confusion. "Yes? Why? I don't recommend any missions until I'm sure his concussion is—"

"Nothing like that," I assured her. "I just need a minute to talk to him."

"Oh, of course. Yes, he's fine, and he is okay to leave the room. Maybe not the camp just yet."

"Excellent. Owen?" I turned more fully, resisting the urge to cross my arms over my chest and speak to him like a child.

"Yup." He stood up and moved over to the door. I followed him into the hall, closing the door behind me.

As we walked past my old bedroom, Owen informed me, "Henrik's in there at the moment—he's been moved to start his physical therapy without disturbing Quinn."

"I see," I murmured, and reached over and opened the door to the small bathroom across the hall from Dr. Tierney's room. "Here will do."

If Owen thought it was odd for us to have this conversation in the bathroom, he didn't say anything. I moved in, and he followed, closing the door behind us. I didn't turn to face him just yet, facing the faded blue tiles of the wall just to compose my mind, trying to calm down the turbulent mix of emotions racing through me. There was a lot of anger and mistrust built up in me, making it difficult to view the situation clearly. I decided to start there.

"I'm angry at you," I announced quietly in the small, slightly echoing confines of our room. "Angry... and hurt... and frankly, I don't know if I can trust you anymore."

"I know," Owen said from behind me, and I turned.

"You don't know," I seethed, the words tumbling out. "You

don't have any idea what it was like, what I had to go through to get us all out alive. And Tim! Did you even think to check him? I mean, how did you even do all this? How could you do all this? It wasn't even your idea to go to Ashabee's! How could you have known?!"

Owen took a step forward, his body language and facial expression pleading. "Violet, there are no words I could begin to use to let you know how sorry I am. You're right—what I did was beyond wrong. I see that now. I should've…" He took a step back and looked away, hiding the shame burning brightly behind his eyes. "I should've seen it then," he finally admitted hoarsely.

I fell silent, feeling the hot press of tears behind my eyelids and pushing them back. "I don't even know if I can believe you." The words were hard to get out, making my heart ache fiercely at what his decision had cost us.

"I know," he replied hollowly. I saw something drop from his eyes and splatter on the floor, and I realized Owen was crying. That only made me want to cry more. I turned away, facing the tiles again, and clamped my teeth together, hovering between despair and wrath and wishing none of this had ever happened. If only so I could have my friend back.

"You need to tell everyone," I said. "You need to tell them everything. I won't lie for you. I won't, and you shouldn't expect me to."

"Violet, I would never—"

"I don't need your reassurances right now. Because right now, they mean nothing to me. You do this… you accept their punishment… and then… then we'll see. But right now, I just… I just need you to let me process this."

Owen shifted behind me. "Of course I'll do it," he said, after a moment. "I was already going to."

"Good. You'll have your chance at lunch. We're having a meeting, and I expect you to tell them then."

I didn't wait for his reply. I didn't think I could bear it if he started making excuses or trying to get out of it. I hated thinking that he even would, but that was where I was with him. I felt like I couldn't even trust that the person he had been in the past was the person he actually was. It was unfair, yes, but it was how I felt.

Pushing past him, I walked out, making a beeline for Dr. Tierney's room and closing the door behind me, just so that Owen wouldn't be tempted to follow me. I inhaled a deep breath, and then turned, pausing when I saw Dr. Tierney leaning over Quinn's bed, a sponge in her hand.

"Am I interrupting?" I asked, suddenly nervous.

"No," she said, shaking her head. "I'll pull the curtains, but he's sleeping. He doesn't like it when I do it when he's awake, although it's more difficult this way."

She dropped the sponge into a basin next to her, and then pulled on the curtain that some of the refugees had helped her rig to hang from the ceiling, blocking my view of Quinn's bed. I tried to push away the image of the rows of sutures crisscrossing Quinn's body, making him seem more like a patchwork doll than a human. I couldn't—they would be forever imprinted on my mind, and it was heartbreakingly sad, in spite of his efforts to handle it with humor.

Moving over to the chair Owen had been in earlier, I dragged it over to the side of Tim's bed and dropped into it. I settled back, adjusting my seat slightly, and then looked up at Tim, surprised to see his eyes open and watching me.

"Oh my God. Tim!"

I was up again in an instant, hovering over my brother's head. He squinted up at me and then started to raise his hand, wincing when he pulled at the IV. "Violet? Where?" He cocked his head, studying me closer. "Hair?"

I reached up and touched my hair, frowning. "I… I got hurt at the palace. I'm okay, but… they needed to cut my hair for an operation. And we're at a farmhouse in the country. We're safe. Are you okay?"

He closed his eyes and then nodded. "Head hurts. Little… thirsty."

"I can do something about that," I said. I bent over to the little nightstand by his bed, picking up the glass jar filled with water that always seemed to be present in the sickroom, and poured some into a cup. I pulled out a straw from the drawer, slipping it into the cup, and then presented it to Tim with a flourish. "See? One glass of water."

I pressed the straw to his lips, and he began to suck, drinking more than half the glass before he was satisfied. I set the cup back down on the nightstand and sank down on the bed next to him, being careful not to actually brush his legs with mine. He'd suffered enough skin damage from his condition already. "Tim, before Ashabee's, what happened to you? I was so worried."

Tim blinked, and then shifted slightly, easing himself up on the pillows. "At palace. I cover Jay. Thomas. Then… explosion. Wall fall. I… sleep. Wake up—still night. Crawl out. Wardens. Everywhere. Grabbing people. Dead. Injured. Put in trucks. Then barrels. Big red ones. Put in different truck. I run. Then… lost. No can call. I look for home, but… don't find. Three days in forest. Eat corn. Apples. Stolen."

He gave me a guilty look, and I shook my head at him,

impressed all over again at his sweetness. "That's okay," I said. "You had to eat. How'd you get back to Ashabee's?"

"Walk. But lost. Took time. Find, and then hide. Wait for you."

I bit my lip. "Tim, I am so sorry we didn't find you sooner. We thought if you had found your way back there, the wardens would've grabbed you."

"I smart. More smart than wardens."

My smile was sad. "But Tim, you were there for so long. I should've looked for you, should've come back sooner."

Tim frowned and then shook his head. "No. You hurt. In palace. Head and hand. You sick. *I* find *you*."

"That's not your responsibility!" I insisted. "I'm supposed to take care of you."

Tim smiled crookedly at me, and shook his head. "No. Take care Violet, take care me. Team."

I gave him a doubtful look, and he shifted his hand over, resting it on mine. "Team," he repeated, his eyes stern.

I smiled softly under his scrutiny, and then nodded. "Team," I said back to him, and he relaxed visibly, leaning back into the pillow. "I love you."

He smiled back. "Love you too."

CHAPTER 10

Viggo

I was so glad Violet had told me about Owen's confession before he had given it. Although, sitting there in the kitchen at our noon meeting, it was hard not to act upon my initial instinct and get up to punch him. The only things holding me in place were the fact that Violet had begged me not to hurt him, and the tiny voice inside me, still whispering that all of this was my fault.

The room was tense and unhappy, people's expressions ranging from shocked to disenchanted to faces that said this couldn't get any worse. We'd already had one conversation, the night before, when Ms. Dale and I had brought back four unconscious people—Violet, Owen, Tim, and Desmond. I was glad Violet had been asleep for the argument that had followed. Nobody liked Desmond being here, but try as we might, none of us could think of a solution that didn't end in the possibility of disaster. We were stuck with her. And we all hated how she'd played us, even if her story *was* true.

Now, as Owen's story emerged, it felt like just another blow to our group's tight-knit dynamics and carefully made plans. I tried to remind myself that everything wasn't falling apart—that we were not terribly worse off than we'd been before.

Owen stood in front of the room, his expression flat, his words bare. "When I got the coordinates for Tim's location from Thomas, I didn't think we would actually find Tim there. I realized how close the coordinates were to Ashabee's mansion, and, despite knowing it was a bad idea, I reached out to Desmond."

Everyone in the room gasped except for Violet and me. She reached out under the table to take my hand, squeezing my fingers, but her eyes remained locked on the table surface in front of her. I squeezed her fingers back, knowing how difficult this was for her to hear.

"I told Desmond that I would take her up on the deal she offered Viggo on the night… on the night that Ian died. If she let the rest of the boys go and promised never to hurt them, I would give her the king's location, the real egg, and… Violet."

The shocked silence spread across the room like oil and water, broken only by Amber saying in a voice that was half snarl, half whisper, "You told her about the *egg?*"

Owen looked down, and I saw Violet's face tighten, but she murmured, "Amber, let him finish."

Owen swallowed, and it seemed that everybody in the room could hear the sound. "I bargained with her. I told her she had to promise not to hurt Violet, and she could only bring a few guards, even though I knew she wouldn't honor the first promise for long. I thought—" He stumbled, then his voice grew clear again, and he looked up at the crowd with a frankness I couldn't help but respect, albeit grudgingly. "I was being reckless, but I thought that if the two of us got her to come out to a remote location with only a few guards, we could take her down once and for all. End all of this. But I knew that Violet would never agree. Desmond taught me well, it seems." Owen's tone was a strange kind of soured wistfulness, his admission tainted by whatever guilt was tearing at him. "I knew that if I drove Violet around, and pointed out how close Ashabee's manor was, she'd want to go. I even resisted at first… I played her."

He looked at Violet, and then at me, and I met his gaze head on, the urge to hit him temporarily silencing the voice of reason. Violet squeezed my fingers again, and I released Owen's gaze and shifted my attention to her, noting her watching me from the corner of her eye. Her face was impassive, but her shoulders stooped.

"I know what I did was wrong. I see that now. But it doesn't change what I did. And I know what you're thinking. You think that… that Ian's… that what happened was affecting my judgment, and you're probably right. But it doesn't matter. I have to own what I did. So please, just don't let that affect your decision. I deserve whatever punishment you decide."

He fell quiet, and the silence grew. I risked a glance around the table, trying to get a read on the room. Ms. Dale's face was twisted with a scowl, her brows down, her eyes glued to the table. Amber's cheeks were flushed red, and she was leaning slightly away from Owen, distinctly uncomfortable. Thomas, on the other hand, was staring at Owen, his face in a surprising configuration of openhearted compassion and understanding. I envied Thomas that—so quick to forgive, to understand, even in the face of betrayal.

Owen closed his eyes after a moment, and then exhaled. "I'll go outside," he announced quietly in the silence. "Let you all talk."

He left, the floorboards creaking as he strode determinedly from the room. I kept my hand in Violet's as the blond man closed the door behind him with a click. Then I heard the boards outside thump as he headed down the stairs, presumably to his tent or to the barn, to await his sentence.

The seconds ticked on as we sat there, the entire group silent save for the sound of breathing and the occasional squeak of a chair.

"How should we handle this?" asked Violet finally.

Her question seemed to rouse everyone from their deep thoughts. Ms. Dale blinked, and then straightened up in her chair. She cleared her throat. "Well, I guess the first thing we should do is decide if he should be punished. After that, we decide what the punishment is."

"He just admitted to being a traitor. Of course we should punish him." Amber's voice was bitter, and I could taste the anger and hurt as she spat the words out. I was surprised by her vehemence, yet also realized that, with how volatile Amber was and her personal history, her feelings made sense. Amber's father had once tried to sell her hand in marriage in order to settle his debts. I was certain Owen's betrayal struck a very deep chord in Amber, especially as it pertained to a man selling out a girl he was supposed to care about. Owen would have a long way to go with Amber before he ever earned her forgiveness.

"If you want to blame anyone, blame me," said Thomas. I frowned, noticing a similar confusion roll across everyone's faces. "I miscalculated. I thought more highly of Owen's mental and emotional state than was reasonable for his loss. Siblings are hard to account for. Some are friends while others are…"

He paused, and then looked down at the table. "I'm sorry.

I realize that thread of conversation might not be completely relevant."

"We're not going to blame you, Thomas," announced Ms. Dale. "As admirable as it is that you want to take the blame for your friend, I won't allow it. We need to try and figure out a solution. I'm curious—Violet? What do you think?"

Violet frowned, her brows drawing together. I watched her take a deep breath in, and then another, and recognized she was picking her words carefully. "What Owen did was wrong, but he did it with good intentions."

"How can we know that for sure?" Amber said, slamming her hand against the table. "He called Desmond and lied about it. Why wouldn't he lie about this? How do we even know that he hasn't been working for her all this time?!"

"Because I was there, Amber!" Violet said, her voice rising to a shout.

Amber leaned back, alarm and surprise filtering over her face. Violet licked her lips and looked up, taking in another deep breath, and I reached out to take her hand in both of mine. She gave me an appreciative smile, and then turned back to Amber.

"I'm sorry," Violet said. "I shouldn't have yelled like that. It's just, I believe Owen when he says he intended to trap her. Not just because he said so, or because I could see this… desperate need for vengeance in his eyes. When Desmond had us cornered in the basement, we had a fight. At first, he tried to make me stay and help him, but when I refused, he told me to run and save myself. He said he'd made a mistake bringing me. He wanted to face Desmond and all her guards by himself, if he had to. I believe that was his real intention." Her gaze was hard to read as she looked toward the door, her eyes clearly seeking Owen.

Ms. Dale rocked back in her chair, her arms folded over her stomach as she studied Violet. "We put it to a vote," she announced after a moment. "All those in favor of exacting punishment on Owen?"

"Aye," said Amber, her violet gaze hard and uncompromising.

"Aye," said Ms. Dale, her face grim. She looked at me, and I shook my head. "Opposed?"

"Me." Violet's voice was soft, but I heard the thread of steel there. I was simultaneously surprised and unsurprised. Then again, even she seemed a bit surprised by her own admission. She shot a glance at me, her eyebrows drawn high.

"Me too," said Thomas. "Although, for the record, perhaps I should recuse myself, as my decision is purely emotional."

"Noted, but this is emotional for all of us, Thomas." Ms. Dale looked at me. "Viggo?"

I hesitated, knowing that I hadn't said much—nothing at all since Owen had spoken. It was partially because I wasn't sure what to say. I was also partially afraid of what I would say.

Even under everyone's scrutiny, I felt frozen. Torn between anger and guilt. The choice sounded simple—it was just a yes or no—but it wasn't easy at all. On the one hand, Violet was fine. We had Desmond. Owen's act hadn't damaged us, and it had possibly even bolstered our chances of getting valuable intelligence. He'd apologized. On the other hand, he could've gotten Violet, and really, all of us here, killed.

"I'm sorry," I said, breaking the silence. "I need more time. I can't come up with a decision on it right away."

"But we're tied—" started Amber, her cheeks flushing red.

"Viggo has every right in the world to want to weigh a decision like this more carefully," Ms. Dale admonished, cutting

Amber off. Amber froze for a moment, and then clamped her jaw shut, sitting back. "Although, I do have a question: what do we do with him until you reach your decision?"

I considered the question and then shrugged. "Whatever grunt work you can find for him around the camp. Have him chop wood, or put him on cooking duty. Keep him out of the meetings and away from Desmond and anything else important." I grimaced. "*Especially* sensitive information."

"We could make that work, but not for the long term. We'll need a decision before we move base again."

I nodded. "Any objections?"

Everyone was silent, and I exhaled, thankful I didn't have to choose right then.

"All right. And on that note, I—"

"Excuse me, this is where you are having the meeting, yes?" An unexpected male voice from the door caught everyone's attention, and as one we turned. I felt a deep flash of annoyance to see Cruz standing there, a debonair smile on his face. "Ah, my friends! Of course you are the leaders around this place, huh? You choose to lead by doing! You are indeed people who are worthy of my respect. Where should I sit?"

Violet turned toward me. "Cruz?" she whispered, and I winced. We had talked for so long about what had happened to her that I hadn't been able to catch her up on the finer points of what had happened to me.

"Why yes, I am," Cruz exclaimed from behind me, moving over to Violet. "But who is this ravishing beauty? I do not believe we have been properly introduced."

Violet turned in her seat, her eyes wide at his sudden proximity, and merely at the intensity he radiated. "I'm Violet," she said, tentatively stretching out her hand. He grabbed it and pulled it to his lips in a gentlemanly kiss, and I resisted the urge to smack him.

"A pleasure to meet you," he said, flashing a smile, and my urge to deck him increased.

"What are you doing here, Cruz?" I asked, crossing my arms.

"This is where all the leaders meet, yes?"

"It… is…" Ms. Dale drawled, shooting me an alarmed glance.

"And you are discussing strategy on your next move, yes?"

"Well, yes, but—"

"Perfect! This is exactly where I should be. Do you have a chair for me, or should I just stand?"

Ms. Dale gaped at him, her jaw nearly slamming into the floor. I felt at a loss too—nobody had ever barged their way into our meetings before, not like this. It was unprecedented, and a little disconcerting. We had no rule against it, per se. We had always operated on the trust of the people we had recruited or rescued and had tried to provide safety, training, and vital necessities for them. They trusted our decisions, and we trusted them to follow orders.

Ms. Dale looked to me as if to gauge my reaction, and a look flashed between us that told me that neither of us was ready to deal with the intrusion. I shrugged; she raised her eyebrows at me while shrugging back and jerking her chin toward Cruz, a complicated series of gestures that seemed to express sympathy with the weird situation—but that told me I should deal with it. Well, fine.

I glared at her as she coolly answered Cruz's original question. "Um, sorry, no extra chairs at the moment." Cruz nodded and then leaned against the wall, his smile never faltering. When

Ms. Dale jerked her chin at him harder, I cleared my throat.

"Hey, Cruz, can I have a word with you?"

"Yes, my friend?"

He was making this difficult. "Outside," I clarified, getting up and moving toward the door.

"Of course," Cruz said, his tone sounding a little offended, as though he was surprised I would dare to imply that he hadn't known what I'd meant the first time.

"What is the matter?" he asked as soon as we were outside. "Am I in your way?"

I tried to think of ways to say this tactfully and came up with nothing. "Cruz, you can't barge in on our meetings. You just joined. You don't have the clearance."

I saw his eyes widen, his mouth turning sullen. "Croft, that is ridiculous! I have every right to be there. And I have lots of information that can help you. I was close to the heart of the Matrian guard at Starkrum. I listened. I heard what was happening—"

I cut him off. "And that's exactly why we can't trust you in our command room yet." He drew a breath to speak, but I continued, trying not to think too hard about why I even needed to have this conversation. I tried to keep my voice as even as possible. "Believe me when I say it's not personal. Everyone else has had to go through this too. I'm glad to have you here, and I appreciate your input. But if you want to be part of the command chain and sit in on meetings, you'll have to build up some trust first."

Cruz looked down, his good humor dampening, and his constant stream of talk dried up for the first time since he'd yelled at me when we'd kidnapped him. I tried to judge whether he would man up, or just resent me, and I couldn't tell. If his pride was wounded and he was threatened, who knew what he would do?

But on the other hand, if *this* was going to break him down, he wouldn't be a successful part of our team. I had to know now.

Before he could stop to think, I pressed on. "Look, this is just how we do things here. If you don't like it, you can move on—we won't stop you. But if you want to stay, think of it as a challenge. You've gotta do what everybody else did. If you work hard and focus, you could do it faster. Better."

Cruz grunted, and for a moment I was afraid he would still just ignore me, or worse, challenge me to a fight. But then he looked up, and there was fire in his eyes.

"Of course I will do it better," he said grandly. "Mark my words, Croft—I, Anello Cruz, will make you forget you ever doubted me. You'll realize that you need my help in no time!"

"Uh, good," I said, relaxing a little as I realized my ploy had worked… as weird as it was. "Thanks for understanding. Now, I gotta go back in."

As Cruz still stood there, nodding gleefully, I tried to nudge his attention toward the hall. "The kitchen will be open after the meeting," I told him, hoping he got the hint. Then, not having time for any more of the argument, I simply slipped away and left him standing, staring, in the hall.

I came back into the meeting to the sight of Ms. Dale shifting through some papers in front of her, then clearing her throat. "Have we received any update from Tiffany?"

"Yes," said Thomas, "but just a text message, and a short one at that. It reads, 'Riots in city, relocating to safe place. Will contact ASAP.'"

"Riots?" said Amber, her eyes growing wide. "That's good news, right? It means the message got out there."

"It could be good news," chimed in Ms. Dale, "but until

Tiffany contacts us with more details, we'll hold off on classifying it. Let's have our scouts keep an eye out for any refugees out of the city, though. We might get good information out of them. We also need to consider moving our base. Especially with winter coming, we need to find better shelter for people, and that will mean breaking our forces up into smaller groups and working in cells."

"How much time do you need to scout?" I asked, leaning forward.

"Probably about a day or two," Ms. Dale replied. "We can't really use the heloship, as it's running low on fuel."

"King Maxen will probably know a good place to check for the kind of fuel we need," said Amber. "We actually don't need much. Unlike cars, the heloship actually runs on a specialized cell, one that requires a very small amount of propellant to operate. But regular gas won't work—only T-136."

"I'll have someone ask him, though all but two of the depots we searched today had been emptied, so I wouldn't expect much. On that note, we did recover eight vehicles, fifty barrels of gasoline…"

Ms. Dale droned on, going over her report. Then the topic changed, discussing the move and areas in which to search. It was toward the end that Dr. Tierney wandered in, heading over to the fire to grab a pot of coffee. We were still operating on minimal electricity for the house, which meant we only had the communal coffee pot over the fire, and it was in use practically twenty-four hours a day.

"All right, that's all I can think of right now," Ms. Dale said. "We'll reconvene tonight and update each other on where we are with organizing our teams and equipment."

The meeting finished, and we all milled around discussing the various other chores we had overlooked, letting the conversations run into the general brainstorming session we regularly had after a meeting. I was listening to a discussion between Ms. Dale and Violet regarding possibly modifying the two remaining drones, when I noticed Cruz slip into the room, look around, and then make his way over to Dr. Tierney. Curious, I took a step back, shamelessly eavesdropping on their conversation, but feeling completely justified by the fact that Cruz was supposed to be impressing me—he knew I was going to have eyes on him, so why not start now?

"Pardon me," he said as he approached Dr. Tierney, his tone husky. I rolled my eyes. "Madam, it is a pleasure to see such radiance thriving, in spite of these primitive conditions. May I have the honor of your name?"

Dr. Tierney cocked her head at him, an incredulous look on her face. "No," she said decisively. "Absolutely not."

I bit the inside of my cheek to keep from laughing as the small doctor stepped around Cruz and walked out, still cradling her mug of coffee. I should've known better than to doubt even for a second Dr. Tierney's ability to handle unwanted attention from a male. As for Cruz, well… I hadn't exactly expected better from him.

Moving back closer to Violet, I watched as the man left, my smile growing as he approached the door, then deepening when I saw Jeff standing on the other side, about to come in. He stepped out of Cruz's way to enter the kitchen, bustling over to both of us.

"Oh, Violet, I'm so glad to see you're okay!" he said, interrupting Ms. Dale. He must have been truly emotional about it—I'd never seen Jeff interrupt anybody before unless he had to.

Ms. Dale just grinned at the intrusion and leaned over to Violet to finish her thought. "I think you might be onto something. Bring it up at tonight's meeting, and maybe find time to talk to Thomas about it." With that, she left.

"Hi, Jeff," Violet said, reaching up to hug the taller man. He hugged her as if she were a fragile thing, and then quickly let her go.

"How ever did you survive?" he asked, his eyes wide.

"Actually, I was saved by that weird elevator that led to your room. It allowed me to sneak out from under Desmond and get the drop on her."

Jeff's mustache twitched and he took a step back, his cheeks flushing. "I see."

Violet took a step forward, clearly concerned by his distress. "Jeff? What was that thing? Why was it so small?"

Jeff met my gaze, and then hers, and his flush deepened. "Ahh, I suppose you would never have seen a dumbwaiter before," he said, with nothing condescending in his tone, only a bit of embarrassment. "It's meant to carry food from one part of the house to another. Not people. At one point in the house's life, that room used to be a kitchen."

"Oh," she said, her face screwing up as she digested the information. Most of the time, it didn't show that Violet had grown up in an orphanage—and a series of terrible work camps—but at moments like these, I could see the people around her remembering.

"Then why did it lead to *your* room?" she asked Jeff, and I could almost see the gears in her head turning. When she'd told me that story, I'd had similar questions.

Jeff stroked his moustache, perhaps nervously. "Well, you see… Mr. Ashabee didn't want the other servants to know about his secret armory. I was the only one he would trust with his secret, and the only reason he did that was because…" His moustache turned down. "I was responsible for maintaining his collection, you see. And also, of course, for checking on him to make sure he didn't dwell down there too long when his more creative manias struck him. With the dumbwaiter left over, he told me I had to move into the room it was in so that I could go help him in secret. Oh, I begged him to modify it and make it bigger, but he refused on the grounds that constructing another would be too obvious to the other servants. I quite disliked that thing. It was… humiliating. But… if it saved your life, then I am grateful for it, and to him, for having any kind of elevator there at all."

Violet's face softened, and she pulled the butler in for a hug. "Ashabee was not a good man," she said as she hugged him tight. "And *you* are. Here."

She pulled something from her pocket and handed it to Jeff. He grabbed it, and I realized it was a picture. Inside it was an image of Jeff and an older woman, probably his mother. "You took this for me?" he said, his voice slightly strangled.

"I hope you don't mind. I just saw it in your room and thought… Well, I'm glad I did now. Especially with what happened."

Jeff smiled, his eyes glistening. "I left all my pictures behind," he said wistfully. "I didn't want to carry too much, anything that would slow me down."

Violet nodded, her hand on Jeff's arm. "I understand. I know what it's like to lose pictures. I'm sorry I didn't grab the rest."

"This was the best one you could've grabbed, under the circumstances. Oh, thank you, Ms. Bates."

The emotional butler wrapped his arms around Violet, embracing her in another heartfelt hug. I watched it all, realizing with a strange jolt that somehow, Violet had managed to find one more beautiful thing in the whole ordeal with Owen.

I just hoped I would be able to as well.

CHAPTER 11

Viggo

Three days seemed like an eternity when the whole world felt perched on the edge of a knife. It was exhausting not knowing anything, and the waiting was downright stifling. Yet the camp continued about its business, ignoring the feeling of a long-held breath, waiting to learn whether it should exhale slowly, or scream.

Everyone had their own ways of ignoring the looming questions, little mindless jobs to help achieve a feeling of accomplishment in the face of the unknown. I, for one, thought it was a good sign. For good or for ill, there was a sense of accomplishment within the group. A camaraderie that was beginning to form between us from all the trials and tribulations we had endured. In leading the way, Ms. Dale, Amber, and I had demonstrated that we could fight back.

Yet, without any word from Tiffany save the brief updates assuring us she was still alive, there was still this question mark involving the city. It cast a shadow, a taint, over the day-to-day routine of the camp.

All of us were trying to figure out what to do with the seven-day deadline Desmond had given us. According to her, the boys would be executed when she didn't return to whoever she had with them. Wherever they were keeping them. If there was such a plan, there would have to be safeguards, or else Desmond would never have been able to go anywhere without checking in with her cronies. We had our spies scrambling for information on where they might be, but it was hopeless.

Desmond hadn't been allowed to see any of our base or the route to it. We'd gotten Dr. Arlan to treat her broken leg and drug her heavily as soon as we got to camp—making sure her blindfold stayed on the whole time—and, while the group of us who acted as leaders had held a furious conference, we couldn't justify killing her after what she had said... at least, not yet. Not until we had more information. She was in the den right now; we'd converted the room into a makeshift but fairly secure prison cell, to hold her until we could make a more permanent decision.

At the moment, our best plan was, if we still knew nothing in a week, to take her to the middle of the city via heloship, drop her blindfolded with her hands tied where a Matrian patrol would come see her, come back before we were seen, and move camp... again.

It was a pathetic plan, a joke, and I dearly hoped we could figure something out soon. If we'd known where the boys were being kept, who knew about them, how to find the Matrian command... then at least we would have had a start at figuring out how to rescue them before time was up. But we had no leads. And who knew, even if we did release her, that Desmond wouldn't kill some of them anyway, just out of spite? She'd done it before. She wouldn't waste all of her precious weaponized humans, I knew that, but she was not above sacrificing some of them just to make us suffer. The thought had us all running scared.

With this weighing on our shoulders, none of us had much free time. But we spent what we had recovering, preparing, planning, and watching each other to make sure none of us broke from the stress.

Violet visited her brother for the first day, and then helped him move into a nearby tent with Jay. She flew the drone around the countryside, looking for signs of the boys or other people to recruit into our small army. But if there were any refugees, she hadn't found them yet. A part of me was beginning to believe that we wouldn't find any—Mr. Kaplan was the last civilian I remembered seeing in what felt like forever, and he had been taken away by a Matrian patrol.

Violet had also been spending time with Cad, Margot, and their children. Eating meals with them was becoming a regular pastime for all of us, Jay, Tim, and myself included. It felt good to have those moments—Violet was continuing to strengthen her relationship with them, as we all were, really. Although at times, I found it hard not to think about Alejandro. I was worried about him, and I prayed he was safe. He and Jenny both.

Ms. Dale spent a majority of her time away from the camp, leaving in the early mornings and returning late into the night. She pressed farther each day, searching for a suitable base of operations and coming back with dozens of options, most of them rejected due to their location, lack of power or facilities, size, or proximity to the city. She was playing our move cautiously—not that I blamed her. With winter drawing ever closer, and the threat of snow looming, it was only a matter of time before, more than the Matrians, the weather itself began to threaten the lives of our people.

Amber avoided Owen like he was a plague bearer. She spent most of her time with Thomas, Jeff, or some of the other refugees who were interested in learning how to pilot the heloship. She'd said that she wanted there to be backup pilots in case anything happened to her, but honestly, I believed she cared more about her role being flexible, so she could be free to do fieldwork. I didn't like it, but there was no arguing with her logic—or with Amber in general—so I let it go.

Between watching the radio channels, strategizing about Desmond and the boys, and keeping all our electronics working smoothly, Thomas continued working on the egg, studying the technology that held the embryo in stasis. Because it *was* in stasis, according to Thomas' analysis of the thing. Frozen in time until it could be implanted in a surrogate. That was the highlight of his discoveries thus far, although the fact that he hadn't learned much else didn't seem to deter him from handwriting new reports and sticking them in with our personal files three times a day.

I also noticed Thomas trying to coax Owen into talking a few times. There was no telling what they actually discussed in the short exchanges. They mostly started with Thomas coming over, saying something, and then Owen moving away, leaving Thomas standing there with a sad slope to his shoulders. I admired his resilience. He never gave up, never wavered in wanting to be Owen's friend, in spite of what he had done. He'd forgiven him. I envied that… that unconditional affection he held for his friend.

Owen kept his head down. He avoided most human contact,

although Lynne and Morgan managed to get close to him from time to time. Never for long, not even for a meal, but it was there. In some ways, I was grateful for it. I hated the idea of him going through everything alone, trapped with the awareness of what he had done.

And then that silent anger would return—rush into me like a whipping whirlwind or the backdraft from a fire. It set a violent edge to my teeth, made me strain for air while my heart pounded hard against my ribs, as if it wanted to break free from my chest and throttle Owen itself. During those moments, I wanted to scream at him. I had put my trust in him, and he had used it to stab me, Violet, all of us, in the back. Because his selfish need for vengeance had overwhelmed his common sense.

I wasn't objective enough to decide whether he needed to be punished. I couldn't make up my mind.

So I worked through it, spending my time doing all the manual labor I could get my hands on. Helping with the latrine work or splitting cords of wood. I washed dishes and clothes with some of the women in the camp, listening in on the snippets of conversation, letting their words provide a distraction from the ongoing problem of what to do about Owen.

And when that stopped working, I turned to physical activity, waking up early to run around the camp and through the guard posts, just to keep them on their toes, before returning to our tent and running through sit-ups, push-ups, and various other strength-building exercises. It was a good distraction, and a familiar one.

In spite of everything I had been doing around camp, there was one thing above all that I both dreaded and looked forward to: my daily visits with Cody, the surly kid who'd made a habit of challenging my authority ever since we'd met back in The Green's facility, and whom we'd brought back to our base along with Ian's corpse after the incident at Desmond's death camp.

We'd been keeping him in the barn. Its doors had been thrown wide open as I approached now, and several tables piled with equipment sat in front of the building. People were performing various tasks around the tables, from divvying up the inventory into three separate groups, to dissembling the guns for transport—there wasn't anyone sitting idle. We were starting to divide the supplies, as it grew more and more likely we were going to have to splinter off into smaller groups for the winter.

I stepped around the chaos and into the barn, the old boards under my feet sagging slightly. It was several degrees cooler inside the barn than outside, since it didn't get any good exposure from the sun. Inside, the smell of mold and musk filled the air, marking the old age of the structure.

Here, more of our people were fast at work, but it was an organized chaos, easy to navigate around. I headed for the back of the animal pens, to the largest one, where Cody was being kept. It had undergone some serious renovations since we had brought him there, in order to make the area feel more like a room and less like a stall in a barn.

I didn't like that we couldn't find some way to bring Cody into the house, but with Henrik's convalescence (and his risk of infection), we just didn't have the room. Which was why we had renovated this space, covering the walls with thin boards to prevent the draft and give him some semblance of privacy. I pushed open the door, the hinges creaking, and stepped into the lantern-lit room, a smile on my lips.

Dr. Arlan was in the middle of giving Cody the booster shot

for the mild muscle relaxant we were administering to him. There had been a lot of debate on how to handle Cody when we had rescued him, and it had been a hard sell all around. Violet and I were adamant about giving him some semblance of freedom, but Ms. Dale was adamant about keeping the members of the camp safe. She wasn't wrong to insist on the measures—at the end of the day, Cody didn't want to be with us. From his perspective, we had kidnapped him, and we were the enemy. So, compromises had to be made, and in order to circumnavigate his enhanced abilities, we had agreed to drug him.

I hated it, but I understood that it gave people—not just Ms. Dale, Amber, or Thomas, but the entire camp—some peace of mind when it came to Cody. I just wished that translated into people being more open and less guarded around him.

"Hey, Cody," I said with a wide smile. "You ready to go for our walk?"

Dr. Arlan pulled the needle out of Cody's arm and set it down on the tray balanced on his knees. "All done," he said affectionately, as he stood up and moved over to the small desk in the corner. I watched him go, smiling at the painting hanging on the wall just over it. The walls were a bit worn, and honestly, sad-looking under the dim glow emitted by the lanterns distributed about the room. Jay or Tim must've found it in the stuff we had taken out of the den to make room for Desmond, and hung it up for Cody.

There was a rap at the door and then it pushed open, revealing Jay, Tim and Samuel the dog, who barked when he spotted me and bounded over, his tail wagging. I knelt, and immediately Samuel lay down and rolled over onto his back, presenting his belly to me. I scratched his stomach a few times and looked over to see Cody staring at me, a sullen expression in his eyes.

"I don't want to walk," he said.

I smiled at him. "That's okay. We can play a game. I'm pretty sure there's a deck of cards floating around."

"It'll be fun," added Jay, leaning into the room. "Although the forest is beautiful right now—the trees have all pretty much lost their leaves."

Cody's eyes flicked between us, and he gave a reluctant sigh before standing up. I watched him put on his jacket from my position on the floor, still rubbing Samuel's belly. He zipped his coat up and then walked past me, burying his hands in his pockets. Jay and Tim stepped aside to let the young boy pass, and then turned to follow.

I lingered a moment, slowly rising to my feet. "He asked about Desmond today?"

Dr. Arlan sat down his pen, and sighed. I turned to see him leaning back in his chair. "It'll pass," he said after a moment. "Honestly, I don't even acknowledge the question anymore, and neither should you."

Frowning, I nodded, and turned to follow the boys, thrusting my own hands in my pockets. I trailed behind them as Jay and Tim cut through the chaos outside and toward the house, aiming for the bit of forest resting just behind it. Dr. Arlan's recommendation didn't sit well with me—but then again, it could have just been personal for me. It was hard to tell.

Jay led the way, pushing through the lower bare branches and making sure there was a clear path for Cody. I eventually caught up to them, and we continued to hike in relative silence through the forest. It was beautiful. The red, gold, and yellow leaves were strewn on the forest floor like a thick carpet that rustled together as we walked through it.

Samuel raced through the leaves, his legs kicking them up as he ran back and forth across the trail. Sometimes he'd spook a rabbit and take off after it, barking loudly. The rabbits always seemed to slip away, but I didn't think he honestly wanted to hurt them, given how wildly his tail waved back and forth as he ran. He just found joy in the chase. I only wished I could be as carefree.

We eventually reached a clearing, and Tim slipped off his backpack and pulled out some water bottles and two cans of peaches. I felt a little guilty as I popped them open—peaches were Violet's favorite—but they also doubled as a treat for Cody, so I doubted she would mind.

We all sat down on a nearby log and took turns eating the syrupy fruit. I had one, but passed on the rest, leaving it for the boys to enjoy. Cody took one as well, but he nibbled at it half-heartedly while his eyes surveyed the forest. I could see the gears turning in his mind, and knew he was trying to calculate some sort of escape into the forest.

I leaned over. "Think you could make it?" I whispered teasingly, and his head snapped around, his eyes wide in alarm. "Hey, it's okay," I tried to reassure him, and he softened a little. He lowered his gaze back down to the ground, and fidgeted slightly.

Tim and Jay shifted beside me, and then stood up. I looked up at them, and Jay nodded toward the wider part of the clearing. "We're going to go play catch with Samuel. Cody? Want to come play with us?"

Cody looked up at them for a long moment, studying them. It was like he was waiting for the other shoe to drop—maybe he wanted it to. If one of us lost patience or got angry, it would only confirm what he believed to be the truth about us: that we were the bad guys.

I gave them a nod, indicating they should go ahead alone. Their shoulders slumped in disappointment, but they went, shifting through the thick blanket of leaves toward the other side of the clearing. I watched Jay bend over and pick up a stick, and before he could even whistle, Samuel bounded over, his tail wagging in excitement.

They threw the stick for him a few times, and I smiled when Tim said something to Jay that made him start laughing. A quick glance at Cody told me he was watching as well, but he didn't seem to be enjoying the picturesque scene as much as I was. Instead, he seemed to resent it, judging by the sour downturn of his mouth.

I sighed and leaned back. Each one of these outings seemed to have the opposite effect of what I had hoped for. Dr. Arlan said it was too early to judge whether any such methods were completely effective or not. We just had to remain patient.

"Can I please see Desmond?"

It was the first time he had asked *me* that question. Unfortunately, our camp was too small to keep her capture and imprisonment a secret, and Cody had learned about it the first night. Although we hadn't heard about it until the next day, when Dr. Arlan had marched in to give us an earful about it.

"We talked about this, Cody. I'm sorry, but no—you can't see her."

Cody gave an irritated sound and turned his back to me.

"I hate you." The words were barely a whisper, but in the still of the forest, with him right beside me, I could hear them.

"That's okay," I replied softly. Gently. "You're entitled to your feelings."

He turned, cocking his head up at me and squinting. "What's

'entitled' mean?"

Hesitating a second to ponder the best way to explain, I looked up at the light gray sky. "Entitled means... that it's something you were born into. When I use it to talk about your feelings, what I mean to say is that you are allowed to feel however you want."

"Oh." He frowned. "Doesn't it make you angry that I hate you?"

I shook my head at him, and then met his gaze. "It just makes me feel sad."

He frowned then and looked away, considering this. I continued to watch Tim and Jay play, but my attention was focused on Cody. I kept hoping he would say something back, but he didn't. He just sat there, staring off blankly, deep in thought. After a while, I stood up and waved Tim and Jay over.

"Cody?" I said softly, and he looked up, as if surprised to see me still standing there. "It's time to go."

CHAPTER 12

Violet

Tiffany's round face filled the screen set up against the wall separating the kitchen from the den area where we were keeping Desmond. I frowned when I took in her face, noting the dirt smudges over her button nose and the wild tangle of her light brown, corkscrew curls, which looked like they hadn't been brushed in days. The bags under her autumn-brown eyes were tinted with blue, clearly indicating that she hadn't been getting any sleep, but her eyes were wide and jumpy, only looking at the screen periodically while constantly surveilling her environment.

"Tiffany, are you safe?" Ms. Dale asked from where she was seated, a pen and paper in her hands.

"Not really," she said, her voice brimming with the distress of raw nerves. "Nobody on the streets right now is safe."

Even as she said it, the sound of automatic gunfire wafted in through the speakers, and I watched as she ducked her head down even farther.

"What's going on out there?" Amber asked.

"It's bad, and I'm sorry for not being able to keep proper contact. I've been having to move around a lot."

"Why? Are the Matrians after you?" Thomas leaned forward in his seat, his eyes regarding the screen intently.

"What? No. No, it's weird, actually. The Matrians have pulled back their forces. They haven't been in the city for days. Well, except for one area." She looked away from the camera, and then there was a shuffling sound as the camera jerked around. A few seconds later, her face was back. "Sorry, I dropped it. I thought I heard something, but it was a cat."

"What do you mean 'one area'?" Ms. Dale cut in sharply.

"Wait," I said, taking a step forward. "Let's just slow this down a bit. Tiffany, what is going on in the city? Start at the beginning."

Tiffany's round face froze for a second, and then she nodded. "Right, well, from what I've pieced together, your video got to every stadium around the city. The Matrians tried to kill anyone who saw it, but there were just too many people for them to handle—and the attack pushed them over the edge. Rioters took to the streets, setting fires and targeting any Matrians they could find. They'd kill them, take their guns, and then use them to kill the next group. By the morning, several troops of Matrian wardens were killed. Then, during the day, the wardens retaliated. They fired guns into apartment buildings and into crowds of scared people on the street, before racing away. Or at least, that's what I've been told.

"The guard posts they set up leading in and out of the city have been turned inward, and are now preventing people from leaving. But most of the Matrian forces have been spotted leaving the city, save for a handful who got surrounded and caught up at the water treatment plant. Everything seemed like it might calm down once they left, but that's when people figured out that they weren't allowed to leave. And when the power went out?" Tiffany's face fell, her large eyes luminous with unshed tears. "Then people just started fighting each other. Everyone's trapped in here, Violet. And they're scared, and they're armed, and they're violent. Gangs have been staking out territories, making it difficult to move through the city unless you're part of a larger, more armed group. Women are getting grabbed off the street by a faction of the Porteque gang, and they've staked out a bunch of apartment buildings on the south side of the city. Other gangs are cropping up left and right, fighting for territory and food."

"Tiffany, how did you come by this information?" Ms. Dale's eyes were narrowed suspiciously at the screen.

She blinked and then licked her lips. "Well, I managed to locate some people who… well, they're not a gang. They're rebels."

"What, pray tell, is the difference?"

"The rebels are trying to help the people," Tiffany replied without the slightest pause. "They provide safe zones, forage for food, and keep guard over the people who can't fight. They are more organized than the gangs, and they've been focusing most of their fighting on the Matrian forces. There were more groups in the early days, but the three I am in contact with now are the largest in the city."

That was interesting. I took a step closer to the table, pressing in between Thomas and Amber. "What can you tell us about them?"

"Well, they were operating independently of each other. I, uh, actually sort of got them talking about unifying, but there are… some political differences that are being hashed out."

"Political differences?"

"Just ideas on how they want to proceed after they get the Matrians out. It sounds stupid, I know, but they don't want to unify unless they are all on the same page with how things would be handled in the aftermath."

"That is literally what putting the cart before the horse means," scoffed Amber, tossing her head, her mop of red curls dancing.

"I know, I tried to tell them that, but... yeah." Tiffany's face was a resigned mask that only made her look even more exhausted. I admired the way she was holding it together, all things considered.

"Is any one of the leaders looking like they are going to be *the* leader? You know—the one that the others defer to?" Viggo had stepped in behind me, and I leaned back against him as he spoke, enjoying the solid feel of him.

"Mags," replied Tiffany, once again automatically. "It's strange, I know, but she is magnificent. And terrifying. She's not very tall, but she is a whole lot of mean. Well, not mean, exactly, but direct. Painfully so. I've never quite met anyone like her."

"I like her already," said Ms. Dale, an unusually smug grin on her face. "Could always use a few more girls filled with piss and vinegar around here."

I chuckled at Ms. Dale's quip. I had to admit, I liked the sound of this Mags too. I was just curious about all of the... political discussions that these newly minted rebels were having. They were already constructing plans for afterward, but as far as I knew, our group had never even talked about it. Then again, I'd never thought that *after* might come this quickly.

"Do you think they'd be willing to meet with us?" asked

Viggo. "So we can talk about us breaking the Matrian blockade together? If we pooled our resources, then maybe we could help achieve both our goals."

I looked at Viggo and smiled. His eyes were glued to the screen, giving it his full attention as he waited for Tiffany's reply. Her frown deepened. After a moment, she inhaled. "I might be able to arrange it, but I would need to reveal key bits of information. Namely the fact that we're holding King Maxen prisoner."

"Are you asking for permission?" asked Ms. Dale.

"Yes."

"If you think it will help prove who we are, then do it."

Nobody objected to Ms. Dale's directive, not even Thomas. It was a calculated risk, but one worth taking if it got us allies inside the city.

"I'm on it," Tiffany said. "I'll try to send you a message in twelve hours."

"Good luck," I said, right before the screen shut off.

"Do you really want to go into the city?" asked Amber, turning in her chair to look at Viggo.

"I do. The people there need help, and I think if we can break this Matrian blockade, then we can start getting things calmed down." Viggo's voice was firm, brimming with conviction. I knew he was worried about the people trapped inside, and feeling more than a little responsible for their predicament.

"Has anyone considered why they are keeping people from leaving the city?" asked Thomas. "To me, that is the more critical question."

"If I had to guess, then I'd say it's to buy time while Elena finds another way to subdue the populace. Knowing her, she's trying to do it as efficiently as possible." Ms. Dale's mouth was pinched as she spoke, and I could practically taste her disdain.

We all fell silent for a moment, and then Ms. Dale sat upright, her back going ramrod stiff. I recognized her posture: she had just had a thought. "The water treatment plant," she said. Turning, she speared Thomas with a look. "Do you have the blueprints for that?"

"I do, but why? Tiffany said that the Matrians had taken refuge up there after being cut off from the retreating forces. They're probably waiting for a rescue team, or possibly even an evacuation."

Ms. Dale shook her head, a line forming between her eyebrows. "For over twenty-four hours? I don't think so—they're going to do something to the water."

"Are you *joking?*" exclaimed Thomas, his lips twitching in what I presumed was humor. It was hard to tell, rarely having seen it in Thomas before. "The plant is almost impossible to tamper with. I researched this in painstaking detail when I was looking into ways to dismantle Patrian systems, and I estimated it would take a minimum of forty soldiers. And even then, they would need three to four days before they could do anything to the drinking water. It's not possible."

"Did you ever tell Desmond this?"

"Of course I did, I… Oh." Thomas's face fell as he settled back into the chair he'd been gradually inching forward in. "I see what you mean now."

"There's an easy way to figure this out," announced Viggo loudly, his voice cutting through the room, challenging. "We merely need to ask the woman in the next room. And, as far as I know, her dose of sedative should be wearing off soon."

I looked at the people around me for their reaction: this was part of the fight that we kept having amongst ourselves. Viggo wanted to use Desmond for information while we were forced to keep her captive. Many of us just wanted her dead. I was torn over the decision, every fiber of my being wanted Desmond dead. But I didn't want to have to play executioner. And I didn't want her people to hurt the boys.

Ms. Dale sighed, settling back into her chair, her fingers and thumbs digging into her temples. I knew what she was thinking. I felt the same way: Desmond was never going to talk. Keeping her around was jeopardizing us all. Even unarmed and chained in the next room, she still had use of her most lethal weapon—her mouth. "Viggo," she said, "we've gone over this."

I worried about having Dr. Arlan in with her. He had zero experience with her, which meant that if she could, she would find a way to lure him in and try to gain his trust. Which was why I had insisted that Dr. Arlan never be left alone with her. Bad enough she was here, but I would be damned if I let her get her hooks into any of our people. These people were more than just fellow rebels who'd had their lives torn apart by Elena and Desmond. They were becoming my friends. And I didn't want to give her any opportunity to hurt any of them ever again.

"We haven't even begun to formulate a plan for what to do with her," Thomas interjected to the generalized muttering that had erupted around the room, drawing everyone's attention to him. "There's only a three percent chance she'll reveal anything of relevance to us."

"We have a *resource* in the other room," Viggo insisted. "We should at least attempt to use it."

"You cannot trust a word out of Desmond Bertrand's mouth," Ms. Dale said, her voice heavy with bitter wisdom. "She will lie and manipulate to confuse and distract us. Honestly, the only thing we should do when we go into that room is put a bullet in her head, and leave her body in the woods for the crows to find. It won't be the first time I've killed in the name of the cause, but at least this time, it'll be the right cause."

Her words rose to an avalanche of conviction, and I felt them resonate deep within me, making me inclined to agree with her crude and brutal thought process. I knew it wasn't right. Executing her would only make me more like her, and less like myself... but, more and more, it was feeling like a hit I was willing to take in order to spare us all her brand of evil. What else could we do? Surrender her to the nonexistent Patrian authorities?

Viggo shook his head at Ms. Dale, his brows drawing together. "I don't disagree, Ms. Dale. But you know we can't do that yet. We have to find out if harm will come to the boys if the Matrians don't hear from her."

Ms. Dale's eyes narrowed. "I know that's what we agreed on, but the more I think about it, the more I find it a farfetched story. It's highly likely she's lying, and I wonder if we shouldn't just call her bluff."

Viggo's voice was low. "That's a chance that we absolutely cannot take. We can't gamble on the boys' lives!"

"Ms. Dale, Viggo, calm down! Both of you!" Amber slapped her hand on the table and leaned forward, her mouth twisted in a scowl. "Desmond is already winning if we fight about what to do with her. I suggest a compromise. We can't execute her now, and we all know how dangerous she is. Let's go in and see what she has to say."

"About what?" asked Thomas.

"About *anything*. Bring the gun; let her think we made the

decision to off her. See if she says anything."

"I'll agree to do it if I get to carry the gun," Ms. Dale finally said, resignation thick in her voice. "But it won't help and it won't work."

"Let's not jump to that," I said, trying not to catch the volatile emotions whirling around the room. "Viggo, you and Ms. Dale go in and let her know we've decided to execute her. See what she says. If we are convinced she holds nothing of interest, we continue with our current plan—find out whether or not the threat to the boys is true, and make sure we're in the clear before we execute her. It won't be a lie then."

"Let's put it to a vote," Ms. Dale said after a long moment of silence. "Just for this exact plan. All in favor?"

Thomas, Amber, and Viggo's hands shot up, the three of them saying "aye" at almost the exact same time. After a moment of hesitation, I raised my hand as well, resolving to see the decision through to the end.

Ms. Dale's face was impassive, but I could tell she still wasn't happy with the decision. "The ayes have it," she said softly. "Let's get ready to talk to Desmond."

A chill raced down my spine in trepidation about what was in store for us all. There never was any telling, where Desmond was concerned.

CHAPTER 13

Viggo

The den had suffered massively in our attempt to create a prison for Desmond. The animal heads and pictures that had adorned the wall had been stripped away, although their former presence was still distinguishable by the dark sections of paint that hadn't faded like the rest of the walls. We had cleared out every knick-knack and every keepsake, every object in the room, creating a wide-open space.

We had given her a big fluffy blanket and a couch cushion (with no zippers on the upholstery) so she could make a small nest on the floor—Ms. Dale had warned us about the many dangerous uses of sheets. She'd also been very upset that we'd even given her something besides bare floor to keep herself warm, but I'd been adamant about it. We weren't animals, and wouldn't treat our prisoners as such. Cruelty in itself had never been justice. That was what separated us from people like Desmond.

The windows had been boarded up from the outside, and I

had personally knocked out every pane of glass and removed any shards. I did not want her to have any shot at finding a weapon. I couldn't risk anyone here, especially given how much I knew everyone wanted her dead.

I did too, and that was what made me hesitate. As a warden, I was used to doing things a certain way—a legal procedure, a trial, some impartial witnesses—even in the continually biased environment that was Patrus. This was all uncharted territory to me, and in reality, executions as a whole didn't sit right with me, especially when it came to women. It may have sounded weird, but it only made me think of my late wife, and how she had suffered in the hands of a justice system working against her. We were a group of people basically enacting vigilante justice, and I didn't want to make the decision until we had to—though that time was rapidly approaching.

At first, our route had seemed so clear to me: we would take Desmond, question her, and finally figure out all of the plans she and Elena had discussed and put into place. All that knowledge would become the lynchpin, and we could finally attack head on, unraveling the thread of their plans, making everything fall apart.

These were all woefully naïve thoughts. They had been from the start. Even from my vantage point at the door, I could see the intelligence glimmering in Desmond's eyes. The calculations, the strategizing. Everything her eyes touched seemed to be undergoing an intense analysis.

"Come in if you're coming in," she said, shifting her hands under her hips and lifting herself into more of a sitting position. As she moved, the chains that connected her wrist and foot cuffs clinked against each other. Her left shin was encased in a bulky white cast, making the task of moving slightly harder for her, but she managed.

Ms. Dale stepped into the room first, her eyes taking in the surroundings as if she were seeing the room for the first time. Desmond watched her former protégé, a small, secret smile playing on her lips. "Not that I'm sure where I am, Melissa, but my congratulations on making this slap-dash of a prison so boring."

"Well, you know us, Des," Ms. Dale replied, coming around to face her. "We do so love accommodating you."

Desmond chuckled, her eyes flicking to me. "Well, considering that I'm still in one piece and Mr. Croft isn't throttling me, I guess that means I didn't kill Violet. Bulletproof vest?"

I took a step down into the room, letting the door close behind me. "Maybe you missed."

Her smile deepened knowingly. "Or that," she amended dismissively. "So, we've moved out of the triage part of our little melodrama. Is this when the torture starts? I'm curious to see what the so-called good guys have planned for little old me."

"No torture, Desmond," Ms. Dale said flatly. "We've come to inform you that we'll be executing you tomorrow."

If Desmond was surprised by this, she didn't show it. Instead, she pursed her lips thoughtfully, her hands flexing in her cuffs. "Oh my. So you've gotten tired of chasing the boys all around the countries, then?" She met my gaze, and I felt a flash of hate so strong it left me balling my hands into tight fists, the still healing scabs on my knuckles threatening to rip open. "I'm getting rather bored with them myself. I'm glad you all are getting the right idea."

I couldn't respond through the surge of fury that ripped through my body at the thought of abandoning the boys to their fate. I took a breath, searching for a way to turn this to my advantage. Ms. Dale stepped in, her training allowing her to maintain more cool than I was able to—but barely.

"You don't think we really believe that tripe that you tried to feed us?" she said sharply. "There's no way Elena would allow you to kill a bunch of her precious experiments just out of spite. She doesn't believe in emotions. The whole concept is ridiculous. I expected better from you, in fact."

"But it worked, didn't it?" Desmond said, the corners of her mouth turning up just slightly.

"Not for very much longer," Ms. Dale said, although the pause after Desmond made the remark was a little too long. "But we've made up our minds. Your days are numbered. The number is very short."

"So where am I to die? Here in this room, or shall we go for a lovely stroll in the forest?"

"Forest. We don't want to expose the children to that level of violence." Ms. Dale gave Desmond a tight smile. "We had a sort of compromise—Viggo didn't want to execute you, but he was outvoted. Then when it came down to timing, there was a bit of an argument, hence the compromise." As she spoke, Ms. Dale paced the room slowly, her arms crossed under her chest. "Basically… you get a final request, within reason."

Desmond looked at each of us in turn, and then gave a surprised laugh. "Dear God, is that the best you can do? This… little sashay around the room with a hokey story about how you all agreed to execute me… Please. You are too soft to do something like that. You can't even muster the practicality to sacrifice a few orphans."

I emitted a bitter laugh. "I can't believe that I spent forty-five minutes in a meeting arguing to keep you alive, even though I know you are never going to provide any information to us."

My retort caught her off balance, and she considered me with a long smile. "It's a pity you didn't consult me before you voted. I could've helped your argument immensely. But I suppose, since you're so set on executing me, it doesn't matter now."

I ignored the hook she was trying to set, and took a step forward, changing tact. "Aren't you tired of all this? All this fighting and killing people? I know *I* am, and I'm half your age."

"Closer to a third, actually," Desmond corrected me primly, her fingers coming up, jangling the chain through the gray and white hair hanging in curls around her face. With her hair down, she looked less severe and more elderly. Frail and fragile. I noticed the translucency of her skin, how the tips of her fingers were slanted down, likely from arthritis. Like this, she appeared almost… soft.

She met my gaze, a sardonic smile playing on her lips. "As for my request, where's my son?"

I already had my answer for that. "You're not going to see him."

"Is that his decision, or yours?" The question was delivered casually, but it packed a solid blow. I hadn't had a chance to ask Jay what *he* wanted—I had just made the decision. "That's what I thought," Desmond whispered, her lips curling up and around into a circle as her smile grew. "You know the difference between you and me, Mr. Croft? At least my soldiers know that I'm going to be making all decisions on their behalf, with their lives, before I go off and do it."

"That doesn't make it right," I snapped back.

"Winning makes it right." Desmond rested her shoulders back into her pillow. "And, by the Mother, I will make sure that

I take everything away from you, starting with those boys, and ending with Violet. And if dying is what it takes to do it, I accept that price gladly."

The hatred was back, thick and acrid on my tongue, as I thought of the way Desmond had fired at Violet, and how Violet had dropped, lifeless, to the ground. For Desmond, it had been as simple as breathing, but to me... In that moment, I'd thought she had robbed me of any last hope I had for the future. The despair alone had threatened to crush me—I couldn't bear losing Violet. Not now, not ever.

Ms. Dale noticed my rising temper and stepped in between us, blocking my view of Desmond. I moved around her as she spoke, but also took a step back, cautious enough not to get too close to her. "You've given us your request. We're done here."

She turned and pressed a hand to my chest, sternly mouthing the word 'go.' I robotically moved back a few steps, and then turned, gaining control of myself. I left the room, Ms. Dale hot on my heels. I watched as she locked the door, then hid the keychain in the next room—with our team coming and going, we needed an accessible place to keep it.

The hatred that had cloyed my chest a moment ago had started to dissipate, my anger draining away bits at a time. I had never felt so out of control in an interrogation room, but then again, I had never had the chance to interrogate Desmond. "I'm sorry," I said roughly. "I thought I could handle that better, but—"

"It's Desmond," Ms. Dale said, her voice bitter. "You're not the only one who can feel her like something greasy on the skin. She's an expert at this, so it's going to take a while to break her."

"That last part... she didn't sound like she was lying," I said, hating that I even had to entertain that thought.

Ms. Dale scowled, flipping her braid over her shoulder. "Well, at least we haven't taken any steps backward. Viggo, the two best ways of breaking someone are through fear or guilt. We tried fear, but Desmond is old. She doesn't have much left *to* fear. She'll lie through her teeth to save her life, but it doesn't help us much if we have no cross-references. Maybe we should try guilt, see if we can't shake something loose."

I frowned. "You want to use Jay?" I did not like that idea at all.

"Ask, yes. Use, no. But… she did ask for him."

"Please. She was just doing that as a mind game, trying to throw you off balance. We shouldn't ask Jay if he would be okay with…"

Ms. Dale shot me a warning glance and then nodded to a place just past my range of vision. Turning, I paused when I saw Jay standing there, his arms full of split wood, staring at both of us. His dark hair clung wetly to his forehead, his cheeks stained red from exertion. "Shouldn't ask Jay if he'd be okay with what?" he asked, bending over to deposit the wood into the pile next to the hearth. The bits of wood clattered as they hit the stone floor. It was the only sound in a room gone silent.

I licked my lips, suddenly nervous. This wasn't an easy thing to talk to anyone about, but especially not the son of our prisoner, a boy she had personally sacrificed to Mr. Jenks' terrible experimentations.

"Do you want me to—"

"No," I said, cutting Ms. Dale off. Jay dusted off his hands, watching the two of us, and then shook his head.

"You were in with my mom," he said after a pause. "Trying to ask her questions?"

"Kind of," I hedged. "She… um… She asked about you."

Jay didn't say anything, didn't even move, for a long time, his eyes drifting toward the door separating them. "She wants to see me?" Even after all she had done to him, there was no denying the slim sliver of hope amid the naked pain that his neutral voice didn't begin to mask.

I moved over to him, unable to stop myself. "You don't have to see her," I told him. "Not if you don't want to." Dropping an arm over his shoulder, I tugged him a little closer to me, relieved that he let me, but still worried by the tension radiating from his frame.

"She knows things," he said hollowly. "Things that would help us."

"She does," announced Ms. Dale. "But Viggo is right. You don't have to see her. In fact, it's probably better that you don't."

"Why?" Jay cocked his head, his gaze on the door finally breaking as he regarded Ms. Dale.

Ms. Dale hesitated, and then reached out and took his hand. "You know, for a second, I honestly wanted to convince you to do it. But after thinking about it, I realized that no information is worth you being hurt for. And that's all Desmond would do—she'd try to hurt you."

Jay considered this. "When I was little, before… before the facility… she used to be away for long periods of time. I never knew where she was or what she was doing. But… I always knew when she got home. It was usually late at night, but the first thing she would do was come in and check on us. It would always wake me up, and I would get so excited she would climb into bed with me to keep me from waking Lee. She'd hold me and tell me stories…" His voice cracked, and he looked down, tears dripping down his face. Even though he was a young man, he looked very much like a small boy in that moment—hurt and lost. It made my soul hurt, seeing him that way. "How can I talk to her, when she isn't even the same mother I remember? What if all that was a lie and... and she never really loved me? I couldn't even believe her if she told me that those moments were just as special to her as they were to me... because... because..."

"Because if they were, then her putting you into the facility would make you hurt even more," I supplied softly.

He sniffed, tears rolling down his cheeks in big fat drops. His shoulders shuddered slightly, and I took a step forward, wrapping an arm around him and holding him tight. "You only have to see her if you want to," I told him as he bit back a tiny sob. "No one is going to judge you for not wanting to. Not one bit. We all love you, Jay, and we just want to make sure you're okay, no matter what you decide, okay?"

Jay nodded stiffly and stepped back, scrubbing his face with the sleeve of his dark green sweater. He began to move, but I held on to him. "If you need to talk, we're always here for you."

Jay sighed, his shoulders heaving under my hand. "I know that, Viggo—I do. You, Tim, and Violet are like family." He paused and looked over my shoulder, shifting awkwardly. "You too, Ms. Dale."

She chuckled knowingly. "You won't hurt my feelings if you don't want to make me your battle ax of an aunt, Jay. What's important is that you feel safe, and happy."

He nodded again, wiping his nose. "Thanks. I, uh, I'd like to go. I kinda want to be alone... so I can think."

I nodded. "Of course."

With that, Jay turned and fled from the room as if Desmond herself were chasing him. Watching him go, I felt my heart ache in response to his pain. He'd find someone to talk to about it— Tim, Violet, Quinn. He wasn't alone, and we wouldn't let him be.

That was what family was for, after all.

CHAPTER 14

Violet

"Look, we need to have a plan together before we talk to these rebels," said Ms. Dale, her cheeks flushed. "If we present them with two different ideas, then we'll only be sending mixed messages." I suppressed a smile. The argument had been going on for the better part of fifteen minutes, and I could tell Ms. Dale was not going to give up.

Then again, judging from Viggo's body language, neither was he. "I *understand* that, but we cannot overlook the water treatment plant! There is something going on there. Elena wouldn't leave the city alone for this long without having something up her sleeve."

Across the table, Amber met my eyes, an impish sparkle in her own. She held her mouth in a slight pucker, giving her a vaguely fish-like appearance, and then began puffing out her chest. I hid my smile behind my hand, recognizing the joke for what it was—Ms. Dale had a habit of sucking in her breath before going on a particularly long tirade, and Amber had pulled it off perfectly.

Ms. Dale didn't break Viggo's eye contact, but she snapped her arm out in front of Amber's face, wagging a finger in warning, and I hid my smile again as Amber made a comical face of alarm, her mouth turned downward in exaggerated mortification.

I sank down in my seat, trying not to laugh as Ms. Dale began sucking in her breath to respond. Laughing in the middle of a heated debate between Ms. Dale and Viggo would only result in instant attention, and I wanted to remain *out* of this fight. It had become circular at this point, and frankly, it was beginning to grate.

I understood both sides well enough to know this was a difficult choice to make. Viggo wanted to commit all of our resources to the water treatment plant, just in case something was going on there. Ms. Dale wanted to commit them to eliminating all the Matrian forces keeping the citizens inside from leaving, as well as the contingent stationed on the bridge. Both arguments had valid points, with one big exception—since the interrogation of Desmond had gotten us absolutely nowhere, there was no evidence anything untoward was going on in the plant. Viggo was working purely from conjecture at this point.

Still, in my mind, he was right. The Matrians holing up in there was too odd an occurrence for us not to take it seriously. I understood that the math supported Ms. Dale's plan, but it seemed like we were forgetting one important thing: Elena would stop at nothing to get what she wanted.

"All right," I said loudly, rudely butting in during Viggo's rebuttal. "Let's stop arguing and think this through rationally."

Viggo bit off a growl and Ms. Dale gave me an irritated glance, but they both sat down. I shared a crooked smile with Amber and then looked at Thomas, asking the strategist, "How—in the simplest terms possible—does the plant work?"

"It's quite simple. Water is pumped up through an underwater spring, and then processed for purification. It spends several days in the ponds out back, so the ultraviolet radiation from the sun can kill some of the bacteria that came up from the recesses of the earth. Then the water is pumped in through the first initial filter—but this one is only designed to keep out larger bits of sediment. The water is moved inside to the massive vats, boiled, and then processed through a pipe system that has more fail-safes than a bank. The result is clean water."

"All right. So, could Elena get enough access to the system to dump something in there? Like a toxin or poison or something?"

Thomas looked up, his eyes shifting back and forth behind his glasses. I liked to think of it as his thinking face, and I could imagine all the vast calculations he was doing as floating numbers scrolled before his eyes. After a moment, he nodded. "In most of the scenarios, I theorized that the water treatment system could be overcome if the mechanical, electrical, and technological backups were simultaneously taken down. But the timing on this would have to be flawless. In addition to that, parts of the system would have to be reprogrammed to be allowed access to the recycled water. King Julian—King Maxen's grandfather—was paranoid about keeping the water as tamper-proof as possible, and he managed to create quite a fascinating puzzle."

"Okay, so, in theory, what is the minimum amount of time the Matrians would need before they would actually be able to begin dumping something in there?"

"Seventy-two hours, give or take."

That meant that if they were trying to crack the system, they had at least twenty-four hours on us—closer to forty-eight at this point. "Thank you," I said. Licking my lips, I considered the puzzle. "Let's pretend they *are* doing something at the plant. Do we think Elena would be trying to kill or incapacitate?"

"Wouldn't she just want to kill everyone?" said Amber, swiveling from side to side in the computer chair she was spread out in. "I mean, if she does, she gets the land. In fact, why are we assuming she's doing something to the water? How do we know she's not trying to demolish the plant, leave everyone here to die of dehydration?"

"But she loses any experienced farmers, as well as the source of water with which to grow the crops," said Viggo, crossing his arms across his chest. "Considering Patrus has the best farmland, I'd doubt she'd want to lose either."

"The farmers are already missing," Thomas pointed out. "I mean, some of them could've traveled to the city, but Mr. Kaplan was grabbed. No reason to think she wouldn't have collected the others as well."

"If she did in fact capture them, then that would mean she could kill everyone else here without damaging her plan," said Ms. Dale. "If anything, it would be simpler. She could just send Matrians over here to start taking over and restore the infrastructure with the Patrian farmers as their captive guides."

"Actually, I doubt very much it is poison," announced Thomas. "The amount needed to poison the water at a concentration high enough to be effective would be extremely difficult to achieve."

"I'm sorry to interrupt, but that's not necessarily true," a voice behind me spoke. I turned and looked at Dr. Tierney, who was standing in the little dinette area, a mug of coffee cradled in her hands. If she was made uncomfortable by everyone looking at her, she didn't show it. "There are certain toxins that would be effective, even if only a microscopic amount were used. But, I do think it might be possible that she wouldn't even use poison."

"Why not?" I asked, curious to hear her reasoning.

"Because she'd never be able to cover that up from her own people."

I shook my head, trying to clear it from the simplicity of her argument. She was right, of course. Elena had too many people on this—there was no way she'd be able to hide mass genocide. And she still had her own reputation in Matrus to uphold. My former home. They hadn't seen our video, and Elena would take pains to ensure that they wouldn't. But simply killing everyone in Patrus and then taking over? There would be no way to explain it. That would possibly thwart her future plans, especially if the people decided to oust her.

So, if they were dumping something, it had to be something that would incapacitate the Patrians. Or worse.

"What if it's the Benuxupane?" I asked, looking around the room. "It would make sense, right? Make the population more complicit with her demands?"

"That wouldn't work either," said Dr. Tierney. She moved across the room to an empty chair between Thomas and Amber, dropping into it with a sigh. "As good as that idea is, they can't have had time to prepare a stockpile large enough to dose an entire population."

Viggo sighed and ran his hands through his hair. "The other problem with using the Benuxupane is that it doesn't help her public image either. It would cause a panic in Matrus if she did that."

I nodded in agreement, and then sighed. We'd tried to make an argument for going to the plant, but wound up starting to convince ourselves that maybe there wasn't anything more going on there than a bunch of stranded wardens. It was odd, yes, but at the same time…

"There's still a dozen things they could be doing there," Viggo went on. "Sabotaging systems so that the water halts temporarily, or maybe even trying to rig it so it seems like the system failed. What if they reversed the system and somehow started to drag water in from Veil River? She could chalk it up to an unfortunate accident."

"There's no way for water from the river to get into the water in the plant," said Thomas. "I considered that option, but the pipes leading from the plant to the river for disposal hang *over* the river, to prevent any chance of contamination."

A sharp rapping sound punctuated Thomas' remark, and I shifted in my seat, surprise rolling over me as I saw Henrik leaning a shoulder against the wall, his arms folded over his chest. "Is this a private party, or can I join?"

"Henrik," Ms. Dale breathed, already halfway around the table in her hurry to get to him. "You really shouldn't be out of bed," she chided. Henrik smiled fondly at her, his face softening slightly. He held up an arm as she drew close, slipping it over her shoulder.

"I'm fine, Mel," he replied, his voice soft. I exchanged glances with Viggo, who mouthed the word 'Mel' to me, his eyes as shocked as mine must have been, and I couldn't hide the smile on my face. "And you guys have been talking so loudly, it's been impossible to get my mandatory bedrest."

"Dr. Tierney, back me up here. He really shouldn't be—"

"Actually, Ms. Dale, I told Henrik he should be getting up and moving around at this point. Although, he is confined to the house." Dr. Tierney shot Henrik a stern look, and in response he gave her a lazy salute. Ms. Dale's mouth was pinched, and I could tell she was biting her tongue to keep from arguing with the doctor.

"Is that what I look like when people are thwarting my plans to keep you healthy?" Viggo asked me, his eyes glittering with humor, his voice lowered to a conspiratorial whisper.

I gave him a considering look, and then shook my head. "You look grumpier, more like a caveman."

He laughed, once, and my smile grew. Then he was gone—up and holding out his chair for Henrik. The older man smiled as he approached, and the two drew in for a quick hug. I shifted my seat over a little as he lowered himself in.

Seeing him out of the bed was good. He looked less like he was on his deathbed, and more like the strong, imposing, grandfatherly type I had always seen him as. But still, there was a fragility in him, in how he lowered himself down into the chair in slow motion, or how he seemed winded, in spite of how short the walk was from the hall entrance to Viggo's chair.

I got out of my seat to make room for Ms. Dale, and moments later I was sitting where she originally had been—opposite Viggo and me—with Viggo leaning in behind me, holding the back of my chair with both his hands. Henrik took a moment to settle in, and then looked around the table with a bemused twinkle in his eyes. "I hope you don't mind that I was eavesdropping. It was kind of hard not to before you all stopped arguing. Mind if I offer some insight?"

Nobody objected. Who among us had ever had a problem

with Henrik's advice? He'd even been able to talk Amber down when she was in a murderous rage.

After taking a look around the room full of nods, Henrik began, "You guys have been debating this plant thing to death, and honestly, right now, it doesn't matter. You aren't in the city, and you won't be in the city until you can get the rebels on your side. And we won't have that unless you have something to offer."

"We are planning to offer weapons, but that's about all we have," said Ms. Dale.

"Actually, you have more than you think. You have Thomas."

"Thomas?" I said, just as Thomas said, "Me?"

"Yes, you," Henrik confirmed with a nod. "Or rather, your access to the cameras in the city. You can offer them intel on something they desperately need—the city itself. Matrians, movements of rogue factions, even this water treatment plant."

"But all my stuff… it's in the city. In my safe house. When I left the sewers, I disconnected it so Desmond couldn't have access to it."

"Could someone put it back together?"

Thomas hesitated, and then nodded, tugging his shirt down over his paunch. "Yes. Provided nothing has been damaged."

"That's where you start, then. If you give them that gift, then they might be willing to get us more intel on the plant."

I opened my mouth. Then I shut it. It was as good as plans got, all things considered. And it was an idea we hadn't even thought of. Looking around the room, it wasn't hard to see that everyone was in agreement.

"It's good to have you back, Henrik," announced Viggo from behind me.

"It's good to be back, my boy," he said with a wink.

CHAPTER 15

Viggo

"**A**re you really sure that you want to go?"

I turned and smiled when I saw Violet stepping down off the porch. I gave the bag I had been stuffing into the trunk of the car another shove. "Somebody's got to go," I said. "Might as well be me."

"Yeah, but it's Maxen," she replied, her eyes rolling and a look of perfect distaste dramatizing her face.

I fought off the urge to laugh, but a small chuckle slipped through. "You better not make that face when Maxen gets here," I warned her playfully, taking a step forward and closing the distance between us.

She stuck out her hip and rested her fist on it. "I never agreed to those terms!"

"You will," I promised darkly. She lifted a challenging eyebrow and took a step closer, her face angled up to meet my gaze, just within the reach of my arms but not touching me yet.

"Is that a threat?"

I smiled, a lazy, slow, predatory smile, all of my teeth showing. "Just a promise, love. Just a promise."

"Hmmm…" Her eyes narrowed to silver slits, her finger tapping her chin. "All right, then. But if you're making me promises, will you *promise* not to punch the king if he annoys you?"

"Of course not. But I *do* promise to feel really bad about it afterward. Well… maybe not really bad. Maybe just a smidge."

Her chuckle was low and husky, and after keeping her body inches away from mine for so many long, agonizing moments, she pressed in close, wrapping her arms around my waist. "It's going to be a long day, isn't it?"

She wasn't wrong. We were moving today, and we'd managed to secure a call with the rebel faction leaders in the city later in the evening. Technically, early morning. Ms. Dale had managed to find several farmhouses that suited our needs nearer to the city, and, after some debate, we had decided to use them as our new base of operations to be in a closer position if we had to go into the city.

But that meant our small army was being pared down to three little teams. Which meant a lot of coordination, planning, and sheer madness for those in charge. Namely, Violet. I leaned over and pressed my lips against her forehead. "I should be asking if *you* want to change jobs, huh?"

Violet laughed and shook her head. "You're being a very good fiancé," she said, "but I've got it under control."

I beamed at the praise, fighting off the urge to say 'I know.' As much as I knew she'd laugh, I didn't want to let humor get in the way of what I wanted to talk to her about. I pressed her tighter to me and then sighed. "Are you sure you're okay?"

She leaned back in my arms, her eyes studying my face. I returned her look, not letting it deter me. "Viggo, I told you, I don't want to—"

"You woke up covered in sweat last night, Violet. Your breathing was labored, and you were crying. Was it... Was it about the guard at Ashabee's?"

Violet looked away, but not before I could see the flash of horror on her face. She pulled back slightly, and then completely, crossing her arms and moving away from me. She stopped after a few paces, and I waited for her to push through whatever she was processing.

After several painfully long heartbeats, she turned back and sighed. "Yes, it was the warden. I just... I can't stop seeing her face, every time I close my eyes. The smell... I can still smell it. I'm fine when I'm awake—it's like it didn't even happen unless I really think about it. But when I go to sleep..."

She sighed again, her arms twitching in frustration. I closed the distance between us again to grab her hand, pressing it flat between my own. She rocked back and forth on her feet, her eyes distant and vacant. "Hey," I soothed, reaching out with one hand to cup her cheek. Her eyes danced back, and I could see the tears there. My heart bled for her, and I bent over and gently pressed kisses to her forehead, her eyebrows, her eyelids, the tip of her nose, and then, finally, a small chaste kiss to her lips. "I know exactly how you feel."

"Ian wasn't your fault," Violet said automatically, crushing herself to my chest. "He wasn't."

I shook my head, my heart a stone in my chest, listening, but not really understanding. "It doesn't matter. It doesn't change what I see in my dreams. How it feels."

She didn't respond, but then again, this time, she didn't need to. We just held each other, drawing strength from the support and compassion we found in our embrace. It helped soothe the pain a little, and gave us this one small place of solace that we could only find in the other. I didn't know what I would do without her, and I didn't want to find out.

I could happily lose all awareness of time, standing there. Yet, as inevitable as the sun rising in the east, it was impossible to prevent the moment from being shattered by the eagerness of a young man hellbent on being the perfect soldier.

"Hey, guys!" shouted Jay as he rushed over, a long duffel bag swinging casually from his hand. "Whatcha doing?"

Violet nuzzled in a little closer, her eyes still closed, and I could tell she was content to ignore Jay in order to steal a few more moments with me. It made me smile, and even, just for a moment, consider doing the same. But in the end, I couldn't—it was Jay.

"Talking about politics," I said sarcastically, and Tim, who was following Jay at a more leisurely pace, snorted. He moved up around Jay, pushing my bag deeper into the small trunk, and then took the oblong bag from Jay.

"Yeah? I bet you guys were smooching. Which brings me to an important question! Can you guys explain sex to me?"

I froze, feeling very much like a deer facing an oncoming truck. Looking down at Violet, I saw her fighting back a laugh, burying her face into my chest so hard, it felt like she was physically trying to shove her head into my ribcage. I let out a little cough that turned to a laugh halfway through, aware of how uncomfortable and awkward it sounded, and then cleared my throat.

"I… um… What do you want to know?"

Jay shifted uncomfortably, and then ran his hand through his hair, his shoulders shrugging halfheartedly. "I don't really know," he admitted honestly. "I heard someone say 'sex,' and then say a bunch of stuff that I didn't really understand. I know it has something to do with a—"

"And this is the point where I *leave*," Violet practically sang, her eyes sparkling in humor. "I've got a lot of work to do."

"You cannot leave me like this," I hissed, taking a step forward to grab her arm.

She danced away, moving faster than she probably should have, and gave me a little wink. "Relax! You got this."

"But wait, Violet… don't you want to tell Tim? I mean… he should know too." Jay's stare was wide-eyed with concern over Violet's looming departure.

Tim snorted again, laughing as he finished loading the last bag and closed the trunk. "It okay. I know sex."

I pressed my lips together, trying to fight the urge to laugh. Tim's English was fragmented as a result of years of isolation in his solitary confinement. I knew—absolutely knew—that he did not mean it how it sounded.

Violet cleared her throat, clasping her hands in front of her, her smile widening. "Our orphanage had sex education once a year," she announced primly. "It was mandatory. But the first time I heard it, I was so horrified that I had to tell somebody about it all… And my brother was the only one around. Uh, he didn't seem too traumatized."

With that, she waggled her fingers and disappeared into the house. I gaped at her departure, and then turned to Tim. The young man tossed his head, and then gave me a little shrug. "Busy," he said, before turning and ambling away, trying to whistle.

Which left me with Jay, who was staring up at me expectantly. I closed my eyes, inhaled deeply, and then met his gaze. "Let's talk about it in the car, buddy. We need to get out of here soon anyway."

If possible, Jay became even more eager. "All right. How can I help?"

"Go inside and do a last check with Violet and Ms. Dale—see if there is any more leftover equipment for us to share or any final jobs we might be needed for before we go."

Jay gave a little salute, and then bounded off, hot on Violet's trail. I smiled as I watched him go, wondering how I was ever going to give him the talk, and then turned toward the barn. Owen was busy there, carefully packing rifles into a bag, oblivious that I was only a minute's walk away.

I took a deep breath, trying to clear my mind from the anger that was beginning to build in me just watching him, and then walked toward him. At first, he didn't notice me. He was so absorbed with his task of breaking down the gun and making sure the chamber was clear, magazine out. When he did notice me, he froze, and then slowly sat the gun down, standing up from the bench he had been perched on. I stopped just on the other side of the table, keeping a healthy distance between us.

Owen met my gaze, his face and eyes revealing nothing as to how he was feeling. I just stared at him, still not entirely sure how to say what I had to say. After a moment, he ran his hand through his hair and reached down to fiddle with the gun he had been breaking down. "Just say it," he said, after a moment.

"We made a decision," I announced.

Owen's head snapped up, his eyes searching my face for any

sign of his fate. Then he sighed and nodded. "I'll go get my things. I'll be out of the camp before the move is fully finished. Don't worry—I have no idea where you all are going, but even if I did, I wouldn't follow you."

I shook my head and held up my hands, the urge to correct him compelling me forward a step, my knees brushing up against the bench. "We're not exiling you, Owen."

Owen froze in the middle of his step away from me, a resigned expression coming over his face. "Yeah," he said bitterly. "I figured I'd never get off that easy. So I guess Amber's suggestion of execution was the popular vote, huh?"

I blinked, his statement hitting me like a stiff jab in the face. "Um, Amber never advocated execution. No one did."

Owen's confusion deepened, and I felt pity for him, and irritation at myself. This was an important moment to Owen, and I was fumbling through it like an idiot, dragging out his torture.

"Oh. I guess maybe that was Amber's way of…" He trailed off and sighed, crossing his arms against his chest. "I'm talking too much."

"I was just about to say," I agreed, before I could stop myself. Owen met my gaze, his eyes steely in spite of the vulnerability that hid there, and I cleared my throat. "Look, the punishment we decided for your actions is probably one of the most difficult and dangerous jobs we have at the camp. It comes with a high probability of violence, and a strong chance that you will be injured, maimed, and/or killed in the line of duty… I want you to be Violet's bodyguard."

Owen's eyes bugged, and he blinked, as if disbelieving that I was actually there. "You have got to be joking," he said—practically shouted. "Why in the world would you ever trust me with her life after what I did to her? How did they even get you to agree—"

"It was my idea," I shouted back, shutting him up. "It was. Because… in spite of everything, I know you truly care about Violet, and now that the guilt of what you did to her is chewing you up, I *know* you will lay down your life to protect her."

The look of intense thought on Owen's face had deepened, as if he were weighing each word carefully, searching for some hint that I was wrong in my estimation of him. I knew he was looking for a reason to get out of this—not because he didn't want to do it, but because he didn't believe he should. That was how I knew it would be the perfect punishment for him. It would force him to deal with his guilt and shame, every day, until he got over it. Or until the job actually killed him. It was a possibility we couldn't ignore.

"How does Violet feel about it?" he asked after a moment, and I knew he had failed to find something to disapprove of in what I was saying. He was fishing for any excuse.

"Honestly, she's fine with it. I think… I think she's ready to forgive you. She might have already done so."

"And you?" Owen's question was loaded, and I could hear the conflicting emotions there, threatening to strangle out his voice.

This was my precipice, one I couldn't begin to describe. "I honestly don't know. On the one hand, I feel like I shouldn't hold you to your actions. I know you said not to factor in… what happened to you… but it's impossible for me not to. On the other hand…" I met his gaze, letting some of the anger creep through. "I really want to punch your lights out."

Owen nodded, biting his lower lip. "I don't really blame you," he announced. "I deserve it."

We both fell silent, uncertain how to follow up. There really was no follow-up to be had. I was just hanging back, out of habit, waiting for him to say goodbye, make a joke, say something pithy. I had almost forgotten that things were different now.

"I gotta go."

Owen's eyes flicked up to mine at my declaration. "Right. I'll… uh… get my stuff ready to join you guys in the farmhouse. And, it goes without saying—but I *will* keep her safe, Viggo." He held out his hand, stretching his arm across the table. I looked down at it for a moment, indecision raging. Then I accepted his handshake, shaking twice before dropping his hand.

With that, I turned and walked away, heading back to the car where Jay, and now Cad, were waiting for me.

I didn't look back.

CHAPTER 16

Violet

"**G**regory—I found them. The box shifted behind some of these old crates."

I had to resist the urge to swipe my hand across my face as I spoke. Phantom spider webs were abundant, especially against my still exposed scalp, but with the amount of dirt and grime on my hands, I had made my decision not to try to brush them away, and I was sticking to it.

"I've got it, Violet," said Gregory, the lanky Patrian man who was in charge of the guards, and I stepped back, allowing him to grab the box that had been lost for the last half an hour. Looking around the barn, I nodded to myself as I took in the vast emptiness of it, save a pile of odds and ends that needed a final inventory and decision on which house to be sent to.

"Violet! This car is ready to go to C house. Do you want to check the manifest or—"

"I trust you, Lynne," I told the brunette woman standing at

the entrance to the barn. She smiled and waved in acknowledgment, then disappeared back out the door, presumably to finalize the instructions.

Eric, one of the other men helping me, handed me a clipboard, and I began to read his carefully handwritten notes regarding the contents of each box. We'd come up with a little alphanumeric code to help track things easier, which was Ms. Dale's biggest concern about dividing up the teams.

All in all, I thought we had done a pretty good job of splitting everything up as evenly as possible. Some things couldn't be evenly distributed, but I was pretty proud of the tradeoffs I had made to compensate for the discrepancies. It would work. And, in a stroke of luck, Ms. Dale's last and final hunt for weapons, ammunition, and general supplies had yielded something. Several others and I had spent hours inventorying the five thousand rounds of ammo, the boxes of comm devices, a dozen boxes filled to the brim with foil-sealed protein blocks, medical supplies (along with some much-needed antibiotics), fifteen barrels of fuel, and even more guns. The last was an added bonus: it meant we could arm more of the rebels.

I paused, noticing something on the list. "Wait, are there really... one thousand units of waterproof bags? Why haven't I noticed this before?"

Eric turned and gave a little shrug. "Maybe it was in one of the older inventories, and just got overlooked when we redid them? Either that, or they somehow manifested out of thin air."

"Show me."

Eric led me over to the small pile of miscellaneous items, and opened one of the larger boxes, revealing the compact, packable black bags, each with a large, stylistically blocked 'A' emblazoned on the side. "Ashabee Industries," I murmured. "I guess this must've been a gift bag for his clients?"

"I have no idea," replied Eric. "You should ask Jeff—I bet he'd know. What do you want me to do with them?"

I smiled slowly. "Distribute them as equally as you can to each group. This is actually a really good find, considering where we might be heading in a day or two."

Eric knelt down and began separating the bags into three piles. I moved around the rest of our pile of miscellaneous items, considering them all and then carefully writing down which base to send them to. Some things I had already separated out, but others were just too insignificant to actually dole out to any one house. However, nothing got wasted until we were sure there was no use for it, so I sent those to the house with the biggest storage room. Namely, the house Thomas would be operating out of.

I was almost finished when I heard the sound of pounding feet racing up from behind. I turned in alarm, and then relaxed when I saw it was Morgan, Tim hot on her heels.

"Violet, we need you at the house, right now."

I frowned and put the clipboard down on one of the boxes, hearing the urgency in her voice. "What's wrong?"

"I saw Cody go into Desmond's room," she said.

"Locked door," added Tim, his face tense and unhappy.

A curse slipped through my lips, and Morgan nodded. "I knew I couldn't break in there, because you don't want Desmond knowing that the Liberators have joined you, so I—"

"Did the right thing," I finished for her. "Do me a favor and go find Owen. Oh, and the car with…" I paused, grabbing the clipboard and quickly shifting through some papers, trying to locate the car and driver with the cargo I needed. "Harry—we need one of those lock-picking devices he's got."

"I've got Owen," said Morgan, whirling and running.

"Harry," grunted Tim in reply, keeping pace.

"Eric, keep working," I said as I began to jog toward the field as quickly as I dared. Several people looked up at me as I moved, but I ignored their glances, my focus entirely on the house, worry gnawing at my spine. Cody in there with Desmond was not good—who knew what she was saying to him.

I climbed the stairs of the porch, the muscles over my ribcage spasming painfully, reminding me that, yes, I did still have bruised ribs. It riled me that I couldn't comfortably run yet. I could have been there in seconds, rather than the minute it took me to cross the yard. I threw open the door to the house, my feet thudding heavily on the aged floorboards as I entered.

Lynne was pacing nervously just in front of the door, rubbing her thumbs across the side of her knuckle. "Violet," she said softly, stepping over to me. "Thank God you're here. He was playing hide-and-seek with some of the other children, and I lost track of him! He must have found out about the key's hiding place somehow—I can't get him to open the door."

"I got this," I said, stepping past her and moving over to the door. "Cody!" I shouted, pounding on the door. I pressed my ear against it and listened, but could only hear the faint sound of voices.

"Violet!" came Owen's voice from behind me, and I automatically stepped aside, making room for him. Owen dropped to one knee and inserted his lock-picking tool into the lock, the mechanics inside whirling. "Tim went to find Harry like you said, but they were looking in the wrong place. Luckily I remembered where they wound up."

I looked at Morgan, who was crossing over to Lynne, taking the brown-haired woman's hands and patting her on the shoulder.

"You both should go," I said quietly. "We can't risk her seeing you."

Lynne's face grew tight, her lips thinning in displeasure. I could tell she didn't want to leave. Morgan, however, laid a hand on Lynne's arm. "She's right. Let's go." Lynne hesitated, and then nodded. I watched as they both left, leaving Owen, Tim, and me alone.

There was an audible click as the mechanism finished manipulating the lock, and Owen stood up, slowly opening the door. I slipped in, my heart thudding against my chest, prepared to see the worst.

Cody stood mere feet away from Desmond, his back to me. I could see Desmond from my slightly elevated position, her eyes on his face, in spite of my noisy entrance.

I paused, trying to assess the situation. Cody looked over at me, tossing his hair. He stared at me, and then looked back at Desmond. "Goodbye," he said, and Desmond gave him a beatific smile.

"Until next time, dear Cody," she said, extending one shackled hand.

The movement broke me out of the state of surprise I was in. Cody hadn't done anything to try to break Desmond out. That was… decidedly odd. "Don't touch him," I ordered as she continued to stretch her hand toward him, and I took a step into the room. Desmond froze, and then sighed, slowly lowering her hand back into her lap.

"Cody, can you please come to me?" I said.

Cody licked his lips, hesitating. "Am I in trouble?"

"Not if you come to me right now."

He hesitated another second, and then crossed over to me. I held out my hand, and he took it, allowing me to push him toward the door and out of the room, where Owen was waiting. I moved to leave, when Desmond's voice stopped me.

"I was beginning to think you'd never come visit me," she said.

This was an obvious barb, one designed to get my defenses up, but I wasn't in the mood to play. Turning, I crossed my arms over my chest. "Tell me about the boys," I replied.

Desmond gave me a kind smile. "Are you still going on about that? My, my... it's like you people have nothing to do!" I shrugged and turned to leave, but her voice stopped me yet again. "Are you not visiting me because I shot you?"

"You missed," I lied, and she gave me a knowing look.

"Tut, tut, Violet dear. Don't waste your lies on something as absurd as that. You are such a capable liar. I really did have high hopes for you."

"Then you shouldn't have set up my friend," I replied tartly, thinking of Owen and the bomb she'd had him carry into Matrus.

Desmond laughed at that, and shook her head. "You mean the friend who led you into a trap with me? Pray tell, where is Owen? Did you have the guts to execute him in the basement?"

I bit back my response, realizing with my last one I had fallen into Desmond's trap. "Tell me about the boys, or I—"

"Violet?" Jay cut me off, and I turned as the young man sprinted into the room. "What happened with Cody?"

"I don't know," I replied.

"Jay?" Desmond's voice held a slender note of hope, making me turn back to her.

Jay looked over, and seemed to realize where he was. He blinked at her and then looked away. "I shouldn't be in here," he mumbled, making for the door.

"I did not raise you to be a coward, Jason Alexander Bertrand!" Her voice rose to a shout, and Jay froze in place, his shoulders cringing forward. I saw Tim enter the doorway, an alarmed expression on his face, but I ignored him.

"Don't talk to him that way," I hissed at her. "Or I'll make Tabitha's little torture chamber look like something out of a fairytale."

"You think you can intimidate me?" Desmond scoffed, her eyes crinkling with amusement. "I'm a *mother*. Can you even imagine what I sacrificed for him? The lengths I went to in order to get him into that program? And what? He wants to sulk about it?" She tsked in that way all mothers seemed to have, the one that universally told offspring everywhere that they were a disappointment. After a moment, she added a small shake of her head. "I gave him inhuman strength. I did what any good mother should and would do—I gave him a tool that is going to help him succeed and thrive. So you don't get to sit there on your high horse and tell me how I can and cannot talk to my son."

Oh dear God, was Desmond being genuine? If I ignored the angry bite that was directed at me, I found I felt a strange surge of empathy. It urged me to believe in the sorrowful cadence of her voice, the soft remorse, regret, and disappointment painting a picture, not of a monster, but just a woman willing to do anything for her son. Her actions may have been twisted and deplorable, but was it possible that she had been doing what she thought was right for her sons?

The thought left me feeling uncertain, and agitated. Especially since it seemed to take a toll on Jay. He seemed to… curl into himself a little. His shoulders rounded and hunched, his nose dropping down to point at the floor.

"C'mon," I said as I pressed my hand on his shoulder, gently nudging him out of the room. Closing the door, I saw Owen sitting with Cody at the table. He tossed something at me when I met his gaze, and I reached out to grab the keys Owen must've gotten back from Cody. I reached out for them, but Tim's hand snaked out and got them first, and he went back and locked Desmond's prison door.

Moving to let him do the job, I stepped closer to Jay, placing a hand on his cheek. "Are you okay?"

Jay hesitated. "Yes. No. I don't know."

"That's understandable. She… She really shouldn't have said those things to you."

He shrugged, his eyes drifting away for a second. "I don't feel like I have a mother," he said hollowly. "Sometimes I don't even feel like I have a family."

"Brother." Tim's hand touched his own chest as he spoke, his fingertips tapping lightly against his sternum. Then he reached out and touched my shoulder. "Sister."

I smiled, playfully bumping his hand with my shoulder. "He's right. We're your family now, like it or not. If you'll still have us."

Jay gave a halfhearted smile. "Of course I will," he said, and then sucked a deep breath in, pushing his melancholy aside. "I mean—I shouldn't have said that last part, about feeling like I don't have a family. You already are. I was just… not thinking." Some of his sadness still lingered, and on impulse, I pulled him into a hug. Tim draped his arms over both of us, and we just stood there, holding each other tightly.

From behind us, there was a choked sound, and I turned to see Owen standing behind us, his eyes tearing up. "Excuse me," he said stiffly, and walked out. Cody watched him go, and then swiveled around to look at us.

I took a step forward, realizing that our little session had triggered Owen's grief, but Jay stopped me. "I got this," he said, looking even better than before. "And I'll be okay… after some time. Tim and I will make sure he's okay."

I hesitated, but then nodded. He was right. Things between Owen and me were still too tense. There was an awkwardness, a void of space between us filled with things left unsaid. A part of me wondered if they should continue to be unspoken.

"Thanks," I said. "I gotta check in with Cody anyway."

Jay flashed me a thumbs-up and then headed out the door. Tim was already waiting for him by the doorframe, twitching impatiently. I watched them go, then moved over and dropped down into the seat next to Cody.

He stared at me warily, and then fidgeted. "You said you wouldn't be mad," he reminded me, tugging at his shirt sleeves.

"I'm not mad," I replied patiently. "But I am worried about what you and Desmond talked about."

"We didn't talk about much," he said defensively, and I sighed.

"Cody, I want to believe you, but we both know you don't want to be here. You could be lying."

Cody looked away, and then frowned. "Viggo said something the other day. He said that I'm entitled to my feelings. Do you feel that way?"

I chewed on my lip, wondering if this was a distraction technique, or if there was a point to this. I wasn't sure which it could be, but decided to let it play out. "I do," I informed him.

"I thought so." Cody shifted in his seat. "It made me think about a lot of things, you know. About how Desmond gives us the medicine, but it doesn't make us feel anything, and it made me wonder if... if she would like me without the medicine."

"Is that why you went to see her?"

He nodded slowly, his eyes fixed on the table. "She told me I was such a good boy for finding her, and then asked me to unlock her. I... I thought the key for her chains was on the keyring, but when it wasn't, she got mad at me. Started saying really mean things, like I was stupid."

I saw a tear roll down his cheek and reached out to lay a gentle hand on his back. He sniffled, and then wiped his cheeks with the cuff of his jacket. "I'm sorry," he muttered, and I smiled at him.

"You're entitled to your feelings, remember?" I said. "I'm just sorry that Desmond said mean things to you."

Cody met my gaze, his eyes rimmed red. "Can I go back to my room now? I want to be alone."

"It depends—are you going to be okay?"

He thought about it, and then nodded. "I think so. I just... I need to think."

"Okay," I said, standing up. I held out my hand, and, after a moment's hesitation, he took it, allowing me to lead him back to the barn. It was not hard letting myself hope, even for just a moment, that this was a step forward for Cody. The only thing that kept that hope in check was my sense of caution, urging me to wait and see what he would do in the days to come.

CHAPTER 17

Violet

I yawned and flexed my lower back, trying to alleviate the ache that had grown there, and in my shoulders, after several hours of sitting. I'd been awake for sixteen hours, organizing, distributing, moving to our new location, and then unloading. The unpacking process was ongoing, but I had been forced to stop participating, as Henrik wanted me to do a detailed analysis of the barricaded roads into and out of the city.

Releasing the stretch, I fought off another yawn and manipulated my fingers, slightly adjusting the position of the drone I was piloting so that the image on the screen swung around, revealing more of this guard post. Using my thumb, I put the drone into hover mode and grabbed the clipboard next to the box containing its remote controls.

I studied the post, trying to analyze it for weaknesses. Truthfully, the wardens here had not spent their time waiting around while the city had erupted into chaos. For one, they'd made barricades—sometimes with those large concrete slabs that often served as borders between road lanes, but mostly with cars and bits of metal welded together. Regardless of what the block-ades were made of, their configuration was usually the same. Two or three concentric rings of barricades, typically with some room in the road for the barricades to be rolled back to allow vehicles to pass through, but heavy enough to seriously cripple any car or truck trying to punch a hole through.

The office building's defenses were fortified with bits of wood and metal barring the windows, save for small square holes, large enough to fit the muzzle of a rifle through, and with enough room left over to be able to sight down the barrel. A generator connected to massive lights helped illuminate the surrounding area, and many of the places where trees or other objects had obscured the lines of sight from the building were now stripped clean, impossible to sneak through without being spotted well before reaching the barricades.

At most of the guard posts there was also heavier artillery of some kind, mounted on wheels or, more typically, a car. Most of them sported .50 caliber machine guns, but a few had some sort of mortar or grenade launcher of some kind. I wasn't entirely sure which this one was, but took screenshots using the function Thomas had installed.

I was just finishing noting my observations on blockade number four when the door to the basement opened, breaking my tunnel vision. Looking up, I smiled when I saw Viggo standing on the wooden landing, looking down at me.

"Hey," I said, setting my clipboard down on the table. "How'd it go with King Maxen?"

Viggo's boots thumped loudly on the steps, descending in a

languid fashion. "Well, he doesn't get better with time, that's for sure."

I winced sympathetically. "He give you a hard time?"

Stepping off the final step, Viggo gave me a droll look. "'Hard' would be a massive understatement at this juncture. I can confirm he gave me a headache, though."

"Oh, poor thing," I cooed teasingly, standing up and moving over to him. He met me halfway, pulling me into a hug.

"I am a poor thing," he whispered in my ear, the touch of his breath on the delicate skin sending delicious tendrils of pleasure racing up and down my spine, pooling at the base of it. As if sensing my dilemma, Viggo placed a firm hand over the area, drawing me even tighter against the long solid line of his body, making my breath stutter out of me. "Poorer for having been denied seeing you all day."

I smiled, losing myself in his embrace for a moment. "You always say the nicest things," I said, resting my cheek against his chest. "I don't think I'm as good at that as you are."

"That's okay. The relationship can only withstand one awesome partner."

I pulled back and punched him lightly in the stomach, but I still couldn't help smiling. Viggo chuckled and tugged me back closer, stooping over so he could press his forehead against mine. "Inconsiderate and violent," he chided. "Whatever am I going to do with you?"

"Taking me to bed would be nice." My last words might have gotten lost in the yawn that overtook me, but Viggo understood.

"I thought I told you I wasn't that kind of guy," Viggo joked, and I laughed as I slipped free of his hold, moving back over to the remote control. I slid my fingers back into the metallic slots, the cold metal tingling slightly with an electric charge, and then clicked the drone off of hover mode.

"You know what I meant," I said as I plotted a route to bring the drone back home. I angled it higher, so I could have a less chaotic view of the earth below, and watched the screen closely as the ground flew by in the bright green definition of night vision.

"I do, I do." I heard him move up behind me. We fell into a comfortable silence while I navigated and he watched. At one point, he picked up my clipboard and began reading. "Your handwriting needs work," he teased.

"Bite me," I replied tartly, still smiling.

"I might just do that."

The silence returned, and I marveled at how pleasant it was to just be around him. We didn't have to talk; we could just be. I didn't think I'd ever felt that sort of relaxed sense of safety in my entire life, but if I died tomorrow, I hoped whatever happened next would feel a lot like this.

"How much longer, Vi?"

I blinked my heavy eyelids and crunched some quick numbers. "About five minutes," I replied.

"Why don't you just set it down in the field? It'll keep until morning."

"Are you sure?"

"We've got our meeting with the rebels in a little under five and a half hours, and we've been going since, what, six this morning? We could definitely use the sleep."

He didn't have to ask me twice, and I quickly landed the drone in one of the empty corn fields. I clicked off the remote control, knowing we needed to conserve its energy as well, and then stood up, taking another moment to stretch the aching muscles in my back.

Viggo waited patiently for me to be ready, and after I dropped my clipboard with a note on Henrik's table, I headed toward the stairs with him following, grateful to be going to bed.

My first stop was on the first floor, at the small bedroom across from the stairs. I unlocked the door and pushed it open, looking at where Cody was lying on the bed, Gregory lounging on a plush chair tucked off in the corner, a book in his hands. He looked up as I pushed opened the door, and gave a friendly smile as I poked my head in.

Cody sat up, his blanket falling off his shoulders. "Violet?" he asked, squinting at me, and I realized I might have woken him up.

"I'm sorry, Cody," I said, taking a step inside. "I just wanted to see how you were settling in."

He rubbed his eyes and then shrugged. "It's a nice room," he said awkwardly, his fingers playing with the edge of his blanket. "The house sounds weird."

"Is it scary?" I asked, and he gave me a sullen look.

"I don't get scared," he said flatly, and I fought back a smile, sensing the bristle around him. He didn't like that for some reason, so I didn't prod. Things with Cody after what had happened with Desmond had been going surprisingly well. Granted, it was all through baby steps, but there was something there.

"I'm sorry," I said ceremoniously. "I didn't mean to offend you. I just wanted to see if you wanted anything before Viggo and I went up to bed. Some water, or a snack?"

Cody cracked a yawn and then shook his head. "I'm good," he said, lying back down on the bed.

I turned to Gregory. "You need anything?"

The older man smiled broadly and shook his head. "That was kind of you to ask, but no, I don't."

Smiling in response, I closed the door and turned back to Viggo, noting the pleased smile on his lips. "He's doing better, isn't he?" he said.

"He is," I allowed. "I just wish I could trust him completely."

Viggo didn't bother to object. We both shared the same fear. Viggo was just being a bit bolder with his hope than I was allowing myself to be.

Another insufferable yawn had my voice cracking as we climbed the stairs leading to the next floor and the three bedrooms there.

Ms. Dale and Henrik had taken the master bedroom—not that we had minded, of course. Since Henrik's wound still needed dressing, it had seemed best to let them take the room with an enclosed bathroom attached.

I moved for the door on the right end of the hall, pulling it open and looking at Tim and Jay splayed out on the twin beds inside. Both of them were fast asleep, and I could see that they'd had dinner in their room, evidenced by the tin plates, devoid even of crumbs, sitting on the nightstands adjacent to their beds.

Smiling at the picturesque sight, I lingered, trying to commit every detail to memory. Then I closed the door, eager to fall into the soft embrace of our bed. I paused when I saw Viggo looking at me, a hungry spark in his emerald eyes.

"What?"

"Nothing," he said quickly. A little too quickly.

"Nuh-uh. Spill. Why were you looking at me like that?" I crossed my arms over my chest and stared at him, waiting for his answer.

He smirked, and then nodded to the room. "I was just watching you check on the boys, and I thought about how you might be as a mother. I was not opposed to the idea."

Neither was I, but with everything developing more quickly and feeling more out of control than ever, I hedged the thought, afraid to even entertain the possibility for fear of dreaming of it and then having it cruelly ripped away. I took a deep breath, trying to settle the sudden onset of turmoil, and carefully pushed it to one side.

"Are you okay?" Viggo asked, ever keyed in to my wellbeing. It drew a smile to my lips.

"I'm not," I admitted honestly, not wanting to push him away. "But it's the same old doubts as before. What's going to happen, are we going to make it, will this ever stop feeling so… terrible?"

"Will we ever get to stop saying goodbye?" he added dryly, and I nodded, the smile on my lips tilting up some before going back down, his humorous jab barely softening the weight the truth always brought.

"It's getting a little old," I said, and he gave a half chuckle, a quick sound escaping him. "And our luck is going to run out eventually."

"Don't say that," Viggo said darkly, reaching out and grabbing my hand. "Don't you dare. I'm not dying like this, and neither are you. We're going to go in our sleep at the exact same time, after we've seen our children grown and our grandbabies as well. I want to be a crotchety old man whose nagging wife makes him go out and spend time with his friends. I want to sit by your side on our porch and hold your hand while we watch the sunset. I want every ridiculous moment for every terrible one, and I expect you to give them to me, with no doubt."

I felt that warm, tingling glow that always flooded me when Viggo talked about the future, his words setting my imagination aflame as I thought about us growing old together. How wonderful it would be to spend a lifetime with my best friend. To raise our children together and watch them grow and develop interests of their own.

"Thank you." I grinned up at him. "Once again, you always know what to say."

The intense look in his face softened, and he stepped in close to embrace me. "I just speak from my heart," he said roughly. "To be honest, though… that *growing old* thing made me question my heart for a second. I was afraid that picture would be a deal breaker."

Delighted by his words, I laughed, and pulled back so I could reach up and cup his cheek. "Any picture that involves me and you, any setting, any circumstance—I don't care if it's… robots from the moon or whatever! If that's your picture of us, then I'm happy, because I'll be with you."

Viggo gave me a stunned look, and then smiled a deliciously slow, smoldering smile. "That's the type of language you use to tell a man you appreciate him," he said, his voice husky and rough, making me shiver slightly. "That's how you win the most awesome partner."

My grin widened, and I pulled away from him, reluctantly, heading to our bedroom. I liked our bedroom; it was quaint. The bed was a bit old, but it was sturdy and big enough to hold the two of us, and that was what I cared about. Viggo and I moved in comfortable silence around the room, undressing and preparing for bed. I brushed my teeth in the bathroom, and then washed my face, using a little bit of the face cream Amber had given me.

I had never considered myself a face cream person, but Amber had sold me on it the first day I'd begrudgingly tried it, when my face didn't feel so dry.

The bedsprings squeaked and rattled as Viggo got into bed, and I turned in time to see his long legs disappearing under the covers. His chest was bare, and I felt my mouth go dry as I saw the strong lines of his pecs crossing his chest, almost leading my eye to the deep furrow that defined the center of his abs, straight down his body, until it disappeared beneath the covers. The only imperfections were those small puckered scars, still pink and fresh, one over his heart, the other on his upper ribcage.

I myself was only wearing a pair of shorts and a thin shirt. While there was a definite chill in the air, I had learned a long time ago that sleeping next to Viggo was like sleeping next to a furnace. I didn't need much on to stay warm, and it was something I was entirely grateful for, especially as the nights grew colder.

He smiled in the periphery of my vision, and as I looked up to meet his gaze, I could see the knowing look he was giving me. His hand patted the empty space next to him, and I moved over to the bed, drawing the cover back and lying down.

We had just started to settle into each other, taking a few moments to adjust our limbs and bodies until we were intertwined and pressed together closer than should've been possible, when a sharp rap sounded on the door.

"Are you decent?" Henrik's deep voice rolled through the door, and I exchanged a brief and confused look with Viggo. My first thought was that he didn't like where I'd parked the drone.

"Ish," retorted Viggo. "But you can come in."

We disentangled ourselves as the door swung open, and

Henrik entered, shutting the door behind him. Viggo stood up and put on an old t-shirt while Henrik waited. Once he was properly attired, he went over and shook the older man's hand.

"What's up?" he asked.

Henrik just smiled as Viggo grabbed a chair, bringing it to the foot of our bed, where Henrik dropped into it like all his strength had deserted him. "Thank you," he said.

I shifted down on the bed some, but kept the covers draped over me, unwilling to face the cold again. Viggo sat down next to me, but we were both focused on Henrik.

He stared at us, and then leaned back in the chair slightly, resting an elbow over its wooden back. "I was going to start with small talk, but, well, there's no sense in dragging the suspense out. I have something I want to give you—both of you."

"What is it?" I asked, intrigued.

Henrik hesitated, and then reached into his pocket and pulled out a small wooden box, about half the size of my palm. "Here."

He offered it to me, and I took it, examining it. It was simple, plain, although the stain on the wood had a slight red tinge to it. As I shifted it to examine the seams, I heard something inside bounce and jingle, as though two metal objects had hit together. My curiosity intensifying, I examined the box more closely, and then finally pulled back the lid, revealing two wedding bands resting inside.

My head snapped up, the words coming from my mouth taking on a life of their own in their haste to understand what I was looking at. "Where did you get these, and why are you giving them to us?"

"Call it a belated engagement gift," Henrik announced politely. "I didn't steal them, if that's your worry. Nor did I scavenge them. They belonged to my daughter and her husband."

Viggo and I exchanged alarmed glances and then focused back on Henrik, listening, aware that whatever he was about to say, it was going to be a story… and likely not a happy one. "When my little girl announced she wanted to get married to a Matrian male, I had my reservations. But if she was happy, I was happy. Her husband Edgar was a kind man. Simple, but he cared for her far better than any Patrian male would have.

"Mathilda wrote me diligently, at least once a week. We scheduled times to call. I had just retired from being a warden when she called me up one day, out of the blue. She was pregnant with my first grandchild."

He smiled then, his weathered face nostalgic, lost in his own story. I leaned my shoulder against Viggo.

"I put in an extended travel request to go see them, and, after calling in a few favors, it got approved. I showed up at her house with bags in hand." He paused, and shifted slightly in his chair, his face going pensive. "I got to extend my trip twice while I was there. So I could spend time with my grandson and my daughter. Eventually, I had to go. We kept in touch, and I got to see Connor growing up through the pictures my daughter sent me, and the letters she wrote. But as his eighth birthday got closer, our conversations always centered around the test—would he pass or fail? There was no option to bring him to Patrus. Matrian law would never allow an untested male across the river. We talked the issue to death, all of us clinging to the hope he would pass.

"Then the call came. He'd failed. He was taken right from her arms, in spite of my Mathilda trying to resist. She called me on my handheld, distraught, begging me to come help her, but it wasn't that easy. Permission takes time and patience. I put in my application, tried to get it rushed through… but before I had even made it through the process, the wardens called me. She and Edgar had committed suicide. Overdose."

Henrik fell silent, his eyes glistening with tears, and before I could stop myself, I reached out and took his hand. He blinked, tears dripping down his face, and met my gaze. I squeezed his hand, and he exhaled shakily.

"I didn't get to see them buried, but they left me their rings, at least. You guys know the rest of the story, really, but…" He broke off abruptly and stood up. "It doesn't matter. Just, please accept the rings. I would consider it a great honor if you decided to use them as your wedding bands, but don't feel obligated. You're both like family to me, and because of that… well… I've said what I needed to say."

Viggo broke the silence first, speaking softly. "I'm not speaking for Violet, but I would be deeply honored to use them."

"I would too," I said, finding my voice. I met Henrik's gaze with a smile, and he smiled in return.

"Good," he said, backing up toward the door. "Now if you'll excuse me, I'm going to try and get some of that sleep stuff all the kids are talking about."

I chuckled, a smile blooming on my face as I watched him turn and swing the door open. "Of course. Good night, Henrik."

"Good night, kids," he said, and pulled the door shut behind him.

Viggo and I sat there for a moment, still stunned by the unexpected gift and Henrik's tragic tale. After a few minutes, I reached over and picked up the smaller, more slender ring, pinching it between two fingers and examining it closely. It was beautiful—gold, with tiny stylized flowers etched into the side.

"Do you like it?" Viggo asked.

"I do," I said after a moment.

Viggo reached out and plucked the ring from my fingers. Examining it closely, he nodded in satisfaction. "I would have picked it out at a store for you," he replied, taking my hand in his and slipping the ring over my ring finger. It hung lightly on my finger, but it was slightly too big, and I felt like it was going to slip off.

"We have to get it resized," I said, pulling it off and dropping it back in the box.

"We will," he replied. "In the meantime, do you know what this means?"

I adjusted my bottom, pushing back from the end of the bed, and then flopped back into my pillow. "Not really."

Viggo stretched out beside me, propping his head up on his hand. "It means we are now officially ready to get married."

I snorted and turned onto my side, presenting him with my back. He immediately slid up next to me, his arm coming over and around my waist and his legs slipping through mine. "After all this is done," I reminded him, my eyelids already beginning to grow heavy and cumbersome.

"Of course," he breathed into my ear.

And then I was out—sleep pulling me down and under.

CHAPTER 18

Viggo

"Just remember that we have to convince…" Henrik trailed off, his head swiveling around to regard King Maxen, who was standing on the landing of the stairs to the basement, his eyes bleary from sleep. I couldn't blame him. My eyes burned, and I felt like my head had been swaddled in coffee—the five hours of sleep we had tried to grab had ultimately turned out closer to three, but in batches. The ordeals Violet and I had faced were beginning to weigh on us both. Her nightmares woke me, and mine woke her. I was beginning to wonder what a good night's sleep even meant anymore.

Maxen stood at the top of the stairs for a span of time, glowering down at us, and I sighed. I was not particularly eager for another interaction with the king of Patrus. He was a fundamentally selfish man, both entitled and arrogant. In retrospect, I kind of wished I had let Henrik, Amber, and Quinn shoot him instead of kidnapping him.

BELLA FORREST

Maxen broke the silence by clomping loudly down the stairs, each sound making me fight off a wince. He'd gotten a bit thinner, there was gray blending in at the sides of his temples as well as his eyebrows, and he had exchanged his finer clothes for simpler ones, although I suspected that hadn't been as much of a choice as a necessity. I could tell he was miserable—it was in every deep nook and cranny of his face not obscured by the beard that had fully grown in around his goatee. He was also angry—it was subtle and slow burning, but it was there, glimmering in his blue eyes, and it winked at us every now and then in every interaction.

He sat down at the head of the table and folded his hands atop it. "Good morning," he said stiffly, not meeting anyone's gaze.

Ms. Dale, bless her heart, didn't even bat an eye. "Good morning, King Maxen. Thank you for joining us."

"It's not exactly like I had a choice," the king snapped back, and I had to bite my tongue to keep myself from interjecting. It would only turn this situation from uncomfortable to worse. Maxen was clearly spoiling for a fight. Luckily, Ms. Dale wasn't going to allow it to escalate.

"That's entirely correct," she replied cheerfully. "So sit down, shut up, do what you're told, and maybe we'll get around to finally restoring your kingdom. And if you do it quickly, there might actually be some of it left to save!"

"Like it or not," added Henrik, leaning back into his chair and smiling broadly, "you need us and we need you. So why don't you stop fighting us at every turn, and start helping?"

The king raised an eyebrow at Henrik. "Aren't you dead yet?"

Ms. Dale literally growled, standing up so abruptly I was surprised her chair didn't go anywhere. Violet leaned over.

"So much for not getting into a fight," she whispered to me,

180

and I nodded, and then stood up.

"Enough," I bellowed. Whatever Ms. Dale had been gearing up to say stalled out. Maxen looked at me in surprise, but I ignored him. Turning to Ms. Dale, I gave her a stern look. "Ms. Dale, maybe we could all try to be sensitive to the king's... predicament. I'm sure this situation, for him, hasn't been without hardships."

From the corner of my eye, I saw King Maxen give me a considering look, and then a congenial smile. I let him bask in that for a moment, before turning and spearing him with a hard stare. "And you. I know you still cling to this ridiculous idea that we kidnapped you to... I don't even know what, but let's be honest: every person here is your ally. We share a common enemy—one that wanted you dead and would've killed you had we not intervened, I might add—and we have kept you safe, fed, and housed. You owe everyone here for that, so you might want to be a little more civil."

My voice ended in a growl, and the king stiffened, his eyes narrowing to slits. "Never presume to lecture me, Mr. Croft," he sneered.

I didn't reply. I just held his gaze for a long moment, trying to convince myself that punching him that one time hadn't been *that* satisfying. Eventually, the king's eyes flicked down and away, and I sat back down in my chair, satisfied that he had gotten the severity of the message. The tension was growing too high for any derision. We had to convince these rebels to join with us if we had any chance of stopping Elena from doing whatever it was she was doing at the water treatment plant. I just had to hope that showing them King Maxen's face would be enough—if they were expecting much else from him, they were going to be woefully disappointed.

The screen on the table against the wall beeped, and Henrik gave a nod. "Game faces, everyone. It's time to make these rebels think we got it all figured out."

I bit back a smile at the truth in his words, and then Ms. Dale connected the channel on our laptop. Instantly, Tiffany's face filled the screen, her wide eyes searching. "I got 'em," she said over her shoulder.

She moved out of view, the camera on her handheld shaking, tilting right and left as she adjusted it. Once it settled, I stared at the three people who were sitting a few feet away from the handheld, seated in what was clearly an apartment's living room space. I took stock of each of them, finally putting some faces to the names Tiffany had briefed us on.

At the right of the screen sat a brunette woman. She was wearing all black, her hair gathered in a messy bun on top of her head. She was young—young enough that there was still some baby fat clinging stubbornly to her cheeks, but she had a wise look in her bright blue eyes. This was Mags. Of all the three leaders, she was the one we were all the most interested in meeting. Tiffany had practically sung her praises in her reports.

Next to her, in the middle, was a man in his early twenties with a shock of black hair tied in a neat ponytail on the crown of his head. The effect should've made him appear more feminine, but there was a masculine edge to the rest of his features, one I was sure women fell head over heels for. His eyes were also blue, but partially obscured by the thin wire glasses perched on his nose. This was probably Logan Vox. When a couple of us had commented about the surname, it had come up that this one was in the public eye—Logan was the youngest son of the owner of the company that produced Deepvox pills, but had eschewed the family business to become a heloship pilot, though he'd had some pretty public scandals even so. Now, of course, he was a rebel. He had cobbled together a pretty formidable force, even if it was the smallest one of the three.

The last man was the oldest of the trio, probably in his late thirties, early forties. He was bald, but sported a thick auburn beard. His eyes were small and his figure rotund, but he was still quite strong, gauging from the set of his shoulders and the bulge of his muscles. He had probably been quite muscular some time ago, but my guess was that after a few years of not maintaining his weight, the muscle had started to give way to fat—slowly. He was the man we knew the least about. Andrew Kattatopolous, Drew for short.

I opened my mouth, prepared to speak first, when Mags spoke up. "So you are the ones responsible for getting that message into all the stadiums?"

Her voice was lilting, curious. She cocked her head at us inquisitively, and I nodded.

"We are. My name is Viggo Croft. This is Violet Bates, Melissa Dale, Henrik Muller, and, of course, you know King Maxen."

The three people on the couch exchanged looks as Maxen stood up. "Can you have him stand closer to the camera?" asked Logan.

I glanced at King Maxen, who rolled his eyes and then moved over to where the handheld was perched at an angle, leaning on the television. "How's that?" he asked, stooping over slightly.

"That's him," came the deep gravel of Drew's voice. "His beard's grown in, but that's him. They are who they claim to be."

"Yes, Drew," drawled Logan, and King Maxen moved back from the screen, revealing that the lanky man was leaning back, his hands clasped behind his head in a youthful sprawl. "We can see that. The question is, what do they want from us?"

Mags reached out and touched Logan on the arm. "We'll get to that in a minute," she said. "King Maxen, it is good to see you in one piece. Tell me, are you safe?"

King Maxen was in the process of lowering himself into his chair when she asked, and he paused, half in, before dropping into it. He looked around the room, cleared his throat, and then nodded. "I am, dear, thank you for asking."

"Excellent. And your health?"

"Never been better." Maxen's posture became more relaxed under the questions, his smile growing more genuine as attention was given to him.

"Really? No broken bones, missing limbs?"

The question caught me off guard—Maxen as well—and I glanced at the screen, seeing that Mags had closed the distance between the couch and the handheld.

"Of course not," he said, his smile flickering and fading. "Why ever would you ask?"

"Oh, just seeing what was so dire that our king had to abandon us."

Violet snorted, and then hurriedly hid her smile behind a cupped hand. I couldn't help but appreciate the irony as well, but to be fair, this wasn't entirely Maxen's fault. We had kidnapped him, after all.

"That was our fault," announced Ms. Dale, tugging at her braid. "We... removed the king to keep him safe from danger."

It was the king's turn to snort, but he remained quiet, thanks to a stony glance from Henrik. Mags's eyebrows rose up to her hairline, and then she nodded. "It makes sense. If Elena wanted him dead, they'd be tearing up the countryside for him."

"Not just him," added Violet quietly, and I reached over and clasped her hand, squeezing it gently.

"I'm sure," Mags demurred. "Still, it doesn't change the fact that many of his people view his sudden reappearance with a certain level of... derision."

"What?" the king sputtered, affronted. "Why?!"

"No offense, King Maxen, but there are many who feel you abandoned your people by running. What makes you think that you showing up with friends to help is going to make them inclined to want your help, let alone you?"

The king fidgeted as her statement came through. We watched as Mags moved back over to the couch and sat down, tossing her hair over her shoulder. "And while we're on the topic of your help—what do you want and what are you offering?"

Ms. Dale blinked and then smiled. "I knew I would like you," she announced.

"We need *your* help, actually," I said, standing up. "You have people on the inside, we have people on the outside. As individual pockets of resistance, we probably can't accomplish much. But, perhaps if we could work together, we could—"

"We are desperately low on ammo," announced Drew, leaning forward slightly. "And even weapons. We scavenged what we could, but—"

"There are lots of things we need," cut in Mags smoothly. "But even with guns and weapons, without knowing where the other groups are, we can never move across the city without calling attention to ourselves."

"We can help you with that," said Violet. "We have a friend who hacked into the camera system in the city years ago. If you can get to the correct location and turn his system back on, you can access it through your handhelds."

Mags arched an eyebrow. "Years ago?"

"It's a long story," cut in Henrik. "For another time. But if you can get the system turned on, then we can begin thinking of how to take back the city."

"Take back the city?" scoffed Logan. "We've got civilians who need to get out of the city!"

"What, exactly, do you want to do?" asked Mags, once again ignoring the interruption.

"Tiffany informs us that there's a group of Matrians holed up at a water treatment plant in the city. We've come to believe they have a plan to do something to the water that will help Elena achieve her goal, possibly contaminating it with a drug or a poison. If that's true, she just has to keep you in there long enough for it to spread." Henrik paused as Mags, Logan, and Drew exchanged looks. "What is it?"

"We had water in our buildings until a few hours ago," announced Logan.

"That's… one of the signs Thomas told us to watch out for." Ms. Dale's words were delivered softly, but they were as heavy as lead.

"Except for the fountains," added Drew. "The big fountains all over the city are working, and they still deliver most of our drinking water."

"Everyone will flock there," Violet cut in, horrified. "Those people will not only fight over the water, but if they drink it…"

"So the water is already toxic?" asked Mags, alarm making her rise in her seat.

"No," Henrik soothed. "Or very unlikely. Calm down,

everyone, please. We still have some time—but not long. A little over a day, if Thomas' models are correct."

Everyone fell silent at that, and Mags sat back down, but on the edge of her seat. "I need to confer with Drew and Logan. Can you give us a moment?"

We nodded, watching as they slipped from the room. Tiffany moved back into the screen. "I'm sorry, guys. I didn't even know the water had been shut off. I spent most of the day with Logan, getting across the city."

"That's all right, Tiffany. So, what do you think? Will they help us?"

She gave a little shrug. "I honestly don't know, but I hope so."

We lapsed into silence, waiting for the rebel leaders to return. They didn't keep us waiting long. Almost five minutes later, they were back, Drew and Logan arranging themselves on the couch. Mags moved closer to the camera, but remained off to one side, so we could still see the two men. "Send us the instructions for how to get the cameras on. If that checks out, we'll hear your plan to get into the city and free the water treatment plant. If it's good enough, we'll join you. But we have a stipulation."

"What is it?" asked Ms. Dale, wariness worming into her voice.

"You can't fulfill it—only the king can."

Maxen jerked in his seat, surprise dancing across his features. "What can I help you with?"

Mags's face split into a wide, impish grin. "You have to agree to let the people who remain decide if you should continue on as their king. And if they don't, you step down and let the people decide who will lead them."

Everyone turned and looked at the king, whose face was

wide-eyed with shock. Even I was a bit stunned by her demand. Not that I disliked it, but for them to go straight for the throat like that, have it out in the open, was definitely unexpected.

The king seemed to be aware of all eyes on him, and his face quickly changed.

"Of course," he replied smoothly. "I am but a humble servant to the will of my people."

"That remains to be seen," Mags said honestly. "I gave Tiffany my contact info. Send us the coordinates and the instructions for the camera stuff. I'll get a team on it. We'll call you back when it's done." Before we could reply, she had reached down and killed the connection.

We sat in silence, every one of us pondering the interaction.

Finally, Ms. Dale swiveled around in her chair, a crooked smile on her face. "I *like* her."

CHAPTER 19

Violet

"I really hate this idea," I repeated for the third time as I watched Jay open the trunk of the car, revealing Desmond.

A pillowcase covered her head—Dr. Tierney had administered a sedative before they transported her.

"Me too," replied Viggo, squeezing my hand. "But there was nowhere else we could put her, short of our safe house, and I don't want to leave her there with the children and the doctors, if we can avoid it. Besides, it's better to keep her close, but not too close, right? This is a good compromise."

I knew Viggo was right. But it was still unnerving. We were on the verge of a major mission, and Desmond would be kept in a shack Harry had discovered a little over a mile away from the farmhouse, near where we had parked the truck with Solomon, just to keep him safe and calm. Loud noises seemed to set him off, as evidenced by the impressive dents in the container in the back. People from several locations who weren't leaving for the raid were already going to be coming to the shed to help feed and care for Solomon; Desmond's guard would have plenty of backup. None of this was ideal, but we were too short on time and resources to find anything better. There was just so much on the line, and things were falling into place faster than we had imagined.

Mags' team had made it to Thomas' safe house in an apartment he had rented out long term before any of this had gone down. He'd hidden his server in there, for fear of the damp interfering with it, and could remotely link with it once it was turned on. Within four hours of our conversation with her, Mags had called to report that they'd followed the instructions we'd sent her. Thomas confirmed, and the conversation with the three rebel factions continued. It seemed that they were satisfied with our exchange after all—his cameras had bought their trust, or at least their cooperation.

Henrik explained his plan at each stage, from taking out the guard posts—specifically the ones that were particularly vulnerable *and* close to the water treatment plant—to the plan he had cobbled together for taking the water treatment plant, based on images from the nearby cameras pointed at the street. Questions were asked and answered, new ideas proposed and improved upon, and just like that... the time to start was now. And though it felt like we were moving at breakneck speed, it was good: if Thomas' projections were correct, and if Elena's forces *were* tampering with the water source, we had less than thirty-six hours to stop them.

Viggo helped Jay pull Desmond out of the trunk, but Jay took the brunt of her weight, holding her on his own. My mouth pressed in a thin line, but I ignored it. It had been Jay's choice to help with this, and I wasn't about to stand in his way when it came to him and how he wanted to handle his mother. I just knew that if she said anything out of line to him again, I would…

I sighed. Desmond's stalemate had us stuck. We still had no way of knowing for sure whether or not she was telling the truth regarding the boys, and wouldn't even be able to try to formulate a plan to check until after this current insanity was done. It was imperative that we deal with the water treatment plant first—if only by the sheer numbers of people who would be affected by anything sinister that went on there. For now, we were doing the best we could.

Jay hefted Desmond up and carried her across the overgrown yard, stepping onto the sagging collection of boards that made up the shack's front stoop. Lacey, a young refugee woman, was already holding the door open for him. The room was already lit—a fire burned in the small wood oven to the left of the room, generating enough heat to keep the chill outside from fully permeating the dilapidated one-room building.

Desmond didn't stir as Jay carried her, or when he settled her on the sagging bed in the corner of the room. Lacey held the door open for Viggo and me as well, then closed it behind us, the hinges creaking. She gave me a warm smile before moving over to a small table with a chair next to it, seating herself primly.

I turned to find Jay and Viggo working together to loop Desmond's chains through the bedframe. Viggo was doing the weaving, while Jay held her by her free wrist, making sure she didn't try anything while the chains were off. Still, Desmond remained motionless. It wasn't until Viggo moved in to pull off her pillowcase that she even started to move. Her hair clung wildly to her face as her eyes snapped open. She looked around groggily, focusing on me. She flexed her jaw as though testing her weapons, narrowing her gaze.

"Welcome to your new, albeit temporary home," announced Viggo. "Now, don't let the sparse surroundings fool you—this quaint place holds a lot of charm. There's curtains and boards on the windows for privacy, and even a bed, for the ultimate comfort."

Desmond gave the room a onceover and then leaned back into her pillow, the chains that once again draped around her wrists clinking together as the small amount of remaining slack slipped against the mattress. If it had just been her hands, I would have been worried about her using that slack as a weapon, but with the chain hobbled to her ankle shackles as well, there wouldn't be much she could accomplish within her limited range of motion.

She smiled slowly and arched an eyebrow. "I see I continue to live. How is dear Cody? I hope I didn't upset him too badly in our discussion yesterday?"

"Don't get too comfortable yet," Viggo said, ignoring the question. "We need to go over some rules. First of all, the chains remain on. Obviously, this place doesn't have an actual bathroom, per se, but upon request, you will be given a bucket. We will not be giving you any privacy, and your guards will be changed every four hours. This is Lacey. She'll be your first guard of the evening. The guards are in charge; if they say jump, you say nothing and do it."

"With this leg?" she asked, bemused.

"With that leg," he confirmed, not batting an eyelid.

Desmond's eyes studied him closely as he spoke. There was an expectant pause, and then she looked over at Jay. "You are really okay with them treating your mother like this?" she asked.

Jay looked up at her and fidgeted, and I immediately went to grab Jay and separate them, at least visually, from each other. Viggo stopped me, nodding to Jay, who had begun to speak, his face clearing.

"I don't think I *have* a mother," Jay announced softly. "I did once, a long time ago, but she stopped being my mother after all the horrible things she did to me and my brother."

"I did them for you," Desmond sniffed at him. "I did them to make you *strong*. Why can't you—"

"They killed me," Jay said flatly, meeting her gaze. "Over and over and over again. I've been drowned, suffocated, and electrocuted, all in the name of that science you volunteered me for. I lived in a ten-by-ten box for almost ten years while they pushed me to my limits. And you know what the worst part was? Even from day one, I didn't have any hope I would ever get out of there."

His eyes glittered and he shook his head at her, his lips trembling. "That's not love. That's not what you do to someone you care about. You don't know how to love, and I feel sorry for you. So yes, I am okay with them doing this to you. It's nicer than you deserve, and I am glad that I have found such good people who will still treat someone who has done only terrible things to them with such kindness."

Desmond stared stonily at her son. "That's the first time I've ever seen you be strong," she said after a moment. "Such a shame you have it directed at the wrong person."

"Eventually you'll realize that what you did to me was not love—it was selfishness. Stop acting like you were doing me any favors, and—"

"I *was* doing you a favor," she hissed. "I wanted you to be strong, so you could survive and grow up and be remarkable."

"Well, I was traumatized. Do you know that when people touch me, it actually hurts me? Not like Tim, just… emotionally… because it means so much to me to feel someone touching me? I cried when Viggo shook my hand when I first met him. Not in front of him, but later, alone… I didn't realize how long I'd just been waiting for somebody to hug me. Or to touch me at all. I'm sorry if that doesn't make me strong in your book, but I don't care. I don't exist for your approval."

Desmond stared at her remaining son, and I was surprised to see her eyes beginning to glisten, as if she were tearing up. She blinked it back and sucked in a deep breath, looking tired. "What do you want from me, Jay? I did the best I could. I didn't even want to be a mother in the first place, and then to have boys on top of it! And still I tried. I could've dropped your brother off at the orphanage and never even had you, but I stayed. You may think what I did to you was selfish, but you know nothing about the world I live in, and the people I deal with. You—"

"He knows enough to know how he feels about things," I said calmly, interrupting her. "And I, for one, am glad that his apple fell so far from your tree." Jay gave me an appreciative look, and I held out my hand to him. "Let's go, Jay."

Jay looked at the hand, and then gave a small shake of his head. "In a minute. I'm not finished." I lowered my arm, but nodded, knowing I needed to let him say his piece. Jay looked back over to his mother. "Mom, this is… probably going to be the last time we see each other. And while I despise everything you've done to me, Lee, and everyone… I'm glad that I got to find an amazing family with Viggo and Violet. Their love for me is unconditional. Limitless. And as screwed up as it is, I would've never found them if you hadn't put me on this path. So, thank you. And goodbye."

Even I blinked in surprise as the young man excused himself and left, Desmond's eyes burning a hole in his back on the way out. She stared after him even after the door closed, and then eventually rolled onto her side, presenting her back to the room.

Lacey stood up from the chair. "You should go," she said in her ever-sweet voice. "I'll be here on guard duty. Everything is taken care of."

"You radio for anything," I told her as Viggo passed over the spare keys to her cuff. "And if she talks too much, gag her."

"Don't worry," she said, beaming so wide that a dimple formed in her cheek. "Ms. Dale gave me a debriefing on her I won't soon forget. I'll be careful—I'll just shoot her in the leg if she starts something."

It seemed odd that her voice continued to be sweet, considering the harshness of her words, yet I smiled. "You do that."

Viggo and I left and climbed into the car. Jay was already waiting for us in the backseat, and as soon as I got in, we exchanged a big hug through the gap between the driver and passenger seats. "I'm so proud of you," I said as soon as I let go of him.

"Thanks," he said, blushing slightly. "I just… wanted to get it off my chest."

"Well, it was good," said Viggo. "You really got your point across."

Jay flushed even deeper as Viggo turned on the car, executing a U-turn on the uneven dirt road that was more dirt than road. We drove the short distance to the house in silence. Viggo parked up front—mostly because he would be leaving soon—and we all got out.

"I gotta pack," said Jay, and he scampered for the stairs.

I smiled at his exuberance, but it dimmed some when I realized he and my brother would be walking into multiple dangerous situations tonight. Anxiety suddenly struck me, and it took me a moment to pull myself together. We followed behind him at a sedate pace, heading upstairs to our room.

Viggo's backpack was already packed, still lying on the bed where he had left it. I entered the room first, and then went over to the bag, picking it up. Turning, I saw Viggo closing the door behind him. I handed him the bag and watched him sling it over his shoulder.

"You packed everything you needed?" I asked.

"Even three of those surprisingly nifty waterproof bags you found," he replied with a smile, a slightly teasing note in his voice.

"Everyone's going to be super glad I included them in all the bags, considering you're all going to a place where the stuff is practically everywhere."

"It's a good idea."

We lapsed into silence, and a feeling of déjà vu fell upon me. It took me a minute to realize why: we had literally just done this less than a week ago. Said goodbye and had our last, lingering kisses before the mission began. I was beginning to hate it.

"Are you thinking what I'm thinking?" Viggo asked, his green gaze studying my features.

"These damn goodbyes?" I quipped.

He chuckled ruefully and then smiled. "I've been thinking about it, and… maybe we shouldn't this time. If everything goes according to plan—" He stopped, and then shook his head.

"Nothing ever goes according to plan," I said, vocalizing what I was certain he was already thinking. "You're not going to make me promise not to go into the city, are you?"

Viggo sighed heavily. "Of course not," he said. "I know better, and to be honest, even with a broken arm and a still healing skull, you are formidable. Besides, who knows what's going to happen? You might wind up having to."

"I knew there was a reason I liked you," I said with a smile. "You're a smart man."

"I know," he replied with a wink. I smirked at him and then rose up on my tiptoes, pressing my lips against his in a kiss. It was short, barely a peck, but it still sent a pleasant hum coursing through my body. I settled back down on the soles of my feet and opened my eyes. "We should go."

In response, Viggo threw open the door and moved into the hall. I followed him as he moved to the master bedroom—Henrik and Ms. Dale's room—and raised his hand to knock. With the impact of his first knock, however, the door swung open, revealing Ms. Dale and Henrik, pressed together so closely that it was hard to tell where one ended and the other began.

Henrik's face was buried in Ms. Dale's neck, his hands around her waist, clasping her back firmly. Her eyes were closed, but she wore an expression of happiness and good humor, laughing huskily, her back arched as though she were pushing away from him, but her hands clinging firmly to his shoulders.

My jaw dropped at the sight of them, and I looked over at Viggo to see him wearing a similarly stunned expression.

Ms. Dale's eyes drifted open—then she froze when she saw us standing there.

I couldn't help myself. "Ms. Dale, is this really the appropriate time to be making out with your boyfriend?"

That was when Viggo and I burst out laughing. It was

impossible not to. Quickly, stiffly, Ms. Dale disentangled herself from Henrik's embrace, smoothing her hands over her shirt and hair in jerky motions. Adjusting the bag on her shoulder, she met our gazes one by one, as if we had not just walked into the make-out scene of the century.

She cleared her throat. "Shall we?" She pushed past us without waiting for a response, but that only made us laugh harder. The sight of Ms. Dale actually flustered, her movements hurried and tinged with the mania embarrassment had caused… It was just so not *her*.

The stairs behind us creaked as Ms. Dale began to descend. "Pull yourselves together," she said primly. It did nothing to help stop our laughter, which had simmered down to chuckles.

"Oh, just have a laugh about it, you old woman," Henrik called down the stairs after her, and I looked up to see him resting his shoulder against the doorframe, his arms folded across his chest. A spark of humor shimmered in his eyes.

Without even breaking her stride, Ms. Dale called back, "I do not entertain the whims of children."

Henrik chuckled at that, and then gave Viggo and me a nod and a wink before disappearing back into his room and closing the door. I guessed that he still had a few things he wanted to get done before we started, which was fine. We had approximately an hour before everything hit the fan.

Once we had pulled ourselves together and wiped the tears from our eyes, Viggo and I headed downstairs, where Tim, Jay, Ms. Dale, and Owen all stood near the front of the house, two vehicles waiting to take them to their different destinations. The rest of their teams were already on their way, being transported in every vehicle we could spare.

Our forces had been split into three groups, led by Viggo, Ms. Dale, and Amber. Drew's people formed a fourth team, while Mags' and Logan's were being brought in to bolster our remaining forces with enough people that we could splinter into several smaller groups if necessary, depending on what happened. Viggo and Ms. Dale's teams would take on the task of entering the water treatment plant. Amber's team and a group of Logan's people would stay behind to refortify the position, in case we attracted any hostile action, and then leave behind a small guard and move into the city, to a third position overlooking the water plant, to provide sniper fire.

Viggo and Ms. Dale would enter the city separately, not only to take down two guard posts, but in order to secure two exits for us in case something went wrong. We had debated this one for a while, but in the end, we'd decided we had to risk both teams at once: the more soldiers we could get moving in on the plant, the more likely we would be able to put a stop to whatever Elena's plan was. It didn't make it feel any less like a suicide mission, and as I stood there, looking at some of the most important humans in my life, I felt the uncertainty hit me, the anxiety of the real possibility that someone in front of me was going to die tonight.

I moved over to Jay and Tim, immediately kneeling down and opening the bags lying in front of them, following an impulse to try to just... prepare them as much as possible, in the best way I could in the short time that remained.

"Violet, you can trust us," Jay said.

"Everything on list. Here." Tim pulled a piece of paper out of his pocket, smiling at the fact that he had presented me with the list I'd written for him.

"I'm checking down here," I said, rummaging through the

items in both young men's bags and mentally checking off the list again. It took me a few minutes to sift through all the items—but everything was there. "You got everything," I needlessly informed my brother and Jay, while they threw each other annoyed looks. "Good job."

Then I pulled them both in for a hug, taking special care with Tim. "Please try your best to be safe," I whispered. "And smart. Nothing beats being smart."

"We promise," said Jay, his voice tight.

"Promise," echoed Tim.

I held them for just a few seconds longer, savoring the hug, and then released them. "Good luck," I said, watching them as they scooped up their bags and headed over to the cars, each one of them moving to a different vehicle to deposit his bags.

I felt a strange mix of pride and apprehension flowing through me at that moment. I was so proud of how much they had accomplished for themselves, in spite of their traumatic experiences. They kept on fighting, unwilling to yield or compromise. On the other hand, they were heading off to a battle with no defined rules. I was worried about them.

Viggo caught me in a hug as he went by, catching me by surprise. He lifted me up, spun me around once, and then dropped a kiss to my forehead. "I'll see you soon," he said, his voice rumbling from his chest.

"I know," I replied.

Then he was gone—moving toward his car and climbing into it, Tim by his side in the passenger seat. He put the vehicle in gear, graced me with one more look and a wave, and then drove off, heading down the narrow lane to the main road that would lead him directly into the city.

I watched them go, trying to convince myself they would be all right. I was so absorbed in thought that I didn't notice Owen suddenly beside me, his eyes also following the red taillights that were all pulling away from us down the road. There was a hunger in his blue gaze, and I knew how he felt.

Still, we hadn't really talked since the incident with Desmond. Apparently, forgiveness had been the easy part—I knew I cared about Owen too much to stay angry at him forever. I knew I would still fight beside him. But being comfortable next to each other again? Comfortable enough to laugh and joke as though everything were okay? The weight of what had happened was still too great. It held my words inside me, taking the levity out of me every time I saw him.

"Let's go," I said softly, and then I turned, heading toward the door, the basement my final destination. There was a lot to do, and not a lot of time to get it done.

CHAPTER 20

Viggo

The view down the scope of my rifle wasn't promising, but it wasn't unexpected, either. The hip-high barricades formed three lines—the first one sat about eighty feet away from where the buildings started. It was wide and deep, where the second one was narrow and only formed a semi-circle across the road. The last one was flat, a line across the road where the city ended just as abruptly as the farmlands began. The parts of the city that they had blocked off were heavily populated and had little open space between buildings—which had made it easier for the Matrians to cut off most escape routes. Beyond the barricades, it was hard to see anything. Some places in the city seemed to be lit with streetlights, while many of the areas were dark, the buildings just silhouettes against the night sky. Even from this distance, I could see the flickering light of fires here and there. It didn't look pretty.

There were twelve wardens milling around inside the barricades. I didn't need the scope to see them. The massive lights that had been attached to the roofs of both adjacent buildings shone extra bright, lighting up the road on either side. I tracked one olive-clad woman as she headed toward the building Violet had identified as their base.

"We're in position," Ms. Dale reported over the main radio channel, her voice muted and soft, almost as though she were whispering. I didn't blame her—I also felt like whispering, even though we were hundreds of feet away. Truth was, her target was the more difficult one to take, so I could understand. To compensate, she had more soldiers than I did, but I still didn't envy the task.

Taking the guard post was the part of our mission plan I liked the least, but then again, it was the one I knew the most about in terms of defenses. It was too late to rethink anything now, anyway. I looked around at my team, all lying next to me in the thick, decomposing cornstalks of the field we were hidden in. A massive harvester loomed behind us, providing additional cover, as the rest of the area was barren, devoid of life and trees. I knew there had been some at some point, but it was clear the guards had been busy cutting down any tree impeding their view. While their focus might have been on keeping people in, they weren't naïve enough to think nobody could get them from behind.

Margot found my gaze and offered a tight, nervous smile before turning and sighting down the sniper rifle she had been given. Cad was lying beside her, his own rifle pointed toward the barricades, but his eyes were on Margot. I could tell he was worried. We all were, really. Cruz, Gregory, Harry… there were fifteen of us out there—a mix of refugees and Liberators—most of them men and women I had had a hand in training. The air around them ran from excitement to nervousness, but the commitment was there. For now, anyway. Regretting that there hadn't been time to say just a few more words to them, I exhaled and turned back to the barricade, trying to clear my mind of all the apprehension.

"Roger," I replied softly to Ms. Dale, pressing my gloved thumb and my forefinger together to transmit. "We're ready." I switched over to the team channel and pressed my fingers together again. "Get ready, guys."

Because there were so many moving parts to our mission, we had to work on multiple channels. Violet, Henrik, Ms. Dale, Amber, Thomas, and I were all authorized to be on the main one, trading information and modifying plans as needed. However, Ms. Dale, Amber, and I would probably spend most of our time on the channel with our team members, while Violet, Henrik, and Thomas would switch between them, delivering updated orders and, more importantly, information through our two remaining drones.

"In position. Viggo, be aware that there are ten more guards in that building." I pressed my eye back to the scope, angling the gun up slightly, as Violet spoke into my headset. Violet's drone was hard to make out in the darkness above the street, but I caught a glimpse of it as she began lowering it into position.

A round cage jutted out from the bottom—one of the innovations Violet and Thomas had spent several days conceptualizing and putting together. The design was deceptively simple, just grenades that had long strings threaded through the pins, so that when the doors beneath them opened and they dropped, the pin would pull and the grenades would explode. Hopefully, it would work.

"Releasing in five, four, three, two, one." As she counted down,

I held up my hand and followed along in my head. Through the scope, I could see the guard I had been tracking stop short of the building entrance and look down. There was a pause, and then her head snapped back up, her mouth moving. I couldn't tell what she said, but the look of panic on her face made it easy to read. She started to run. Three seconds later, the six grenades Violet had dropped from the cage went off, and I lost my mark in the flaming blast of the explosion.

"I missed the vehicle!" Violet exclaimed in disgust, and I acknowledged automatically, then turned to Margot and the rest of my troops. "Two are down, but that's it." I could hear Violet's disappointment, and I understood it. She had wanted her drone contraption to be more effective, if only to help me out.

"Margot," I said, pushing the sentimental thought out of my head. She was already peering down the scope, and I heard the soft puff of air as she squeezed the trigger, the silencer muting the round. Instantly, this side of the barricade went dark as she struck her target—the massive light perched on the roof on the right side of the road.

"Forward," I ordered loudly, already feeling like we had lost precious seconds. I pushed up off the ground, cradling my rifle to my chest, and loped forward, keeping my body low. I could hear the rustle of clothes and grass as everyone moved with me, forming a long line.

The next sound of a gunshot came from my line, the crack of it loud enough to drown out the early sounds of alarm from the enemies still standing.

Seconds later, bullets began to whiz past, accompanied by the flash of fire from muzzles wielded by the women rushing toward us—at first in slow, random pings, and then picking up in speed, until the area was filled with a cacophony of *pop pop pops*, going off irregularly. I raced forward, keeping my feet high to avoid tripping on the uneven ground, and hip-fired at a woman starting to stand up from behind one of the concrete blocks that made the first barricade, catching her in the side. She dropped, her cry merely adding to the din of noise, and the firing increased.

"The blast didn't damage the entrance," Violet reported through the earpiece. "More people are coming out."

"We need that first ring!" I transmitted to my team, switching before she'd finished speaking. "Don't straggle! That makes you targets!"

I didn't pause in my run, but I did look to the left as I spoke, where I could see several wardens emerging from the damaged face of the building. I pushed forward, firing wildly at them as they came out, and they scattered. I was pretty sure I'd hit one, but it was hard to tell—my head was swiveling around looking for more enemies.

Margot raced beside me, her long legs churning as she held her heavy sniper rifle high to her chest, her breath coming in harsh gasps. I turned, and shouted, "Keep moving!" as I angled for one of the barricades on the left side. A woman on the other side popped up from behind the barricade, swinging her gun around at Margot, and without thinking I shot her three times in the chest, a rush of adrenaline driving my hands.

The sound of battle was growing, with shouts and gunshots echoing all around us, both our own and the enemy's. I made it to the barricade, diving down below it as shots whizzed all around me. Margot was seconds behind, and she dropped down next to me, pressing her back to the three-foot-tall barricade. I looked around, checking to see where everyone was, and noticed that

Margot and I were among the first to hit the first ring—the rest were still straggling behind, taking pot shots at targets.

"Run, people!" I shouted into the microphone for the second time. "Teams, report!"

"There are so many of them!" Margot shouted beside me, panting as she pulled out her handgun and clicked the safety off.

"Just keep firing!" I replied, and then peeked up from the barricade to find my next target.

"Tim, Tasha, myself, and about four more are on the right side," reported Gregory through the channel. Even though the earbud sat directly in my ear canal, the sounds of battle and shouting were already starting to mix together, and threatened to drown him out.

I fired twice, and then the gun clicked empty. Dropping down, I slid an extra magazine from the side pocket of my black cargo pants. I took another glance as I ejected the clip and slammed the fresh magazine in.

"Cruz here. Harry, April, Marna, and... two other people are here with us in the center." I grated my teeth together and fired a few more shots, narrowly missing a woman as she raced toward the second barricade. She grabbed cover just behind it, and I kept my gun trained on the area she had disappeared behind, searching for signs of movement.

"Only Margot and I are on the left side! We need more people over here!" I transmitted as I scanned.

"Cad here. We zigged when we should have zagged, and now we're closer to Gregory. Should we try to send people to you?"

I squeezed off a few rounds as another target crossed my line of sight. I wasn't sure if I was the one to hit her, but she fell all the same. "No—Cruz, send me some of those extras you have."

"On it," said Cruz.

Adrenaline surged dangerously in my veins, and my eyes skated back and forth around the chaotic battlefield. Too quickly—I almost missed movement farther back along the road into the city. I did a double take, jerking back in time to confirm that the .50 caliber machine gun mounted to a truck was moving.

"Viggo—"

"FIFTY CAL!" I shouted over the din of the gunfire, cutting Violet off. Margot met my eyes, her own large with fear. I grabbed her, practically jerking her across my lap and then curling my torso over her body as the .50 caliber began to fire. The sound was akin to a cannon in my ears, a nonstop, relentless staccato, and red streaked across the sky, a sign of the tracer bullets they were using to help them better identify targets. I looked up in time to see one of the men hurrying toward me—Jeremy—go down, his body convulsing as the massive bullets tore through his body. I turned away from the bloody sight, cringing. At this time in our attack, we had no way of recovering the bodies.

"WE HAVE TO MOVE," I shouted to Margot, practically pushing her forward along the edge of the barricade. Violet's cousin scrambled on her hands and feet. I followed, angling right and around. Concrete exploded behind me as the machine gun continued its relentless attack. I pressed my thumb and forefinger together, activating my microphone.

"We're pinned down," I shouted over the roar of the guns. "Somebody take that gun out! Go around and to the sides!"

"I have a better idea!" replied Cruz.

I ducked down as shards of concrete rained down over my head, trying not to imagine the inevitable bullet finding its way through the barricade. "What is it?"

Cruz didn't respond. It was Violet who replied, after a long moment, "Cruz ran into the field."

"What?" I cast a look over my shoulder, and in the low light, I could see a figure loping across the field, heading back the way we came. "Damn coward."

"Try genius," replied Cruz in the headset, surprising me. I scrambled forward a few more feet to the metal barrier Margot was crouched under, noting the lack of bullet holes. A quick check revealed a vehicle parked a few feet in on the other side, but beyond it, I could see the truck with the mounted gun, and the woman standing in the back, manning the machine gun.

"What are you doing!?" I radioed him as I caught Margot's eyes and pointed to the other side of the vehicle. She shakily got to her knees and peeked over, then ducked back down, her eyes wide.

"Helping!"

I grated my teeth together and released my fingers. It wasn't worth arguing with him, but if we survived this, I was going to give him an earful about leaving us behind and going all cowboy. Leaning closer to Margot, I looked her in the eye. "Can you get her?" I asked.

A vein was ticking hard in Margot's neck, her lips parted as she panted. She was afraid, but even so, she nodded. "I can do it. Just watch my back."

I nodded, then, pulling my rifle up to my chest and sucking in a deep breath, gave her a look—one that said 'GO.' Margot swung up, using the barricade as a brace to steady her gun. I rose right behind her, firing on the surrounding guards while she lined up her shot.

A woman was racing from one barricade to another, but

from my angle, I could see her. I aimed low, for her legs, and she pitched forward with a scream indistinguishable over the sounds of battle. Margot's chin was pressed against the muzzle of her gun, and, just beyond her, toward the city, my eye caught a woman pressed against the corner of the building inside the second barricade. She was just drawing a bead on Margot when my bullet caught her in the left shoulder.

The gun jerked in Margot's hands, and then she ducked back down, her eyes squeezed shut, an expression of revulsion curling her mouth downward. The .50 caliber fell quiet. "C'mon," I said to her, the silence spurring me into motion, and I leapt over the barricade, surging forward toward the second ring. It would only be seconds before someone replaced the woman who had been manning that machine gun—so we had to get to that vehicle. I pressed my back against the car, using the tires to hide my feet, and then swung around its tailgate as the sound of automatic gunfire again blasted into the night.

Margot slipped up beside me, still panting, her eyes wild, and I realized that had been her first kill. If we made it out of this alive, I would make sure to get a moment alone with her to ensure she was all right, but for now… We were at war.

I shot at a woman as she began to climb into the back of the truck, and she went down. On the other side, I saw another woman fall. The six remaining guards fired back, and I spun around as two began firing at me, the bullets pinging as they hit the vehicle.

"Get down on the ground and shoot at their legs," I said to Margot, and she shook her head, her face tight.

"I can't," she cried, rubbing her eyes with her hand and jerking down farther as more bullets impacted the car. I heard the thick edge of desperation in her voice. I was worried, but I couldn't stop to help her now.

"Somebody get around them—Violet! Where is Mags' team?"

"Her team was held up by gunfire from buildings," Violet reported. "She's almost there, maybe two minutes aw—"

"Hey, Viggo—you might want to get down, eh, friend?"

Cruz's voice cut over Violet's in the radio, and I turned in time to see the giant harvester slamming into the concrete barricades right behind us. The barricades peeled open as Cruz drove, going under or tipping over as he pushed the three-ton vehicle through. The engine whined as he surged forward, and I pulled Margot down just as the extended metal bars that jutted out of the side smashed into the car we were hiding behind. Glass shattered as the vehicle jerked forward, the tires refusing to spin. I covered my head as the glass rained down on me, watching as our precious cover was slowly jerked away from us.

"C'mon!" I shouted, grabbing Margot's arm. I forced her up, moving to keep us behind the vehicle. As soon as she was on her own two legs, trying to keep up with the car as it was forced forward, I swung my rifle up and fired on any sign of movement. I heard Cruz curse over the line, and turned to see him leaping out of the cab of the truck, noting the bullet holes in the glass.

The harvester, however, continued to roll forward over another barricade, and the car that was being dragged along in front of us smashed against the barrier, the metal on the roof rending and tearing under the heavy arm of the harvester before finally ripping free.

Margot had pulled out her pistol again, the heavy sniper rifle bouncing on her back as she pressed against the second barricade, just past where the mangled remains of the car had settled. The harvester was rolling slowly to a stop, and I pressed the advantage. "PLUG THE HOLES," I ordered my team over the radio as I vaulted over the next row of barricades. "They're boxed in."

The harvester came to a full stop as the arms impacted on the walls of the buildings on the side of the barricade, but the cab punched a hole through the remaining barricades—they went flying a few feet back. The firing was dying down now, but there was still a big gun and a few of the enemy just beyond, and they were quickly getting ready.

A flash of movement across from me drew my eye to Tim, and I watched as Violet's brother used the barricade as a step, leaping up and spinning gracefully around, shooting a woman who was kneeling down on the other side. Margot was moving behind me again, and I altered my run so that she was partially hidden behind me, fearing a stray bullet.

"Cad here. We're approaching the harvester from the right side. Did any backup get to you?"

"No," I said as I approached the huge bulk of the harvester and slowed, the sound of gunfire disappearing completely. Pressing my back against the wheels of the hulking red behemoth of a vehicle, I slowed to a crawl, caution overriding my need to move into the city street beyond and put a stop to all this insanity. "If you are heavy on that side, I'll take what I can get."

"Sending people over now," he said.

I waited, and two refugees and a Liberator crept around the rear of the harvester. Margot flinched when they appeared, and I pressed a hand on her arm. "Wait here," I told her, and she nodded, clutching her gun in a tight-knuckled grip. I waved the others forward and began to move.

The corner loomed ever closer, the gap between the front

and sides of the harvester and the wall of the building seeming to grow as I moved forward. I caught a glimpse of the tail of the vehicle and came to a stop, collecting myself. Taking a deep breath, I closed my eyes, taking a moment to picture Violet's face.

My nerves settled down a bit, the tension easing as I tricked my body into a slightly calmer state. I needed to focus. At last count, there had been six wardens left. Five on the ground around the vehicle, and one on the machine gun.

Then I opened my eyes and stepped forward, dropping down into a low crouch as I neared the gap, the enemy vehicle waiting somewhere in the street beyond. I peered down my sights and eased inches forward as the corner, and then the tire of the enemy vehicle, drew into view. Twenty feet back, judging from the narrow view provided. I eased forward a few more inches, knowing that once I could see them, they could see me—and not even my bulletproof vest was going to stop these bullets.

Just as a leg in Matrian uniform was coming into view, rapid gunfire caused me to jerk back, and it took me a minute to realize the gunfire wasn't at us. It was at *them*.

"Who is that?" whispered Margot, and I turned to see her pressed behind Cruz and Harry, their faces pensive.

"Viggo, hold your fire—those are Mags' people."

I let out a breath at Violet's news. Then I stepped out and approached the gap more confidently. Three women were already dead, their bodies on the ground next to the truck. I stepped out as a woman broke off, running for the gap, and she faltered. A bullet from behind caught her in the shoulder, and she fell, screaming. I kept my rifle up as I moved forward, dropping another woman as she popped up to fire on the street behind the truck.

The last one's hands shot up, just above the bed of the vehicle. "I surrender!" she cried, and I lowered the gun.

"I got her," said Harry, slipping around me and heading over toward the truck. My people began to creep in around the vehicle, and I noticed Tim and Gregory heading over to me.

"Don't fire!" I shouted down the road, and I watched as men and women began to creep in cautiously from the neighboring buildings and the alleys between them. A short, curvy brunette pushed forward through the crowd, and I recognized Mags from our handheld conversations as she made a beeline toward me.

Turning, I nodded to Gregory. "See what you can do to straighten this up for the guard team," I ordered quietly, and he gave me a thumbs-up.

I turned back in time to see Mags only a few feet away. I opened my mouth to say something, but then froze when I saw a familiar, slightly bowlegged figure behind her, a cap perched on top of his disheveled gray hair, his mustache turned up in a smile.

"Heya, boyo," Alejandro greeted me, his blue eyes sparkling. "Long time no see!"

CHAPTER 21

Viggo

I pulled Alejandro into a tight embrace, surprised to find tears welling in my eyes. I'd had no idea he was coming, no idea he was there at all… no idea he hadn't died fighting fires in the weeks of Matrian-dominated chaos.

He hugged me right back, his hand thumping on my shoulder blades. "Oh, my boy, my boy!" he kept repeating. I laughed, and we broke apart, but my hand was still on his shoulder and his on mine.

"What happened to you? Is Jenny with you? Is she okay?" I asked, the questions pouring out of me. I looked around and realized we had a bit of an audience, but I didn't care. I was elated to see Alejandro again. I had worried endlessly about him since our parting, and now, seeing him here, I just had to know what had happened to him.

"Jenny's fine. She's back with the others, holding down Mags' fort." He nodded at Mags, who was standing patiently to one side, a hand on the strap of her rifle. Her blue eyes sparkled in amusement as she watched both of us, and I did a double take, staring from Alejandro's eyes back to hers. They were definitively similar, and Alejandro's grin widened. "Oh, come on, boy—don't tell me you haven't put it together."

"She's…" I trailed off as it clicked. "She can't be."

"The very same," Mags replied, smiling broadly, and I let go of Alejandro and immediately pulled her into a hug as well, laughing heartily.

My command line beeped, and I switched to hear, "Viggo, what the hell is going on, and why are you hugging that woman?"

I laughed harder at the sound of Violet's voice coming through my earpiece and pressed my fingers together. "Because she's family," I announced, pulling away from Mags and looking up. "She's Alejandro's niece! I haven't seen her since she was, what? Seven years old?"

"What? Really! Alejandro's there?"

"Sorry, guys, gotta cut the family reunion short—Thomas! Where the hell is Vox's team? We're pinned down out here." Ms. Dale's sharp retort cut through the rest of the chatter on the command line.

"He's almost there, according to the thermals. Just hold on." The line went silent, but I was immediately sober. The transmission we'd just heard meant that Ms. Dale still hadn't captured her position yet, meaning she and her team, people we all cared about deeply, were still in great danger.

I turned to the two rebels in front of me and dug around in my backpack, producing twelve sets of handhelds and earbuds. "These are for you and a few of your men. The rest need to get to Drew's team. We have two channels, but you'll only need to worry about the team ones for now, although we might need you on the main channel from time to time. We also have backup channels in case these are compromised—your team leader will brief you on that when you get connected. We don't have enough to go around, so we separated our men into teams with leaders who receive orders."

"Smart," she said as she and Alejandro donned them. "Carmen! I want you, Pete, and Stacy to get these over to Drew. He's waiting in what remains of the quartermaster's office. You know where that is?"

The short, dark-skinned woman with a downturned mouth listened carefully as Mags continued her explanation. I paid attention with half an ear as I began directing people over the radio about what needed to get done. I could see Gregory had already gotten a jump on it, so I avoided giving orders regarding anything he was working on—namely, removing the bodies. But the harvester needed to be moved and barricades righted, if only so the gate team could have defensible cover, in case trouble came knocking.

Once Mags was finished, the woman repeated the instructions correctly, and then turned to get ready to go. Mags watched her go for a minute, and then gave me a thoughtful look.

"So, I was actually eight and a half," she announced softly. "Before my father and Alejandro had that fight." I frowned, remembering how broken up Alejandro had been about that argument. Not because of what had happened between him and his brother, but because by ostracizing that part of the family, he had lost his chance to see Mags. And since he and Jenny had never had kids, it had been a blow to him.

"But that is in the past," Mags added with a smile.

"Congratulations on your engagement. Did you actually propose on a sinking boat?"

I gave Alejandro a look. "You told her that?"

Alejandro's smile was unapologetic. "My boy, I told *everyone* that story. The romance, the excitement… the drama. It was one of my better tales about you two." He winked.

I shook my head at him, unsurprised by his response, and looked at Mags. "Let me warn you, his stories are mostly second-hand, and grossly exaggerated."

The radio in my ear beeped, and I switched over to the next channel. "Objective B captured," Ms. Dale announced, her breath coming out in a sharp pant. "That was a doozy, but the good news is, the barricades here are mostly intact, so you can send in the guard team."

"Excellent," came Henrik's voice. "Viggo, status update."

I did a quick scan to check everyone's progress and pressed my fingers together, prepared to transmit, but the comm beeped as Cruz came on the line, interrupting me. I clenched my jaw, reminding myself to pull him aside to have a little conversation about teamwork and the radio—and why he was failing at both.

"We had one casualty, and have taken one prisoner. But even now, we are working together to clear the road and repair the defenses."

"Unless Viggo is injured or dead, get off the main channel, Cruz," grated Henrik. "You're mucking up the system otherwise."

Cruz made a quick Cruz-like apology, but the man's excuse that I seemed busy debriefing Mags and Alejandro, while technically true, didn't mean I wasn't capable of multi-tasking. Or just doing my job.

"Cruz is right," I said once he was done, unapologetic that

we'd kicked him off regardless. My people were still busy, but it was a vast improvement over minutes earlier. Several of the bodies had been moved to the side, while the harvester had been moved back slightly, blocking less of the street. The engine had never stopped running, even after its impact with the wall, and someone must have managed to back it up a few feet. I doubted they could get it back any farther than that, recalling the mangled wreckage of the barricades it had left in its wake, but it did provide additional cover, should any patrols swing by. I noticed the hole it had broken in the barricades was wide enough to get the truck through, and felt confident that our guard team could at least hold this position should trouble come knocking. "We're progressing a little bit ahead of schedule."

My eyes paused over Margot, her stillness drawing my attention amid the rush of people. Her eyes and face were vacant, staring at a fixed point on the road in front of her. She still held her gun in her right hand.

I quickly switched channels. "Violet, tell Amber's team to move up with the guard team." I quickly excused myself from Mags and Alejandro.

"They're on their way now," Violet replied as I weaved through the bustle of refugees and rebels toward Margot. As soon as I was close enough, I gently reached out and took her by her arm, leading her off to the side. She gave me a confused look, and then seemed to realize she was standing in the middle of everything, her gait increasing until we were out of the way.

"Are you okay?" I asked, looking deep into her eyes.

Her lips twitched, and she hesitated. "Not really. You?"

I thought about it. The adrenaline surge that I had gotten during the battle had departed, and now I felt shaky and raw. A lot of things had happened during that fight—things my mind hadn't had time to process in the moment, things that were suddenly pressing in, trying to flood my mind with a horror I hadn't registered earlier. I pushed it back slowly, and then shook my head. "Me neither," I admitted, and she smiled.

It wasn't a big smile, but it counted. It counted because, just for a moment, it had chased some of the haunted look from her expression, leaving her looking just a little bit more innocent than she currently felt. Still, it faded, and I was left with an uncertain feeling as to what I should do about Margot's emotional state.

I frowned, the image of Margot's two children flashing in my head. I couldn't even contemplate how she was feeling right then and there. What could I ever tell my children about what I had seen? What I had done? The enormity of it all hit me as I stared at the lost look that had returned to Margot's face.

"Do you want to stop here?" I asked her, needing to give her an out. "It would be okay. No one would judge you."

She thought about it. Her mouth opened, and I could anticipate the 'yes' that was already forming. But then she hesitated and looked away. I followed her gaze, and saw Cad helping to right one of the less damaged barriers that had been in the path of the harvester.

"No," she said softly, dragging my attention back to her. "No, thank you. I have family in the city, and... I just can't let him do this alone." Her tone was pleading, raw and naked, and I saw that she expected me to be disappointed in her for some reason. I couldn't fathom that, couldn't even relate.

"Margot, don't be silly," I chided her, and she gave a surprised laugh. "I totally get it. If it were Violet, I absolutely would not let her go in alone."

And she would've come to support me, too, if she weren't injured, I thought to myself, smiling. Margot stepped in and threw her arms around my waist, giving me a quick hug. "Thank you, Viggo."

"Ooooooohhhh, I am telling Violet and Cad about this. They are going to be heartbroken." I rolled my eyes at Amber's childish taunt, and turned to see her standing behind us, her arms crossed, one auburn eyebrow arched in challenge.

"Hey, Amber—any trouble getting the vehicles through to the city?"

"Are you kidding? Cruz wrecked the place. But Cad and a few others are almost finished making a path. We'll get them in."

"Our checkpoint is secure. Vox and I are ready to proceed to the next objective," radioed Ms. Dale.

"Roger," replied Henrik. "Keep an eye on those street cameras, and be careful. We may not have a lot of time, but there's still a little wiggle room, so play it safe."

I looked at Amber, and she nodded. "We got this. We'll finish getting everything set up."

Hesitating, I looked around and took in all the work that had been done, trying to gauge how vulnerable I would be leaving her. "Five more minutes," I said. "Then we'll go."

"Right—I'll go help everyone speed that up so we can get this over and done with." Amber turned to go, and Margot stepped forward.

"I'll help," she announced, squaring her shoulders.

I watched them go, and then went to find Mags and Alejandro. Within a few minutes, I had pulled them off their jobs, and we'd gathered around the handheld and a map of the city, checking the nearby streets via Thomas' cameras and charting the optimal route to the plant.

"It's a little bit close to the Porteque territory," concluded Mags, "but it really is our best and fastest option. You sure you don't have any cars to spare?"

"If only," I lamented. She chuckled and began folding the map. I watched her for a minute, and then leaned a hip on the car. "Why didn't you tell me who you were during that meeting?" I asked.

She looked up at me and smiled. "Two reasons. One, it would've taken away from the issue at hand, and two… I didn't want you to try to pull the family card if your plan sucked and I called you on it."

I snorted out a laugh, and then turned to start collecting our people. We had a really long way to go.

CHAPTER 22

Viggo

"Logan, hold up. I'm detecting thermal signatures on the street ahead of you."

"Roger that. Could it be fires?"

I listened idly to Logan and Thomas' transmissions over the main channels, my attention completely on the intersection in front of me. My group was holding our position, our small force pressed into every nook and cranny of the front face of a brick building we were using to conceal ourselves as we moved deeper into the city. The shadows on this lane were deep, dark, and ominous, and a periodic red glow flickered through, marking the next small fire like a beacon.

"Viggo, I need you to wait one more minute—I got some screwy thermals on the screen here."

This time, it was *my* drone scout on the line. I acknowledged Violet's transmission, trying to ignore the tension twisting my guts in knots. I felt exposed and vulnerable out on the street like this. Especially if all the streets looked like this one did.

It stood deserted, but trash and cars were littered across what once had been a picturesque little lane. The cars were everywhere, all of them wrecked—some of them burned-out frames, others wrapped around trees, and still others strewn about, making it look like a small war had taken place here.

Then again, maybe it had. I reached up and touched a jagged bullet hole in the staggered brick pattern of the building next to me, then slowly pulled away, unsettled, as I realized the hole was wide enough for me to put my entire middle finger into, with a little bit of space still left on the sides.

"Thomas, something is really messed up here," said Violet in my ear. "I don't think the drones are powerful enough to read deeper into the building."

"I'm experiencing similar problems—they may not be," came his reply, as I sighed and kept my eyes flicking over the scene, searching for any sign of movement around us.

The sound of running feet behind us, punctuated by rapid gunfire, caused me to snap around, the hair on my neck rising in alarm. It took me a minute to realize the footsteps were running away from us, as was the intermittent gunfire, and I shook myself. Even then, it was hard to relax. I threw a significant look at Mags, who was situated right behind me, and she returned it as though she shared my sentiment.

"I knew things would get bad. I just didn't think they'd go this bad this fast." Guilt churned through me as I looked around the street, my eyes taking in the carnage. "What happened here?"

Mags pushed some of her heavy brown hair off her face, sighing. "All the info we have to go on is rumors, but it looks like the Matrians tore through here as they were retreating. Some people tried to stop them, but…" She trailed off, her bright blue eyes drifting down. She shifted slightly, and then looked up. "It's easy to believe, because there were so many other places like this. People slaughtered."

"Who's cleaning up the bodies?"

Mags nodded up to the apartment buildings surrounding us, and then shrugged. "It's safer in the day, and there are a lot of little areas like this, where the neighbors work together instead of fighting each other. It won't last for long, though. The gangs are getting bigger, and food, weapons, and ammo are in short supply. Most people have improvised melee weapons, but the bigger gangs, they're armed to the teeth. If they need something, they'll take it, and they won't care who they have to kill to get it."

"This is our fault."

She blinked in surprise and turned to face me, shifting a little closer. "You mean because of the video at the stadiums?"

I nodded and sucked a big breath into my lungs, trying to press down the guilty feeling in my stomach. While it had been a group decision, it was hard not to feel deep personal responsibility. That video had been the catalyst for the chaos the city had fallen into, and now there were people—most of the population of Patrus—trapped inside with no laws, and no protection from the Matrians or from each other. We had known what the ramifications would be, had known there would be fallout… but this destruction, and violence on this level… It was jarring, and hard to push away the guilt. "Yeah."

Mags gaped at me and then a chuckle escaped her, her head shaking ruefully. "No offense, Viggo, but are you always this arrogant?"

Surprised by her censure, I shook my head, certain I hadn't

heard her correctly. "Excuse me?"

"You think that—"

"Viggo?" Mags' lecture was cut short as Violet's voice buzzed in both of our earbuds.

I looked at Mags. "Hold that thought," I said, and pressed my fingers together. "Yeah?"

"The road ahead is clear, but be cautious with the buildings. Our sensors can't seem to get much deeper than about fifteen to twenty feet into them, so anybody could be hiding in there. I know for sure there are people in some of the buildings, but they are farther back, probably trying to keep out of view. Just be careful and keep your eyes open."

"Roger that. Keep the drone in front of us until the next turn, and keep an eye out. I don't like all these fires on the street."

"Neither do I. They're also messing with our thermal scans."

"Roger. Switching back to team channel." I quickly changed the channel and gave everyone the lowdown. "Cruz, you and the people behind you break left on the street to the intersection. Let's get around the corner—keep an eye on the windows."

"Roger," said Cruz, and he peeled off across the street, weaving through the vehicles. The men and women behind him followed closely, using whatever they could as cover to keep their advance into the intersection unnoticed. I gave them fifteen seconds, and then stood up.

"My side—go," I transmitted to the men and women behind me, and crept into motion myself.

Once we had gotten around the corner without anyone taking potshots at us from the questionable buildings, I motioned for everyone to relax a bit, and we began to creep less and walk more, a few people shaking legs out and breathing in slight relief.

"Pair off and stay close to the buildings," I ordered. "I want one person in each pair watching the windows above, and another one checking the alleys. Call out anything you see. Mags, you're with me."

Mags lifted a dark eyebrow, the corners of her lips turning up and then down as she fought off a smile. She gave a nod and followed me up onto the curb, her footsteps light behind me. "Ready to finish that talk?" she asked.

"Windows or alleys?" I asked, adjusting the rifle strap on my shoulder. This area was mostly residential, with both wide and narrow buildings lining the streets, nestled tightly together. The tallest building had five floors, but most were only four. Like several residential areas, the bricks on the building bore similar shades of color, but the patterning on them was so varied and different. It had definitely been a beautiful street before.

"Windows," she said, her head tilting up to peer at the line of them above the street. "And don't try to dodge the question."

"Of course I want to know what you meant. No offense, Mags, but you haven't seen me in over ten years. Not to mention, you saying that around our soldiers kind of undermines my authority. It makes it hard to execute a plan if my soldiers are looking to you instead of me."

Mags made an irritated tutting sound, and then sighed heavily. "You know what, you're right, and I'm sorry. I just don't like it when people try to take responsibility for stuff that wasn't in their control. It's a waste of energy."

I pulled to a stop just short of the alley I was approaching. Mags must not have noticed, because she bumped into me, making a startled sound. I turned, steadying her, and gave her a frown. "It's my energy to waste. Besides, the things that make me feel guilty are the things driving me forward, making me do something to right these wrongs and help these people."

Mags gave an indelicate snort as she took a step away from me. "You sound just like my papa. He also tried to take responsibility for things that were out of his control. Look, if you hadn't done something, someone else would've, and we'd be *right back here*. Different faces but same scenery."

"You can't know that for sure."

"Sure I can. This place was a powder keg even before your video, Viggo. It was about to blow."

I considered her information carefully. "We had two people embedded in the city. They seemed to think most people were happy with the status quo. That's why we chose to show the video."

This time, Mags' chin trembled slightly as she shook her head. "Then your people were missing out on a lot. There were already small resistance pockets forming—Tío Alejandro was very involved with one, and I got sort of dragged into it after my papa got taken for one of Elena's little… workgroup trainings. Tío tried to warn Papa, but… Papa's anger was too great. He wouldn't listen. They came and dragged him away from me." Her voice was ragged and harsh in her whisper, and I could tell she wanted to scream out her anger and rage at her father's loss. "He's an arthritic old man! What could he have to learn?"

I looked over to her, and saw tears running down her cheeks. Her eyes continued to scan the windows, and I felt a rush of approval for her maintaining control like that. I reached out and placed a hand on her shoulder, and she blinked in surprise, then gave me an appreciative smile. Alejandro and Tim gave us curious looks as they passed by, and I just shook my head. Mags sniffed loudly, and then let out a chuckle. "Dios mío, what a mess I am."

"From what I hear, you are quite a formidable leader. I liked that idea of cross-training people you started implementing. It's smart."

Mags sniffed and smiled, finally looking up at me, her eyes sparkling. She nodded a few times and then emitted a small chuckle, wiping her eyes. "Did they see?" she asked, nodding ahead to the other members of the team.

"What?"

She smiled, her eyes finally dry. "You were worried that no one would follow your orders," she said dryly. "Me crying on you ought to have restored your image." She reached up and patted my cheek affectionately, then moved past me.

A small chuckle of surprise escaped me. She'd made her point—that I was arrogant—but she'd also explained why releasing the video wasn't the whole reason things had gotten so bad. The people in the city had known something bad was going on. They had been planning to stop it. Our video had just been a catalyst to accelerate their plans. And it *had* been arrogant of me to assume we were the only ones who had thought of resisting.

I moved to catch up with her, stepping over an overturned mailbox. "So when did you become so scary?" I teased.

She flashed me a sardonic look and rolled her eyes. "You think only Matrian women are capable of being badass?"

My eyes flicked up the street to where Margot and Cad were moving. They were clearly chatting, and I saw a smile creep across Cad's face as he tipped his cap at her. "Not at all," I said to Mags, recalling the times Violet, Tim, and I had come to have dinner with Margot, only to be put to work, her tone brusque and commanding. She reminded me of my training officers when I had been a cadet: no nonsense, no disobedience, and everything would go along great. And then I thought of Amber, her fear-lessness and resolve, and shook my head. "Not at all. Not even remotely."

"I always knew you were a more evolved male."

I smirked. "Thanks."

"Viggo, one of those fires I thought was stationary just start-ed moving."

The alarm in Violet's voice stopped me short, and I pressed my fingertips together to activate my mic. "Where?"

"They're on a perpendicular street, heading toward the same intersection you're aiming for. They're spreading out now. I count… maybe fifty people? They're carrying things as well—weapons, most likely, but I can't tell what kind. The torches are messing with my night vision."

I looked around at the various alleys between the mangled apartment buildings on the street, not certain where each one led. "Give me options, Violet."

"Silence Lane, fifty feet up from your position. Follow it to the cul-de-sac with the big building at the end. That offers the best strategic position if the mob approaches you."

"Roger. Find me that alley, people." I deactivated the link and moved forward, checking the alleys quickly.

Seconds later, Alejandro transmitted, "I've reached it." I searched the street for him, spotting him waving a slow arm up ahead of me. Mags and I made a beeline for his position.

It was a small road, only wide enough for one vehicle at a time, and it had no sidewalks, the only border the tall twin walls of the building curving around to the right. I thinned my lips, whistling a high-pitched note. The pairs of people up ahead stopped and turned, and I pointed toward the lane, flashing the hand signal to move fast.

They began to move toward us. "Mags, Alejandro, get them inside and in position. I'll make sure everyone gets off the road."

Mags nodded and jogged ahead, moving deeper down the cobblestone lane, disappearing from my sight as it slowly curved around. I kept an eye on the intersection we'd been heading for, and began to notice the shadows start to move against the buildings, a soft red glow chasing them away.

CHAPTER 23

Viggo

"**H**urry," I hissed, waving on two stragglers—Alicia, a refugee woman, and one of Mags' men. They raced by me just as the red glow grew brighter still, and I saw the first person carrying a torch step out from behind the building at the corner into the intersection. I slowly stepped back into the small curve of the road, not wanting to risk catching the torchbearer's attention, and then turned and trotted away more quickly. The walls of the buildings on either side of the lane were smoothly built and curved, continuing on for fifty feet. I kept my back pressed to the wall and moved silently as I began to hear the sound of feet, the crunching of incautious steps almost drowning out the low hum of talking.

Nearing the end of the cul-de-sac, the lane widened into a slab of pavement made for parking, but there were no cars—only wide, empty spaces before a simple gray building with white trim and a stylish glass front. A few feet beyond, a handful of steps led up into the concrete block structure, and I ran toward them, moving up and through the double glass doors into the hall inside. I moved deeper, slightly relieved to see Mags sitting on the right a few feet away, her back to an inner doorframe and her gun angled toward the street.

"We have line of sight to the street from this room," she whispered, and I drew closer to her, peeking around the first doorframe in the hall to see members of our team kneeling or lying on the floor, their guns drawn and ready. My eyes did a double sweep of the room. It was an L-shaped reception area, with wide, cushioned furniture and coffee tables, a few desks pushed together to form a counter in the back. The entire building face was composed of glass looking into the street beyond. The room was upended, however, furniture displaced and scattered across the floor. I didn't care how it had happened at this point. It provided many hiding positions for my team.

"All lights off, people," I ordered softly into the gloom. "That will be the first thing that gives us away." The room dimmed as the remaining flashlights clicked off. Then I moved to the other side of the door, deeper into the building, and stood over where Mags was sitting, her back against the frame. "Has anyone cleared the floor?"

Mags shook her head, and I pressed my fingers together. "Cad, Cruz?"

Cad, who was kneeling behind a chair, looked up at me and then scrambled over. Mags laid her legs flat while he crawled over her. Cruz was right behind him, abandoning his desk and sliding over on his elbows before crawling over to Mags. He didn't say anything to her, something that, knowing Cruz, I was grateful for.

"Viggo, it's hard to tell how many," said Violet through the line, "but some of the group with the torches broke off and are heading toward you. It might just be two."

I acknowledged and turned to Cad and Cruz.

"I need you two to start checking this floor. I'd hate for some-one trapped behind us to get caught in the crossfire. Or try to kill us."

"We're on it," Cruz whispered, moving toward the T-shaped junction at the end of the hall. Cad followed him, but I didn't have time to watch him, as my eyes were trained on the orange flicker growing on the building wall across from us, under the light of the moon.

I went down to one knee, swinging the stock of my rifle up to my shoulder and sighting down at the lane beyond, where the people carrying torches would emerge. When they did, I moved my finger slightly away from the trigger, waiting, watching as a man and a woman came down the alley, torches held high, as if they were exploring rather than hunting. They were carrying weapons—the man had a bat dangling from one hand, while the woman brandished a kitchen knife.

They drew closer to the glass, the red glow lighting up more and more of the parking lot in front of our position, and I grit-ted my teeth. "Don't shoot unless you absolutely have to," I whis-pered loudly to the team.

"We aren't equipped to take people captive," whispered Mags more softly, and I knew her comment was directed at me.

I didn't answer—it was a moot point anyway. As the two ex-plorers drew nearer to us, the man stopped and put his hand on the woman's forearm, drawing her attention away from the build-ing. The two exchanged a few words, and then, simple as that, they were leaving, hurrying back the way we had come. I let out a breath of relief and relaxed against the wall for a second.

As soon as the flicker from their torches had disappeared, I straightened. "All right, everyone," I said to the room, keeping my voice low. "They're gone. You can get up."

"They joined up with the main group and are continuing down the street," reported Violet, confirming that the explorers weren't coming back. "I recommend waiting for them to clear out before proceeding."

I considered her suggestion as I watched everyone slowly climb to their feet, reaching down to help Mags to hers. She straightened up, shaking her legs out a little, and looked up at me. "We've got a bit of time. You want to give our people a few minutes?" she asked.

I was about to answer when my command line beeped—a sign that someone wanted the attention of one of the leaders. I switched channels hurriedly in case it was me.

"Thomas?" It was Ms. Dale speaking, her voice carefully neutral. "Those signs you told us to look out for that the Matrians are tampering with the water supply. Wasn't one of them that the tunnels in the sewer would be flooded?"

"Yes. Why?"

"Well, I'm looking into one, and they are. This is going to slow Logan and me down a bit. We were counting on the sewers to get through a rough neighborhood."

"It's much worse than that," said Thomas softly. "Flooded sewers means our timeline is cut in half. We're now down to five hours until water that's been tampered with makes its way into the city... possibly even less, with how quickly the Matrians have been working. We need to move the rendezvous times up by at least half an hour."

"How are we supposed to do this when our best route has just been blocked?" Ms. Dale's voice over the radio was testy.

"I'm looking for alternate routes for you now," Thomas said, seeming to barely register her annoyance.

Henrik's voice came on next. "All teams, we need to move up our timeline. This means that if you can find a shorter route that has a slightly higher risk, now is the time to try it. But don't do anything excessively reckless—clear with me first."

I turned my eyes toward Mags, who had clearly been listening as well, meeting her blue eyes as they came up to me wearing an expression that I recognized. I guessed she felt the sinking in the pit of her stomach, too. This meant I'd been right to attack the water treatment plant. But this time, being right was making me feel worse.

"Well," I said slowly, "I guess we don't have time to take a minute."

"Let's take a look at the map," she said in response, already pulling her copy from a back pocket.

The area we'd been sent into was closer to the south side of Patrus City, an area I wasn't as familiar with. When I'd been a warden, this area had been full of nice neighborhoods and high-end institutions. I'd been patrolling the city center, where some of the best shopping, entertainment, and bars existed—and also much higher rates of crime and gang-related activity. Now this area was literally a warzone, and I couldn't even begin to imagine what the city center looked like. I was glad to be on the team with Mags, who knew it better than I did.

"We're here," she said, tapping on a small dead-end road eight blocks from the warehouse district. "We were going to go around, use Drew's territory to cover us and then come up an adjacent street. It's safer, but it'll take us two hours, an hour and a half at a minimum."

I shook my head. "With the accelerated timeline, we can't spare the time."

She nodded, her face grim. "I know, but the fastest route skirts dangerously close to Porteque territory. If they've expanded their turf or claimed another apartment building... we might get bogged down."

"How much time would we save?"

She sighed and crossed her arms over her chest. "An hour," she said. "Maybe more. Unless we get pinned down, in which case we could lose hours. It's a gamble."

"Henrik, we can get there in an hour, maybe less, but it's dangerous," I transmitted, turning away from the table and the map and looking around the room. The team had relaxed somewhat, seeing the torches disappear, but all of them were watching me and Mags closely, knowing something was going down. "And we'd be going close to Porteque territory, but I think it's worth it. We can still make our rendezvous."

"You sure you want to go that route?" There was no judgment in Henrik's voice; he just wanted to make sure I was confident in the decision.

I was, though not for a lack of doubts. But since they'd confirmed something was happening at the plant, I knew every second mattered. It wasn't enough to arrive at the water treatment plant on time. We still had to fight our way inside, and then input Thomas' ridiculously long string of commands into the system to purge all of the water from the plant into the channels reserved for waste water. That had been our final decision—even if we had no idea what the Matrians were doing to the water, we could reverse it all, just in case.

"Time's stealing other options away from us," I said. "But if you're asking whether my people can handle it, I know we can."

"I'm not, but that is good to know. All right. Amber, Ms. Dale—what's your ETA?"

Thomas answered. "Given their current rate of travel and the obstacles in their way, I'd say an hour and twenty minutes. Give or take. Viggo, soon I'm going to have to move Violet's drone to Amber's team for a while."

Violet and I both acknowledged him, our voices coming through the line at the same time, sending a little surge of amusement through me—we were on the same wavelength, it seemed, even now. Then I was back in the moment.

We had an hour and twenty minutes, give or take. "All right, guys," I called out to my team, looking around at the faces watching and listening to my transmission with serious expressions. "We've had a change in plans. We've just confirmed that the Matrians are tampering with the water treatment plant. So we're going to have to take a rougher route than expected to get there before contaminated water can make its way out on the streets. This just got a lot more vital, but I trust you all to be able to handle it. If anybody wants to go back now, you have the chance. No judgment."

I surveyed the room. A chorus of disgruntled voices greeted my announcement, a woman named April and some others saying, "We're not giving up now!"

Nobody volunteered to leave, and I breathed a sigh of relief.

"Okay, great. Let's get ready and get on the street. Gregory, I want you checking the street cameras for us. We're moving more blindly now, so we need to play this smart. Take a small team back out to the main road and check it out. Everyone else... you have five minutes to move out. Let's get ready to go."

CHAPTER 24

Viggo

The light from the handheld illuminated the angles of Mags' face as she clicked through the video feeds. "Any movement?" I asked, turning back toward the street.

"No," she whispered back. "But the cameras are only at the intersections, so I can't tell if the streets are clear."

I scanned the street. This one reminded me of the one we'd pushed through earlier, burnt or damaged cars scattered everywhere, windows on shopfronts broken, stores looted, trash and debris littering the sidewalks. The tall buildings that lined the road were bathed in shadows, but at an intersection a few buildings up, fires burned in barrels on every corner, creating a dome of red glow. "We've been through thirteen intersections just like this, Mags."

"Yeah, well, right now we're dangerously close to Porteque territory," she replied. "We need to be ready to run like scared rabbits. Trust me, I know this area particularly well."

"Rabbits freeze when they're scared," I replied, standing up and waving for everyone to move forward.

Offering a hand to Mags, I helped pull her up from where she had been seated against the building, ducked down behind an overturned newspaper stand. "Same old Viggo," she said dryly as she tucked the handheld into her satchel. "Doesn't change the fact that those barrels are lighting up the intersection like a beacon. Somebody really wants to see what's going on down there."

I shot her a look and began to move away, threading my way through the chaos of broken-down cars. My boots ground against shards of glass coating the street as I walked, but I managed to mitigate the sound, trying to keep our approach as silent as possible. Mags and Alejandro moved similarly to me—the trick was putting weight on the outside edge of your foot when you stepped, rolling your foot down rather than planting it. It had felt odd when I'd first started practicing it, but after a while it had become ingrained.

But the limited time we'd had to train with our refugees—and even a few of Mags' team—meant that many people were making more noise than necessary. I kept a sharp eye on the building windows on either side of us, but didn't stop until we were a few feet from the intersection. I motioned with my hand, and we split into two teams, one on either side of the street. At least they were all fairly proficient at following my signals.

I glanced over to where Alejandro stood up front. He was peering down his scope at the building on the adjacent corner. I turned to Margot and nodded, and she slowly raised her rifle, scoping the building on the other side. Our practice was to stand at the corners and appraise the other team's side of the intersection for better visibility.

"The building opposite you is four stories tall, set behind a small park," said Alejandro on the team channel. "The park creates a wide-open space, which gives the building behind it a better view of the street."

"The one on your side is two stories, and pressed right up against the street," I replied. "It's doubtful anyone's holed up in there."

"Which means if there is anybody watching, they will be in the building Alejandro has eyes on." Mags' voice sounded grim. I hesitated, and then pushed up closer to the intersection, heading for the sharp corner of the building. "What are you doing?" she asked as I crossed the threshold from darkness to light, the glow extending beyond the actual intersection.

"I want to see what we're dealing with," I said as I eased forward.

I kept my eyes on the building on Alejandro's side, just in case, but there was no movement in any of the windows. As I reached the corner, I knelt down, and then slowly peeked around the side, staring at the building across the street. The gray concrete building Alejandro had noticed rose above the small park, the windows dark and eerie. I watched it for a long moment, knowing I was exposed from either side, and then moved back to the shadows.

"It's too good an ambush spot," I admitted to Mags. "We need to go around."

Mags crossed to me with quick, silent steps, pulled out her map, and spread it open on the hood of one of the many broken cars nearby, using a penlight with a red glow to illuminate the large piece of paper. I bent over it to find our location while Mags pulled the handheld from her satchel, flicking it on and searching through camera feeds.

"Mulbury and Doxit?" I asked, tapping on the intersection back and to the north.

Mags began speaking into her radio on the other channel, asking Henrik about the camera numbers for the intersection, and I continued to examine the map, feeling more and more dejected as I studied it. If Mulbury and Doxit weren't clear, then we'd either have to head four blocks back or two blocks to the east before we could start another trajectory, easily losing half an hour in the process.

"Viggo?" I turned and found Tim standing there.

"Hey, buddy. What's up?"

The lanky young man looked over my shoulder at the intersection. "What problem?"

I frowned. "You're not supposed to break rank, Tim," I said. He gave me a sardonic look, and I sighed. "The fires in the intersection might be bait meant to draw people out, and there's a building that has a good view of the street. If we move into the open, and there are people in there with guns, they could easily kill a lot of us."

He frowned and tossed his hair. "Take out lights?"

I glanced down the road at where he was looking, studying the barrels. They weren't secured by anything, but I didn't see a good way of putting the fires out. They were too large, too spread out, and too likely to cause chaos if they tipped. Maybe someone could get one, but if there *were* shooters in the building, I doubted very much that whoever went in would be coming back out.

Opening my mouth to explain this all to Tim, I was interrupted by Mags snapping her fingers at me to get my attention. I followed the line of her arm up to her face. "Main channel," she said, turning her handheld around and showing me a strangely dark screen.

Clicking over, I came in on the middle of Thomas saying, "—hacked. It's only a matter of time before the Matrians—ninety percent chance it's the Matrians—get into our system."

"What's getting hacked?" I asked, straightening in alarm.

"The cameras!" he practically shouted, and I could hear the stress in his voice. "I'm hacking her back, but she's good, and she's clearly got better equipment than I do."

"How long do we have, Thomas?"

"A lot longer if you'd all stop bugging me," he bristled. "So stop bugging me!"

I switched back over to our channel and moved over to Mags. "How did that other intersection look?" I asked.

"Not good," she said as she turned the handheld around and held it out to me. Two of the cameras were out and a third was transmitting upside down—presumably having been torn from its mount—but it only showed a small fraction of the street, the remaining screen filled with the blank surface of a pole the lens was facing. The last camera was upright, but the angle was bad on that one, too.

In the view from that camera, two dark shadows were grappling with each other in the orange flicker of a fire burning just off screen. One man's face was visible, and I could see wet blood coating half of it. They pushed against each other, the man's mouth opening in a roar, and then something cut in from the side and tackled them both, pulling them down and off screen.

"I've seen at least four different people since Henrik gave me the numbers," she said softly. "I think we gotta risk it."

"Viggo, what's going on?" Alejandro cut in over the team

channel, and I turned to see his dark form still pressed against the building.

"The other route is a no-go," I informed him and everyone who was listening. "People are rioting in the streets. We need a minute to decide how to get past this intersection without attracting any attention."

"No, Viggo. I mean why is Tim heading into that intersection carrying all that stuff?"

I turned and gaped as I watched Tim enter that red-orange halo of light, holding several big, flat objects against his side, under his arm. He looked around the intersection for a moment, then moved over to the first barrel, his pace calm and confident.

"Everyone get guns on that building now!" I ordered into the link, taking quick steps toward the intersection. Clicking off the safety to my rifle, I jogged down the sidewalk and then knelt by the wall, using the corner for cover as I sighted down at the building. There was no movement that I could see.

I heard the sound of thin metal flexing, and turned to see Tim standing fifteen feet away, holding a piece of metal that looked like it might have come from the hood of a car at some point.

He lay the metal down over the rim of the barrel, his face going from orange to shadow. "Clever boy," Alejandro praised him through the earpiece, but I found it hard to agree. Tim was out in the open, exposed to anybody who might be looking. While his idea to smother out the fires might have been clever, his execution was—

I would've missed the muzzle flash if I hadn't been staring so intently at the suspicious building. The crack of the gunshot sounded loud in the quiet street, and I whirled back toward Tim with a cry. But he was still standing. In fact, he was nonchalantly approaching the next barrel, this one near Alejandro.

"Shooter—fourth floor, third window from the left!" I transmitted.

"How the *hell* did he do that?" Mags cut in, and I could hear the alarm in her voice—and maybe a touch of awe.

Another gunshot sounded, and this time I kept my eyes on Tim. If I hadn't, I would never have believed it. One minute he was holding an undersized garbage lid out over the barrel, and the next moment, he had moved back a step, so quickly that it was hard to see—a ping sounding from behind him where a bullet bit into some trash near where he'd been standing.

Tim moved the step back and dropped the garbage lid into the can, covering most, if not all, of the flames. Then the gunfire began in earnest. Tim went low, leaping back and forth in a zigzag as he raced for the third barrel. He made a graceful roll, holding his collection of firefighting objects tightly to his chest, and ended in a crouch behind the third barrel.

I recovered from my amazement, the feeling that I was watching some kind of scripted dance. "Give him covering fire, NOW!" I shouted at my team, and began to shoot at the windows where the muzzle flares had come from, randomly, just to put up some resistance, even though the chances of hitting someone blind like this were incredibly low. The gun kicked against my shoulder as I depressed the trigger, shells ejecting from the side and clinking against the pavement.

"Margot can't see anything," reported Cad. "The building isn't lit inside, or if it is, it's only giving enough light to benefit *them*."

"Just keep firing—anything helps. Give Tim a chance to get those fires out!" I ordered, coming back around the corner to eject the magazine. My hands moved almost automatically, working the gun as they'd done hundreds of times before, as my eyes found their way back to Tim. He was still hiding behind the third barrel. Bullets bit into the pavement beside him, but he didn't panic as he carefully lifted up a third flat object. I couldn't tell what it was, but he slowly, almost leisurely, slid it over the rim of the barrel, pushing it with his fingertips.

A bullet pinged off the lid, and Tim yelped, dropping his head back down. In the orange light, I could see enough sweat on his skin that it glistened in the firelight, but he didn't stop. He reached back up with one arm and finished pushing the object across. The flickering light cut off immediately.

Tim turned around slowly, placing his back to the barrel. "Tim, come back!" I shouted at him, knowing he was eyeing the last barrel. And while most of me was growling in a protective conniption fit… part of me wanted, somewhere deep down inside, to see him go for it—to see him win.

But the gunfire from the building was increasing, a hail of bullets hitting the pavement on either side of him, and I continued shouting at Violet's brother to stop. Tim ignored me, and, in one fluid motion, stood up and began racing toward the final barrel. He seemed to weave himself through the air, his body flowing sinuously around bullets, pulling himself out of the way of the oncoming fire with incredible grace. He had flipped over the barrel and dropped to a knee behind it, preparing his last cover, when something caught it and flipped it toward him.

Almost without ceasing his motion, the young man flipped backward in a controlled flail as a red-hot spray of embers and flames crashed out from the mouth of the barrel, spreading in a flurry across the street. The barrel right in front of me went next, spinning wildly across the intersection toward the one closest to

Alejandro, the contents getting dumped everywhere. Clanging and hissing added to the unending barrage of rifle shots echoing across the intersection.

Still upright after all of that, Tim darted right as the other two barrels fell to a similar fate, vaulting over the hood of a burnt-out car and diving for one a few feet away, tucking up under its trunk. Bullets pinged all around him, but his cover held, for the time being.

I realized I'd been holding my breath. Staring at the fire pit that now made up the intersection, and Tim's position just beyond, I felt a sinking sensation in my stomach. The fear, hope, and startled awe I'd felt as Violet's brother had braved the intersection were subsiding into a much more practical, uglier fear. With all these obstacles, I just wasn't sure how I was going to get him out, *or* us through.

CHAPTER 25

Violet

"**S**tay on this road, Amber," I said, studying the screen. "You're in the clear for about five hundred feet."

"Copy that," Amber said, and I watched as she and her small team fanned out in the street, moving from vehicle to vehicle. Now that Amber's team was making its way through the city to meet up with Logan's people, I was splitting time between Viggo and Amber. It was becoming a little bit of a headache, especially with Viggo nearing Porteque territory. Every part of me just wanted to be by him, being his mechanical eyes, keeping him safe… but right now, according to Thomas, Amber's team needed me more.

I manipulated my fingers, and the drone slowly moved forward. I tilted it back and forth, so that the belly swung up toward the buildings on either side of the road, and switched my thermal scan back on, rechecking each structure for any sign of movement.

Owen stood behind me, staring at the screen from over my shoulder. It would've been unnerving, but truth be told, I could use the extra eyes at this point—almost three hours of staring at the screen had left mine feeling dry and a little bleary.

The command line beeped, indicating someone was transmitting on the line, and I used my thumb to quickly change to the main channel, disappointment surging in my stomach when I heard Thomas' voice instead of Viggo's. It was silly, I knew, but I liked hearing him on the line. It was the only connection I had to him at the moment, now that my drone wasn't watching over him.

A variety of voices checked in on the command line, and I added mine to the chorus; when it seemed we all were there, Ms. Dale's voice announced, "Everyone switch to beta six. This channel has been compromised."

Beta six was the code name for the next channel in the frequency list we had developed before sending everyone out. Even though we didn't have enough comms for everyone, we still had more than enough to worry about our enemies getting their hands on one of them. So we had developed a protocol, at Ms. Dale's insistence, that when we lost—or lost contact with—a team member with a communicator, we would switch to the next frequency in our list, one we'd all memorized to make sure that no physical copy fell into the hands of the enemies.

When we had all found our way to the new channel, Ms. Dale continued. "Logan's advance team met with fire from a heavily armed group twelve blocks away from the objective. The hostile group retreated, but in the direction we need to go."

"You need a new route?" asked Henrik, and I glanced over to see him sliding a big map of the city in front of him, standing up, and pulling out a red pencil.

"We weren't expecting to have to come topside," Ms. Dale said on the line, irritation sharpening her voice. "So yes, please, we need a new route. Again."

I understood her frustration. It had been building over the last half hour as every move her team made seemed to be two steps forward, one step back. And since she and her team had started out farther away than Amber and Viggo's teams, they had even less time to deal with delays.

"I've been trying to tell her that we need to just cut through the bigger buildings," came a deep, masculine voice, similar enough to Viggo's to make me start to smile, then shake the expression off when I realized it was just Logan Vox. I continued pushing the drone forward, scanning, then flying again, idly listening to the chatter.

"It's too risky," Henrik told Logan as he circled something on the map. "Too many scared and desperate people we can't control. We would risk hurting them in order to keep them from hurting us. I'd like to keep the loss of civilian life to a minimum. We certainly won't be earning any favors by showing up in their hiding places armed to the teeth and looking for a fight. So I'm going to have to side with Ms. Dale."

There was a long pause. "Are you two dating or something?" Logan asked. His tone was flippant, like he was making an off-color comment out of spite, but also inadvertently stumbling into the truth. Still, it made me blink in surprise, wondering just how much longer Logan Vox had in this world. It depended on where he was standing in relation to Ms. Dale, I supposed, but then again, a bullet never traveled for too long before hitting something.

I could just picture Ms. Dale standing next to Logan, giving him that same look of unruffled disapproval that had so famously, and so continuously, painted her face during my martial arts classes with her. It was a chilling look, and I didn't envy Logan for being on the receiving end of it, even if he had brought it on himself.

"I found a new route," announced Henrik, ignoring Logan's comment entirely, though I saw the side of his mouth twitch up across the command table. "You'll need to check cameras..." He trailed off, flipping through some papers and scanning the rows of carefully handwritten print. It was the only hard copy we had of the streets and their corresponding camera numbers, and even that was mostly because Thomas hadn't been able to transfer everything to the handhelds—there wasn't enough space on the data chip. "178-21-D through H to confirm."

"One second," Ms. Dale replied. I busied myself by doubling back to Amber's group and rescanning the building faces, in case someone had snuck back in after my last pass. It was so frustrating to be limited like this by the equipment's size and range. Even going two hundred feet ahead of them made me feel clammy with nervousness. I didn't want anyone to get the jump on Amber or her team if I could avoid it.

Owen shifted behind me, his arm reaching around to point at the screen. "There's someone in that room," he said, tapping on one of the multiple windows in the screen.

I bit back the urge to tell him to back off. He was bored, and guarding me wasn't exactly the most glamorous job. I knew how he felt—even sitting here and being productive, I still felt pretty useless. "Thanks," I said as I manipulated the drone again. "There's a lot of small movements inside, but if you can't make out a person, that's generally because they're hiding in their home. Or at least, that's what I've seen so far."

"Ah." There was a long moment of silence, then, "Did you get Desmond all set up?"

I frowned and turned so that I could properly face him instead of trying to comment over my shoulder. "Owen, I know you don't like it, but the place is secure and—"

"It doesn't matter how secure you made it. You cannot expect to keep her in it. I still can't believe that we're even keeping her alive."

"It was a group decision, and her execution hasn't been lifted, only postponed," I replied automatically, and then froze, realizing how insensitive I was being. Owen had been a pretty big part of the group of us in command, but after what had happened, he was still being excluded from those meetings. Not that he complained, but when it came to Desmond, and Owen's attitude toward how to handle her... Well, Ian's loss was still coloring his emotional state. But I knew it still hurt him that we couldn't trust him yet.

That's his own fault, the dark, angry side of myself argued. *He created this mess, and now he's got to lie in it.* I pushed that part down, deep inside, and mentally closed the lid as hard as I could. I did not want to be angry at Owen. I wanted things to go back to the way they had been. If that meant biting back some callous remarks, I could do it. Soon.

"Mags, this is Drew. Do you copy?"

I came back to the discussion as the man's gravelly voice filled the line. Henrik leaned forward in his seat, and I flashed him a nervous look. With all these new elements joining us, the whole operation was beginning to have a 'too many cooks' feeling. Still, we needed him, so all we could do was hope he would be a team player. Switching channels, I quickly informed Mags that she was being summoned, and then changed back.

A few seconds later, she was there. "Hey, Drew, can't talk right now. Listen to these guys."

Silence filled the line. "What's going on?" asked Drew.

"Drew, this is Henrik. I'm glad you received your communications device all right. We were beginning to worry."

"The runners I sent with Mags got held up and had to lay low for a few minutes to avoid one of the other gangs. But they got here. What's going on with Mags?"

The line beeped, and I switched back over to Amber's channel while Henrik began to explain to Drew about Viggo and Mags having to take on a building filled with Porteque guys. Hopefully he wouldn't feel compelled to go after them and jeopardize the rest of the mission. The situation had become very messy very quickly, and I was frustrated, itching to break free of this tiny basement room and get into the city. Find Viggo, help him out, and then complete the mission… all in time for breakfast.

Things never worked that way, however. Not even when I had gone out on reckless and wild solo missions.

"Violet?"

I shook my head, trying to clear my fanciful thoughts. "Sorry, Amber. Repeat last transmission?"

"You haven't told us if the next part of our route is clear."

She delivered the line without any accusation, but I felt a kick of guilt in my stomach anyway. I took a deep breath, trying to untangle my thoughts, but couldn't seem to break free of them. It took me several seconds to realize I needed a break. Now. Before a distraction on my part meant that something vital on Amber's part got overlooked.

"Amber, hold on. I'm having Owen take over for a minute."

There was a long pause, and I felt a moment of regret for dropping Owen on Amber. She didn't seem even remotely ready to forgive him, and had even railed at me for being too nice to him after everything was said and done. I understood where she was coming from—I just didn't agree, so I hoped she'd be able to put her differences aside to work with Owen. "Roger," she acknowledged after a second, and I was relieved to hear professionalism in her voice.

I switched the drone over into hover mode and then turned in my seat, my mouth open to formally ask Owen to take over for me for a short period. The words died on my lips when I saw him scowling, his posture rigid, and I realized he was still thinking about Desmond and how close she was to him right now.

"Owen," I said, and he started and turned, giving me a surprised look. "Stop thinking about her."

"I can't," he said. "She's dangerous, and after what happened with Cody—"

"Cody's actually been doing a little better since that whole incident," I told him irritably. It was true. Since meeting with Desmond, Cody had been showing little bursts of improvement here and there. Nothing major, mainly just talking a little more and being a little less sullen with people. I still wasn't sure what had been discussed between them, and I still harbored a few doubts, but I *hoped* that somehow, in talking to Desmond while out of the influence of the Benuxupane, Cody had gotten a peek at the person inside, and it had made him change his mind.

"See, that's another thing. Is it really wise keeping Cody here under so light a guard, now that he knows about Desmond?"

I didn't disagree with him, but felt very much like I wanted to. That tightness was back—the walls of the room were beginning to feel like they were drawing in on me. I really needed to step away. "Owen, this isn't the time or the place for this discussion. Can you just please sit here and scan the next portion of the road for Amber? I need a minute."

His blue eyes immediately filled with concern. "Are you okay?" he asked, and I nodded as I stood up from the chair, the stiff muscles in my lower back protesting after being seated for so long.

"Fine. Just need fresh air. You remember how to do this?"

"Please. I'm so good you'd never know I spent the last two days learning." I smiled nervously at him, accepting the joke for the olive branch that it was, and he quietly slipped into his seat, put on the headset I had been wearing, and then slipped his fingers into the hollow tubes that were the flight controls.

Once I was certain Owen did understand the controls and had picked up where I'd left off, I made my way up the stairs, down the hall, and right out the front door. The air outside was crisp and chilly, and I sucked in a deep breath, letting the subtle smells of winter wash over me. The temperature had been steadily dropping the last few days, which had not made tent living at our other location fun, even with Viggo's furnace-like body next to me... but I still loved it. Loved the smell of winter and the pure promise of snow.

It helped to center me a little bit, and I tilted my head back, looking at the stars. The heavy clouds that had filled the sky over the mountains earlier in the day were clearing up, and the stars shone brightly above the wisps that remained. Everything else was silent, still. It was the opposite of how I felt, but something I deeply wanted to emulate.

"He's going to be okay." I breathed out the words, the resulting sound less of a whisper and more of an escaping of air. "We always get through these things."

It wasn't much of a pep talk. Even I wasn't naïve or arrogant enough to believe that just because we had come out on the other side of too many fires to name, this one would follow the same pattern. There was no guarantee of that. But rather than give in to more nihilistic impulses, I chose to believe in that miniscule sliver of hope that we would defy the odds once again.

"Violet?"

I turned and saw Morgan standing in the doorframe, Cody by her side, holding her hand. I turned more fully to face them and offered a wave. "Hey. What's up?"

She gave me an odd look and then pointed her thumb over her shoulder. "You left the door open. The draft dumps right into Cody's room, so I thought I better check it out and… You okay?"

I gave a shrug. "Honestly, I have no idea," I admitted. "But I'll get there."

Morgan gave me a sympathetic look. "I get that. To be honest, I'm not so good with people. They make me feel… uncomfortable." She fidgeted, and looked down at Cody. "Cody and I have that in common."

Cody gave her a sleepy smile, and she reached down to tousle his hair. I had to admit it was weird seeing Morgan and Cody getting along so well, but somehow, miraculously, after the meeting with Desmond, Cody seemed to have taken to the dark-haired woman.

Cody shifted his smile to me and nodded. "We're aliens," he announced, before his mouth spread open wide in noisy yawn.

Morgan gave him a smile and then looked back at me.

"I should really get him to bed, but… you sure you're okay?"

"I'll be fine," I reassured her, a little surprised at how invested she seemed. To be honest, before the showdown with Desmond, we hadn't spoken more than a handful of sentences with each other, and my first impression of her had been that of a person who went along with orders but sometimes seemed to be sullen or overly skeptical. But since then, she'd also surprised me with moments of sweetness. She never sugarcoated her judgments, but that meant that when she really cared, you knew it. And she clearly cared about Cody.

She shrugged and nodded, and then headed back down the hall toward Cody's room. We were short on manpower tonight, having sent every available human into the city, so she and Lynne, from the only other group at our main hideout, were taking turns with Cody. We still didn't want to leave him alone.

I watched her go, and then sighed, knowing my break—as short as it had been—was over. I maybe had time to relieve my bladder before I needed to get back down there. I headed back inside, regretfully closing the door behind me.

There were still many hours before dawn.

CHAPTER 26

Viggo

"**W**e could just charge it," Alejandro said. "It's what, a hundred feet to all those cars? We grab Tim as we go, stay low and behind the cars, and disappear behind the next building!"

We stood back twenty or thirty paces from the still burning ashes in the intersection, small bits of wood glowing with pulses of embers. A breeze through the buildings caught some of them, sifting them around in a circle before scattering them farther.

If anything, this was worse than before. The lighting on the street may have dimmed some, but the embers were still blowing hotly. Attempting to cross at anything other than a reckless run would be suicide, and even that seemed too risky.

I considered his question. The shots from the building were slowing down, and I felt certain the people inside were gearing up to bring the fight to us. They didn't know how many of us there were—with Tim pinned down out there, they could even be planning to storm the intersection and take him prisoner, or worse. Clicking over to the main channel, I pressed my fingers together. "Thomas, I know you're busy right now, but I have a question."

"I just threw up my final firewall," replied Thomas. "That'll buy us at least twenty minutes, and then the cameras are gone. What's up?"

"How long is the distance between neighboring manhole lids?"

Mags shot me a curious look, clearly wondering where I was going with this. To be honest, even I wasn't sure if it was worth a shot. But I had the kernel of an idea rooted inside of me.

"On average… three hundred and fifty feet, but in older parts of the cities, the manholes are spaced out a bit farther."

"And the water in the sewers right now… can it kill me?" I wanted to double check. "Does it have any water from the river in it?" I watched Mags' confusion disappear, and she made a face, as if she had smelled something rotten. I understood that look—but if I could get into the sewers, then I might be able to get us out of our current predicament.

"No, the sewers drain from the city into pipes that extend over the river. King Patrick's father was adamant about not having any chance of the river getting into his system. As for the cleanliness of it… They had to flood the system with clean water from the building, while also preventing it from draining. However, the ratio of fresh water to… mmm… soiled water is about 93.7 to 6.3."

I took a deep breath, setting my mind to fully understanding what this alternative path could offer and whether it would be worth it, and then checked my watch. We had thirty minutes before Ms. Dale hit her rendezvous. Amber had hit hers ten minutes ago, and Drew had been at his for twenty. My and Ms. Dale's teams were the last ones, and we all needed to make it on time, or this mission was a no-go.

"Wait one minute," I said into the mic. Turning to Mags, I looked at her, prepared to ask her a question, when she started speaking.

"I can't swim," she blurted out. "Papa never let me learn. So if your plan is to just have us follow the street down to cross, that isn't going to work."

I faltered. That had been my plan. However, I had overlooked the fact that not everyone in the group would know how to swim—or be strong enough swimmers under the dangerous conditions of the sewers. I was certain Alejandro was, but... Could Tim even swim?

I looked over to where Tim was crouched behind the trunk of the car. "Any minute, they're going to send people out of the building," I said. "They'll try to flank us, come at us from both sides. We need to get out of here, and the only way to do that is down that street. Do you see any other options here? I really am looking."

Mags hesitated, and then stood up and scooped the map into her hands. "C'mon," she said as she darted over to Alejandro's side of the street, moving over to her uncle.

The man standing next to Alejandro moved to one side as she shouldered her way into their line, looking up at the building, studying it. I moved in close to her, apologetically shoving the man next to Alejandro farther down, and looked over her shoulder as she considered the building and the map together.

"Okay, this might sound crazy, but could we use the sewer to get in under the building?" She lowered the map, and I blinked at her.

"I have no idea," I said. "One sec." I quickly transmitted the question to Thomas.

"Absolutely, but the entryway will be narrow and difficult to see," he affirmed. "It would be very easy to miss in the dark."

Mags smiled widely, a dimple forming in her cheek. "You and a few men get into that building and ambush them from behind," she said. "We'll get in a shootout with them down here to distract them, while you go take their advantage away."

I found myself nodding approvingly. I liked her plan instantly—but I would need help. "Alejandro, Mags, get me anybody who can swim. Five is good, but ten would be better. Split the difference if you can. You're going to need the manpower too."

Mags nodded and darted back up the sidewalk to race across the street. I moved away from Alejandro, heading back down the darkened part of the street, out of view of the people who guarded the intersection, to the nearest manhole. The heavy metal lid was covered partially by a few charred pieces of rubber, and I squatted down, tossing them to one side. I slid my fingers into the slots on either side of the crescent emblem for Patrus emblazoned on the top, and then lifted the lid up a few inches, until I could catch the edge and slide the whole thing back.

I pulled out my flashlight and clicked it on, setting it on the softest setting. Dark water flowed only about eight inches below street level. I stared at it, trying not to think about what was floating by down there, and then pulled my backpack off. Reaching into the side pockets, I pulled out one of the waterproof bags Violet had given to everyone.

She's cleverer than I give her credit for, I thought with a smile as I yanked my earbud, microphone, and gloves out and dropped them into the slit in the bag. Grabbing one edge, I pulled it hard, stretching the pliable fabric, and then folded it across the gap and around the odd bundle that my communication devices formed. The fabric stuck snugly against itself, sealing the entire packet. I inspected it, but the lines had almost disappeared, with one corner visible to make it easier to reopen with a stiff tug.

Tucking the packet into my pocket, I slid my rifle off my shoulders. It was too bulky for this job; it would have to stay with the team. I would have somebody collect and redistribute the larger weapons from my team of swimmers after we went down.

I was just wrapping up my pistol and extra ammo when I heard the sound of padding feet moving over. "There was movement on the first floor," Mags said as she hurried around the car with a group of our people in tow. I counted six, including Harry, Cruz, and Alejandro. "Margot took two shots into one of the rooms, but she doesn't think she hit anyone." She gave me a thin-lipped, grim look.

"I'm sure she didn't miss on purpose," I replied, pulling out my gas mask and screwing down the filter valve until it was sealed shut. I couldn't use it to breathe, but it would help protect my eyes and allow me to see underwater. I looked up at the volunteers and gave them a quick rundown of what we were doing and how to use the bags to protect their weapons.

"Here," Mags said when I was finished, holding out a mesh bag with ten objects in it. I lifted them up, inspecting them closely. They weren't really round, as I had first thought, but rather rounded out by a trick of geometry, small alternating black and white pentagon shapes. I recognized them immediately. They were wharf-markers. The white pentagons contained bulbs that would flash every few seconds to mark the path for a dockworker on days or nights when the fog on the river got too thick to see through. And they were waterproof, at least for a little while—it was a useful quality when you were working on the docks. "And here, I made sure the other men took these instead."

She held out a pistol, this one with a silencer on it, and I quickly unwrapped mine, exchanging it with hers and then putting it into one of the bigger pockets on my pants. "Thanks," I said, looping the strap of the bag containing the wharf-markers around my bicep. "They're going to be coming soon. Make sure you have a team ready in the back, in case they try to flank you."

Mags gave me an odd look and patted me on the shoulder. "We're gonna clear out and take position in the building Alejandro's against," she said. "It's not as tall as theirs, but it will give us an advantage. And the stairs are easier to control. I'll get a second team on the roof across the street to help out, and send a few people to the next checkpoint to play watchdog. I got this, so don't worry. And I'll keep a close eye on Tim."

She bent over and picked up my vest and backpack, adding them to the pile of heavy gear the rest of the swimmers had dropped. I couldn't take the vest—none of us could—because the armor would sink me in the water. "Be careful," she called over her shoulder as she moved back to the building.

Positioning the cinched-down gas mask atop my forehead, ready to deploy, I sat down on the edge of the manhole, dangling my feet into the water. I felt my pockets, double checking that my pistol, ammo, and comms were in place, all tucked in the waterproof bags, and then handed my rifle to Gregory, several more dangling from straps over his shoulder. It was painful having to leave my rifle behind, but given that this gang had been known to stockpile weapons, I was betting there would be plenty of larger guns for us to filch inside.

"Thirty seconds between each person," I said to the group of swimmers. "I'll drop a wharf-marker at every breathing spot, so you won't miss it, but there will also be a left turn, and I will drop one there at the junction, okay?"

"Do not worry, my friend," said a voice from behind me, and I turned to see that the first person lined up to swim with me was Cruz, crouching behind me, his gear ready to go. "We are going to be big heroes after this, no?"

I rolled my eyes and turned back to the cold water that was already trying to suck me down through my pant legs. Alejandro moved over to me and knelt next to the hole. "I've been meaning to ask you—where'd you pick up Cruz? He seems a bit crazy, even for how you folks operate."

I shook my head, and my mouth began moving before I realized what I was saying. "It's a long story, Alejandro. I miss Owen."

Alejandro patted me on the shoulder, and then I sucked in a deep breath, lowered my mask, and slipped into the dark water.

CHAPTER 27

Viggo

Where the hell is the damn manhole? I swung the flashlight around while desperate thoughts taunted me, screaming that I'd already swum past it, and now I was trapped, suspended in this watery tunnel until I couldn't take it anymore and I breathed in the murky water—I felt the pressure build in my throat, my body fighting with my mind to convince it to exhale, and I applied logic to the primal fear, going through the options in my brain.

It was possible that I'd missed it. The water was dim, and in spite of the flashlight in my hand, everything down here seemed a lesson in gray. Colors were muted, shadows exaggerated. And always, just behind the light beam lurked the slow, heavy press of the darkness. It loomed, a reminder that the only thing keeping me from certain death was the flashlight I held in my hand.

And it was hard to gauge distance down here. Thomas had given only an average when we had talked about the distance, but that didn't mean each gap had been three hundred and fifty feet exactly. Which meant I might not be as far down as I thought.

I kicked, shifting myself so that I was more on the left, so I could see the branch off to the building we were headed for. Swimming on this side, I might risk the next surface point, which was more in the middle of the tunnel... But I had to find this turn. My heart pounded hard in my chest, reminding me that oxygen was essential for life, but I was fine. Safe for just a little bit longer before I would even contemplate panicking.

Even taking painstaking care, I almost missed the turnoff. It was a narrow passage just behind a section of protruding wall, but the shadow the wall cast as I swam by it made it almost disappear. If I hadn't looked back twice, needing to know for sure, I might have missed it entirely. I swiveled around in the water, making for the opening, my lungs feeling compressed and my motions seeming impossibly slow. Reaching into the mesh bag, I scooped out one of the few remaining wharf-markers and switched it on. The halogen lights pulsed brightly, and I dropped it just past where the wall jutted out.

I could reach out and touch the sides of the walls in this passage, but I focused on the ceiling, using the natural fingerhold of the bricks to propel myself along. Resisting the urge to gasp for breath, I rolled my head back, looking for some sign of the next manhole, but found nothing. The urge to panic was back, my body starting to shake violently. My vision dimmed and went gray for a second, and I had to clamp my teeth together to keep myself from inhaling.

I began to stretch farther forward, my hands grabbing the bricks in claw-like fashion. My chest burned and my neck clenched. I was so focused on fighting back the impending unconsciousness that I almost didn't notice it when my hand hit empty space. I followed it forward and up, kicking my feet as my hips dragged against the corner of the brick. I was already trying to inhale when I surfaced, suctioning the mask tighter to my face.

Ripping it off, I gasped, and then gagged and coughed, my body's instincts stepping over each other in relief. I sucked in another gasp of air, this one better, more familiar, and felt the deep satisfaction of being alive. Reaching up with shaking arms, I slipped my fingers through the small holes on the bottom of the lid, giving my legs a moment to rest.

I breathed in sharp pants, water blowing off my lips. I fought back a shiver, my arms and limbs aching from the cold and oxygen deprivation. I desperately wanted to sit there for longer, but I knew that whoever was coming behind me was going to be just as desperate for air, and I couldn't block their way. I also had to check whether this was actually our exit.

Flexing the arm that held me up, I raised my torso a few more inches out of the water, turning my ear toward the holes and listening. I heard the rustle of leaves overhead, and realized I was somewhere under the park. Which was good—it meant I only had one more stop to go.

After exhaling slowly and sucking in an equally slow breath, I replaced the mask and dove. I dropped the marker and kept on, using the brick stone like a ladder. The next manhole felt significantly closer, and even though I surfaced quickly, I was less winded than before. I raised myself up a few inches, listening to the street.

Gunfire popped loudly overhead, and I heard the sound of heavy feet moving. A shadow carrying a bright torch passed by, and I quickly slipped my fingers out of the holes in the lid, not wanting to risk the chance of being discovered.

"BOY!" bellowed someone overhead, and I pressed myself even lower into the water. "WALK OVER HERE OF YOUR OWN FREE WILL, AND WE SHALL LET YOU LIVE! YOUR FRIENDS HAVE ABANDONED YOU!"

There was the sound of distant gunfire, and I heard boots scuffling back, some men cackling. "A mother never abandons her young!" I heard Mags' voice clearly, and shook my head. If she'd wanted the men's attention on her, then she had gotten it.

Something tugged hard on my pants, and I realized how much time I had wasted listening. I sucked in a deep breath, re-placing the mask, and just as I was pushing back into the water, I heard the leader start giving orders.

Under the water, I made out Cruz's face in the mask. He pointed up, and I stopped him, pointed to my ear, and then pointed up. He made a circle with his finger and thumb, and then shot up. I let him pass, dropping a marker down under him, and then continued swimming, hoping that Cruz would hear part of the orders.

I kept moving along the ceiling, pausing for just a moment to shine the flashlight around the tunnel. The next opening slowly revealed itself, and I swam up to it, pausing when I realized it was a grate placed right against the surface of the water. It was large enough for a fully grown man to squeeze through, but I was wor-ried it wasn't going to open.

I planted my hand against it and pushed. The grating wob-bled, but held fast. Pushing off it, I allowed myself to sink down to the bottom, planting my feet on the rock below. I sank down farther, folding my knees up and pressing my butt down to the bottom—then pushed off hard from the floor, thrusting my arm up toward the grate with as much energy as I could muster.

The flat of my palm connected to the grating, and a side of it pushed up. My lungs starting to squeeze again, I continued to press on it, forcing it out of the way.

I climbed out of the hole in the floor, and a wave of cold air hit me. Water splashed all over the dark orange floor. I slid my mask off my face, letting it drop, taking slow and steady breaths as I moved the flashlight around the room.

It was small. One door, closed, stood ten feet away from the rectangular hole leading to the sewer. Rows of pipes lined the wall, some leading back into it, others moving through large metal drums or branching into new pipes. A bare wall was behind me.

I dropped a wharf-marker down into the hole, and then stripped off my shirt, twisting it into a long line and squeezing as much water out of it as I could. There was a swish and slap in the water, and then Cruz surfaced, his hands gripping the sides and hoisting himself up until he was sitting with his legs dangling in the water.

The mask made a popping noise as he broke the seal and took it off, and he managed a deep breath, his chest heaving. "The leader, he ordered his men to go to the roof of the building across the street from Mags," he said, running a hand over his short hair to slick some of the water out. "He sent another group of men to come in from Tim's street, so she's pinned from three locations."

Digging into my pocket, I used my still damp shirt to try to collect any residual moisture from my face, especially my ears. The bundle with the earbuds slipped into my hand, and I quickly unwrapped the items.

"Get your legs out of the hole," I told Cruz as I slipped the bud into my ear, and tugged on the glove. Pressing my fingers to-gether, I quickly transmitted, "Mags, we made it to the building. We overheard the leader—he's going to approach you through the building east of you, and down the street north as well. They're going to go for the roof across from you, so tell your men to be ready."

"Well, that'll buy us a few minutes," she replied. "And if you get up to their shooting position, you'll have a clear line of sight on all of them."

I heard someone surface and looked over to see Harry pull-ing himself through the hole and crawling forward, his clothes sucking wetly over his paunch. "That's the plan," I told her. "Be careful, okay?"

"You too," she replied. "Over and out."

Quickly unwrapping the rest of my gear, I pulled the wet strands of my hair back and retied them behind my head. I pulled the shirt back on, pocketed the extra ammo, and then grabbed the pistol. As I did, we were joined in succession by Carl, then April, then Marna. That was five volunteers. Alejandro brought up the rear, surfacing with a small splash. "Heavens above!" he spat as he grabbed the edges. "I thought that tunnel would go on forever."

"All right, that's everyone," I said, my voice low. Around me, everyone was getting ready, unwrapping their gear and trying to squeeze the water out of their clothes. "We don't have time to scout this one, so I want you treat any man with a weapon as a hostile and drop him—quietly. Kill if you have to. These are Porteque guys, according to Mags, and I doubt anyone will miss them. The mission is simple: go to the fourth floor, shoot the guys in the window, and take their place to fire on the men attacking

Mags. Any questions?"

"Can I get out of the water first?" Alejandro looked up at me from where he held himself up by his elbows, his lower torso still in the water. I quickly reached down to help him up and out.

"Time is of the essence," I reminded him as he slid his hands over his wet clothes, trying to force the water out. The entire floor was covered in a puddle by the time we were finished. I gave Alejandro a moment to catch his breath, then crept over to the door, gently testing the handle.

I turned my flashlight down a few clicks, and then opened the door slightly. Gunfire rattled, the sound muted by the building around us, but the hallway before us remained silent. I pulled the door open a few more inches and poked my head out, taking a quick glance. The hallway stood empty and straight, only one other door within view of my flashlight.

"I'm heading in," I whispered over my shoulder, and then opened the door more fully, moving into the hallway. The other door led to the electrical system, but the room was completely empty, and I closed it again, moving farther down the hallway as the flashlight slowly revealed it to me. The passageway finally stopped at a small landing of narrow, switchback stairs, heading up.

As soon as the rest of the team had gathered, I began to climb, keeping my footsteps as silent as possible. I approached the ground-level landing slowly. It was completely dark, and there was no sign of flashlights or any other sources of light, so I felt confident keeping my flashlight on.

The light revealed a door, and I dialed the flashlight even lower, until it was only emitting a small glow, as I moved up to it. The door was locked, so I stepped to one side, wordlessly pointing at the lock.

Harry pushed his way through, rummaging in his pockets, and slipped the lock-picking device into the keyhole just under the knob. The machine whirred softly, falling silent as the lock clicked after a few seconds. Harry pulled it out and tucked it back into his pocket, and I motioned for him to move back down the stairs as I ever so slowly peeled back the door, trying to ensure that it wouldn't creak, and peered through the small gap.

Red light flooded the crack, and as I peeked through it, I could see it flicker, indicating something was burning. I pulled it open a little more.

Double glass doors stood twenty feet away, just past another set of concrete stairs heading up. Outside, two men stood with their backs to me and the door, staring down at the streets. I could see the straps cutting across their backs, and one shifted slightly, the long muzzle of his rifle coming into view. I ducked back, swinging the door shut extra gently to avoid even the slightest click, and took a moment to think.

"We've got two men on the other side of double glass doors that lead to the street. The opening for the stairs is directly behind them. There's light coming in off the street, but that only works for us now, when their backs are turned—it works against us if they turn around."

Everyone leaned forward as I whispered, listening intently. Cruz raised two of his fingers, meeting my eyes. "The stairs—is there an open side? A banister?"

I blinked, trying to remember my split-second picture. "Yes."

"Then we use the shadows and climb up and over the banister," he said easily, a smile twisting the corner of his lips. "Limited exposure time, and we take advantage of the shadows, right?"

"I'm not sure I'm that spry anymore," whispered Alejandro.

Cruz's smile grew, and he grabbed Alejandro on the shoulder. "It would be an honor to give you a boost, my friend."

I looked at Cruz, wanting to find a flaw in his plan, but unable to do so. Yes, it involved a little risk, but it was actually minimal compared to trying to sneak past the guards, or even trying to take them out.

"Sorry, Alejandro," I said, meeting his eyes. "But Cruz is going to give you a hand."

Alejandro hesitated, and then shoved his gun into the wet leather holster on his hip. "Let's get it over with," he grumbled. We opened the door wide enough to let him and Cruz slip through, keeping low to their stomachs. I watched as they crept down toward the doors, using the shadow to mask their approach. Cruz gripped Alejandro and rose, and within seconds, Alejandro had rolled over the banister and dropped onto the stairs with barely a sound. Cruz scrambled up behind him, and the two crept up the stairs, disappearing from sight.

"Next two," I whispered, allowing Harry and Marna to go through the door. I watched them both as they slipped over the banister and onto the steps. There was a tense moment when I heard Harry's shoe slap on the ground, but the guards continued to watch the street, their backs to us.

April, Carl, and I went last. I covered Carl while he helped April up, and then climbed up after her, using the banister as a handhold and the steps, appropriately, as a foothold. I kept my gun in my hand as I climbed, rolling over the thin banister and onto my hands and toes on the stairs. I moved up them quickly, passing through the red light that illuminated a section of them and slipping onto the next landing.

Alejandro helped me up, and I noticed a pair of legs sticking out of the doorframe just behind his left shoulder, illuminated by candles placed strategically around the hallway. The man on the floor was slowly being dragged deeper in. "There was a guard. Cruz shot him. Harry and Marna are checking the apartments."

The feet disappeared completely into the doorway, and then Cruz stepped out. He wiped his fingers on his chest and pulled the door closed. "That room is filled with ammunition," he whispered as soon as he noticed me watching him. "We should stock up if we can."

"We think this floor is being used as a warehouse," whispered Marna from behind me, and I turned to stare at her as she and Harry approached, her gun out but pointed at the floor. "There's a ton of supplies in each apartment, food, water… There's an entire room filled with toilet paper."

"So stupid," muttered Harry.

Alejandro huffed, his beard twitching. "You kidding, boyo? If it were the end of the world, I'd trade the lot of you for a double-ply roll."

I managed to keep from laughing. I couldn't afford to let my guard down. "Not the place," I said gruffly. "If this floor is clear, then let's get to the next floor. Cruz, take point."

The dark-haired man nodded, and moved past me to the set of stairs above the ones we'd just climbed. I followed him closely, my gun back in my hand. The landing at the top was clear—at least from our angle—but I remained vigilant as we crept up the stairs.

Cruz threw up a hand across my chest, and I froze. He craned his neck, then held up one finger, indicating one guard. I gave him a thumbs-up, and then he sprang into motion, sprinting up the stairs, not bothering to silence his steps anymore. I followed at his heels, keeping my gun trained on the area just left of the landing as it came into view. I fired at the leg I saw a second later, the shot puffing softly out in the quiet we'd established, and then again as the guard fell, hitting him just over his left eye. Continuing up the stairs, I kept my gun trained on the hall as I cleared the steps.

Cruz knelt next to the man on the floor, pulling his weapons from him. I motioned for Alejandro and Harry to check the rooms, while I pushed past Cruz, aiming for the corner room. I pushed open the door, and froze when my light cut across a long pair of bare feminine legs, bruised and dirty. I raised the light a little higher, revealing dirty underwear, a thin pink tank top, and finally a woman's face, her hands raised up to block out the light. Her back was to the wall, and she was sitting on a thin, dirty mattress. I immediately lowered the light out of respect.

"Please," she pleaded softly into the darkness. "Don't."

Every instinct in me was screaming for me to help that woman. "Viggo?" said Harry from behind me, and I held up my hand.

"I'm going to get you out of here," I announced softly. "Wait."

I stepped back and pulled the door closed, wishing I could block out the vision of her bruised arms and tangled, knotted hair. "Viggo," Harry said, "there are—"

"Women on this floor," I finished for him, and he nodded, his face pale. I felt a seething anger come across me, settling into my bones and muscles, disguised as calm—the heavy calm that promised death. It gave me a clarity of purpose, a vision of a future that would make the Porteque gang suffer for what they were doing. "This ends now. I go first, then Cruz. April, you bring up the rear."

The middle-aged woman nodded, the freckles spread liberally

across her cheeks and nose bright in contrast with her pale skin, but her eyes held a hard edge in them. I could tell she was feeling the same anger.

I moved forward, my pistol in my hand. Heading up the stairwell, I saw a man's bald head come into view. His eyes widened as he saw me, his mouth opening to warn the others, but I pointed and pulled the trigger, ending his warning before he could even draw breath. Red spattered on the wall behind him, and I kept moving. I heard something drop in the hall to the left, but I kept my eye on the partially open door in the corner and the muzzle flashes coming from it. I pushed the door open and stepped inside.

Two men were at either side of the room, one kneeling, the other standing. Both were firing their guns out the window, and I noticed the night vision goggles strapped to both of their heads.

I shot the one standing first, in the back, before he could even turn, and he dropped. The man opposite him started to turn, and I squeezed the trigger again, feeling no remorse as he dropped lifelessly to the ground. These men weren't men, and didn't deserve to be recognized as such.

I moved back toward the hall, where Cruz was waiting for me, his gun trained down the hallway. I waved April over from where she was perched a few steps short of the landing, and made room for her as she moved over to us. Gunfire came from the four other doors down the hall, two on the left, and two more facing the street.

Holding up four fingers, I used hand signals to explain that I wanted two people to a door. They partnered up, and as a unit, we crept down the hall. Cruz and Carl peeled off first, stopping by the door on the left, just past the stairwell. Then April and Harry stopped, this time on the right. Alejandro and Marna held up just shy of the right, and I took the corner apartment on the left. I squatted in front of it and counted down on my fingers, starting at three.

On one, I threw the door open and quickly fired two rounds. One man dropped, but a second squeezed the trigger as he turned, his gun going off loudly as it fired into the wall. I dropped to my belly, shouting "Duck!" as the bullets tore overhead, and I squeezed the trigger twice.

The man cried out as my bullet struck him in the chest, his arms spreading as he tumbled forward. His weapon continued to fire as he fell, coming to a stop only after he hit the floor and it skidded away a few feet. I held my gun up and searched the room.

"Clear!" I shouted.

A chorus of 'clear' met my ears, revealing the apartment building had thin walls. I slowly got up on my feet, looking around, searching for injuries. "Everyone okay?" I asked.

Cruz gazed about, and then nodded, wiping the sweat off his forehead. "We are fine, my friend," he said with a smile.

"Any enemy left alive?"

April wiped her mouth with the back of her hand and shook her head, her eyes unremorseful. "No."

"Excellent. Everyone pick a room and get ready—we're going to give Mags a little overdue backup. April, take a rifle and cover the stairs from the top landing. Alejandro and Cruz, get in the windows and fire a few shots, just to make sure everyone below thinks their people are still up there. Just don't aim for our people. I'll let Mags know the same. Carl, Marna, go downstairs and get us as much ammo as you can carry for the rifles left in this room, then get back up here. I'll be in the corner apartment."

I gave the orders rapidly, feeling the familiarity of it return. We didn't have much time before the rest of the Porteque gang was in place for their ambush on the streets, and I wanted to make sure to flip this little trap on its head.

I moved up to the window that had a view of the street below. Looking around, I found the car Tim had sheltered behind, and though I couldn't see him, I couldn't see anybody else in that area either—definitely no sprawled bodies. That was a good sign. Hopefully, he was still hunkered down beneath his cover, waiting for the right moment to escape.

"We're in their roost," I transmitted to Mags as I set up my position, using the wall next to the window as cover. "There are no more enemies up here at this time. Don't shoot at us; we're going to hit their men once they start moving toward you. I want you and your teams to start pulling back to the stairs. Come around the opposite building through the alley and then come right for us. Use the park for cover, and we'll give you cover from above."

"Roger," she said, as gunshots sounded from Alejandro and Cruz's room. I picked up the rifle lying over the floor, next to the man I'd killed, and cradled it against my shoulder, taking a moment to check the magazines. There were a few more on the table next to the window, so I checked them too.

I took a few shots, but then noticed a large group below as they began to move out, heading for the park in low, crouching runs. "Get ready," I transmitted, pulling the rifle up. "Fire on them and break them up. Shoot to kill—we don't need any of these guys running around." I thought of the woman in that room and gritted my teeth. "Ever."

The men below began to creep farther into the park, spreading out and moving silently. I saw another group of men break away and head right, cutting across the street and using cars for cover. They were closest to me, so I angled my sights toward them.

"Everyone ready?"

"Ready," announced Cruz.

"More than ready," added Alejandro, his voice grim.

"Good—fire."

CHAPTER 28

Violet

"Amber, hold up. I got a big group emerging from the building just around the corner from your position."

I tracked the small crowd silently from above, watching as it continued to grow, their heat signature becoming larger and stronger. The steady stream of bodies leaving the building stopped—I had lost count at about fifty people, as the bodies blended together on the scanner, but it was probably between that and a hundred—and I held my breath. The orange blobs at the head of the group turned right, and I cursed.

"Amber, they are heading your way," I said, swinging the drone around and heading back toward her. "You've got maybe a minute to hide."

"You want us to go into the buildings?" she asked, her mic popping.

"No," I said, remembering Henrik's warning. It had worked for Viggo's group, but I didn't want to take any more chances. I ground my teeth, thinking. "Up the fire escapes," I said. "As fast as you can until my mark, then slowly."

"Roger," she replied with a grunt, and I pulled the drone to a stop above the intersection, watching.

I tilted the nose of the drone up some, exposing more of the street to the sensors, and watched as the crowd grew closer, marking their speed closely. I waited until the last second, trying to buy Amber's team time to get as high off the ground as possible. I hoped she hadn't put her entire team on one single fire escape.

"Now," I transmitted, swinging the drone around and heading down Amber's street, the mob of people just reaching the corner. I maneuvered the craft higher as I moved, and slowed to a stop when I caught sight of Amber's team spread out on the fire escapes, slowly climbing up. They were on the same side of the street, but split between two different fire escapes, a narrow alley separating them.

Amber was squatting in the corner of the third-floor balcony, her gun trained on the street below, while her team crept by her, heading straight for the fifth story. "I'm thinking I'm just going to do this Violet-style," Amber whispered softly, and I smiled nervously.

"What's Violet-style?" I asked, rotating the drone around to do another sweep of the buildings across the street.

"Running pell-mell across the rooftops in order to escape a mob."

I chuckled ruefully and shook my head, switching from the thermal scan to the night vision and maneuvering the drone around so I could peer through the windows of the buildings her team clambered on. Maybe I was being too thorough, but with the thermal scanner unable to reliably read through building walls, I was not taking any chances.

"Owen really loves to exaggerate that story," I replied, my eyes searching the green image on the screen for anything out of the ordinary.

"Hey, you aren't the only one suffering in that story," she said testily, then affected a deeper, dramatic voice. "'Amber was barely conscious, her life slowly draining out of her with every step we took. We were surrounded by the enemy, and I knew that if we were caught, she would surely die.'"

I bit back a laugh as I shifted to the next building to repeat the process. Then we fell silent, and I didn't say anything, in case she was moving or doing something that required her concentration. After a moment, she asked, "How's he doing?"

My eyes flicked over to where Owen was sitting on the stairs, his back pressed against the wall, and frowned. "He's… He's here."

I moved up to the next windows, letting silence fill the line. "I really want to hate him, you know," Amber admitted softly.

I said the only thing that came to mind. "I know."

Blinking at the screen, I leaned closer and squinted my eyes, trying to discern what I had just seen. It had looked like a flash of movement, which wasn't uncommon, but there was something about it that was weird. It hadn't been dark… It had been light. I peered a little closer and stroked a finger across the screen, running my fingers over the thin vertical line that was now jutting out the window. I switched over to thermal, and blinked when the red-hot body of a person lit up, standing just behind the wall next to the window. I realized what that vertical white line was— it was light shining brightly off of a silver muzzle, reflecting the light of the moon.

"Amber, adjacent building, two o'clock from your position.

Individual is armed and pointing at your position."

"Most of my team's up on the roof. The civilians just passed us and are moving away. We'll be clear in—"

Whatever she said I lost as the door to the command room I sat in slammed open and the basement went dark.

"What the—" I heard Owen utter, then he grunted, and I heard another clatter and a slam. Almost in the same moment, my chair was pulled out from under me, and I fell, hard, on my rump. Pain jolting my body, I scrambled forward on hands and knees, under the table that held the screen. Then it seemed that things were flying all around me.

I heard the flutter of papers followed by the crash of something breaking. Ducking under my table, I was almost hit by something heavy as it crashed to the floor in front of me, skidding off to one side. Henrik shouted, but the sound of rushing wind grew, and I became aware of a breeze that seemed to fill the basement.

"Cody?" I asked, daring to lean out slightly from under the table, and then ducking quickly back in as something long seemed to come right for me. There was a hard metallic thunk on the side of the table, making my shoulders hunch for fear that it had somehow broken through. The breeze stopped, and the door at the top of the stairs slammed closed. I heard a sharp click, and then there was silence.

My heart beat hard against my ribcage, and I pressed my hand against it, fearing that it was too loud in the sudden silence of the room. I waited a few seconds, my eyes finally growing used to the darkness. There was light coming from somewhere. Likely the kitchen lights were on, and shining through the cracks in the closed basement door. I hurried out from under the desk.

"Violet?" Amber's voice made me start in alarm.

"Amber, are you safe?" I asked.

"Yes, but the—"

"Hold position and keep the line clear. Something's happened." I was sure my words were going to worry her, but there was nothing to do about it now. I couldn't report anything when I knew nothing. "Henrik? Owen?"

"I'm here." Henrik's voice came from the left of me, and I moved around the table, blinking in the dimness, to find the older man leaning back on the floor with his hand on his side. I knelt down next to him.

"Are you okay?" I asked, moving his hand away.

"I'm fine," he rasped, although he let me pull up his shirt to check on his wound. The bright white bandage taped just left of his bellybutton was stained with blood, and I carefully peeled back the tape, revealing the stitches underneath.

From what I could see in the dim light, one of his stitches had popped out, but the wound was far enough healed that we could fix it with some butterfly tape. I pressed the bandage back down, leaning into the tape to make it stick a little bit longer, and nodded. "It's an easy fix," I said. "Can you get up?"

"It's a gut wound, girl," he grumped, but he let me help him up.

"Violet?" Owen's voice was a rasp in the darkness, and I turned my head toward the stairs leading up to the door, studying them in the orange light creeping in through the door's seams. Something opposite of the stairs moved, and I saw Owen's shadow emerge from the darkness in the corner, lumbering toward the table. "Are you okay?"

"I'm fine," I whispered. "Are you?"

"Got the wind knocked out of me. Something just slammed into my chest."

"It must have been Cody," I breathed.

Owen leaned on the table with one hand, his other wrapped around his stomach, cradling it. "I know," he replied, his tone resigned. "I'm sorry."

"Desmond's the one who's going to be sorry," I muttered as I moved over to the stairs, picking my way across the debris-ridden floor. I climbed to the top of the stairs, and then felt around the stone for the light switch, clicking it on.

Much to my relief, the bulb immediately switched on, and I glanced down the stairs toward the chaos of the room—papers and equipment everywhere, a length of pipe lying on the ground next to the desk, the drone controls knocked over, and various pieces of the unfinished basement room having been strewn about randomly. Turning back to the door, I twisted the handle, but it refused to turn.

"Who's got the keys?" I asked.

"They were on the table a minute ago," said Henrik, sinking to one knee and beginning to sift through the papers that had been scattered there.

"Were those the ones that also had the keys to Desmond's chains?" Owen asked suddenly.

I felt a splash of fear and immediately hit the transmit button, cutting to the channel that connected us to our other houses. "Lacey?" I called for the guard who'd been stationed at Desmond's prison.

Henrik and Owen looked up at me and then exchanged looks. "How would Cody know where we stashed her?" Henrik asked. "I don't think we talked about it in front of him…"

"Children always have a knack for hearing information they shouldn't be hearing," I said, thinking about Tim when he was young. "We shouldn't have let him wander around, even with his guard... Oh God." I pressed my fingers together again. "Lacey?"

Silence and the occasional pop of static filled the line. "Everyone, change frequency to Delta nine," Henrik announced on the command channel.

"Does anyone have a lock-picking tool?" I asked, although I knew they didn't.

"No," said Henrik, heaving back on to his feet.

"Damn it!" exploded Owen. "Right now, he's probably getting her free, and then she is going to go tell the Matrians about our base, ruin our plans for the water treatment plant, and continue this horrible game she's playing! Why couldn't you just have executed her?!"

"Because she threatened the boys, Owen! And if there was even a remote chance she wasn't lying, we couldn't risk it!"

Silence met my statement, and a glance at Owen nodding angrily revealed that he had already known this—he just hated the feeling of impotence it brought. I could understand that. I didn't envy the turmoil that was running even hotter inside him than it was inside me, but I didn't have time to entertain it. We had to get out of this room. I had to check on Morgan and stop Desmond. If she'd escaped, she now knew the location of one of our newly found bases. And as much as he would hate it, I had to get Cody back from her.

"Violet?"

Viggo's voice in my ear made my thoughts tumble apart, and I turned, expecting and wanting him to be right behind me, even though I knew he wasn't.

"Viggo? Are you okay? Did you make it through the Porteque territory?"

"We're almost there. We've got a few more issues to clear up, but so far, everyone is fine."

"That's the best news I've heard all night." The little reminder that the men I loved most in the world were still all right made things feel a little less grim. I was going to ignore the strain in Viggo's voice, until I had a chance to extract the whole story from him. *If* I did. Right now, I was just glad, so glad, he and everyone were safe.

"Glad to hear you're okay," said Henrik, echoing my thoughts, and I looked over at where he was leaning against the table, his hand still pressed to his side. "We've got problems here. Cody came in and wrecked a bunch of stuff, and we're currently locked in the basement. He's got the keys, and we think he went for Desmond."

Silence met Henrik's statement.

"*Cody* got her out?" Viggo said, his voice coarse with disbelief. "How? We've been sedating him."

"We don't have all the details," I said. "All we know is it was Cody, and he was using his enhancement. The place is a mess."

"Violet?" Amber's voice cut in softly. "I'm not sure if this is the best time to tell you this, but your drone is dead. It slammed into the wall of a building."

"What?" I raced down the stairs again, my eyes finding the heavy briefcase-like remote control a few feet from the table, propped up on its side. I rolled it over and lifted the heavy lid a few more inches, revealing spider web cracks in the screen, cutting black lines across the screen that was supposed to display the feed, which was now showing only red static. I exhaled slowly and closed the lid. "Crap."

"Use the roofs, Amber," Ms. Dale said over the radio, her voice sternly practical. "You're in a pretty dense part of town, structurally speaking, and it'll give you the advantage of elevation." It was a good suggestion, and now more than ever we needed the groups to get to their rendezvous points on time.

I sifted through the debris lining the floor and found a few paperclips. Straightening the rounded edges, I climbed back up the stairs and knelt in front of the door, slipping one into the keyhole on the doorknob. I started to unfold the second one, when I realized that I couldn't pick the lock with a cast on my hand. Of course I couldn't. And even with all the training I'd been doing, I didn't think my left hand was going to be up to the job.

I waved Owen over and let him take my spot in front of the door. Picking a lock was difficult in the tensest of times, and doing it with a paperclip wasn't easy. Minutes ticked by as he fiddled with it. Henrik stayed below, giving orders over the radio as he sifted through the papers, mechanically trying to organize them.

The doorknob rattled and I looked up, barely hearing Amber's voice in my ear. Owen pulled his gun and stood, motioning for me to move past him down the steps. I did so just as the rattle stopped, and then there was a distinct jingle of keys. The lock clicked, and the door swung open, revealing Morgan, one hand cupped over her eyes. "You guys okay?"

"Morgan," I said, taking a step closer. "Are you okay? What happened?"

Morgan looked away and then slowly lowered her hand, revealing the quickly purpling flesh under her brow, the mark wrapping around her orbital socket. "Cody blindsided me. One minute I thought he was sleeping, the next thing I knew, *pow.*

Violet… as soon as my head stopped spinning, I took off after them down the road in the car. I got there just as she was pulling away. I would've kept chasing them, but I needed to see if you guys were wounded. I couldn't handle it if one of you bled out while I chased down Desmond."

I took in a deep breath through my teeth. "Did you see Lacey while you were there?"

Morgan's face went from weary to appalled, and she shook her head wildly. "Oh no, I didn't even think about it. I'm so sorry—I hope she's okay."

"It's all right," I said, though we both knew that if it wasn't, there wasn't much we could do about it now. Morgan bit her lip and nodded as though trying to convince herself.

"Violet," she said, "one more thing. Desmond was driving the truck. With Solomon in it."

I was unprepared for the flash of dizzying anger that coursed through me and left me feeling burning white and hot. "What?"

"They took the truck—" Morgan began, wrongly interpreting my question.

"I know, I know," I snapped, unable to stop the current of flame that was eating up my insides. "She'll use him if she has to. She'll turn him on anyone who gets in her way." I turned and leveled a look at Henrik. "I want to go after her."

Henrik looked unsurprised. "Guys, Violet wants to go after Desmond. We have just learned she took Solomon in her escape."

There was a pause on the line. "Do you think Desmond will try to jeopardize the mission?" Viggo kept his voice calm and even, but I knew he didn't want me going into the city without having a really good reason.

"I do. I'll bet she gleaned that we were going to target the water treatment plant, and if there's something going on, she'll head there to warn them—and because she has a vehicle, there's a chance she could get there before our people."

"If she even goes there, but Violet, if she doesn't…" Amber trailed off. She had unwittingly helped me to understand another angle to this argument: if Desmond didn't go for it, then it meant nothing was happening at the plant to begin with, and we could call off the attack and focus on freeing the city completely.

"We *have* to go, regardless of where she goes. By the time she gets to the city, she will know our location, or something close enough to it to make life bad for us. And we have to get Cody and Solomon back from her before she can put them on the Benuxupane and use them for her plans again."

"No offense, but Cody made his choice," Amber said, and I couldn't help but snap.

"We have no idea what Desmond said to him in that room, but we do know that he is a traumatized little boy, suffering from abuse and neglect. Desmond has a drug that he feels he needs in order to… stop feeling the way he does about all of the horrible stuff that happened to him. And you want to blame him for that? Blame her, for making him take it in the first place, and then convincing him it was a good thing he was doing. You can give up on him if you want, but I'm not ready to."

I didn't mean to become so passionate, but the whole situation made me quake with anger. Desmond escaping was a dash to our hopes—but it was almost expected, almost a relief to be rid of the burden of her unwanted presence and the threat that what she'd said about the boys was true. But to force Cody and Solomon back into their lives of being used as tools? I couldn't let that happen. I hadn't wanted to go into the city in this condition.

It very likely could kill me. But if there was a chance of stopping Desmond from interfering with our plans, I had to take it. Everyone else was busy with the mission. It had to be me.

The other people on the line seemed to take my shout as all the convincing they needed.

"Owen's going with you, obviously," said Viggo softly. "But you need more people if you're going after her. Who's left?"

"Morgan," I said, and I turned to where she still stood on the landing, looking up at her. She hesitated, her eyes flicking over to Owen, and then Henrik, before nodding.

"Lynne will want to go too," she said softly.

"—and Lynne as well," I transmitted. "We've still got one of Ashabee's special cars. We'll gas it up and track her. But we've got to go now—we've already wasted too much time."

Henrik met my gaze and nodded. "Go," he said. "I can give you my mobile comm set, with the glove, and use the headset you were using with the drone. I'll send someone out to check on Lacey."

"Thanks." I nodded to Owen. "Get whatever you need and meet in the car. Morgan—"

"I'll go get Lynne," she said, turning and leaving the room at a run. I raced after her, my mind compiling a rapid list of what I needed. We hadn't had much time to begin with… and now we had even less.

CHAPTER 29

Viggo

I fired another round at a group of cars that several men had scrambled behind, picking them out using the night vision goggles I had scavenged from one of the dead gang members. I pushed them back from the building, trying to keep as many of them as possible from getting to the doors before Mags got there. When we'd begun firing on the Porteque gang members from their own building, the intersection had erupted into chaos—I'd seen fighting between the members well before they'd even thought to fire back at us, and the sight gave me a savage pleasure.

The gun clicked empty, and I ejected the magazine. In the room beside me, Alejandro continued to fire. I heard a rifle go off in the hallway and gritted my teeth.

"Report!" I roared, into the microphone and down the hall at once.

"Tim's on the move, as are we. Entering the park."

"Two down on the stairs."

April and Mags spoke at the same time, but I picked out what was said simply by context as I slid a new magazine into place, my eyes tracking Mags' group's progress down the sidewalk in the park below. My eyes flew right as I saw something shift on the building across from us, and I pressed the stock of my gun into my shoulder, firing in short, controlled bursts at the rooftop several hundred feet below.

"Marna and I took out the group trying to flank us on the left. She is an amazing shot. Tells me she had a good teacher." I acknowledged Cruz's report, not having time to really register the compliment, just satisfied they were holding their own over there. My rounds streaked red, giving the goggles a bit more light, and I readjusted and fired another burst, watching the man who had been creeping up on the edge of the building jerk and fall. I stared at the shadows for a second, looking for movement, and then glanced at Mags again.

"We got guns out front," she shouted into the mic, and I saw her leap back a few steps, bright white flashes on the screen making her disappear and reappear. She was firing, as were several of the group around her, creating havoc in my vision.

"I'm sending a few people down to help you," I replied, disconnecting and looking at Alejandro. "Get down there and take one from each room… and April. You'll be in charge until you get to Mags. Take out the guys who are pinning them down, and get our team into the building."

My main channel beeped, and I quickly switched over while Alejandro moved out of the room.

"Viggo, I'm in position," Ms. Dale said. "What's your status?"

Before replying, I fired another few rounds at the car. I must've gotten too close for comfort, because the Porteque members behind the car were running, and a little bit of satisfaction grew in me. "We're two blocks away. Mags and her team are in a firefight, but we've got the advantage on them, and we'll be able to control the situation and get there soon."

"There isn't a lot of time—"

"I know. But this needs to be done too. I'll be there." I fired at the men again, two falling while the other two made it out of my sight. Switching over to the team channel, I pressed my fingers together. "It's going quiet down there. Anyone have visual on any targets?"

"No," replied Cruz over the comm, which was good, considering he was two apartments down. Even with the thin walls, I doubted I could hear him over the sound of continuous gunfire. "They are dead or have fled."

"Not quite yet," I said. "Alejandro's heading down to handle the people in front of the building." My eyes returned to Mags and her team, huddled down low behind the brick half-wall that surrounded the park.

"I'm already down here, boyo," Alejandro replied in my ear, and I heard the *pop pop pop* of the guns below suddenly pick up and increase. Through the goggles, I saw Mags and her team start firing, the sound rising to a steady cadence for a moment, and then falling silent.

"Street's cleared," Alejandro said, and I relaxed a little, watching as Mags and her team raced for the glass doors below me and out of my sight. I pulled off the goggles and set them down by the window. "We got a few scrapes and bruises," the older man continued, "but nobody's been shot."

"Resupply with ammo on the second floor," I said, pressing my fingers together. "I need four volunteers willing to stay behind and defend the position. I'm not just leaving a group of unarmed women in a city that's tearing itself apart, so we'll free them, find them some clothes, and arm them. For the volunteers, that means missing out on the showdown at the plant, but hey— this is the first taste of battle, and it's okay to admit it if you can't handle it. Now, hopefully that doesn't mean *all* of you will race to take one of the volunteer positions..."

I heard Harry give a loud laugh in the other room, glad that it could ease the tension a little, in spite of what had just happened. I hoped other people who had heard it laughed as well, because that would help soften the blow that followed. "We have no time to rest, people. I'm sorry for that, but everyone is waiting for us at that plant. Once we get there, things are going to start immediately, and it'll be a lot like this, possibly even worse. And I know it's scary. I feel it—we all do. But we have a chance, a very real chance, to save this city, and show Elena that we are no longer running! This is where we make our stand. This is where we show her we can stop her. Let's put a little fear in *her* heart for once."

It was hard to tell how my speech went over, considering I was all alone in the room, but as I came out into the hall, Cruz was lounging against the doorframe to his room, one foot planted on the wall, his rifle balanced over his knee. "That was some speech," he said with a twisted grin. "Very motivating."

The way he said it made me suddenly doubt myself. I stared at him for a minute, and then moved downstairs, the compunction to immediately free those women overriding everything else for the moment. I'd ordered Gregory to help find the volunteers needed to hold the building for a few hours before we could come back for them. Hopefully.

Margot was exiting the corner room, pulling the door closed

behind her, when I came down. She gave me a small smile. "That was a good speech," she said softly. "It almost makes me feel bad about volunteering to stay behind."

"I think that's a good idea," I said. "This has been…"

"A very different experience than I thought it would be," Margot elegantly supplied, her mouth warm but her eyes grim. "And I can apparently give a repeat performance." It took a second for her meaning to sink in, and when it did, I sighed. She'd killed again, probably in the street when they were running across the open space toward the apartment building. Licking her lips, she looked at her hands. "I'm a mother, Viggo. I have given life, and now I've taken it away." Shaking her head, she met my eyes again. "It's not right."

I sighed and closed the distance between us, capturing her slim hand in between mine. "I meant what I said, Margot. There's no shame in staying behind. I presume Cad will be staying?"

"He will. You know how hopelessly in love with me he is."

"Well, we never said he was the brightest bulb in the—yow!" The sting from the palm of her hand on my shoulder was… impressive, and I rubbed the spot, trying to soothe away the pain. "Just kidding! Mercy!"

Margot chuckled, and I let go of her hand, glad that she'd gotten a laugh out of it. The smile chased away some of the darkness lurking in her eyes. On impulse, I pulled her against my chest and gave her a quick hug. She clung to me tightly for a moment, and then let me go, sniffling. "Please take care of yourself," she said, reaching up to smooth down my shirt. "I have such a good wedding planned for you and Violet."

I chuckled, then nodded. Glancing at the doors in the hall, my smile slipped, and I sighed heavily. "You need any help with the women the Porteque guys were... keeping prisoner?"

Margot gave me a look—one that told me I should know better—and shook her head. "Viggo, a man going into those rooms is not going to be well received right now, even if he is setting them free. Some of them are so drugged up they can barely speak. They've all been tied up and..." She trailed off, her eyes drifting down. "It's just better if you go. We'll handle it—stop wasting time with me."

I let her push me toward the stairs, and after one last goodbye, I headed down. Mags and Alejandro were on the second floor, where the stockpiled supplies had been kept, watching carefully as ammo was being distributed, magazines refilled.

I slapped my empty one down on the table next to Gregory as I went by, and he didn't miss a beat as he continued to slide bullet after bullet into the chamber. "You can do it yourself, Croft," he said as he tapped the magazine and handed it back to the owner.

"Didn't put them there for you to do, Miller," I shot back, and he laughed.

"Arthur and Marna volunteered," said Mags hurriedly. "So did—"

"Margot and Cad," I finished for her, trying to speed things along. "I ran into her on the steps. We almost ready to go?"

Mags smiled and pulled out her map, tapping her finger on our position. "After you left, I realized there was another good reason to go after this building in particular," she exclaimed. "We can just cut straight across here"—her fingers indicated—"using the alleys. They're not on the maps, but I know they are there. Two blocks, Viggo, and we're there."

"What about the Porteque guys?" I asked.

"The ones who got away will seek shelter within other

buildings, and the others will avoid the streets until they know what's going on. Either way, it's two blocks, and practically a straight shot. We should take it."

I studied the map and then nodded. "Let's do it."

Moving back over to the table, I blinked as I picked up my magazines, the rounds packed in them. Gregory smirked as his fingers continued to move, and after a moment, I slipped them into my pocket and clapped him on the shoulder. "Thanks. Almost done?"

"Four more and we're good," he said, tossing a completed magazine into a duffel bag on the floor beside him. "I'll meet everyone on the ground floor."

I exited the room, practically plowing into Cad as he stepped onto the top step. "Hey, did—"

"I know you're staying," I said. "Margot told me—and I'm glad for it. Just be careful, okay?"

"Of course. Good luck at the plant."

We exchanged a brief hug, and then I moved downstairs. Mags was already waiting by the door, a crowd of our men behind her, filling the hall. She surveyed the street, her blue eyes flicking up to me as I slowly pushed through the crowd, angling for the young man standing at her side.

Tim beamed up at me as I reached out to gently ruffle his hair. "You okay?" I asked. "You had me a little worried with that superhero thing… But I've gotta admit, it was pretty awesome."

"I sit. Good duck." His reply was flippant, but I knew he had been a little rattled.

"You did a good job, Tim. I mean that… Just next time, wait for me, eh?"

"No promises," Tim said, and I sighed. I often forgot that Tim and Violet shared the same trait for being headstrong and stupidly brave. I was going to have to keep my eye on both of them from here on out.

"How's it look?" I asked Mags.

"Just waiting for the all clear from the fourth floor," she replied.

I studied the street through the glass doors, looking past the bullet-riddled bodies and the torches still burning on their sides on the black street, to the park across from it. It offered plenty of cover. If I were lying in wait to shoot someone, I'd do it there.

"Park is clear," announced Cad through the bud, and I heard people passing out the message to those who didn't have comms. Then a beep at the command channel had me switching once again, hoping it wasn't Ms. Dale telling me they were going to start without us.

"Guys, we got a big truck rolling up on the guard post," said a less-familiar feminine voice instead, and I recognized it as Tasha, the Liberator who headed the small group we'd left to hold the guard post and cover our escape route, just in case. "It's coming up fast."

I checked my watch and cursed. It had been twenty minutes, give or take, since Desmond had escaped, and we had anticipated she might go for the nearest guard post, which was incidentally the one we'd captured—the worst way to puncture a hole in our defense.

"Roger," said Henrik's voice. "Violet is behind her by a few minutes, so just fend her off. Be careful."

"We got this," Tasha replied confidently, and I had to clench my teeth together to prevent myself from saying anything for fear it would make that confidence diminish. Moments passed with no update, and then thirty seconds… Even though I wasn't there, I felt tense for them. I just hoped they had stopped her.

Forty-five seconds, then a minute… Still nothing. That wasn't a good sign. Mags was raising her eyebrows at me, waiting for the sign for the final dash to our rendezvous, but I held on a minute longer, hoping something would come through.

"Tasha, report," Henrik's voice cut in finally. Silence greeted us both. I held my hand up to my earbud, clenching my teeth together as Henrik repeated Tasha's name.

His voice was resigned as he said to everyone, "With no response from Tasha, I am ordering us to go to tango foxtrot. I'll let Drew know we changed the main channel."

A sinking feeling in my chest, I acknowledged his order and then switched channels, first to inform my team, then to check in with the rest of command.

Finally, I looked around at my team. "Desmond is coming up on the plant fast, guys," I said, both to those around me and over the team radio, trying to keep the worry from my voice. "She might already have taken out one of our guard posts. So we need to get to the rendezvous posthaste. Let's make it count."

I gave the signal to go, and Mags leapt out the door of the building ahead of me, her face grim. She took the steps two at a time, and I kept close on her heels as she moved down the street, hooking a left into the narrow alley between the apartment we'd cleared and the adjacent building. It was a tight fit. I had to move sideways, but we made it through, the rest of our group silently squeezing in behind us.

Mags ducked low, her weapon in her hands, and led us on, weaving through the cars on the street to the alley on the other side. I hung back, checking the buildings as the team moved past me, with Mags holding her position on the other side, clearing the windows on her side of the street before letting them continue. As soon as the last person exited the alley, I sprinted over to the other side, and then slowed to a jog as I moved past the single line of people who stood with their backs to the wall.

When the next alley opened up, there were no buildings on the street it opened onto, but rather another park, this one larger than the last one. Recalling the images Violet and Thomas had captured of the park just left of the plant, I felt a rush of appreciation toward Mags.

We crossed the empty street at a run, entering through a metal ironwork gate and heading left, following the ground's gradual slope up. The left side of this park bordered the road leading into the plant. We made our way through the dark trees and over part of a brick wall.

As soon as I saw the trees thinning, I raised my fist, ordering the group to stop. I slipped onto my belly, using my elbows and knees to move through the leaves on the ground. A road slowly came into view as I crept out of the tree line.

I looked up the hill, following the light gray line of the street as it moved several hundred feet farther up a steep incline. I could make out the top of the water treatment plant just above the horizon of the hill, and I moved back into the tree line. Once I was back with my team, I pressed my fingers together.

"We're in position," I announced on the main channel. "Ready to go when you are."

CHAPTER 30

Violet

I was sitting in the backseat, leaning in between the front two seats, my body wedged into the gap. "How far are we from the guard post?" I asked, my eyes watching the pavement as it disappeared beneath us.

Owen slowed and downshifted, expertly hooking a left down a paved road. "We're two minutes out," he replied.

I bit my lip and leaned back into the seat. From beside me, Morgan cleared her throat, and I turned toward her, surprised to find her pressed between me and the door. "Do you mind?" she asked, holding up her hand and flicking the backs of her fingers at me.

"Sorry," I said contritely, scooching over a few inches and giving the raven-haired girl some space.

"Don't worry about it," she said, her eyes drifting out the window beside her. She folded her arm over her stomach and then reached up with her other hand to press on the skin right under her bruised eye.

"Does it hurt?" I asked.

Her turquoise eyes flicked back to me, and she shifted slightly in her seat. "Like the side of my face has been tenderized, salted, turned into jerky, and then shredded right off my skull," she said after a minute.

I cringed at the graphic description, but as I reflected on it, I realized it was an accurate account of what it felt like to get punched by an enhanced human. That was a feeling I'd experienced plenty of times in my life, even before… this. "That is a really good way to describe that," I said in awe, and Morgan gave a surprised laugh.

"What's so funny?"

"Nothing," she said, scrunching her shoulders together. "Just… you didn't find that disturbing?"

"I mean, yes, but not because it was weird. It was disturbing because it was ridiculously accurate. You have a way with words."

The compliment caught her off guard, and she looked forward, considering what I had just said. "I didn't realize Cody could hit that hard," she said, seeming to ignore the emotional content of the discussion, and I let her, seeing that it was making her feel awkward.

"It's kinetic energy," Owen informed us from the front seat. "Cody's speed doubles as strength, hitting with the force in the speed he's moving at. You're lucky you were in an enclosed room with him. He could've killed you if he'd had a bigger head start."

"That sounds like Jay's super strength," I muttered.

"It's not exactly the same," replied Owen as he hooked another turn. "I think Jay's muscle fibers are woven together more tightly, giving him more strength than you and I possess. Cody's enhancement is actually more similar to Tim's—when Tim's reflexes kick in, it looks like he has enhanced speed too, but that's just because the relays between his brain and his muscles move at a significantly faster rate than most of ours do. So he just… reacts in an instant, faster than we can perceive."

"Either way, it's not doing my face any favors," Morgan sulked, still pressing her fingers to her face, and Owen chuckled.

"Don't worry, Morgan. You're still as beautiful as ever."

Just like when I'd complimented her, Morgan didn't reply, but I noticed her cheeks going darker in the dim light from the console. I looked at Owen, who was obliviously heading down the road, then back to her and the casual way she was trying to hold herself. Realization came like a bullet, and I met Morgan's eyes in the darkness.

No wonder she was so interested in what was happening with Owen. I'd thought it had to do with the fact that they had been Liberators together, but it had never occurred to me that there was something more to it. Maybe it had been hard for me to imagine anybody feeling that way about Owen, even before everything had gone down, because he'd always felt like a brother to me. But Morgan liked him. Romantically.

She held my gaze, her eyes flat, expressionless, and then turned back to the window, presenting me with a shoulder. She clearly didn't want to talk about it, which was fine. We weren't really in a place to have that conversation anyway, for so many reasons.

"Slow down, Owen," Lynne said from the passenger's seat, her voice soft. "What is that?"

An acrid smell of something burning filled my nose seconds later, and I wrinkled it in distaste. Whatever was burning wasn't wood. I leaned over to look out the window, and paused when I saw the dense haze we were driving through.

Owen hissed and jerked the wheel as an object loomed out of the darkness in front of the car, narrowly missing it. "I can't see anything in this," he spat. "What was that?"

"I think it was an overturned barricade," Morgan said.

"What is *that*?" breathed Lynne into the darkness. "Is that the guard post?"

The alarm in her voice had me crowding Morgan over so I could shove forward in between the seats again. The dense, dark gray fog began to glow red as we rolled forward, and the smoke started to thin. Owen slowed us down to a crawl as he navigated us past another two barricades—one smashed, the other over-turned—and then the smoke cleared.

At the mouth of the city, a fire raged from inside the crop harvester Cruz had used to crash through the barricades. Angry red flames engulfed the cab, black smoke roiling off the top and pouring into the sky. With the windows of the buildings on either side of it, the image looked like a face screaming in anger.

Right in front of it, resting on its side a few feet away from the burning, was the trailer we'd kept Solomon in, rolled on one side, like some offering to a dangerous god.

"Stop the car," I ordered. "I have to go look at it!"

"Are you insane?" said Lynne. "Solomon could be out!"

"Solomon could be hurt," I snapped back at her, my fingers searching blindly for the handle. I met Owen's eyes in the mirror. "You don't have to come," I told him as I successfully found and opened the door.

"Yes, I do," he said solemnly as he slid open the door and stepped out onto the pavement. "Keep it ready to go," he told

Morgan, and she slid out of the backseat to switch places with him, her face flushed but focused.

Doubt diminished my certainty as I took a step forward on the road I'd witnessed a battle on hours earlier, and I paused for a moment, fighting through it. There were so many fears I could entertain, but unless I kept moving forward, I would never know what the truth was. After what Solomon had sacrificed for me—his very sanity—I wasn't about to ignore him for the sake of convenience.

Owen shadowed me silently as we cautiously walked up the road toward the trailer, his eyes darting around the overturned barricades and past a vehicle with half the roof missing. I didn't blame him for being jumpy—I felt exposed and vulnerable in the middle of that road. The fire lit up the sky, but it created long, creeping shadows, cast by the broken things left over from the battle, which seemed to be reaching towards us. If Solomon was out there, we would step on him long before we ever saw him.

"This is where she swerved the trailer," Owen said suddenly, and I started. He held up his arm and pointed to a set of still standing barricades, set up in an L across half the road. "She took it left, and tried to hook it back around."

I saw what he was talking about. The L-shaped configuration had created a space to the left of it, but it tapered sharply back around. Desmond had smashed through many barricades by this point, and gauging by the view of the front of the cab, it had been smashed to pieces.

Honestly, I didn't care how she had done it. What I cared about was the trailer and the cargo it had been transporting. I pulled my gun out as we drew closer to the cab. With a nod at Owen, I pulled to the right and went wide, keeping my gun trained on the sideways rectangular hole where the windshield used to be.

The cab was empty, deserted, but I kept my gun on it while Owen moved close, making sure no one was still inside. "It's empty," he called, and I let out a deep breath.

"We need to check the back," I told him, moving past him along the long metal shipping container we had been keeping Solomon in. The fire roared just behind it, only a few feet away, and I could feel the heat coming off it in thick waves, making sweat break out on my forehead. "This thing is a steel oven. He could roast alive."

"Violet, slow down!" Owen said, jogging up and catching my arm. "It's my job to keep you safe, and while I knew you wouldn't make it easy, I didn't think you'd be this careless with your own safety. At least let me check the area around us first."

I exhaled and slowed down, but didn't stop. We approached the corner of the trailer's container slowly, but as it grew nearer, I realized that one door was open, the corner of it partially buried under a large mound of grass and dirt, indicating it had skidded slightly when it tipped over.

I moved around it, almost as terrified of hearing Solomon's guttural roar as I was of finding his lifeless, broken body inside— but not quite. Owen stepped in front of me as we came around the corner, keeping himself between me and the potential danger.

The trailer was empty. I stared at it, unsure of my own eyes. "I'm not sure if this makes me feel better or worse."

"It's okay for it to be both," Owen replied.

I opened my mouth, uncertain about how we could continue, when a soft keening noise drifted into my ears. It was barely audible, and I couldn't be quite certain that I'd even heard it over the roar of the fire from the harvester.

"Did you hear that?" asked Owen, his head snapping to the left, looking just past the corner of the smoking harvester and toward several barricades grouped around the edge of the building.

"I was just about to ask you," I replied, flexing my grip around my pistol. "Let's check it out."

I let him go first, trying to be considerate of his new role as my bodyguard. It felt weird to even think of him that way. After all, *I* had been the one to save all three of us at Ashabee's, and with a broken arm and a broken skull to boot. But I had resolved to make this work, for Owen's sake, and that meant compromises like this one. Sometimes.

Owen hunched over as he moved toward the sound, which was louder now—a choked, whining sound that made my heart want to cry out in sadness. He went wide as we came closer to the nearest barricade, creating distance between himself and the other side as he circled around it. I slowed my pace but didn't change trajectory.

The keening continued, and I slowly stepped around the broken edge of the barricade—and froze as I saw Solomon sitting a few feet away. He was rocking back and forth, his knees clutched to his chest, the soft sound that had caught our attention coming from his mouth.

Owen clicked on his flashlight, shining it on the ground next to Solomon, and my heart seemed to stop when I saw golden curls stained with blood. Solomon flinched, his cries cutting off as he held up his hand to shield his eyes from the flashlight. Owen shifted the beam of light a few feet away, obscuring the damaged remains of Tasha's face, much to my relief.

Solomon sniffed, gave another cry, and began rocking again.

"Did they know each other?" I whispered softly to Owen, and he nodded.

"They were friends," he said softly. "I don't know if there was something more there."

I watched Solomon crying, my heart aching for his pain. I had no idea if he'd killed her or not, but the fact remained that he was crying. This was behavior he hadn't exhibited before. Was he changing? Was that medication finally working its way out of his system? Or had the death of somebody he'd loved awoken those feelings in him as nothing else could?

"I'm going to try to talk to him," I whispered.

"Violet, that's not a good idea..."

Owen exhaled sharply, but didn't try to stop me. I moved slowly, making sure to avoid Tasha's body. Solomon stopped his rocking as I began to approach, watching me with dark, glittering eyes. The wetness on his cheeks glistened red from the fire burning behind him, and it made him look like he was crying drops of blood, giving him a sinister appearance.

I shook off the impression, remembering the man I had known. When I had first met Solomon, I had been intimidated by his brooding nature and massively built physique, but it hadn't taken long for me to realize there was more to him than that. This was a bit like that... but this time, the danger was real. I channeled that apprehension as I took another step, emboldened by his lack of protest or aggression.

"Hey, Solomon," I greeted him gently, moving even closer. He growled, a sharp, angry sound, and I froze. He stopped, and I got the message, sinking down to my knees and sitting. "I'm sorry about Tasha."

I meant it with every fiber of my being. Solomon stared at

me, and then his eyes drifted down to where Tasha's body sat in the shadow, his eyes moving like he could see every horrific detail of it. He pressed his fists into his eyes, a high-pitched sound escaping him, almost like steam from a tea kettle.

I watched the pain move its way through his body, my heart bleeding for him. "Are you injured?"

Solomon lifted his head, his eyes a mixture of rage and despair. He struggled, squeezing his eyes shut and rocking his head back and forth, twitching madly. After a moment, he nodded, his eyes opening to watch me closely.

"Will you let me look at it?"

He hesitated. He closed his eyes, squeezing them shut tight. He took a shuddering breath in, and then exhaled, shaking his head no. I sighed, but didn't argue. I could tell he was expending a lot of energy just trying to respond to my questions, and it was frustrating him. If I pushed him too hard, he could snap again.

"Solomon… we're going into the city. To chase Desmond." His head snapped up, and his lips lifted in a silent snarl. "We can make room for you in the car. You should come with us."

Solomon leaned back, away from me. His eyes flicked from me, to Owen, to the car sitting on the road, waiting for our signal. He shook his head.

I opened my mouth to say something new, but Solomon was clearly done, and he stood up in a fluid motion, so abruptly that it took me by surprise. I took in a sharp breath, trying not to move a muscle, worried that he might have reverted back to that angry, screaming monster that wanted to hurt everything around him.

Instead, he vaulted easily over the barricade into the city, cutting through the long shadows, leaping up on the side of the trailer and then over the harvester and disappearing into the city on the other side. I watched him go, half of me still startled by his sudden movement, the other half relieved for so many reasons— but all of me worried about what Solomon would do in the city.

Owen moved away a step and waved to Morgan and Lynne, letting them know it was safe. They pulled up quickly, and I moved to the car, sparing one last look at the rooftops, hoping to see Solomon lurking up there. Then I got in behind Lynne on the passenger's side and fastened my seatbelt.

"Catch us up with Desmond," I told Morgan as she put the vehicle in gear, navigating us around the burning harvester and back onto the road into the city.

CHAPTER 31

Viggo

"Give me just a minute, please," said Jeff over the line, polite as ever.

"We don't have many to waste right now," Henrik warned in return. I lifted the binoculars back to my eyes, staring up the grassy park slope at the dark facility from my position on my stomach. In my sights, four women dressed in olive green and moving in formation approached the hill on foot, and I watched them as they began inspecting, their flashlights cutting across the curb-less road, and then across the grass on either side of it.

We were hundreds of feet away, but there was no telling what other equipment they had on them. I scooted back slowly, dead leaves shifting under my body as I backed away from the tree line. "How's it look?" asked Alejandro as I eased back into line with him.

"Four guards at the top of the hill—a patrol. Jeff better get here soon. If they come down that hill, we're going to have to take them out." A new apprehension surged through me. Combined, Mags' and my group still had around thirty men and women, the largest force out of anyone, and it still didn't feel like enough, even with Thomas' assessment that there were actually only twenty women milling around outside of the plant.

My apprehension stretched as Henrik immediately came on the line. "All right, kids, this is it," he announced gruffly, and I could tell he was feeling it too. I couldn't blame him. It was his plan, after all. That was a lot of pressure to put on one person, and every life lost on our side was something he was going to carry with him for a long time.

"Jeff, are you ready?" Henrik asked. Jeff confirmed, and Henrik continued, his voice firm and commanding. "You start your run in five, four, three, two, one."

I held up my fingers and began counting down as he did, raising my hand up high enough for my team to see. When I made a fist, nothing happened, at first.

Then I felt the wind shift, and shielded my eyes at the dust the heloship kicked up as Jeff piloted it low to the ground, the weird whirring noise growing as the ship moved above us. The tips of the trees we were hidden in swayed under the force of the air displaced by the massive propellers, and I moved my binoculars back to the plant's defenses in time to see one woman pointing up, then running back, disappearing behind the horizon of the hill.

"Hold your position," I reminded everyone, speaking loudly, since the wind from the heloship would mask any sound I made. "Don't move until we see Drew's team."

"Targets acquired," Jeff broadcasted. "Lighting them up."

There was a small, barely discernable hum, and then a

thunderous roar went off as the gun mounted to the wings of the heloship activated, cracking through the silence like a never-ending roll of thunder. Even though I knew exactly where he would be—to the left of us, hovering over some trees—I still couldn't see him until the flash of the guns caught my eye, revealing the heloship's boat-like underbelly. Something exploded just over the hill, the roll of smoke and fire illuminating the hillside in a bright orange flash, dragging my attention to the battlefield.

"Fuel tank hit," said Jeff. "Moving to secondary target." I watched as Jeff adjusted the line of fire, expending every last bit of ammo we had left on the heloship. The line of bullets cut right, and then left, and several other explosions rocked the night.

"Yeah, get 'em, Jeff!" Amber crowed triumphantly over the line. "You are handling that thing beautifully."

"Just doing my part, Ms. Ashabee," he replied, but I could hear the reluctance in his voice. Jeff didn't enjoy violence, so this had been a compromise for him: hit the fuel reserves that helped supply the emergency generators of the plant, and hopefully stop some of the inner workings of the plant without setting it back so far that it would no longer be able to supply Patrus with water. This had the added benefit of making the Matrian forces pull back a little bit, and giving our assault team a chance to move in—before they realized how small our forces really were.

"Good work," announced Henrik. "Drew, bring your team in now!"

"Roger," replied Drew's low voice. My heart began to thud, knowing our time was close, and I tried my best to move past it, settling into the cold and analytical feeling of true battle. I looked down the line, assessing, and saw that several of my people had let go of their rifles to cover their ears, trying to dampen the loud roar of the heloship's guns. I tapped Alejandro on the shoulder, pointing down the line at them. He nodded, and turned to tap the next person down the line, alerting them to grab their guns.

Jeff's guns suddenly fell silent. "Ammo expended, returning to base." The heloship began to pull away, and a dark movement on the road behind us caught my eye. I turned to watch a dark blue car speed up the hill past me and then swerve right, coming to a screeching halt perpendicular to the road, half on and half off it, the passenger side facing the plant.

"Go go go!" Henrik shouted as the second car roared up.

That was our cue. I stood, motioning my team to follow, and charged toward the car, not bothering to stoop over, as it would slow me down. The driver of the first car slid out, rifle clutched to his chest, keeping low. I heard heavy footsteps behind me, alerting me that my team was keeping up.

The next car barreled up past me when I was just emerging from the tree line, the third hot on its tail. The lead car passed the first, and then cut hard to the right, replicating the first car's position on the opposite side of the road, ten to fifteen feet past the first. The third one cut back to our side, staggering the line.

And so it went, the next car becoming the next bit of cover that we could hide behind as we charged up the hill toward our selected entrance to the plant. I made it to the first vehicle and dove behind it as the fifth car passed. "Twenty seconds," I announced over the transmitter on my team's channel. "Mags' team right, Alejandro's team left... my team right up the middle."

Gregory gave me an approving smile from where he crouched beside me, while Tim's face was neutral. The young man squatted behind the hood of the car at the wheel well, his silver eyes watching Henrik's plan unfold. I watched from behind as the cars continued to zoom past, the drivers not bothering to modulate their speed until the very end.

Rifle fire shattered the calm that had settled in the wake of Jeff's departure, sounding from the top of the hill, and I watched one car come to a screeching halt on the left side of the road, in the right position—but with no sign of the driver anymore.

"MOVE!" I shouted, and swung around the back of the first car, charging up the middle. Gregory easily kept pace beside me, while Tim lagged behind, his pistol in his hand. The hill was steep, making it difficult to see the Matrian guards flooding out of the plant until they were at the top.

Tim was the first to fire, three shots in rapid succession. Three women dropped, and I found myself envious of the young man's heightened reflexes. More women took their place, however, and I dove for cover behind the third car as bullets began to spray down the hill.

The next car in the line squealed past, driving directly into their line of fire in hopes of scattering them. The driver—one of Drew's people—didn't let up on the gas, even as bullets ricocheted off the hood and window. I fired my rifle around it, trying to help draw some of the fire off of the car, and then its tires squealed as the driver went over the horizon of the hill... and I lost sight of him.

Gunfire filled the air now, bullets raining thickly on us and pinging and zinging off the cars we hid behind. I continued to press forward, leading the charge up the hill. I darted across the road to the opposite car, firing as I went, and then pulled the back door open. I belly-slid into the backseat, and then sat up, firing on the opposite side of the road from the backseat.

The hood of the car dipped, and I turned to see Carl climbing on it. "Carl, don't!" I shouted in warning as the man began to fire, but it was too late. He had barely squeezed the trigger when his body jerked and fell back. I squirmed back out of the car as bullets attacked the rear glass.

"Is he alive?" I asked whoever was listening, belly-crawling toward the hood.

I came around the corner where Tim was leaning over Carl, his fingers at his throat. He met my gaze over his shoulder and shook his head. I felt a stab of pain, and then pushed it aside, knowing that if I were to fixate on that feeling, I wouldn't be able to move forward. I had to focus on the rush of battle, on the adrenaline surging through my veins, and feel as little as possible. I'd done this before, but it was never easy.

"Take his ammo," I said softly. "We'll find him after the battle."

Tim's lips shook, but he nodded, and began to search for the ammunition on Carl's still form. I slid into a sitting position and looked at Gregory, who was leaning on the other side. "What's going on?" I asked, my voice almost a shout over the sounds of the guns.

"Mags is almost to the top, but she's drawing heavy fire from our side," he announced. "We need to make it to the next car."

"Right." I pulled my legs up and went to a crouch, turning to face the front of the car. Taking a deep breath, I flexed my thighs and moved up a few inches, trying to get the lay of the land before we proceeded. My eyes were just making out the forms beyond the window when I felt something hot bite into the tip of my ear. I jerked back and down, my fingers reaching up and feeling the edge of my earlobe, coming away with the smallest pinprick of blood. A cold sweat came over me as I realized that if the shot had been any farther to the right, I would have been dead.

"Viggo! Someone is in the first car!" Gregory's sharp shout caught my attention, and I turned to watch as the first car that had stopped on the road, far behind us now, came to life and streaked back in reverse. The driver—whoever it was—rounded it out, and then barreled forward, shooting up the road.

I watched it plow toward us, an idea coming to my mind. "Get ready to run behind that thing," I shouted, squat-walking closer to him. Tim loped over on his hands and feet behind me, and I watched as the car drew nearer.

Then it was past and I was vaulting over the corner of the car, one hand planted on the trunk as I flew over. I landed roughly on my feet and rolled forward to shed some of the momentum, and then I was running, my boots hitting hard and fast as I raced be-hind the vehicle. I kept my eyes peeled left, then right, and began firing moments later, managing to hit a woman standing just at the crest of the hill on the left.

The ploy was working, and I heard Tim and Gregory's guns go off around me as they followed. We pushed the last few feet up the hill, and then the car cut right sharply, just past the last car to make it to the top. I sprinted for it, my breathing coming in sharp gasps as the enemy fired upon us. I hip fired, trading accuracy for intimidation, as we ran.

Just behind the person who'd raced up the hill, the final car's windows were shattered, and I could see the bullet-riddled body of one of Drew's men still slumped in the driver's seat. I made it to the car and threw open the driver-side door, using it for more cover. Gregory followed suit with the door behind me, boxing me in slightly.

Keeping my back to the interior side of the door, I quickly ejected a magazine and inserted a new one. I looked up to see the firelit figures of Matrian forces moving toward us, and leveled my gun at them, this time taking a moment to sight down the barrel.

I caught one woman in the shoulder and neck, and another in the leg and stomach. Both fell onto the pavement, and I exhaled, lowering the gun for a second to wipe the sweat off my forehead, then freezing when I saw a long shadow cutting across the scarlet glow of the still burning fires littering the concourse.

I hesitated, and then fired right through the door, not wanting to risk moving in any direction first. As I squatted higher up, I raised the gun, making sure I had hit her. I ducked back down and ejected the magazine, torn between exhaling in relief that it had worked, or grimacing at the sight of her twitching and gasping for breath as she slowly choked on her own blood.

After a moment's hesitation, I stood back up and shot her in the head, unable to let her suffer in her last moments. Then I ducked back down.

Static crackled, and then Mags was there in my ear. "Viggo, they're falling back into the industrial compound!"

"Chase 'em," I replied, chambering the round. "But stay close to the main entrance. That's the goal."

I shot at a form moving toward the car, and then inched forward around the car door. Several olive-clad women ran for me, and I fired on them, catching the one whose gun was swinging toward me in the chest, and the woman next to her as well. I heard Gregory give a triumphant shout and turned, watching as Alejandro crested the hill, his team by his side. He ran past the car, stopping to fire.

Trusting he knew what he was doing—even though I wanted to scream at him for not seeking cover—I twisted around and stood, looking past the car toward the large circular dome of the plant.

By now, women in Matrian uniforms were making for the entrance in a flat-out run, and I could see some of our lines pressing forward, making for it and using the industrial pipes that cut in, over, and out of the concrete concourse as cover.

"C'mon," I shouted to Greg and Tim, and moved around the car, running at a slight jog. The car that had led our way sat twenty feet ahead, the engine and hood wrapped around a wide pipe that had once been seated up out of the ground at a ninety-degree angle before joining an L-curve overhead. Water leaked from a bolted seam several feet above, spattering down on the shattered window and crumpled hood.

I angled to move past it when a movement caught my eye, and I rapidly moved toward it instead. I jerked open the door, the remaining glass shattering with the motion and the hinge heaving and groaning. I looked inside, grimacing when I saw Cruz lying on his back on the glass-littered front seat, which had been tilted all the way back, blood streaking from a gouge in his temple, his shoulder bleeding badly through his fingers. The dash of the car had been driven forward and up in the impact, effectively trapping his legs beneath it.

He jerked his gun up, and then relaxed it down when he saw it was me. "Did we make it up the hill?" he asked, his teeth clenched in pain.

I nodded and ducked down. "Let's get you out of this car," I said, gripping him under his armpits.

"Wait, no!" he shouted, but I ignored it and jerked him back, slowly dragging him. He grunted in pain as I strained around his bulk.

"How did you even get into that position?" I asked through

clenched teeth. "Were you lying on your back when you drove up the hill?"

"I—*madre de Dios*—my shoulder is shot, *pendejo!*" He glared up at me, a muscle in his jaw throbbing.

I ignored his snarl and focused on extracting him from the car as quickly as possible. I looked over and noticed Tim had followed me and was covering our position, but Gregory was nowhere to be seen. Good, he was sticking to the mission and getting the door clear. Cruz groaned as I continued to pull on him, his knees sliding free and spilling more glass on the ground.

The gunfire was beginning to dim, and I became aware of radio chatter in my ear. It had been nonstop since the start of battle, but I had lost track of it in the intensity of the fighting in front of me.

"The south entrance is clear," Ms. Dale said into the main channel. "We're heading in."

"I got a group pinned down behind some pipes by the west entrance," Amber shouted over the din, gunfire blasting in her mic, indicating—I hoped—that she was firing. "But my team is keeping them in place."

I finally got Cruz out, unceremoniously dropping him on the pavement. I grabbed Tim's attention, signaling to him, and we switched places. He started tending to Cruz's wound, and I knelt by the trunk of the car, peering around the corner.

The dead littered the white concrete concourse, and I wished I could have been happy to see that it was more Matrian forces than our own—but ours were there too. Men and women in dark clothes, lying still, blood seeping out from their cooling forms. I knew most of their names, and I determined that if I lived through this, I would learn the rest of them, too. It was a bitter consolation.

I looked past them, my eyes focusing on the metal door beyond. Our entrance. Several women were holding the door, hiding behind industrial barrels they'd hastily stacked around it. Muzzle fire came from small gaps in between them, and they had built them up to converge to a small point in between. It was well defended, and gauging by the muzzle fire, they had more than enough people and guns to hold it for a small span of time.

Time we don't have, and manpower we can't afford, I thought, coming to a snap decision. "Wait here," I told Tim, and I peeled away, heading for the car we had just abandoned back on the hill.

I raced around it, noting the bullet holes that bit into the front of the car, and pulled Drew's dead man out, laying him on the pavement next to it as respectfully as I could, given the circumstances. I slammed the rear door shut and then climbed in, closing the door behind me.

The keys dangled from the ignition, and after a quick prayer, I twisted them. The car shuddered, the engine struggling to catch. I held the key down for a second and then, on impulse, tapped the gas. The engine roared to life.

Throwing the car into gear, I slammed my foot onto the gas pedal and cut the wheel hard, turning on the inner axis. The tires squealed as I swung right, and I cut it back to the left, swerving past Tim and Cruz's car and aiming directly for the barrels, squeezing between them and the massive black pipe on the other side.

There was a moment's lull in the gunfire as their barricade came into view, and then a woman stepped out into the gap between the barrels, a rifle leveled at me. I grabbed the handle and threw open the door, throwing myself out of the speeding vehicle just as she opened fire.

I landed hard on my shoulder, rolling across the pavement as the car plowed into the barricade. I couldn't see it, but I heard the shouts and the crash of barrels and the imploding sound of its mechanisms breaking. By the time the world had stopped spinning and I had come back to myself, Tim was kneeling over me, his face taking up my entire frame of view.

My vision began to jerk to the right, and it took me a moment to realize that he was slapping me lightly on the cheek… and that he had been doing it for a while, judging by the concern lining the young man's lips.

I sat up, my shoulder aching fiercely, and allowed Tim to help me up, rotating the sore limb a few times to determine how damaged it was. It wasn't bad, all things considered, but I couldn't turn my neck as far as I would have liked, and was betting I had deeply bruised the muscle. I gritted my teeth, knowing I had to move on. As long as I didn't let it stiffen, it should hold up through the battle.

The car had smashed against the barrels, scattering them into the Matrian forces. One woman—the one who had fired on me—had rolled over the hood, but the others were down, barrels on top of them. The car blocked the door, but I could see Alejandro and several other people pushing it back, while Mags darted around, checking to see if the Matrian soldiers were dead or wounded.

I pushed aside the feeling of weariness and hobbled over to the entrance, preparing myself to give orders and get inside.

CHAPTER 32

Violet

Morgan downshifted quickly, swerving left around a still burning car in the middle of the street. The tires made short squealing sounds as she cut the wheel back around, rounding out the turn, and I found myself gripping the overhead handle just to maintain my balance.

"You know, for a girl who's done very little fieldwork, you drive like a pro," Owen said as the turn concluded. "Seriously, how'd you learn to drive like that?"

Morgan's attention was fully dedicated to the road, her eyes darting around as she kept a firm hand on the wheel. "Desmond cross-trained me a lot. I guess she really didn't know what to do with me, so it was train on this, with that... over and over again. Until I got relegated to this sort of... security guard slash trainer." She shrugged, and I chuckled.

"Wasn't what you were hoping for?" I asked.

"When is life ever what you were hoping for?" she

retorted bitterly.

I started to reply when the sound of gunfire blared through the street and bullets clinked against the side of our car. I couldn't help but jerk down in the seat, even though I knew I was over-reacting. We had taken one of Ashabee's special cars, a small ve-hicle with top-of-the-line body armor and bulletproof windows.

The gunshots continued, on either side of the vehicle, and Morgan bit off a curse as the window went gray. We were driving into smoke. She slowed the car immediately, reducing our speed to a crawl. "It's insane out here," she said as she inched forward, trying to pick a path through the swirling darkness, the head-lights barely illuminating our path.

I moved back in my seat. The gunfire was still happening, but behind us, and definitely moving away from us, possibly even faster than we were moving. The haze was thick, obscuring most everything in soot and shadow. I peered through the glass, hiss-ing as a dark shape passed close by the window, my hand tight-ening on the gun.

"Can you pick up the pace, please?" asked Lynne, her voice taking on a high-pitched quality. She was nervous, not that I could blame her, and—

"Violet?" Thomas' voice in my ear cut my thought off before it had fully formed.

I pressed my fingers together. "What's up, Thomas?"

"I got good news, bad news, and worse news."

"What's the good news?" I immediately asked, and then re-gretted it. Amber always saved it for last, and maybe it was better that way.

"I found Desmond, or rather, where she was as of two min-utes ago. She's definitely making her way to the plant, and you're right on her tail."

I let everyone know the good news, and Morgan smiled—more a baring of her teeth—and said, "Good."

"What's the bad and the worse news?" I asked.

"The bad news is she's on a safer road than you, so you might be delayed. The worse news is that the rioting in your area has gone from bad to worse."

I frowned. "Thomas, how do you know that?"

"I'm still flying my drone," he replied. "Ms. Dale and the other groups don't need it at the moment. I've gotten all the intel I could for them, so she had me come over to help you with…" He paused, and I waited, keeping an eye on the thick, roiling clouds blanketing the street.

He probably had gone to the other channel. I would've joined him, but now that my drone was down and I was in the field, I only needed to be in there if there was an emergency decision to be made. And even then, I trusted them to handle it. If I got on, it would only distract people from the can of worms they were about to open, if things were going according to schedule.

"It's finally lightening up," breathed Morgan, her spine relaxing a little as she continued to move the car carefully forward.

"Violet! Look out, there's an enhanced human right in front of you!" Thomas' line held enough alarm that I was already shouting for Morgan to stop, even before his warning was fully finished.

She slammed the brakes, and I jerked forward a little in my seat as we stopped, expecting at any moment to see a figure with a gun emerge. The haze in front of us shifted and swam. "Back up," I whispered, slipping the gun out my pocket.

"Violet, you can't shoot through the…" Owen trailed off as a bearded man lumbered into view, the mist parting and allowing us to see him face to face.

His clothes were ripped and dirty, and blood dripped down half his face, making it glisten in the headlights. He was definitely older—maybe mid-twenties—which meant he would be more unstable than the younger boys we'd faced in the past. Stumbling, he slammed into the car, and then screamed, spittle flying in large wads from his lips. He drew his hands together, lifting them high over his head, and then brought them back down.

"Reverse reverse reverse!" I repeated as my whole body clenched, going stiff in preparation for the oncoming blow.

Morgan clutched the gear shift and revved the engine, propelling the car backward just in time. The man stumbled forward as his target moved away from him, his fists landing on empty air. Morgan whipped the car around, and the man looked up and began to charge.

"Go go go!" shouted Lynne, and Morgan went, her foot slamming on the gas as she cut the wheel hard. The man dove for the rear window, and I clicked the safety off of my gun and pointed it through the window at him in case he could break the bulletproof glass. Morgan pulled away too fast, and the man fell and rolled across the pavement.

"Look at the map," Morgan shouted, and Lynne rummaged in her bag, pulling out our map of the city. She spread it open as Morgan hit a hard left, and I found myself reaching for the handle, even though I was twisted around in the seat, watching the smoky fog. The car bucked as Morgan hit something, and Owen's side of the car erupted in red as embers sprayed out across the window next to him.

The fog suddenly cleared, and then we were speeding away

from a thick gray cloud. "Is he back there?" Lynne asked shakily.

I scanned the receding line, and started to shake my head, when the man darted out, leaping over an overturned car and landing on the other side. His face immediately moved toward us, like he was a dog who'd caught our scent, and he roared, cutting a path straight for us.

"He's catching up!" I shouted. "Why are we moving so slowly?"

"There's stuff in the road!" Morgan barked back as she yanked the wheel to avoid yet another obstacle.

The man drew closer, and I felt my heartbeat increase. As much as I didn't want to hurt one of the boys, the inevitability of it was a looming shadow in my heart. Suddenly the gun felt heavy, and I wanted to drop it on the seat.

I looked over at Owen as Morgan swerved around something in front of us, the gravity in the car shifting, sliding me into his shoulder. "We need to slow him down," I shouted. "Look for something—anything—we can throw from the back of the car."

Owen looked at me from where he was pensively staring out the window, and then doubled over the backseat, opening a panel on the flat, felt-like shelf behind us. The panel was a long cutout, and as he lifted it, I squeezed my fingers under the crack to pick it up, the car bouncing under our knees.

We slid it forward, propping it against the backseat, and I looked up in time to see the man running a few feet behind and to the side of us, snarling and snapping his teeth. He pulled back an arm to strike at my window, and Owen pulled me back from his location, forcing his body between us.

"Watch out!" Lynne screamed, and Morgan jerked the wheel hard. I turned as the end spun out of control, trying to see what we'd almost hit, and suddenly we were bouncing back the other way. I landed hard against Owen as Morgan slammed on the brakes, sinking down a few inches into the gap between the seats as we came to a lurching stop.

"It's Solomon," Lynne breathed shakily, and I sat upright, rudely grabbing on to Owen and hoisting myself up from off my back. I moved back to the window as Morgan gunned the engine, and confirmed that, yes, it was Solomon.

By the time I had found where to look in our turned-around car, he had the other man by the throat, his mouth bared in a silent snarl. The red fire behind him caught the definition of his broad muscles flexing as he lifted the wild man up by the throat. The man's legs kicked out, catching Solomon in the jaw, and he stumbled back, dropping his prize. The man pressed his advantage, his fists slamming into the side of Solomon's face once, and then Solomon reached out and grabbed the other man's fist, stilling it, his head snapping back to look at him.

"He's... protecting us," I whispered as I watched him force the struggling man over, step by step, to the wall and begin smashing his head into the brick.

"Good," said Morgan. "We have a mission to complete."

She hit the gas and we sped off, leaving Solomon and the other man behind as they rapidly faded from view. Morgan hooked the next left, and I saw more fire, and people running around, fighting on the streets. A man picked up a rock and threw it at us, but it missed, sailing to one side and onto the street as we sped by.

I clicked over to the main channel, knowing I needed to give everyone a report. "We encountered an enhanced human—male, in his early or mid-twenties, dark black beard," I announced quietly over the line. "I think Elena brought the boys in."

"Yeah, Thomas told us, Vi," said Amber. "But to what end? The place is a catastrophe. She'd lose more of the boys than she'd keep, in all likelihood."

"She could be sweeping in behind us," replied Logan. "Using these enhanced humans to pin us between a rock and a hard place."

I frowned, my mind working. Amber was right. The fact that Elena had unleashed the boys here, and six blocks away from the water treatment plant, seemed careless. Like an afterthought.

Then again, maybe it had been. Elena's plan was coming apart at the seams—maybe she was running out of solutions. Maybe we finally had her scared.

But that didn't feel right for Elena. She wasn't the same as regular people. She didn't have the handicap of fear to distract her from the battle. Frustration, yes, but fear, not so much. The woman was a high-functioning sociopath with power. Whatever was going on, I doubted it had much to do with desperation. Not yet.

"Violet, keep an eye out for them and let Thomas know if you see any more boys." Ms. Dale's voice was firm, but I could detect the notes of exhaustion and concern in her words. "Clear the channel. We need it for the plant."

"Roger," I acknowledged, my heart a stone in my chest as I realized that Ms. Dale and everyone were going to attack soon, and that some of the brave people who were fighting with us were not going to survive.

Leaning forward between the seats, I grabbed Morgan's attention. "Get us there fast," I said. "We can't afford to let Desmond disrupt their plan in any way."

She nodded, her face grim, and sped up as the road in front

of us seemed to clear. I leaned back in my seat, unable to feel relaxed as my eyes darted around, studying the road as we drove by. The streets had quieted down again, but I couldn't shake the unsettled feeling in my stomach at the revelation that the boys were here.

There was something more to this plan, something we were overlooking. I just wasn't sure what.

CHAPTER 33

Viggo

"**Y**ou and Drew's team do your best with the barrels, cars, whatever," I told Ingrid. "Just keep them from coming in behind us."

The pixie-faced Liberator bobbed her head, her blonde top-knot bouncing. She swiped the back of her hand against her cheek, wiping away sweat and leaving a long black smudge along her jaw. "We got your back, Croft," she said. "Stop wasting time."

I nodded and approached the door where the rest of the team—now twenty-six of us—were heading in. The circular building was massive, and the area of the plant we needed to get to was buried in the heart of it. The place was also designed in a maze-like fashion that made it difficult to navigate, but Thomas had pre-plotted our route.

Cruz cursed, and I turned to see where April was finishing wrapping up his still bleeding shoulder. She tied a quick knot, eliciting another harsh sound from Cruz, and then gave him a sharp nod. "It'll hold," she murmured. "But you should really sit this one out."

"And miss protecting your lovely self from harm? You would deny me that honor?" Cruz's face was tight as he said it, his flirtatious tone lighter than usual, likely due to the pain he was in. Still, somehow, April gave him a wide grin.

"You never give up," she teased, and he managed a half shrug as he stood up.

"I was never taught how to." He looked around, his eyes landing on me. "We ready, Croft?"

I looked at his shoulder, and then nodded. "Waiting on you," I replied as I turned back to the small door that led to the plant and the rest of our mission. Apprehension tried to take over my brain, but I shouldered it aside.

We just had to hope for as little resistance from inside as possible, though that hope sounded dim given what we'd encountered just getting here. I nodded to Alejandro, and he pulled back the heavy metal door. A red glow emitted from the wall across from me, illuminating the small service corridor that bordered one of the massive tank rooms. I could hear the loud roar of machines churning deep inside the plant through the entrance.

Pulling out a hand mirror, I handed it to Alejandro, who held it out into the hall, checking the left side. It wasn't something everyone had considered bringing, but I had brought mine, my time as a warden having taught me the importance of it for checking blind spots. Mine happened to be one of three on our team. He dutifully handed it over to Mags, who did the same on the right. "It's clear," she said softly, handing it to me, and I slipped it back into my pocket.

I stepped forward into the hall. The red emergency lighting

lit it up well, revealing only small pipes—probably filled with chemicals to treat the water—lining the wall, periodically feeding back into the wall or into a box.

"Viggo?" Violet's voice in my ear was soft, but there was an edge to it.

"Violet?" I asked, taking a step deeper into the plant. "It's not a really good time."

"I know that, but this is important."

I hesitated, and then turned, disconnecting the microphone so I didn't transmit orders meant for others over the line. "Cruz, Mags, take two teams of five and find the doors. The one on the east side needs to be secured and locked, while the one on the west leads to our first room on the way to the control center."

Mags nodded and began giving orders in hushed tones. I stepped deeper into the hall and then put my back against the wall, giving people room to move by. "What's up?"

"I guess this goes for everyone, really, but there was something off about that enhanced man."

I frowned, confusion coming over me. It took me a minute to remember what she was talking about—which was understandable after everything that had just happened. "What was it?"

"He was… angry. Kind of berserk." She delivered the information matter-of-factly, but I could hear the bomb drop in her words. I suddenly felt rooted in place, my stomach churning in horror as I realized what she was saying.

"Oh my God," I said.

"What?" asked Henrik, confusion roughening his voice. "What are you talking about?"

"Hold on a second," I said. "Thomas, is it possible that whatever they have been contaminating the water with is making it out into the city fountains already?"

"Possible. Especially the ones closer to the plant," announced Thomas grimly. "But you seem to have drawn a conclusion based on some yet-to-be-explained data."

"He was like Solomon," Violet said, her tone bitter, angry. "Angry and prone to attack everything around him. That's not like the boys we've known, especially when they're on the Benuxupane."

There was a long stretch of quiet as we all absorbed this information, and then Violet continued. "What if Elena isn't dumping Benuxupane or poison? What if she's putting in the pill that Desmond gave to Solomon? What if her game is to show the Matrian people how dangerous the Patrian people have become, and wage her war against them openly, with their full support?"

There was another long silence, and then Thomas spoke. "The efficacy of that plan would be astronomical," he whispered, unable to keep the awe out of his voice. "It would incite a primal fear in the Matrians—their next-door neighbors have become monsters capable of incredible feats of strength, but suffering from extreme rage and unable to control their behavior. She could even let the people inside the city tear themselves apart... and just keep them from leaving the city through those checkpoints they set up. It's brilliant."

A loud bang came from down the hall, and I jumped, turning toward it. "Mags?" I said.

The comm buzzed, and it was Henrik, trying to shoot down the idea, but I already knew in my gut that it was true. Everything was worse than we'd feared, and the plant had gotten infinitely more dangerous. I ignored the discussion and took a few steps forward, allowing the curve to illuminate more of the hall.

"Mags?" I repeated.

The bang came again, this time more of a clatter, like loose metal rattling in its brackets. "Viggo?" came Mags' questioning voice, and I came around the curve a few feet back. The hall acted like a tunnel, the walls stopping abruptly and opening into a small room with grated steps leading to the next door. Tim was slowly backing down the steps, toward Mags, who stood by the entrance, her gun trained on the door. Something slammed into it with another loud bang, and the door flew back a few feet and then toppled over, part of it hanging over on the stairs.

I almost knew what I was going to see before I saw it. An olive-clad woman stepped out, her hands balled into fists. The skin over her knuckles was torn and bleeding freely, and she peered at us from beneath a lowered brow, her lips curled up in a silent snarl. She wiped the back of her arm over her mouth, and then screamed, a throaty, angry sound, leaping into the air and coming down in front of Tim.

Tim danced back a few feet and then planted his legs wide, ducking low under the wild, sweeping haymaker the woman leveled at him. He stepped in close as the woman's swing carried her arm past him, grabbing a fistful of her shirt and planting one foot on her stomach. He used her momentum to drag her down as he lowered himself to the floor, rounding his back and then rolling her over him, his foot shoving her forward so that she flipped over him. Her head and shoulder hit hard against the concrete ground.

Quickly scrambling to his feet, Tim turned as the woman began to move, her hands bracing on the floor as she pushed herself up. I didn't give her a chance to get up again—I shot her dead, and pressed forward. "C'mon," I said. "We gotta get into that room." *Because if all of the wardens inside the plant are like that... we gotta make it through as soon as possible.*

I tested the door sitting on the top of the stairs, making sure it could be stepped on without tripping us up, and then moved through the open doorway onto a catwalk, inside one of the water treatment rooms. Pipes wider than I was jutted out of walls in any direction, seemingly at random. I kept my back to the curved side of the building as I stepped past the massive pipes coming through the wall just a few feet to my left.

"Don't shoot!" a feminine voice cried, causing me to hold up. "I didn't sign up for this. I surrender!"

"TRAITOR!" shouted another voice, and I ducked back as gunfire exploded in the room, filling the area with bullets ricocheting off of pipes, whistling at high velocity until they found some concrete to stop their flight. It died quickly, and I poked my head out again, studying the dim shadows under the pipes.

"Anyone who wants to surrender, throw your guns on the ground and put your hands up so we don't shoot you!" I shouted, and launched myself over the railing, down the five-foot drop to the concrete below. I used my right arm—my left still felt like ground meat stuffed into an overstretched sock—and landed solidly on my boots, dropping behind a set of three pipes that rested inches off the ground, rising in a leveled slope up toward the ceiling.

I could see a wide hatch standing open on the pipe opposite me, and a large red barrel tipped on its side, leaking a milky white fluid into the water rushing by. Then gunfire erupted in the room, and I ducked down as it came dangerously close.

"Right side, right side!" Greg shouted, and I stood up and fired at the general area, sparks from my gun and the guns on the area above lighting it up, only adding to the red glow that illuminated the space. I angled left when I saw a dark figure emerge from behind a grouping of smaller pipes, gun in hand. Her focus was on the catwalk, so she never had the chance to see me, or the bullet that caught her in the head.

I turned and saw a woman standing over the hatch, cupped hands to her lips, water streaming through her fingers. She met my gaze, going wide-eyed in surprise when she realized that I saw her, fear crossing her features. Then, quicker than I would have thought possible, her face began to change, and before I knew what was happening, she had ripped off the hatch allowing access to the pipe and flung it at me like a frisbee.

I ducked down under it and squeezed the trigger wildly, and she went down. A few more shots were exchanged, and then it was done, a chorus of "clear" beginning to fill the room. I came around the pipes in a hurry, pulled the barrel off the hole, and righted it, stopping it from polluting any more of the water source while making sure to keep my hands well away from the milky substance.

"Henrik," I said, pressing my fingers together. "I just watched a woman drink from the water she was 'poisoning,' and then rip off a hatch weighing about forty pounds, and fling it at me hard enough to take my head off. They—" I paused as Gregory appeared from around another set of pipes, guiding an olive-clad woman with sleek chestnut hair toward me.

"I surrender," she said immediately, holding up her hands to show she was unarmed. "I didn't sign up for... whatever the hell that was."

"I'll get back to you in a minute," I transmitted to Henrik before disconnecting the transmission. "It's all right," I told her. "We won't hurt you. What's your name, and what happened?"

She tugged at her uniform and squared her shoulders. "Janice Stevenson," she said, swallowing. "We were getting ready for you to come in, and then Vanessa drank the water and… and went insane. There's no other way to put it. Those *were* our orders, but they lied to us! They told us that they got wind of a terrorist chemical attack happening in the next couple of days, so we've been trying to flood the water with these. We were told to drink the water if the terrorists… if you were close enough… They said it would inoculate us against certain poisons if you tried to use chemical weapons. The rest of us thought we were fine, but Vanessa panicked and started drinking the water and just *changed*. She killed Gwen, just like that, and then she came after me, but… then she heard something at the door and went after it instead."

I held up my finger to her as I began to transmit. "It's confirmed," I said grimly. "And the Matrians have orders to drink the water if we get close to them."

"There's more," added Janice, almost impatient to get her story out, flipping her hair over her shoulder. "We were also given pills to take in emergencies to protect against chemical attacks. Now I'm worried they'll just do the same thing."

Leaning back on the pipe, I felt the terse silence on the line as everyone realized the impact that this could have on our battle. I shook my head, a mix of anger, disgust, and fear clenching in my gut as I realized that some of the tainted water was already on the street. It must have been, if that man Violet had seen was affected by it. People were being changed against their will, and then probably killing others. No one could know that it was coming from the water, not yet. And how could they resist drinking it, even if they did? All other sources were already out.

If I hadn't hated Elena before, this move would have made me despise her.

I quickly informed everyone in the main channel of Janice's revelation as I rolled away from the pipe and stood up. When I was done, I pulled apart my fingers and gave her a stern look. "Janice, we can purge this system and save a lot of people. That's what we're here to do. But I need to know—is there a faster way to the control room?"

Janice returned my hard look, her jaw clenching with indecision. Then she nodded, sliding a long strand of hair behind her ear. "Yes. I can show you, but you have to let me go free."

"Agreed, but after the battle is over. There are still rogue Matrian forces outside, and even if you did manage to make it out into the city, there would be no stopping any of the hundreds of angry people in the street looking to make someone pay for what's happening to them."

As I spoke, I could see Janice's half-thought-out escape plan die in her eyes. "Excellent points," she said. "Fine. But I stay right here. I'm not going to get near one of… one of them."

I held out my hand, and she shook it. "This wall," she said, pointing at the wall opposite from the one that separated us from the outside, and moving toward it slowly, "is about twenty feet thick, and holds some of the bigger pipes that draw in and out from the collection pods outside. The king who designed this place was kind of a paranoid guy, so he made it really difficult to overcome the safeguards. But he also did something to help his workers move in and out of the central room in case of an emergency."

As she spoke, she led us closer to the wall in question, thick gray pipes running across the surface of it, the bottom one ending a mere three feet off the ground. I looked at Janice, and watched as she slipped under the pipe and stood up behind it. After a moment's hesitation, I followed her, and blinked when I saw the rungs sticking out of the wall, creating a ladder leading up. "We discovered it on the second day," she said. "It made life a little bit easier."

I could tell she was thinking about the sudden shift in her circumstances, and how different things could look in the span of twenty-four hours. I felt similarly.

"Thank you," I said to her, and she frowned.

"I want to say don't mention it, but honestly, I'm still a little too surprised that I'm even doing this."

"You and me both," I replied, eyeing the ladder leading up. "But probably for totally different reasons."

CHAPTER 34

Violet

Morgan hooked another left, and suddenly it was there—the water treatment plant. From our position on the street, I could see the entire top of the hill, illuminated by orange flames similar to the ones that dotted the rest of the city, but these were bigger, more sinister, filled with meaning. The surrounding city buildings ended suddenly, and then Morgan was speeding past the cars I knew Viggo had used for cover barely fifteen minutes ago, seeing the bullet holes, broken glass, and… fresh blood.

Then our vehicle crested the hill, and the road beneath us leveled off. I stared, unable to fully comprehend the carnage before me—a car wrapped around a pipe, bodies strewn across the ground, billowing fires breathing smoke that disappeared in thick black plumes into the inky, moonless night sky.

Or maybe the smoke was just blocking out the stars, I thought bitterly, remembering the moonlight I'd flown the drone in earlier. It was hard to tell.

I switched to the command channel. "Guys, we've arrived at the plant and are on the lookout for Desmond. Please let us know if you see any sign…" Ms. Dale and several others were acknowledging me when a movement on the left drew my eye, and I paused. The novelty of a car flying toward us, rolling on its side in midair, was a difficult thing for my mind to process.

That second cost us.

The next second, I managed to shout, "Morgan!" and point, and Morgan had time to cut the wheel—then we were spinning, the world rotating around me and then tumbling sideways in midair. Everything in the car seeming to float in the air as we rolled.

Then it all crashed down again. We rolled to a final, jerking stop, landing with the hood of Ashabee's car upside down, the bulletproof glass still intact but webbed with cracks. My heart raced in my chest like a hummingbird trapped in a tiny cage, and I fought vertigo and a sense of disorientation from time and space as I dangled from my seatbelt harness.

"Violet?" Owen said, his voice urgent. "Are you still with us?"

I reached across my body and pressed the button, releasing the seatbelt. I landed awkwardly on my shoulder on the roof of the car. "Yeah," I whispered, rolling myself upright, grabbing my bag from where it had landed on the ceiling. My body felt numb with shock and adrenaline—it would start to hurt soon, but I didn't want to wait for it. "You?"

Something shifted out front, and I saw Morgan pressing her shoulder against her door, gently rocking it open. There was a metallic groan, and then she was out. Owen slid out of his seatbelt and followed Morgan's lead. While he worked on the door, I leaned in between the seats to check on Lynne, who was fumbling with her straps.

"I'm stuck," she whispered, the fear in her words strong enough to carry over the sound of Owen getting the door open. I was just pulling my bag over, grabbing the small knife from one of the side pockets, when I heard Morgan's shout of alarm.

Looking through the cracked windshield, I saw a pair of uniformed legs making a direct line to us, and flipped open my knife, quickly cutting Lynne free. "Move," I told her as I slid back into the backseat, making my way to the door and the pavement beyond.

Gunshots went off overhead, and I heard a feminine, yet inhuman roar that made me cringe, lighting a fire in my motions. I used my casted arm to sweep aside the glass as I moved—finally a use for the damn thing—and then exited the window feet first, crouching just outside the car. Owen was leaning over the belly of the car, shooting at something. I pulled out my gun and hunted for a target.

Oh God. There were so many of them. And they were bounding all over the place, faster than any human should have been able to move. Owen shouted wildly as he shot at another woman who darted toward us from out of the darkness, and she spun out and away. I fired two shots, catching a woman in her side, but she scampered into some of the deep shadows created by the pipes jutting out of the concrete concourse.

"Lynne, hurry up!" shouted Morgan over the sound of her own gun. One woman broke through the hail of her and Owen's fire by leaping into the air to close the dozens of feet between us, swinging her fist toward me. I dodged, off balance on my knees, and then Morgan was there, catching the woman's fist as it impacted on the car with a strength I hadn't expected from her. The woman growled and swung Morgan around by her grip, trying to clutch her to her chest in a deadly hold.

Lynne was still inside, and she whimpered a little as the car groaned. "I'll get out on my side!" she said nervously. As Morgan grappled with the woman in front of me, I tried to find a clear moment to shoot her assailant, but couldn't risk shooting my friend in the process. Owen was keeping the rest of them at bay, picking them off with precise shots before they could get near us.

"Morgan, get her back toward me!" I called, spinning to my other side to shoot at two women closing in from that direction. One went down, and the other cut around the back of the car. I heard the heavy groan of Lynne's door being opened forcefully and her grunting and muttering. Then it broke off, and I heard a scream instead.

Owen cursed, and I whipped around to see a woman pull a struggling Lynne up off her feet, one hand wrapped around Lynne's throat. She was smaller than Lynne by far and shouldn't have even been able to lift her, but Lynne couldn't free herself. As Lynne struggled, going for her gun, the woman stared at her, lips curled in fury.

I brought my gun around to fire, but my aim went wide, my left hand jerking. Owen's gun went off at the same time, and I heard Morgan shout "Lynne!" as she broke free of the woman she'd been fighting with the sound of a gunshot.

She was too late. As I pulled the trigger again, in one quick motion, the enhanced warden jerked Lynne's head around with a sharp snapping sound.

My heart palpitated, and I kept firing, my hand shaking so hard that my shots went wide, pinging off the car. Heartbeats later, Owen and Morgan were there, their guns cutting the warden down. She and Lynne both fell. A part of me wanted to go check for a heartbeat—but I didn't move toward our fallen friend, and neither did Owen or Morgan. We'd all heard the snap, seen her go limp and lifeless.

And we didn't have time to reflect or mourn. I heard another inhuman roar come from our right, and I turned, everything inside me going colder as I saw several more olive-clad women closing in. I raised my gun, but Owen pulled me behind him, his gun already out, firing quickly and expertly.

"Go," he shouted. "I'll draw them off."

"But Desmond—"

"You start heading toward Desmond," he said, pushing me away before darting off in the opposite direction back down the hill. "This is my job."

The blond man fired as he ran, three of the wardens moving after him. I raised my arm to shoot, not wanting to leave Owen alone to face such desperate odds, but Morgan grabbed my arm.

"Don't—it'll draw attention to you," she said, pulling me off to one side. "Owen's giving us a window. We should use it."

The taller girl kept dragging on my arm, and indecision tugged at my limbs as I looked over my shoulder at where Owen stood his ground, firing at the oncoming berserk women. One of them dropped down on the pavement, but the others were still advancing toward him as he danced back.

Morgan fired her gun and dragged me a few more feet, toward a collection of pipes emerging from the concrete, thrusting me in between two of the pipes, boxing me in. "Stay here and keep quiet," she ordered, turning to go, and I tucked my gun under my armpit and reached out to stop her.

"Where are *you* going?" I asked.

Her head turned toward me, catching the light from one of the fires and giving it a blood-soaked impression. "More are coming. I'm going to draw them… *Hey!*"

She yelped as I pulled her into the small cranny with me, dragging her down until we were pressed together.

"Violet, they're—"

Whatever she was about to say was cut off when the pipe behind me shuddered. I turned as much of my body as I could, and saw, through the gaps in the network of gray pipes, a warden's hand pushing the pipes apart, making a hole to try to reach me. I felt a spray of water as the first pipe snapped, and I turned back to Morgan. "Behind me, right behind my head!"

She began to back up, and I felt the brush of fingernails on my neck, making my skin crawl as I slid forward, trying to avoid getting hooked on anything. The pipes shuddered, and the sound of more water splashing out on the concrete sent a chill racing up my spine. It all seemed so much deadlier now.

Morgan raised her pistol as soon as she got out of the hole, and I ducked down, covering my ears as she fired three shots into the small, confined space. The woman bellowed, and Morgan cursed. "I winged her," she said. "But she's coming around from the other side. We gotta run for it."

I slid the rest of the way out of the pipes and began running, cutting across the concrete and heading to the next asymmetrical pipe cluster. My ribs creaked and ached, but I couldn't stop for them—they would either be fine, or I would be dead anyway. Morgan ran beside me, and behind her, I could hear not one, but multiple sets of running feet. Tossing a quick glance over my shoulder, I saw three women in pursuit, and I forced my aching body faster, knowing we couldn't outrun them for long.

We drew closer to another bit of exposed piping sitting closer to the building wall, and one of the women gave a triumphant, bloodcurdling howl, the other two joining in the chorus. I felt myself flinch even as I ran, certain that I was moments away from my death, when a masculine bellow drowned the noise out with sheer volume.

I pulled up short as Solomon landed a few feet away, flying down from some unknown perch, his breath coming in sharp pants. He looked even more battered than before, and I saw red abrasions running up and down his shoulders and chest, like he'd been dragged along the concrete. Morgan pulled up short beside me, and I could hear her little gasp of surprise as she looked at him, the thick ropes of muscle cutting deep lines into his physique, a grim, determined sort of anger tense on his features.

The three women chasing us switched focus, and I ducked as their shadows passed by overhead as they threw themselves at Solomon all at once. "No!" I cried, leveling the gun at one of them and squeezing the trigger, satisfied when she dropped.

The other two landed on Solomon, their fists flying as the large black man was driven back a few steps on impact. He took a blow to the face, and then, barely fazed, began fighting back, kicking one in the chest hard enough to throw her back toward us. I ducked down and moved left, this time pulling Morgan behind me, and we ran.

"You just want to leave him?" I asked.

"It looks like he's got this!" she shouted back as she oriented us both using the main plant building, following the walls around. This area of the concourse had less gunfire and fewer people, but it didn't stop my eyes from jumping from shadow to shadow, alert for any whiff of enemy.

I slowed to a stop at a certain point, my breath coming in pants and my head beginning to spin. Morgan didn't notice at first, but then she jogged back as I tried to regulate my breathing. "Sorry," I wheezed, my hand wrapping around my side, trying to stave off the stabbing pains that ripped through my side at every breath. Now that we were no longer being directly pursued, I couldn't continue ignoring it. "Give me a minute."

Morgan looked around, her lips thinning, obviously displeased. Her eyes darted around the area, and she nodded. "Just one minute," she said, and I gave her a look.

"Wasn't asking for your permission," I informed her, pleased I had enough air in my lungs to do so. "Not to mention, what the hell was that—stuffing me in between some pipes and trying to run off like that?"

"I was doing it for *you*," she whispered, incredulous.

"No, you were doing that for *you*," I replied tartly, my breathing calming down some. "No offense, Morgan, but it was dumb! There's no way I can get Desmond without some help. I already…" I couldn't say *lost*. "…am missing Owen. I can't do this all alone!" I held up my right arm, showing her the cast that still encased the lower half.

"Violet, you took down a bunch of Desmond's guards by yourself," Morgan tsked, annoyed. "And she handpicks them, believe me. You can handle—"

"I had time to think then! I set *traps* and made them come to *me*! This is different. We're chasing Desmond. Lynne's gone, and Owen's…"

I trailed off as Morgan shut her eyes for a minute, realizing she didn't need a reminder of what had just happened. She made a fist and then unclenched it, nodding tightly. "You're right," she said after a second. "Even if it wasn't Desmond, I shouldn't have thought to leave you alone. Not with all this insanity. Anything could happen. To… anyone."

I sighed, suddenly feeling like a jerk. "Look, I know you meant well. It's just… we're a team. I'm not the golden girl who needs to be rescued or protected."

"Then why'd you agree to let Owen become your body-guard?" Morgan asked.

I studied her closely, and instead of finding animosity, I saw only curiosity in her eyes. "Let's talk and walk." Normally I wouldn't have wanted to talk in a combat situation, but for just a moment, I needed to rest my heart and think about something small, and I sensed that Morgan wanted the distraction too.

We began moving forward again, both of us scanning the pipes for movement, and I contemplated her question, not entirely knowing the answer at first. "It's hard to explain, but… when Viggo approached me with his idea, the only thing I could focus on was that he was not going to exile Owen. I didn't care what his punishment was, just that he wasn't forced to go for making a bad call."

"That bad call could've cost you your life," Morgan pointed out as she ducked under a fat pipe running from the building into the ground. "He gave Desmond information about us as well."

"I trust Owen." It was not grounded on any logical argument, but it was the truth. It had definitely taken a leap of faith, but I had done it without thinking.

"That egg thing is dangerous, Violet. Elena—the Matrians knowing that it's still in play could be catastrophic."

I resisted the bitter chuckle that built up in my throat, trading it for a sad nod. "Any worse than what's going on in there?" I asked, and she paused mid-step before pressing ahead.

"Maybe," she said. "Although, knowing the queen, she's got a backup plan. Probably will try to breed with one of the older boys from the experiments or something."

I cringed. "That's gross."

"Yeah. But it's just how she would think."

Considering her words, I stepped out around a serpentine spiral of pipes and paused when I saw a car sitting abandoned in front of the tall metal fence that cut across the yard, separating the concrete from the field containing the collection ponds. I knew from the aerial photos that this area housed the collection vats, where the water was stored and pre-treated before entering the plant proper. There were several massive vats that sat at ground level, each containing several thousand gallons of water.

I could see one of the wide, circular ponds sitting a few feet away just past the fence, the water dark and still, but the reflective surface glowing red.

"She's gotta be in there," I said, pointing to the open gate. "It's a pretty open space, so sneaking up on her isn't going to be an option."

Morgan stared at the fence, and I could see the wheels turning in her head. "I'll go in and distract her," she said. "You sneak around her and put a bullet in her head."

I eyed her wearily, feeling the stitch in my side still pulsing with every breath. "I don't think I'm limber enough to sneak up on Desmond. And while my shooting with my left hand has improved some, I don't think it's a good idea."

"You can use this," she said, unzipping her jacket and revealing a flat black fabric that I recognized as the Liberator uniform. The material had the ability to camouflage the user for periods of time, rendering them practically invisible. "Distance won't matter then."

I stared at it, almost beyond shock, but then shook my head. "No, you keep it. You be the sniper. She'll shoot you, but she'll want to keep me alive. I'm sort of public enemy number one."

Morgan hesitated, and then nodded, pulling off her coat and dropping it to the ground. "I've got your back," she said as she quickly stripped off her street clothes. I envied her. The suit regulated her body temperature, keeping the nippy air at bay. She ran her hand through her short black hair, tamping it down again. "Let's get this over with."

I took a deep breath, pressing my fingers together once more. "Everyone," I told the group via the radio, "we've located Desmond's car near the UV treatment ponds outside the plant buildings. And we have a plan to take her down."

CHAPTER 35

Viggo

The concrete wall that separated this room from the next was ten feet tall, and the tunnel at the top of the ladder was small and cramped, barely wide enough for my shoulders to fit. But I managed, keeping my head low to avoid hitting it on the ceiling above. The sound of rushing water assailed my ears, drowning out any other discernable noises save those coming from our earbuds.

"We're breaching the final door. About to make our assault on the control room," announced Ms. Dale softly into her microphone. "Everyone make sure to keep the shutdown codes handy. First one there starts the process."

"We're moving into position," I told her as I approached the end of the tunnel, taking a step on the catwalk that hung suspended from the ceiling. The thing creaked ominously, but held. I slowly stepped out onto it, fully trusting it with my weight, and it continued to hold firm.

"Viggo." This time, Ms. Dale's voice came on my team's channel, strangely enough. "I need you to do me a favor."

I knelt down on the catwalk, surveying the factory floor below. "What?" I asked guardedly.

"I'm missing Jay. He heard Violet's announcement about Desmond and took off into the plant. I think he's got some foolish scheme going on—I couldn't stop him. There's nothing we can do about it now, but could you please watch out for him in the area you're covering?"

I could hear the concern in the woman's voice even through her professional attitude, and my stomach sank. Jay was running around the plant by himself? He and Tim had done this running-off thing before, but now of all times…

"I'll keep an eye out for him," I promised Ms. Dale, aware that that was probably the most I would be able to do under the circumstances. She answered in the affirmative and signed off, sounding resigned. As much as that worry churned my insides, I couldn't afford to think too hard about Jay now. I refocused on my surroundings.

The catwalk was suspended over a massive vat of water, the drop to the surface a healthy thirty feet. Below, the water churned, a long blade cutting across the surface, displacing the water and making it look as if some large aquatic beast were swimming just below the surface.

Six guards patrolled the ground around the vat, guns in their hands, and their body language and demeanor were extremely confident. It didn't look like they'd drunk any of the water yet. I heard my comm link beep on the team channel, and switched over. "Where exactly is the objective?" asked Mags.

I pointed to the small door posted opposite us on the floor

below, a concrete block with stairs on either side elevating the room to a position at the same level as the water tank. My guess was that it had been designed that way in case something in the system malfunctioned and began flooding the room, so the higher position would keep whatever electrical systems were inside safe. Initially.

"Croft, those women on the floor—we should shoot them, no? We have the advantage of elevated positioning."

I frowned, considering Cruz's question, and looked up at the bolts securing the catwalk to the ceiling. "It's not a good idea," I finally said. "The catwalk isn't that secure, and the ricochet alone could tear us to pieces."

I continued to study the room. The catwalk ran across its length, probably less than a hundred feet across, culminating in another rung ladder of the same design as the one before it, cleverly hidden behind rows of pipes. The ladder ended forty to fifty feet away from the door. The lid of the vat was higher up, but it was hard to gauge how much higher up from the angle I sat at.

"Okay, here's what we're going to do," I announced softly into the microphone, looking back down at my team. "The control box is our goal, so make sure you have the copy of the code Thomas gave us ready to use. First one there inputs the code, the rest of us cover them. Ms. Dale's team will be coming through the door on the other side, but don't expect her to be the only one to come through that door—it needs to be covered as well." I swallowed. "There's no way to know we will make it out of this, but I will try my hardest to make sure that we all get back to safety and our loved ones. You have all fought more bravely than I could ever hope, and I am honored that you let me lead you this far. Now trust me for just a little longer."

The faces that had been so filled with nervous energy at the beginning of the night were grim. Soot made an appearance on every person, and everyone had their fair share of injuries, from bumps, bruises, and scrapes, to Cruz's bandaged shoulder, the white gauze already stained with blood.

I didn't need to see the expressions on their faces to understand how they felt, because I felt it. I had been through it all with them. They were tired and already on the verge of breaking, in spite of the battles we had won. Still, it didn't hide the determination in their eyes, and I felt proud to have them standing beside me in this fight.

"Let's go," I said, and I turned and began creeping across the catwalk. The suctioning sound of the water as it was moved by the massive blade covered up any telltale echoes caused by our boots, but I still took care to move as quietly as possible.

I was halfway across when the catwalk shuddered violently, and I froze. Everyone who had followed me did too. I looked down to see if our presence had been noticed by the wardens down below, expelling a slow breath when I saw that it had not.

"There's too much weight," Mags whispered through the link. "We need to spread out."

I nodded and moved to one side of the path, waving Tim through. Behind him were Alejandro and Janice, followed by Gregory, then April. I waved them past slowly, wanting to build up a bit of distance. I could see Cruz waving people back into the tunnel, trying to relieve some of the weight from that direction.

Harry slipped past me, and I looked over to see Tim arriving at the other side. I raised a hand for him to hold up, and then followed Harry, not wanting the young man to be the first to put boots to the ground. The first one into a room filled with hostile enemies was more likely to get shot, and even with Tim's advanced reflexes, it was my job to lead.

Mags materialized next to me. "I got this," she whispered, indicating my post midway through the catwalk, and I nodded, moving toward Tim.

I was a good twenty-five feet away from him when I heard a surprised shout go up over the rush of the water, and I ducked down as bullets began to ping off the metallic grated flooring of the catwalk. "Return fire," I shouted, pulling my rifle around and shooting down through the railings at the floor below.

A Matrian woman standing by the lip of the pool ducked down behind it as I fired on her, disappearing from sight. I climbed back to my feet, intent on making my way to the other side, when I heard a primitive scream go up. I looked back to where the woman I had been firing at disappeared, and saw her olive-clad form emerge at a dead run, heading toward a wall. I hip-fired at her, but she was unfazed, running headlong through the sparks flying around her.

She leapt into the air, almost eight feet up, and then slammed her fists into the wall. I gaped as she began to leap up it, her hands and feet moving in a blur as she used her newly gained strength to crawl up one of the huge pipes lining the wall, holding on to the sides, and then began to cross toward us on a series of horizontal pipes, moving in huge, impossible leaps. She moved in at an angle, drawing closer and closer to the catwalk, and then leapt out, practically flying through the air and landing hard on the railing near Mags.

The entire catwalk shuddered, Mags' side dropping down a few inches, the men and women on it giving startled screams or shouts and reaching for the handrail. "Back up!" I shouted, turning back, but it was too late. The bolts groaned as they were yanked out of the wall.

"Magdelena!" Alejandro shouted in alarm, and I held up my arm to stop the older man as he leapt forward, uncertain whether our side would continue to hold up.

Mags was already racing, leaping over the gap and grabbing on to the stable edge that my side provided, her fingers slipping through the holes in the grates as she landed. There was another metallic snap behind her, and I lifted my eyes to see the section of catwalk we'd come from tear free, leaving a ten-foot gap in between, most of my team on the other side.

I watched as the ten-foot chunk of metal plummeted, carrying the warden down with it, splashing into the water. The section of catwalk sank into the dark depths, but the warden surfaced and began swimming toward the side of the pool. She was halfway there when the blade came up in front of her, and within seconds she had been swept under, sucked into whatever undercurrent the blade was creating.

Mags grunted as her biceps flexed, pulling her body higher up onto the groaning, tilted surface of the remaining catwalk. I got as close to the edge as I dared and reached out my hand to her. She tightened her arms more, raising herself up a bit higher, and then let go of the grate and grabbed on to my wrist in a talon-like grip. "I can't swim," she reminded me desperately, and I wrapped my hand around her wrist and began to pull, helping her get her hips and legs back onto the catwalk.

The gunfire continued around us as I pushed her past me, and I kept low, trying not to think about all the ways a ricochet could go terribly wrong. "Cruz!" I transmitted, hoping the man had not fulfilled my previous wishes for his demise by falling into the vat below.

"Yeah, I'm here. We are stuck on this side—what should we do?"

"Stay up there and provide us with covering fire," I replied. "Hit the doors especially, but keep them off of us." Another feminine roar filled the air, lashing with a seething violence. "And stay alive!"

"We'll cover you—just get to that room and complete the mission."

I gave a thumbs-up over my head as I continued to push Mags forward. The catwalk swayed from side to side, groaning as we moved quickly across it, trying to duck under the spray of bullets being shot at us. I was certain the catwalk would give at any moment.

I saw Alejandro fire into the room, covering us as we moved up, and seconds later Tim followed suit. He, Alejandro, April, Harry, and Gregory staggered their fire, using short, controlled bursts to conserve ammunition. I made it to the ladder, climbing onto the pipe and then lowering myself down behind it, planting my foot on the fourth rung from the top.

"Follow me," I shouted, and began to climb now. Bullets zinged past me every so often, and a few times I shielded my eyes, more out of instinct than any notion that it would stop a bullet. I felt vulnerable on the ladder, even with the pipes working to disguise our movements. I hated presenting my back to a battlefield. It made me feel like I had "target" written all over me in bright neon colors.

I made it down the ladder, and took a moment to check on Tim's progress. Then I made a quick scan of the ground I could see and stepped out from under the pipes, coming out in a crouch and moving forward without waiting to see what was looking at me. Electrical boxes rose from the concrete around the pool every fifteen feet or so—probably a different aspect of the moving blade—and I flung myself toward the nearest one. Overhead, I could see the flashes of the muzzle fire from our partially stranded group ahead, and I tracked their trajectory to find out where the trouble was.

I made it to the box and knelt behind it, studying the curve of the tank and where the concrete disappeared. I heard a gun go off behind me and turned to see Tim standing there looking in the other direction, a woman on the ground and bleeding, but not dead. He readjusted his arm and shot her again, delivering the killing blow, and then loped over to me.

I turned my head back down the hall as he moved over. "As soon as Alejandro's here, we run for it."

"Viggo, more are coming in from the next room!" announced Cruz in my ear, and I grimaced.

"Scratch that, we need to move now!" I said, standing up to shoot a woman who had appeared around the bend. She dropped, and so did I, ejecting the spent magazine and slapping in a new one. "Are Alejandro and Harry down yet?"

"Yes!" projected Mags over the sound of her gunshots. "Let's go!"

I stood up and began to run for the stairs leading to the door. A woman dropped to her feet in front of me, and it was clear from the deranged look in her eyes that she too had drunk the water, or taken the pill.

April and I fired a long burst into her and then plowed over her as she fell, the door to the control room looming closer. I raced up the stairs and pulled open the door, my body struggling with the weight of the thing, while Tim stepped through, still firing his weapon. Mags got past me next, and I plunged in after them, ready for anything.

At the moment, there was nobody living standing there. Tim holstered his weapon and moved over to the console, studying it, while Mags nudged a woman lying on her back on the floor. I turned and waved on the stragglers from our group. April brought up the rear, her gun firing more and more rapidly as more targets came circling around the vat. I fired over her head at a target. "April, move!" I shouted.

Something growled overhead, and I looked up in time to see a woman leap off the wall twenty feet up, heading for April. I swung my gun up, compressing the trigger and trying to hit her, but it clicked dry. I hurriedly ejected the magazine and loaded the next one, but it was too late—she landed next to the Liberator woman, grabbing her by the arms and tossing her into the pool like a ragdoll, before she had a chance to scream. She turned toward us, and I didn't hesitate to see if April was okay. I finished slapping in the magazine and began to push the door closed. Mags and Alejandro quickly moved in to help me—this door was heavier and had a hand wheel, just like the ones at the facility.

I managed to thrust it closed and stepped back to begin spinning the wheel. Before I could even begin, the door slammed open again, pinning Mags between the wall and the door, as the same warden who'd attacked April stepped through, her face menacing.

I pulled up my gun, but she smacked me across the face, sending me flying. My back hit the floor as the entire side of my face erupted in pain, and I blinked to clear the spots from my eyes. I dragged in a shuddering breath, afraid I had forgotten how to breathe, and then sat up.

Alejandro was swinging at the enhanced woman, Mags' name on his lips as he fought. Harry stood just behind Alejandro, shouting for him to get out of the way so he could shoot, but Alejandro wasn't listening.

I saw her catch his hand with her own, smaller one, and squeeze. Alejandro screamed and fell to his knees as the woman's grip did not let up, and I could hear the sound of the bones in his hand breaking. Harry shot her, but even as she slumped over, she maintained her grip on Alejandro's hand, dragging him with her a few feet.

I could barely rip my eyes from the sight, and I hated having to ignore Alejandro, but the door still stood wide open. I shot at the next woman moving through, and the one right after her. Someone began firing into the room, and I dove to one side as a spray of bullets cut across the space. Scrambling on my hands and feet, I made it over to the door and slammed it shut, this time managing to twist the wheel tight to seal it.

"I need something to jam the wheel," I yelled as I held the wheel fast, knowing it wasn't secured yet. I heard some shuffling behind me, and then Harry leaned over and slid a long-handled wrench through the wheel spokes, bracing it against the long locking mechanism on the back of the door.

I let go of the wheel and turned to Mags, kneeling down next to her and checking her pulse. I heard something slam into the door I had just closed, but I ignored it as I searched for any sign of life.

"How is she?" Alejandro croaked from the floor.

"Alive," I said after a moment. "For now, anyway."

"Just like us," Alejandro whispered, his voice wobbly, clearly in agony. I looked at where he was cradling his hand against his chest and felt the pit of my stomach drop out, leaving me with a slightly nauseated feeling as I saw the... unnatural way his fingers sat.

I looked around the room, considering what he'd said, assessing the situation, looking for options. Tim, thank God, was still at the control board, his fingers flying as he began entering the long series of complex codes and instructions. It was going to take several minutes for Tim to input that code, which meant we had to hold this position for that time. With the enemy on both sides of the room, and no way of knowing how many more were out there, things weren't looking so great. And that wasn't even factoring in an escape plan. I was beginning to wonder if there would be anything left of us to need one.

"Exactly like us," I agreed as I checked Mags' pupils.

Outside, the thudding against the door began in earnest.

CHAPTER 36

Violet

The yard the collection pools sat in was quiet and still. I could hear the faded pops of gunfire behind me, but here, nothing seemed to move. A break in the clouds let in some of the light from the moon, but a haze of smoke seemed to cling to everything—especially over the surface of the ponds, giving the impression that they were steaming. It was eerie for everything to be this still in the middle of a battle. My heartbeat sounded too loud in my own ears.

I tapped my fingers together. "Thomas?" I whispered into the command channel, surprised at how quiet it was. The groups must have all been on their team channels as they moved deeper into the plant… I pushed away all the horrible ideas of other reasons for their absence, focusing on the task at hand. "Do we have a visual of where Desmond went at the water treatment plant?"

It was a moment before Thomas responded. "Violet, all of our cameras have been down for a while. We did have reports from Drew's team of a vehicle coming up after the initial assault but before you got there, though not the same one that she took from us. The likelihood that this was Desmond—"

I cut him off. "I'm near the UV treatment ponds. Could she be there?"

I pictured Thomas' thinking face before he responded, "There is a ninety-three percent likelihood that if Desmond hasn't been reported elsewhere, she will be there. But Violet, that area is the most likely spot for heloships with reinforcements to land—"

"Thanks, Thomas," I said firmly. I couldn't think about all that now. No matter what was out here, I had to stop Desmond. Nothing he could say would change the fact that I was going in.

I tugged my jacket tighter around my shoulders and exhaled, my breath fogging in the frigid night air. In spite of the glow from the fires just around the corner, shadows and pockets of darkness lingered, long and ominous, across the yard. It was there my eyes had searched during the entire conversation, looking for any sign of Desmond or Cody.

It was hard to resist the urge to turn or look over my shoulder every few seconds for fear of finding her standing there, like the boogeyman come to life. It was difficult not to think of her that way—she'd been there at every step, anticipating our moves, throwing more and more awful things at us to try and overcome. I was almost glad she'd escaped so we didn't have to find out if her threat with the boys was legitimate.

The thought made me pause, and I felt a deep anger that helped solidify my courage. I was tired of this, and I was tired of her—and while I wasn't going to stop being afraid, now that I had the chance to end this, I wasn't going to hold back.

"Desmond!" My shout carried loudly across the wide space.

I waited for several heartbeats, and when there was no response, I shouted again. "Desmond!"

I strode across the yard, completely ignoring the hair on my neck and arms standing on end in warning. I was too angry that I had let the fear Desmond inspired in me have so much control over my actions to even allow myself a moment of doubt.

"Desmond!" I shouted again, and then stopped when I heard the distinctive sound of the hammer of a gun being drawn back. I turned, and saw Desmond leaning heavily on a cane. I paused at the sight of it, wondering idly where she had gotten it from, and then pushed the thought aside. She stood forty feet away—an easy shot for her—by the edge of one of the ponds. I searched the area around her, and then met her eyes, their glitter looking even more menacing in the dark. "Where's Cody?"

Desmond gave me a considering look, her eyes narrowing on the gun in my hand, the barrel pointing right at her. "Are you here to kill me, Violet?" she asked.

The anger writhed in me. "That depends," I said, arching an eyebrow. "What I want is Cody."

Her eyes glanced around me, and she frowned. "You're stall-ing," she announced. "For what, I wonder? Is Owen out there?" I felt a stab of fear that she was onto us, and then paused, the reali-zation washing over me as I looked closer. She wasn't onto us; she was afraid. There was a vulnerable curve in her shoulders, and she looked… manic, somehow. Although I hadn't really noticed it before, being taken prisoner must really have had an effect on her.

"I'm not stalling, and I have no idea where Owen is," I told her flatly, and it wasn't even a lie. "I want Cody. That's it."

"I don't want to go anywhere with you," Cody announced,

stepping out from the shadows behind Desmond. "I'm happy with Desmond. You guys suck."

I ignored Cody, not giving in to the twinge of anger his jab left me with, or my impulse to try to coax him back. I was relieved to see the young man alive, but I knew that, ultimately, this was one thing I was not going to give him a say on.

"You see, Violet? He doesn't want to be with you." Desmond smirked knowingly at me, and I resisted the urge to just shoot her. Forty feet wasn't a far distance by any means, but with my left hand… it might as well have been a mile. If I fired and missed…

Where is Morgan? I wondered, fruitlessly searching the long shadows a few feet behind Desmond. Certainly we had been talking long enough for her to get into position. It already felt like too long. "I'll go with you," I announced. "If you leave him behind, I will go with you, and I give you my word I won't fight you."

"Violet…" Desmond trailed off and shook her head at me, her smile curling up farther. "You really do have a flair for dramatic timing."

My brows drew together in confusion, and I took a step back as the wind began to shift, at first swirling the smoke in the air gently, but then faster and faster, until I could feel it along my scalp under the short layer of fuzz that had grown on my head. I looked up in time to see a matte black heloship that seemed to fade in out of the night as it lowered itself into the yard several hundred feet behind Desmond.

The bay door started to extend, and before it was open even a quarter of the way, a girl appeared through the growing gap, coming up and over the door in swanlike fashion. The moonlight caught her hair, making it a silver beacon in the night—doubtless in the sunlight it would have been royal gold. She landed on her feet with liquid ease and began moving toward Desmond.

She might have reminded me of a deer, but there was a lethality to how she moved. I watched her draw near and met Desmond's eyes. "Another princess?" I asked tiredly.

"Lena," Desmond confirmed with a lazy smile. "She and her twin were my best pupils. I would say it's not a boast, but why not take pride in my work?"

I absorbed that knowledge robotically, keeping my mind strategizing on the matter at hand. I had an ace up my sleeve with Morgan—wherever she was—and my blood was boiling for a fight. I'd reached the point where everything was terrifying, so I had to continue as though none of it mattered. Cold fire rushed through my veins. I had already killed my fair share of the seven Matrian princesses. What was one more at this point?

"Do we have a deal, Desmond? Does Elena still want me enough to warrant taking me alive?"

Desmond's mouth pulled tight, and I realized with a start that she didn't agree with Elena about how to handle me. That was interesting, but not at all reassuring. If she just wanted me dead, she could shoot, but now that Elena's younger sister was here as a witness, Desmond risked angering her queen. I could almost see the calculation in her eyes as she weighed the pros and cons.

Finally, she nodded. "Drop the bag and throw the gun on the ground," she said with a wave of her own gun, clutched almost carelessly in the hand not holding her cane. "Walk over slowly."

I obeyed, dropping all I carried and then moving over to her in the way she had asked, with both hands raised. The princess was closing in on her as well, and as we drew close, I slowed when

I began to make out the details of her face, coming to a complete stop a few feet away, reeling from the likeness in front of me. The hair was different in style and color, but the resemblance was there.

"Desmond, what happened to you?" asked the princess, the husk in her voice making it surprisingly deep in spite of her slim, delicate form. Her turquoise eyes flicked over to me, and a smile licked the corner of her wide lips. "Is this her?"

The name dropped from my lips before I could stop it. "Morgan?"

Lena—or was she?—blinked at me in surprise, her lips popping open. "Morgana is *here*?" Her head snapped over to Desmond, her eyes blazing. "You said she'd been taken care of! Where is she?!"

The breath caught in my lungs as Morgan snapped into view a few feet behind Lena, her gun pointed at the princess' blonde head. "Here," she said calmly.

The next moment seemed as if it had been scripted somehow. Morgan pulled the trigger, the gunshot echoing loudly, but Lena had already sidestepped, her body spinning gracefully around as she leveled a fist at her twin's face. By the time the punch would've connected, however, Morgan was out of range, her hands appearing out of nowhere to deflect the blow and deliver an attack of their own.

I could only watch, stunned. The fight was a graceful dance, their moves fluid yet strong. More often than not, they didn't even touch, their limbs coming within an inch of each other as they anticipated and blocked one another's moves. It looked effortless, but I could hear that each of them was straining as they let out grunts and harsh breaths. The battle was beautiful, but it was deadly, and the precision and ruthlessness of the two fighters was terrifying. The gun went off once, then twice more, to no effect that I could see—Morgan was not pulling her punches. She was trying to kill her sister.

I stared for what felt like too long, but must have been less than a minute. Then my eyes flicked back to Desmond. I saw her turning her eyes from the fight toward me at the same moment, and I lunged toward her, trying to take the advantage. But I was weaponless, and she swung her gun up toward me again, shaking her head like a teacher scolding a naughty child. "Are you reneging on our deal?"

I froze. "No," I said, not bothering to hide the regret in my voice. "Just… testing your reflexes."

Desmond took a couple steps and shoved the gun into my side again, dropping the cane and wrapping her arm around my good arm. "Best not to get involved in a family squabble," she said with a flick of her head toward the sisters, pushing me forward. "It'll be over soon enough."

I stumbled forward as Desmond prompted, painfully aware of her gun in my side. My mind struggled to rework our plan, frantically improvising as Desmond pushed me closer to the pool, angling us toward the heloship. Two women clad in sky-blue uniforms—indicating they were royal guards—were already heading toward us, rifles in their hands, but they were still a fair distance away. I took them in, and then looked back over my shoulder to see the twins still intertwined in their delicate and deadly dance. Cody was trailing along behind us, and I focused on him.

"Wait," I said to Desmond, coming to a sudden halt. "I told you I would come quietly… *if* you let Cody go! He's still here. *You're* breaking our deal!"

She started to scoff, but I stepped into her, bringing my face so close to hers that I could count every wrinkle. "Don't you dare," I grated out, meeting her eyes. She pushed the gun deeper into my ribs in warning, but I brought my left hand up to the muzzle, ready to push it away from me. "If you break your word right now, I will fight you tooth and nail. I know I'll lose, but I don't care as long as I do as much damage as possible. You've got a broken leg. And you've already seen what I can do."

Desmond stared at me, and then gave an irritated tsk and turned around to look at Cody. "You heard Violet. Go."

Cody's eyes widened, and he frowned. "No," he said, his voice high with alarm. "I want to go with you!"

Desmond watched him, bored and impassive, as tears welled up in his eyes and he began to cry. "Cody, you're acting like an infant. You're useless without Benuxupane."

At her words, his tears turned to sobs, and she rolled her eyes and turned away. "Let's go," she said, nudging me forward. I tried to ignore the sickness in my stomach that was adding to my anger—if Desmond hurt his feelings, maybe Cody would finally believe us about her... Maybe it would be for the best...

Cody's cries grew, and I gave up and turned back to see him still following us, fat tears rolling down his cheeks and snot dripping from his nose. "Please," he begged hoarsely. "Please don't leave me!"

"I'm not your mother!" Desmond snapped, whipping around. "I have no interest in being your mother! You are a weak, spineless thing, and I could never be a mother to something so pitiable. Now go away!"

Cody's face fell, devastation and heart-rending disbelief on his face. "You're lying," he stammered, his voice coming out at a high-pitched warble that made it sound like his vocal cords were frozen. "You're lying because of Violet. You want me to meet you somewhere—"

A gunshot followed by a loud splash cut off whatever Cody was going to say, and Desmond jerked me farther around, using me as a brace to look back around the curved edges of the pond. Morgan stood at the edge of the pool, her foot planted in Lena's limp back, and as we watched, she pushed her sister's body farther out into the water, a look of grim triumph on her face. Then she looked over at us, the satisfaction on her face vanishing, and she spat out a curse.

"Shoot her!" Desmond screamed over her shoulder just as the guards began to fire in Morgan's direction. The dark-haired woman sprang into action, seeming to move through the bullets, her body twisting around impossibly as she raced across the ground toward us.

Desmond tugged my arm, propelling me forward a few more steps, then paused, turning to where Cody was still following us, tears pouring down his face. She made an irritated growl and whipped around, her gun leaving my side and aiming for the little boy behind us.

I saw Cody's eyes flash up toward her face, and his name was barely a consonant in the back of my mouth when a shadow darted forward from the left, slamming into the boy and pushing him into the pool we stood next to.

Desmond's gun went off with a loud bang, and my heart stopped as I saw Jay look up at me from the spot where the younger boy had stood a moment ago, a hand fluttering to his stomach and blood rushing between his fingers, his mouth opening in an 'O' of surprise.

My throat felt frozen, the muscles in my chest so tight, it was as if the scream that refused to come from my throat was trying to rip the flesh from my bones. Jay dropped to his knees and sagged back, sitting on his heels. "Mom?" he asked, his gaze jerking to Desmond, his eyes those of a young, frightened boy.

Desmond expelled a little breath, the gun in her hand shaking. My eyes dragged over to her, as hard as I tried to stop them. I knew I couldn't see her look guilty. I wouldn't forgive her for it. She had no right to that feeling anymore—it was her fault all of this was even going on! I knew that if she looked guilty, nothing would stop me from strangling the life out of her right then and there, no matter who tried to stop me, no matter how many times they shot me. But my eyes went to her face anyway.

Guilty wasn't even the word for it. The look on Desmond's face was the truest emotion I'd ever seen on her countenance, and it was twisted into a grotesque mask of raw horror. The gun in her hand was trembling so violently that her grip would give out soon. Jay gave a strangled breath, and it seemed to break the spell she was under. "Jay?" she gasped, moving toward him.

Jay saw her coming and recoiled, painfully dragging himself across the ground away from her, blood spilling from the wound in his stomach.

"Jay, we have the heloship! Let me take you to Matrus! The hospitals there are intact, I—"

"NO!" rasped Jay as he whipped himself around to glare at her. He held himself up by his arms, and I could tell by the way they quivered that even he was running short on strength. "I'm not going anywhere with you."

Desmond turned to where the wardens were standing. They had stopped firing, uncertain. I looked around for a sign of

Morgan—or her body—but saw neither. Too many things raced through my mind, and I couldn't stop staring at Jay—*Jay*—I needed to help him—

"You. Get him on the ship," Desmond said to the wardens, and in spite of the panic radiating from her, her voice held the weight of command.

"Ma'am—"

"DO IT," Desmond bellowed, and the warden blinked, and then moved toward Jay, her jaw clenched tightly.

Jay watched her come, his expression thunderous through the pain in his face, and then directed his gaze back to his mother, shaking his head. "You don't get it!" he stated bitterly. "I'd rather be dead than go with you."

He stared at her for a heartbeat longer, and then, with the wardens approaching, pulled himself over the short distance to the pool, throwing himself into the water with a splash.

The fugue of fear and anger that had rooted me to the spot where Desmond had left me was suddenly broken as he disappeared into the water, and I leapt forward, searching it for him. My eyes didn't find him in the ripples of dark water—but there was Cody, splashing several feet deep inside, his limbs swinging awkwardly.

"Jay!" Desmond screamed, rushing over to the water's edge, and I changed tact—I would push her into the pool if it was the last thing I did—when one of the wardens gave a shout cut short by a bullet. I looked over to see Morgan charging for us from just past where Desmond stood, her body springing forward across the grass.

The remaining warden fired on her, and Morgan weaved and dipped, her progress slowing as she was forced to find a less direct route. I felt the gun jab into my ribs again and bit back a curse, turning to see Desmond back at my side—the moment I'd been distracted by Morgan had been a moment too long. Desmond pushed me forward, and I resisted weakly, torn between all the things that needed my attention right now.

"I'm not going anywhere without Jay!" I shouted. "He needs our help! How can you just leave him!"

"It's his choice," she grated out through a tight larynx, her voice cold and deadly. "Now move, or I shoot Cody next. Believe me, I can hit him."

I ground my teeth together and began to move, tears springing up in my eyes, blurring my vision. Desmond jabbed the gun harder into my ribs, and a stabbing pain radiated from the spot, making me cough, but I kept my feet heavy as the heloship drew nearer. My mind was barely on Desmond anymore—how could I save Cody and Jay? Everything in me was screaming that I needed to go to them *right now*.

I could see Morgan, still weaving her way through the hail of bullets, coming closer in spite of the heavy fire. How had I never known she could move like that?

"Morgan!" I shouted over my shoulder as Desmond continued to shove me forward. "Get Cody and Jay! You have to save them!"

Morgan didn't respond, but suddenly her trajectory changed, and without warning she dove into the water, the line of her body as sleek as an arrow. She began to swim in long strokes to where Cody thrashed in the water, trying to keep his head above the surface. She was halfway to him when there was a deep, metallic clanking sound, and the water began to churn.

The treatment system! They had managed to initiate the

purge. But that meant…

I stopped short as the water began to churn, and then I started to struggle. "Jay! Cody!" I shouted as Desmond grunted. I swung my cast, trying to hit her face, knowing that she wasn't allowed to kill me, but she jerked back out of my reach and did something clever with her hand, somehow rolling me over her and down on the ground.

As I scrambled to get to my feet, my ribs and head aching, I could already hear a warden's pounding footsteps as Desmond shouted, "Grab her and let's go!"

CHAPTER 37

Violet

A strong grip grabbed me under the arm before I could make my mad dash to freedom, hoisting me up. I lashed out with my legs, trying to buy time and keep us on the ground, but the woman who held me had already managed to get an arm around my throat and twist my left arm tight behind my back, locking it into place. "I'll break it," she warned in a low voice as she walked me up the ramp—a threat that resonated almost worse than the threat of being shot at this point. I twisted around to try to look back at the pool, but she pushed me through the door, releasing me at just the right moment to upend my sense of balance and have me stumbling across the metal floor in the bay of the cabin.

I whipped around and gasped for air, the tears that the motion squeezed from my eyes making the world swim around me. I watched as the warden helped Desmond on board and slammed the button to close the bay door. Desmond hobbled over to me, her cast thumping against the ground. I could see the pain in her eyes, the agony and hopelessness, but she didn't stop moving. I supposed her sense of duty ran too deep. "Don't make me rethink the decision not to shoot you," she muttered halfheartedly as she drew near.

With my watering eyes, I realized she had something in her hand a second too late, and I winced as the cold metal handcuffs snapped closed around my left wrist—my good one. She turned and beckoned over the warden who had manhandled me onto the heloship. The woman obediently moved forward, and held out her arm. Within moments, we were handcuffed together.

"Search her," Desmond ordered gruffly as she hobbled forward. "Pilot, get us airborne now. We need to fire on the plant."

"Ma'am?" came the surprised voice of the other warden—the pilot—from the front, and I shifted my stance slightly as the woman next to me began to pat me down. "Our orders were to retrieve you and—"

"I'm modifying the orders," Desmond snapped as she stepped into the cockpit, blocking my view. "The plant has been taken over by hostiles. We need to take it out before they can—"

"Stop you!" I shouted loudly. "Don't do it! She's having your people pour poison into the water! Elena's trying to kill all these people—"

My words stopped short with a choke as the warden patting me down straightened and, without prelude, struck me square in the throat. I doubled over, my casted right hand pawing at my throat as I struggled to draw in breath.

I was hauled roughly back, my knees knocking against something hard enough that I lost my balance and slammed my back against the beveled edges of the wall. The warden loomed over me, her hazel eyes flat and disinterested, and I realized she'd pushed me into one of the seats. "Tilt your head up," she ordered, gripping me hard under my chin and forcing me to obey.

My throat immediately relaxed, and I dragged in a shuddering breath as the heloship's engines began to roar. I was too busy gasping for breath to dodge when the guard leaned over me and stuffed the fingers of her free hand into my ear, pulling out the earbud that was part of my communicator set. She tsked, threw it to the ground, and stepped on it, the fragile bit of electronics crunching beneath her heel. Next, she ripped the tiny microphone from my jacket collar and repeated the procedure, and I groaned involuntarily.

"Better," she said.

Desmond and the pilot's voice were masked somewhat, but I could hear them both arguing over firing the missile. Apparently the pilot wanted to make it to the minimum safe distance first, but Desmond just wanted it over and done with. Maybe Jay's refusal of her had affected her more than I'd thought possible—I'd never seen her this angry before.

The fuselage shook slightly as we lifted into the air. I sucked in another breath under the warden's supervision, not trusting myself to speak, and she nodded approvingly. "While you are handcuffed to me, you will be silent and calm." She spoke as if this were any other Tuesday and we were discussing the weather. "In exchange, you may get bathroom privileges and food and water. If you are not, then you can soil yourself and go hungry. Are we clear?"

I felt a burst of déjà vu, followed by a supreme stab of cold rage, and glared back up at her. "She just shot and left her own son for dead," I stated flatly, but my heart felt like it was being stabbed over and over again with each beat. I tried to keep more tears from coming. I had to stay calm so I could get through this. "After she made him participate in an experimental program where they kept him in a cage and traumatized him for years. No—I am not going to be good for you, her, Elena, or anyone else. Monsters like that deserve nothing short of death."

The larger woman opened her mouth to say something, her expression barely changing, when the heloship jerked and swung in midair, violently enough to cause me to bounce around in the seat and the warden to reach over me and steady herself using the wall. "What the hell was that?" I heard the pilot say.

If anybody responded, it was lost in the sound of a heavy, tectonic groan coming from the massive bay door in the back of the heloship. The warden over me leaned back, lowering her arm, and then began tugging me up using the chain connecting us.

"Something's on the back," Desmond said, whipping around and glaring at me. "Do *you* know anything about this?"

I couldn't respond, just shook my head as there was another groan, and I heard the hissing sound of air rushing in as an alarm went off behind me. "I got a seal breech on the bay door," the pilot announced as the alarm went silent with a crash.

The groaning continued, and I slowly backed up, away from the door, this time tugging on the guard's arm. She looked over and then took a healthy step back as she realized what I was doing, opting to move with me rather than order me out of the control area. I saw her reach down into her thigh holster, pulling out her pistol. "Give me a weapon," I said, but she didn't acknowledge me as we continued to move back.

Lights flickered and then fell dark as the air noise began to intensify. "I'm going to shake it off!" the pilot said, and suddenly we were swinging from side to side. I reached out and braced myself on one of the exposed beams, sliding the tips of my fingers into the coarse webbing that was meant for cargo and holding on as best as my casted hand would let me, my body being flung back and forth against the various things restraining it. The creaking sound continued, the rush of the wind growing louder, and then suddenly sparks shot out from the sides of the wall by the cargo door.

There was a sharper, louder groan than before, a squealing of rending metal, and I felt the heloship shudder beneath my feet. Then the wind was rushing in from the open hatch, kicking up papers and sucking them out of it. I jerked back, my spine hitting the wall, as a dark figure swung into the rear. The figure moved, and I realized it was Solomon—he must have forced the hydraulic door open with sheer strength.

The warden next to me recoiled, and I slammed into her out of pure instinct, hitting her with my shoulder. Her gun went off, shooting over Solomon's head, and he snarled and loped forward in a crouch. I spun away from her, trying not to get caught up in what he was about to do, but the chain held me fast, and the next thing I knew, I was flying in the air.

I hit the ground with a thud, and then felt an intense pressure on my wrist. I gasped in pain as the entire joint felt like it was about to disconnect, and looked over to see the warden slipping over the edge of the torn-open bay door. Before I could fully register the implications of what would happen if she fell, I jerked out my hand and grabbed her hip, arresting her fall and then yanking her back with a surge of adrenaline unlike anything I'd ever experienced.

Behind me, Solomon roared, and I heard gunshots going off. I focused solely on moving the warden I was attached to farther and farther away from the edge.

Glass shattered in the cockpit, and I fell over on top of the woman as the heloship bobbed and weaved. I turned toward it, keeping a hand on the now unconscious guard to keep her from dragging me back to the edge.

"Help me!" the pilot screamed as Solomon ripped her chair out from the brackets and tossed it aside. Her scream was cut short by the subsequent crashing noise. Solomon turned, surveying the room around him, his chest heaving.

When his dark eyes came across me, he kept still and looked at me, a raw, hopeless kind of pain in his eyes... and a kind of understanding. I saw his mouth moving, trying to form words.

He'd been following me, protecting me, just like he'd always done.

I opened my mouth to warn him, but then Desmond stepped into the doorframe, her back to me, blocking most of my view. I couldn't see her face, but I could see Solomon's, his eyes staring at the sight before him. I had time to wonder if he'd seen Desmond since he took her berserker pill—if he still remembered her as the leader of the Liberators, the woman whose cause he'd given his humanity fighting—

"Solomon—" I began, not sure what I was going to say.

Then Desmond made a snarling noise in front of me, her arm jerking up, and gunshots sounded—once, twice, a third time. Solomon stepped back, his hand going to his stomach. "No!" I found myself shouting. She was going to kill him. I looked around for something, anything—

Solomon roared angrily, the confusion on his face blossoming into pure rage, and I heard his footsteps as he moved forward. Desmond shot twice more, and then grunted as he slammed into her. I rolled up and over the guard's body as he moved past me, carrying Desmond by the waist with two hands.

"Solomon, wait!" I shouted, but it was too late. Without pause or thought, he pitched her into the black space created by the open bay door.

Her scream quickly faded, practically disappearing in a second. Solomon stood there for a moment, his chest heaving, and then spat into the open space after her. He scrubbed his mouth with the back of his hand before slowly turning around. He locked eyes with me and blinked. Lowering his hand, he flashed me a crooked smile, and then tumbled forward onto his chest, landing hard, a wet glisten beginning to pool under him in the moonlight slanting in from the ripped-off bay door. He'd been shot more than three times. He was going to bleed to death, and fast.

I sat up, ignoring the aches and pains in my wrist, shoulder, and back, fumbling through the guard's pockets, my fingers feeling too fast and too clumsy. "Please tell me Desmond gave you the key," I whispered under my breath as I searched. My fingers brushed against something metal in the pocket of her chest, and I pulled out a ring of keys, trying not to think about how there was no longer a pilot in control of the heloship. One crisis at a time. I searched through them until I found the one that unlocked the cuff, and then snapped the open handcuff around one of the built-in handholds on the bench.

I verified that she was still breathing, and then reached over her to grab one of a set of emergency flashlights out of its mount on the wall. Clicking it on, I scanned the floor and quickly recovered the warden's gun—so she couldn't have it—and then moved into the cockpit.

The chair was lying on its side, the pilot still strapped to it. I straddled the seat to check on her. She also had a pulse, but there was blood coming out of her nose, and her arm was pinned awkwardly between the heavy metal chair and the grated floor. It was definitely broken.

I stood up and moved over to the cockpit, wincing when I saw that most of the screens had been smashed in Solomon's attack. I spotted the comms the pilot was wearing dangling from a cord overhead, and slipped the heavy headphones over my ears.

"Mayday," I started to transmit, and then ripped the comms away from my head as the sharp squeal of feedback transmitted painfully in my ear. Looking at it, I realized the microphone was cracked and barely holding together.

I leaned over and checked out the window, surprised to see that we were now higher up than I had thought, and farther away than I had believed possible. The river was rapidly disappearing behind us, and I recognized some of the buildings below us as belonging to Matrus. It seemed so strange to see the peaceful, tidy streets, lights on, but with very little movement.

Everything calm. Peaceful. Still. Such an unfair contrast to the other side.

I put it out of my mind, and turned to the horizon. The navigation LED, which remained intact, read east, and I realized this direction would take us deep into The Outlands, a place no one had ever returned from. I couldn't even wrap my head around that, so pushed it aside and focused on what I could change. Another glance through the window told me the path was clear—as far as I could tell in the low light of the moon—but it was hard to know how long that would last.

I stared for a moment longer, and then grabbed the first-aid kit from the bracket next to the bathroom. My assessment of the situation was this: I was alive and conscious. We were headed into unknown territory. I didn't know whether the heloship was still running because it'd been set on autopilot or an emergency homing protocol, or if it was randomly going to sputter and die at any moment. The radio was fried, the controls panels busted, the pilot unconscious, and Solomon was bleeding out from multiple gunshot wounds in the bay.

"Basically," I whispered as I knelt next to Solomon and opened up the kit, "we are royally screwed."

CHAPTER 38

Viggo

The bang of a fist on metal came again, and I motioned everyone away from the door. I heard Alejandro hissing, and glanced back to see him trying to pull out the revolver he carried in a thigh holster. He jerked it out with a gasp, panting, and I saw the agony he was in.

I leaned over and slipped Mags' arm around my neck, sliding my arm under her knees. I lifted her up and then began backing away from the door. Harry and Gregory were two steps ahead of me.

"Cruz, we got hostiles on the door." The earbud was silent as I motioned for the three of us to stop halfway in. I moved over to where Alejandro was propped up in a wide and deep break in the wall that functioned as a server room. I stepped over him and carefully set Mags down as the thudding on the door intensified, growing more and more insistent.

"We are retreating, my friend. Several more came in and

climbed the walls to us. We are trying to find a way around." Cruz's voice held deep regret and shame.

My stomach dropped as I absorbed his message—no backup from that end. I heard the metal groan and turned, making my way back over to where Harry and Gregory were crouched on the floor. I moved in between them and pulled the strap off my rifle, moving in front of the control panel.

Beside us, I heard Tim humming under his breath as his fingers flew over the controls, inputting the codes to activate the purge. I glanced over at him, nestled in the alcove, confused about why he would be humming at a time like this, and then noticed that he wasn't taking time to check the instruction sheet Thomas had made for us. What he was humming were the instructions: he must have memorized them.

The metal groaned, and I watched it flex inward. I pulled out my final magazine and set it down in front of where I knelt. "Short, controlled bursts," I reminded them. "When they get in, try to plug the door with their bodies."

Harry and Gregory nodded, shouldering their rifles. I took a deep breath to clear my mind, and then followed suit. The door continued to flex open, the blue-gray paint flaking off the surface as it warped underneath. The top hinge ripped, the rod in the middle of it clattering free.

The sound stopped suddenly, and then the door came flying right toward us. I ducked down, but Harry got caught in the shoulder. The bearded man cried out as he fell over, the door landing partially on top of him.

I began firing at the hole even before I was fully looking at it. Sparks flew as I hit the wall, but I adjusted fire and shot the woman stepping through in the chest. Her body crumpled, but another woman was already there pushing past her falling form. Gregory got her with a single shot to the head. We continued to fire, the loud sound of the gunfire ringing in my ears, making it difficult to hear anything.

The third woman tripped over the first woman as she fell, but the fourth woman wasn't where I expected her to be in the doorway, so I almost missed her as she swung up and over the third woman, landing hard on her feet and then rushing forward. Gregory fired, but she sidestepped him and then kicked me in the chest.

I staggered back a few feet, the breath knocked out of me. Doubling over in pain was a reflex, but it was one that could get me killed. So I straightened and moved, ignoring the panicked signals being emitted by my internal organs. I managed a small gasp of air as I scooped my gun off the floor. Gregory was kicking the woman off of him, having disabled her in close combat, and he turned to confront the next woman coming in.

I had started to fire, when the sharp sound of a thud against the second door behind us had me whirling. The hand wheel shook, but the wrench held fast, locking it in place. The shake stopped, and I turned back to the fight in time to see Gregory being lifted off his feet by one of the wardens, his face purple as he gagged for breath. I leveled my gun at the woman and fired, catching her in the side. She fell, and Gregory dropped to his hands and knees, his hands around his throat.

I started to fire at the next person, but then ducked when I heard the sound of metallic rending coming from behind me. Whirling around, I saw that the door had been ripped outward this time. I squeezed the trigger to fire at the next woman as she came through, and my gun clicked empty. With a curse, I ejected the magazine and reached for the spare, stopping when I realized I had left it on the floor earlier.

Then she was on me, her hand configured into an openhanded tiger paw technique. I recognized it, although I had never tried it out. I dipped under her sweep and landed a stiff hit with the butt of my rifle to her ribcage on my follow-through, using her momentum to my advantage. She let out a sharp chuff of air as she flew by, and I danced back, my eyes sweeping the floor for the magazine.

I saw it sticking out from under Harry's leg, and bent over to grab it. I straightened, slapping it in and turning to fire at her as she was getting back off the ground. Then I fired at the one rushing for Gregory, and at the next one coming through the first door. I expected yet another, but the areas beyond both doors appeared clear—although who knew for how long.

Then I moved over to Tim, kneeling next to him and putting my back to the console.

The air around the doors seemed still, but I didn't trust it. "Status, and I need your rifle."

Tim didn't pause in his motions, didn't even seem to acknowledge me as his fingers flew across the keyboard. "Almost there," he whispered as he shifted his weight to one leg and nudged the rifle propped up against the console. I reached around him and pulled it over, dismayed that it wasn't the same type as mine.

That meant our ammo wasn't interchangeable. A shadow crossing the light from the door to the left caught my eye, and I swung my rifle around to shoot at it. Gunfire came from their side too, and then suddenly died as my bullets found their mark.

"Viggo!" I turned and saw Alejandro looking just past me back toward the right. Gregory lay on his stomach, his eyes wide open, glossy. I stared at the bullet hole in his head, my heart clenching. He had been right there fighting next to me. I had just been joking with him less than an hour ago.

"Alejandro," I croaked. "You got that door covered?"

"I do. I got a rifle, too." The old man's voice was grim, angry, and hard. He knew what I knew—we were probably not coming out of this room alive. I tightened my grip on my gun and thought of Violet, hoping she wouldn't be too angry with me for too long.

Tim didn't falter beside me, the rapid click of buttons being pressed filling the room. I heard gunshots come through in the door I was looking at—the one that led to the other vat room—and noticed the still mostly intact door lying on Harry. In the chaos, I couldn't tell if he was breathing or not, but I couldn't risk helping him just yet.

Taking advantage of the lull in battle, I gripped the detached door and began to pull it toward Tim, intent on giving the young man as much cover as possible. Alejandro watched me in confusion, and then I saw the hard understanding come into his eyes as he realized I was trying to protect Tim until the bitter end.

I propped it up at an angle between the floor and the wall, and it covered most of his torso and one of his legs. His head was still very much in view, but it presented a small target that most people didn't instinctively go for in a firefight. Hopefully it would buy him some time if I wasn't able to cover him.

My heart throbbed hard in my chest as I squatted back down, and I had only reached up to wipe off my forehead when footsteps pounded up and three women burst into the room from my door, charging right in. I grabbed my gun, their unexpected appearance shaving seconds off my response time, and then suddenly I was hauled up, and my legs were dangling.

I didn't bother to try to break the woman's grip on my vest. Instead, I reached up with one hand and undid the fastener on the side, loosening it and slipping out of it. I went low as I landed, scooping up my gun from where I had dropped it and firing up even as I fell back.

That woman fell as I started to straighten, but another was there in her place, her hand reaching out, grabbing the muzzle of the rifle and giving it a squeeze. The metal compressed under her grip, and she yanked the gun from my fingers and then stepped forward, head-butting me.

I reeled back at the blow to my nose and felt blood dripping down my face. The woman before me let out a throaty scream of victory and then launched herself at me, her arms swinging for me faster than I would have believed possible. I avoided the first blow, but her second one caught me in the side. Luckily, the angle was wrong—her fist glanced off my ribcage, barely two knuckles connecting.

That didn't mean it didn't hurt. The pain was immense and immediate, and I dropped down on my hands and knees. The warden's foot lashed out, kicking me in the same spot, and whatever air I had been able to catch from the kick in the chest earlier was gone again. I gasped on the floor, seeing her foot draw back in my periphery, and I knew if she kicked me again, she would probably kill me.

Instinct made me ignore the pain for long enough to pick my knee off the floor and land a hard kick of my own directly to the joint of her knee, picturing a spot just behind it and aiming for it. I kicked her harder than I thought, and her knee compressed backward. She crumpled immediately with a howl and began rocking back and forth.

She came to a flopping stop as Alejandro pulled the trigger, his face squeezed tight in pain. "Behind you!" he shouted, and I rolled forward, not even bothering to look. A hand clamped down on my ankle and began to squeeze, and I heard Alejandro's gun click empty. I lashed out with my other foot, trying to break free.

"Got it," Tim shouted, and a deep, thrumming hum filled the air, followed by a metallic clunking sound. Then I saw the young man turn and shoot the woman who was holding me, using her own pistol. Her grip on my ankle relaxed, and Tim bent over to help me up.

I leaned on him, a little afraid to put any weight on my ankle—it was throbbing so hard.

I tried to straighten, freezing when I saw six more women step in, three from either side. Their eyes quested back and forth, their breath labored and angry, as though there was only one thought in their minds now—destroy the enemy. I sucked in another tight breath, still unable to breathe normally, and just… looked at them. Alejandro shouted a curse and threw his gun at one of the women, but she ducked easily. Tim nervously brandished his gun, his eyes darting around. I could see the calculation in his eyes: he had good reflexes, but even he couldn't kill all six of them before they were on him.

I watched them approach, and then pressed my fingers together. "We initiated the purge, Ms. Dale. You can turn back. We're not going to—"

Heavy gunfire tore through the control room, and I ducked as I heard the loud sound of a large-caliber rifle being fired at automatic speeds, pulling Tim along with me. It stopped seconds later, leaving nothing but bloody carnage on the floor.

I peeked my head out and saw Ms. Dale stepping into the room, the massive, blocky weight of a .50 caliber machine gun gripped firmly in both her hands, steam still piping from the front of it. She tossed it to the floor, giving me a stern look. "Of course we're going to make it," she said tiredly. "Because we just did. I'm sorry I couldn't warn you sooner—my microphone got broken, and then things got crazy."

I turned to look out at the treatment room through the door, and saw the water churning in the vat, the rushing sound growing even louder as the water rapidly drained out.

Lowering myself back to the floor, I rested my head against the console and resisted the urge to laugh in relief. Or sorrow. Or both.

Ms. Dale's people started to press in and pass through the control room toward the other side of the plant. "Cruz is trying to find a way around," I told her, and she nodded and began giving orders to her people, sending a couple of them to help.

I watched as she led a group of them out, and then climbed slowly to my feet. My entire side still burned as I tried to move, and I wound up walking slightly stooped over, unable to fully right myself for fear of pulling the severely bruised muscles. If Cruz had our people coming in the other side, I was certain they could handle it. I had bigger concerns at the moment. I hobbled slowly over to Harry, fighting through the pain, and sank to a heavy knee next to him, putting my fingers to his neck. His pulse was still there, but it was weak. A quick check revealed purple splotches on his chest and stomach. I was certain that wasn't a good sign, but there was nothing I could do for him at the moment.

Standing up slowly, keeping my slightly doubled-over posture, I moved over to Alejandro and Mags, listening to the gunshots filling the air suddenly double. Ms. Dale's group must have joined the fray with Cruz. I pressed my fingers to Mags' neck, and found her pulse beating strongly. Peeling back her eyelids, intent on checking her pupils, I found myself doubled over and gasping for breath as she suddenly lashed out with a small fist, not hard, but catching me in the same side the warden had.

I had to lie down, the pain was that bad. I slowly lowered myself as Mags leaned over me, her face fluttering in concern. "Viggo? I'm so sorry, did I hurt you?"

"I'm fine," I wheezed hoarsely, trying not to breathe too deeply.

I was lying and we both knew it, but she ignored it, looking around at the bodies on the floor and the otherwise deserted room. "Did we do it?" she asked. "Did we win?"

I looked over to where Harry lay, Gregory just a few feet away from him. "I think so," I said tiredly, the statement not fully expressing every feeling coursing through me in that moment. "We purged the plant," I said to Mags. "The contaminated water is gone. There might be a little still in Patrus, but not enough to destroy the entire city."

Mags' eyes glittered with tears, but whether they were of happiness or sadness, I didn't think even she knew. "We did it," she said hoarsely. "We stopped 'em."

"Yes," I said, although the triumph tasted weird in my mouth. "And now we need Dr. Tierney here. We got a lot of wounded."

Mags nodded and began transmitting as I somehow managed to flop over onto my back, thinking of Violet. We'd made it through this; we'd survived the first hurdle. Desmond hadn't appeared and stopped our attack on the plant—I hoped to God Violet had stopped her. I pushed all those thoughts away, imagining how much I was going to enjoy just… holding her tightly and going to sleep by her side. Soon. As soon as all this was cleaned up.

Once Mags was finished on the radio, she leaned heavily to one side, resting her weight on the wall behind her. "I wish we could say this was it," she said. "But there is so much more to do. The city is in shambles; people are still killing each other… We may have saved them, but that doesn't mean we can re-establish order."

I groaned, and slowly worked myself into a sitting position, the fantasy of holding Violet popped by Mags' cold dash of reality. "We need to reorganize and get our people medical attention, food, and rest first," I said. "After that, we'll start with the city. One block at a time if we have to. The biggest thing that will calm people down is restoring power, but some of the seedier elements will have to be dealt with. Luckily, I think having Maxen will be useful."

Mags shot me a hard look. "Our agreement was—"

"The people can't agree to kick him out right now. They aren't even talking to each other. It would be chaos. Restore order—be one of the groups the people start to look up to—then decide who is going to lead. Baby steps."

"And in the meantime, Elena is coming up with something else." Mags glowered angrily, and I sighed. We had fires on all fronts, and they were raging. But I knew we couldn't worry about the fire on the other side of the river at the moment. The people came first.

"We'll deal with it," I said, easing up against the wall a few inches, pushing past the agony that made up one side of my ribs. "You haven't known us long enough yet, but we always do. And this time, we'll end it."

I hoped.

READY FOR THE GRAND FINALE OF VIOLET AND VIGGO'S STORY?

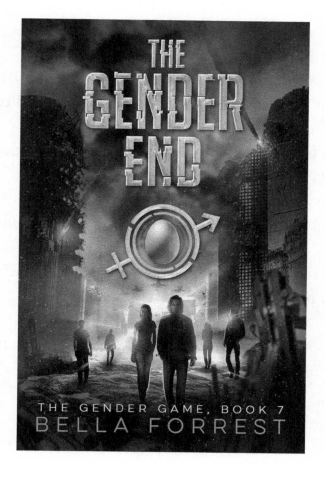

Dear Reader,

Thank you for your loyalty to this series and for journeying through it with me to the end. I'm both sad and excited for the conclusion.

THE GENDER END, the thrilling final book, releases **July 10th, 2017**.

If you visit www.morebellaforrest.com and join my email list, I will send you an email reminder as soon as The Gender End is live.

You can also visit my website for the most updated information about my books: www.bellaforrest.net

Until we meet again between the pages,
—Bella Forrest x

ALSO BY BELLA FORREST

THE GENDER GAME
The Gender Game (Book 1)
The Gender Secret (Book 2)
The Gender Lie (Book 3)
The Gender War (Book 4)
The Gender Fall (Book 5)
The Gender Plan (Book 6)
The Gender End (Book 7)

THE SECRET OF SPELLSHADOW MANOR
The Secret of Spellshadow Manor (Book 1)
The Breaker (Book 2)
The Chain (Book 3)

A SHADE OF VAMPIRE SERIES

SERIES 1: DEREK & SOFIA'S STORY
A Shade of Vampire (Book 1)
A Shade of Blood (Book 2)
A Castle of Sand (Book 3)
A Shadow of Light (Book 4)
A Blaze of Sun (Book 5)
A Gate of Night (Book 6)
A Break of Day (Book 7)

A SHADE OF DRAGON TRILOGY
A Shade of Dragon 1
A Shade of Dragon 2
A Shade of Dragon 3

A SHADE OF KIEV TRILOGY
A Shade of Kiev 1
A Shade of Kiev 2
A Shade of Kiev 3

BEAUTIFUL MONSTER DUOLOGY
Beautiful Monster 1
Beautiful Monster 2

DETECTIVE ERIN BOND (Adult thriller/mystery)
Lights, Camera, GONE
Write, Edit, KILL

FOR AN UPDATED LIST OF BELLA'S BOOKS,

please visit her website: www.bellaforrest.net

Join Bella's VIP email list and she'll personally send you an
email reminder as soon as her next book is out!
Visit to sign up: www.MoreBellaForrest.com

CPSIA information can be obtained
at www.ICGtesting.com
Printed in the USA
LVHW111604061118
596138LV00003B/77/P